"Park's harrowing, emotionally dense debut [is]
set to the music of sensuous prose."
—*TimeOut Chicago*

"Samuel Park's astonishing novel provides mesmerizing
perspective into the life of a Korean wife and lover—intricate
and intimate as only a woman's secret life can be."
—Jenna Blum, author of *Those Who Save Us* and *The Stormchasers*

"Captivating . . . Park's novel can be read as a contemplation of
loss and the angst of unrequited love, much like *Dr. Zhivago*."
—*Kirkus Reviews*

"In his heroine Soo-Ja, Samuel Park has created an emotionally
resonant character that readers will root for and long remember."
—John Burnham Schwartz, author of *The Commoner*
and *Reservation Road*

"An understatedly brilliant tale . . . Through Soo-Ja's eyes,
Park beautifully evokes 1960s war-torn South Korea."
—*Audrey* magazine

Praise for *This Burns My Heart*

"Extraordinary . . . A page-turner of a book, a story of unfulfilled love in postwar South Korea . . . *This Burns My Heart* is informed by Park's keen understanding of how women, circumscribed by the restrictions of their time, expressed themselves the only way they could find: suffering. South Korea provides not only the backdrop of Soo-Ja's story, but also the context for Park's novel, which spans the decades after the Korean War to the beginning of the country's economic boom. In a sense, Soo-Ja's story parallels South Korea's development from a poor, struggling state to a gleaming Asian tiger."

—*Chicago Tribune*

"Memorable . . . Atmospheric and exuberantly filmic . . . *This Burns My Heart* cuts a chunky swath of postwar South Korea from 1960 through the '70s. . . . Park manages to keep readers connected to Soo-Ja throughout the novel, primarily because she soon flips from a petty youth to a more dutiful child and mother, ostensibly matured by expectations of obedience to her new husband's family . . . a simple but visceral romance in a refreshing Korean setting."

—*The Miami Herald*

"*This Burns My Heart* is quietly stunning—a soft, fierce story that lingers in the mind. Samuel Park is a deft and elegant writer; this is a very exciting debut."

—Audrey Niffenegger, *New York Times* bestselling author of *The Time Traveler's Wife*

"Vivid . . . atmospheric . . . Park's descriptions of antigovernment clashes and the martyrdom of a 12-year-old boy, in particular, provide eerily prescient reverberations of recent clashes in Syria."

—*The Boston Globe*

"Park does a good job of bringing the rapidly changing South Korea of the 1960s alive. As cities sprout from beanfields and rickshaws give way to Kias, the world around Soo-Ja and her family is changing at a frightening speed. . . . I especially recommend this novel to readers who were intrigued (as was I) by Lisa See's *Dreams of Joy*, set in postwar China. The contrast is fascinating."

—*The Christian Science Monitor*

"Park melds a captivating love story with a detailed portrait of a nation rising out of the ruins of war."

—*Chicago Sun-Times*

"An understatedly brilliant tale of middle-class dysfunction told with Chekhovian aplomb . . . Through Soo-Ja's eyes, Park beautifully evokes 1960s war-torn South Korea, a country struggling between conflicting impulses to preserve or rebuild. Written with clarity and elegant restraint, *This Burns My Heart* is sure to engage."

—*Audrey* magazine

"A heartrending story with a remarkable heroine who is both maddening and humbling, Park's elegant prose resonates with the quiet force of love in all its guises and a country struggling to be reborn."

—Amazon "Best Books of the Month" pick

"*This Burns My Heart* never loses touch with the human passion at the core of its epic romance. Writing prose with the beauty of poetry, Samuel Park traces a young woman's journey to hard-won maturity, alongside the meteoric rise of post-war Korea, in a novel which shines with eloquence and wisdom."

—David Henry Hwang, Tony Award–winning author of *M. Butterfly*

"[A] harrowing, emotionally dense debut . . . set to the music of sensuous prose . . . like all good love stories, it lets go of the ambiguity it's built when the time is right. The path is long and surprising, the drama is high, there's pain involved, and the twists and turns are reliably, recognizably and realistically unpredictable."

—*TimeOut Chicago*

"*This Burns My Heart* is a delicate yet powerful story of love, loss, and endurance. The emotional world of the heroine, Soo-Ja, is beautifully realized; I found myself caught up in her dramas from start to finish, and was reluctant to part with her at the novel's close. A lovely, romantic, haunting book."
—Sarah Waters, author of *The Little Stranger, Fingersmith,*
and *Tipping the Velvet*

"Samuel Park's engrossing first novel . . . bravely flirts with the fire of melodrama. . . . The best part of *This Burns My Heart* is that its resolution is not the point, not a justification of all the pages that went before but a triggering of sorrow that those pages have passed, like a replay of Soo-Ja's own dilemma."
—*The Seattle Stranger*

"The very talented Samuel Park weaves a compelling, vivid story of one family's evolution that deftly mirrors Korea's development from ancient country to modern society."
—Janice Y. K. Lee, *New York Times* bestselling author of
The Piano Teacher

"Captivating . . . Park's novel can be read as a contemplation of loss and the angst of unrequited love, much like *Dr. Zhivago* . . . First-rate literary effort."
—*Kirkus Reviews* "Best Fiction of 2011"

"*This Burns My Heart* is at once a passionate and sensitive love story and a fascinating historical novel set against the cultural dislocations of a rising South Korea. In his heroine Soo-Ja, Samuel Park has created an emotionally resonant character that readers will root for and long remember."
—John Burnham Schwartz, bestselling author of *The Commoner*
and *Reservation Road*

"An unflappable heroine anchors Park's epic post–Korean War love story . . . But this is no quiet tale of yearning: the plot kicks in with an unexpected fierceness, and the ensuing action—a kidnapping, fist fights, blackmail—make for a dramatic, suck-you-in chronicle of a thrilling love affair."
—*Publishers Weekly*

"Samuel Park's astonishing novel, *This Burns My Heart,* provides mesmerizing perspective into the life of a Korean wife and lover—intricate and intimate as only a woman's secret life can be."

—Jenna Blum, *New York Times* bestselling author of *Those Who Save Us* and *The Stormchasers*

"A vivid and involving novel . . . Park portrays, with penetrating compassion, individuals trapped in soul-crushing, sexist traditions . . . Smart, affecting, and unabashedly melodramatic, Park's novel of adversity, moral clarity, and love is consuming and cathartic."

—*Booklist*

"Both an epic love story and an intimate depiction of life in post-war Korea, *This Burns My Heart* introduces a singular heroine whose passions, struggles, and triumphs are mirrored in our own. Samuel Park is one of those rare writers whose talent transcends the limits of race and gender."

—Wendy Lee, author of *Happy Family*

"With complex, sympathetic characters and vibrant, lyrical prose, Park reminds readers about loyalty, sacrifice, friendship, family and, above all, the enduring power of first love."

—*BookPage* "Best Books of 2011"

"*This Burns My Heart* captured me with a heroine who is both irresistible and flawed, and engrossed me with increasing twists in a triangle of love and sacrifice. The story explores how a fateful choice colors a decade of marriage, and challenges a young woman's ambition already constrained by traditional Korean culture. Sam Park paints all the flavors of post-war Korea in this vivid debut, and his understanding and expression of the human heart is universal."

—Eugenia Kim, author of *The Calligrapher's Daughter*

"Inspired by the life of Park's mother . . . this novel has the added gravitas of being embellished truth."

—*Library Journal*

THIS
BURNS
MY
HEART

SAMUEL PARK

Simon & Schuster Paperbacks
New York   London   Toronto   Sydney   New Delhi

Simon & Schuster Paperbacks
1230 Avenue of the Americas
New York, NY 10020

First Simon & Schuster trade paperback edition March 2012

SIMON & SCHUSTER PAPERBACKS and colophon are registered trademarks
of Simon & Schuster, Inc.

For information about special discounts for bulk purchases, please contact
Simon & Schuster Special Sales at 1-866-506-1949 or business@simonandschuster.com.

The Simon & Schuster Speakers Bureau can bring authors to your live event.
For more information or to book an event, contact the Simon & Schuster Speakers
Bureau at 1-866-248-3049 or visit our website at www.simonspeakers.com.

Designed by Akasha Archer

Manufactured in the United States of America

10   9   8   7   6   5   4   3   2   1

The Library of Congress has cataloged the hardcover edition as follows:

Park, Samuel.
    This burns my heart : a novel / Samuel Park.
        p.   cm.
        1. Women—Korea—Fiction. 2. Self-realization in women—Fiction. 3. Marriage
customs and rites—Korea—Fiction. 4. Psychological fiction. I. Title.
PS3616.A7436T47 2011   2010043441
813'.6—dc22

ISBN 978-1-4391-9961-9
ISBN 978-1-4391-9962-6 (pbk)
ISBN 978-1-4391-9963-3 (ebook)

For my parents
Ryung Hee and Kwang Ok Park

THIS BURNS MY HEART

Prologue

Seoul, South Korea
1963

"You tricked me," she says, lying over a silk mat on the gold-colored floor, her husband next to her. In the dark, her words float above her, not really doing anything, without the punch and bite they have during the day. They hang there like fragments cast off from a comet, lingering over their bodies before lying down to rest.

When I could be with my father, my brothers, and waiting for my future.

She asks for closeness, for a man who pecks her on the cheek for no good reason as she walks by, or whose arm—warm, solid—is always there next to her own, his hands quick to reach for the small of her back. She hopes for the constant brushing of skin; the merging of silhouettes; the way arms and hands greet casually every day. This is what she imagines married life to be—bodies no longer separate, always feeling each other.

Instead, her husband moves around her like a child afraid of his mother, careful to avoid her space, never finding himself that near. His touch is never there, and she can feel its absence, pulling its weight down on her, leaving her cold, and with no memory of warmth. He lies next to her, still as a prowler, pretending to be asleep. He makes no noise, as if he were holding his breath.

You tricked me, you tricked me.

All she hears is the air slipping in and out of his nostrils, his face almost clenched, like a fist. He never tells her much, and she wonders where it goes, all the words and thoughts that he takes in. Maybe she, too, should lie awake, she thinks, storing pins in different parts of her body. And then when she wakes she will once again be with the quiet, distant man who writes beautiful letters but in person says nothing, looking terrified that she might hurt him. But one thing strikes her: he doesn't deny that he tricked her.

PART ONE

Chrysanthemum

Daegu, South Korea
1960

chapter one

Soo-Ja knew about the stranger. The one following her for the last four blocks. She kept her pace even—her instinct in situations like this was not to be scared, but to see it as a battle of wits, as if she'd been handed a puzzle, or a task. She wanted to lose him, but do so elegantly, in the manner of a great escape artist. Her friend Jae-Hwa—walking next to her, her homemade knit scarf blowing in the brisk Siberian wind—hadn't noticed him, and kept on chattering about the lover in the film they'd just seen.

Was the man a secret agent from the North? Soo-Ja asked herself. The war had ended only seven years ago so it was feasible. It didn't help that the other side didn't sit across the ocean, or on a different continent, but rather just a few hundred miles away, cordoned off by an imaginary line drawn with chalk on a map. Soo-Ja fantasized that the man mistook her for the mistress of a high-ranking official, and wanted her to carry state secrets across the 38th parallel. Would he be disappointed, she wondered, to find out she was just a college student? Daughter of a factory owner, born in the year of the tiger?

Soo-Ja pulled her compact out of her purse and looked into the round mirror. There he was, within the glimmering frame, in his white jacket and white pants. Western clothes. Appropriate, she thought. She could not imagine him in *hanbok*, or anything worn by her parents or her parents' parents. From his self-satisfied grin to the rebellious extra inch of hair, this young man looked like a new species, a new breed. He walked behind her at a relaxed pace, his hands in his pockets, a body-guard of sorts, there to protect her from men like him.

"We're being followed," Soo-Ja finally told Jae-Hwa, though she hadn't decided yet how to outwit him. She wouldn't just lose him. There had to be a *scene* of some kind; otherwise the anecdote was too dull, the narrative too brief. Also, he needed to be punished. Not horrendously, as he hadn't done anything terrible, but lightly, so he'd learn that he couldn't just go after a pretty girl like that, couldn't simply claim her as his.

"Who's following us?" asked Jae-Hwa, her voice panicky, vowels already in hiding, her hands hanging tightly to her friend's arm. Was he a "spoiler"? One who damages virgins before their wedding day, rendering them useless? Jae-Hwa, with her short, boyish haircut, lacked her friend's beauty, and in spite of that—or maybe because of it—often found herself overplaying her own appeal. She imagined men coming after her, though they really sought her friend.

"A *meot-yanggi*," said Soo-Ja.

Meot-yanggi: a flashy, vain person, showing off goods, wealth, or physique.

Soo-Ja smiled at the fact that a single word could contain all that: a definition, a criticism, a jab. She turned around and glanced at him directly, boldly, and watched as he smiled at her and lowered his head slightly, a nod. Seeing him in natural scale, Soo-Ja was struck by how tall and lean he was. All around, the sunlight dimmed, as if he were pulling it down toward him.

Soo-Ja knew then how she was going to lose him.

As the street widened in front of her, she jumped into the delicious whirl of bodies, tents, and rickshaws swarming the marketplace. With Jae-Hwa barely able to keep up, Soo-Ja danced past peddlers waving hairbrushes in the air; zoomed by mother-daughter teams haggling with shopkeepers; expertly maneuvered around noodle stands and fishcake stalls. *Tchanan, tchanan,* she heard a peddler yell as he pointed at ceramic pots displayed on the ground on top of white sheets. An old man coughed—his shoulders weighed down by containers of cooking gas—then flashed his broken teeth at Soo-Ja. The arms and legs of children brushed past her, their breaths spicy with chili peppers.

Soo-Ja smiled, her eyes thrilled by the kinetic energy of carts zigzagging swiftly in all directions. Bodies came at her one after the other, faces shuffling as quickly as pictures in a deck of *hato* cards; mobile stands selling used clothes wheeled down unexpectedly, causing her to have to duck and sidestep. When she reached the edge of the market, Soo-Ja stopped and took a breath. She watched as a bulldozer across the street from her dug into a fenced-off patch of soil. It had long been a fascination of hers, watching construction workers rebuild bombed-out sites. It felt miraculous, how a factory could be sliced in half during the war, and then regrown, like the stubborn perennials. Soo-Ja loved this sense of reconstruction, her only complaint being that all the new buildings and houses looked exactly the same. She couldn't tell a newspaper office from a fire station, as if both structures were interchangeable plastic toys in a child's board game. Soo-Ja wondered if the men who erected these stone castles secretly feared that they would be bombed or burnt down once again.

"Is he still following us?" Soo-Ja asked Jae-Hwa, smiling. She already knew the answer.

Jae-Hwa turned around to look and saw the stranger walking toward them. He strained to keep his confidence, though he was clearly out of breath.

Jae-Hwa dug her fingers deeper into Soo-Ja's arm. "I see him. What're we going to do?"

Soo-Ja pulled her friend close, with a daring look on her face, and they started running again. This time, Soo-Ja moved away from the main road and slipped into a tiny little street. She had entered a maze, a corridor about a meter wide. As they raced deeper into it, the two of them zigzagged into never-ending turns—enough to lose hound dogs, detectives, and even the young man on their trail. They squeezed past an old woman carrying a load of laundry on her head; evaded a group of children running in the opposite direction; ignored the hunger pangs from smelling *soon-dae*—the sausage-shaped delicacy filled with vegetables and rice—sold by a peddler on the corner. They giggled like schoolgirls, bumping onto the white clay walls as their bodies emerged in and out of shadows.

They made their way out into the other side of the labyrinth, darting into a second main road—a much quieter one, trodden by tired bodies rushing home. The peddlers here looked more worn-out, and so did their wares. A group of paraplegics huddled around a fire, listening to the radio. In the distance, a streetcar went by, its overhead wires slicing the sky into two.

Jae-Hwa—tired, hungry, confused—turned to Soo-Ja. "I wish he'd stop following us! Should we ask someone for help?"

"Listen, he's not the one following us. We're the ones *leading* him."

"What do you mean?" asked Jae-Hwa.

"I'm taking him someplace where they'll take care of *kkang-pae* like him."

"Where are you taking us to?"

"It'll be a nice little surprise for our new friend."

Soo-Ja took Jae-Hwa's hand again and led her onward, diving into the night like an expert swimmer, splashing dots of black onto the asphalt. She knew she was only a block or two from her final goal—the police station.

Soo-Ja waited for the stranger to turn the corner, as she stood in front of the police station—a one-story brick building with high windows and a pointy spire on its awning. Next to Soo-Ja, a police officer appeared ready to lunge, eager to play hero for the young damsels. He fit the part—burly, with massive hands, wearing his black cap low above his eyes. His dark blue uniform molded onto his large frame, his chest shining with the police insignia.

When the stranger finally turned the corner and realized where Soo-Ja had led him to—saw the punchline of the joke that had been told—he immediately turned around to flee. The officer jumped at him, his hands and arms so quick as to make him seem like an octopus. The man in white struggled—elbows hitting rib cages, hands made into fists, feet on tiptoe attempting to launch. But he looked like a teenager, so much larger was the officer. While subduing the young man, the officer kept taunting him by slapping the back of his head.

"*I-nom-a!* You like following girls? Would you like me following you around all day?"

Soo-Ja watched the complicated mechanics of the fight, the way the officer teased him by letting him go and then grabbing him again. The young man thrashed about like a boy being dressed down by his father, who happened to be a bear. Soo-Ja could see the frustration in his eyes, the long, desperate breaths.

He had hunted her down through the alleyways of Won-dae-don, only to walk into a trap. Finally, the officer tossed the young man onto the ground, face against grime. The officer placed his foot on the young man's chest before he could even try to get up.

Looking at the stranger in white, Soo-Ja realized that he was quite young—probably their age, twenty-one or twenty-two. He was also handsome, with a small button nose, slightly puckered lips, and bright, intense eyes. He had an oval-shaped face, as delicate as if it had been penciled in, and marked by a dimple on his straight chin. Seeing him beaten up evoked a feeling of pity in Soo-Ja. She felt relief when the officer finally let go and let the boy lie by himself on the cement floor.

"What were you doing following these girls?" the officer repeated.

The stranger coughed a little and then spoke, between hard breaths.

"I just wanted to find out where she lived," he said. The cop turned around and looked directly at Soo-Ja, who felt more glad than ever that she hadn't led him to her own house.

Then the officer turned to the stranger again. "Why did you want to do that?"

"So I could come back another day and ask her for a—"

"For a what?" barked the cop, leaning over and slapping the back of the boy's head again.

"For a date," the boy finally said, turning to the other side to evade the cop's large gloved hands.

A crowd had gathered around them. It was now, officially, a *scene*. The other cops looked at Soo-Ja. In a second, the situation had flipped: they saw themselves in the young man's shoes and sympathized with him—rooted for him even.

"Then why didn't you act like a normal person from the beginning and just talk to us?" asked Jae-Hwa. "Instead of following us around and scaring us to death?"

The young man got up slowly. He could probably feel the tide turning, his emotional capital increasing by the minute. He shook the dirt off his clothes and turned to Soo-Ja. His white jacket was no longer white, but rather a combination of sand, grime, and blood. But even like this— his face red, his eyes half shut—he still radiated a certain imperious presence. Soo-Ja could tell that he came from a rich family. They stood there like equals, while the others became mere plebeians, extras in the background.

"Let's start over. My name is Min Lee," he said, bowing to Soo-Ja. "My father is Nam Lee, the industrialist. I should've had the guts to talk to you. If I promise to behave, will you go on a date with me?"

Soo-Ja looked at his dirty clothes, his bruised face. He reminded her of a fig fallen from a tree, its broken skin an invitation to worms. She sensed a kind of spotlight over her, and the crowd holding its breath, waiting for an answer. The world circled around her body, as she weighed the pros and cons of what seemed like a big decision. How could she offer another blow to this young man, who'd already been so mangled and mistreated by all of them?

"All right," said Soo-Ja, and she could feel the collective relief of the crowd watching. "You can pick me up for a date sometime. But you'll have to find out where I live on your own. Because I'm not planning on telling you."

"Where have you been? Your father's been waiting for you!" called the servant, in her gray hanbok uniform, with rags in her hands. Soo-Ja had just rushed past the main gate, entering the hundred-year-old compound that she called home. She stood in the middle of the courtyard, her human presence instantly providing balance to the elements—the dark sky melted into the wave-shaped black tiles on the rooftop, ebbing into the curved eaves connecting the head and the body of the one-story house, which in turn blended into the lighter shades of the thick wooden doors. On the ground, the white, hand-washed stone floors flowed into the roots and stems of a grove of pine trees, their needles swaying to the side, their cones hatching open like chicken eggs.

"Did he say why?" asked Soo-Ja, glancing at the main house.

The round lamp bulbs illuminated her father's familiar, rotund shape, sitting expectantly in the middle of the room.

"What have you done this time? Now go in! Don't keep your parents waiting any longer," said the servant, before heading back to the kitchen.

Soo-Ja ran up the stone steps leading to the main house, but took her time reaching the room, letting her shadow announce her arrival first. She glanced down at the dark yellow paper doors, the fiber thick and rough to the touch, the surface porous, almost alive. Her breathing slowed a little, and her fingers carefully slid the doors open, one in each direction, revealing the waiting figures of her parents inside, both sitting on the floor.

Soo-Ja's father looked up from the account book in front of him on his writing table and put away the square rubric he used to sign checks. Next to him, Soo-Ja's mother held a luminous silver-colored brass bowl, with loose grains of white rice scattered around its rim. They had just finished dinner, and half-empty plates of *banchan* sat on the lacquered mahogany dining tray in front of them: spicy cabbage, soybean sprouts, baby octopus dipped in chili pepper paste.

"Where have you been all night? Never mind. Do you know what this is?" Soo-Ja's father asked, removing his eyeglasses and waving a letter at her.

Soo-Ja sat down across from him on the bean-oiled floor. She tried to look ladylike, with her knees touching and her feet behind her. She couldn't bear to stay in that position long and switched her legs around. "No, Father."

"I received a visitor at the factory this morning."

"Who was it?" asked Soo-Ja, pressing her fingers against the floor, where the shiny laminate had turned yellow over time.

"It was a man from the Foreign State Department. He came to talk to me about a job for you in the Foreign Service. Do you know about this?"

Soo-Ja bit her lip. "What did he say?"

"Some nonsense about a daughter of mine applying for their diplomat training program. Although I can't imagine a daughter of mine would go behind my back and do this without asking my permission."

"But, let's say, if a daughter of yours did apply for the program . . . did she receive news that she'd been accepted?" asked Soo-Ja, anxiously moving her body forward, her back perfectly straight.

Soo-Ja's father looked at her, exasperated. "How could you do this without even asking me first?"

"I'm sorry, *abeoji*. But you wouldn't have let me if I'd asked you."

"For a good reason," said Soo-Ja's mother, speaking for the first time, as she rearranged the oval millet-filled pillow under her. "If you want to work before you get married, you can become a teacher or a secretary. A diplomat? I've never heard of such a thing."

Soo-Ja glanced at her mother. She was a small-boned woman, who looked older than her forty-four years. She kept her hair in a net a lot of the time and wore grandmotherly clothes: layers of heavy wool sweaters, old-fashioned loose pantaloons, and duck-shaped white socks. She never acted like a rich woman, and possessed no jewelry.

"That's not what I want to do. I want to travel," said Soo-Ja. "Can I— can I see what the letter says?"

Soo-Ja's father hesitated, then handed her the letter.

Soo-Ja read it eagerly, and she reached the middle before realizing she'd been accepted. Her heart immediately began to flutter, as if she had a bird trapped inside her chest, madly trying to break away. Soo-Ja looked up at her parents, smiling, expecting to see pride reflected in their eyes. But she found none.

"You must be out of your mind to think you're going to Seoul," said Soo-Ja's mother. She leaned her face over a small container of cooking gas until the tobacco in her pipe began to burn. "What would people say if we let you go live alone in a strange city? That just isn't done."

Next door, in the kitchen, the cook and her helpers had been on their feet for hours by the kitchen furnace. They were preparing the food for the next day's Seollal holiday, steaming *song-pyeon* over a bed of aromatic pine needles in a gigantic iron pot. But no sounds emanated from the kitchen, as if the preparations for the feast were on hold, and the servants, too, were being chastised.

"We have to protect you," Soo-Ja's mother continued. "What do you think would happen with no one to watch out for you? What would our friends and business associates say if they heard we let you go to Seoul on your own? They'd think we've gone mad, that we're incompetent parents."

Soo-Ja could hear noises coming from the kitchen again, as the servants resumed their cooking. She heard the sound of a pig's head being chopped off with a butcher knife, its entrails thrown into the pan, sizzling over the fire. The air in the room felt heavy, and Soo-Ja felt bound to her spot.

"I would work very hard," pleaded Soo-Ja. "I would go from my classes to my room and from my room to my classes. I would not speak to anyone. I would visit Aunt Bong-Cha frequently, so she could verify that I'm all right."

Soo-Ja's father looked pensive. "Your mother's right. Seoul is not a safe city. You hear on the radio every day about clashes between protestors and the police."

"There have been clashes everywhere!" said Soo-Ja, making her hands into fists.

"But not quite like in Seoul," her father retorted. "It's the nation's capital. The Blue House is there. It attracts all kinds of troublemakers."

"These demonstrations aren't going to last forever. They'll be over soon," said Soo-Ja, almost rising to her feet. She made herself as still as a stone pagoda, hoping that their words would slide over her like rain in a storm.

"Stop it, Soo-Ja," said her mother, signaling an end to the discussion.

She took the pipe out of her mouth and waved it in her daughter's direction. "Are you a good daughter, or are you a fox daughter? This is for the best."

With that final dismissal, Soo-Ja knew she would not be able to go to Seoul. She'd never be a diplomat. The pain from this realization was so intense, Soo-Ja had to balance on the floor, for fear it would give way from under her. Soo-Ja asked herself why the ground was shaking, until she realized it was she herself who was.

"You're wrong," she said. "I will go. I will find a way."

At around midnight, Soo-Ja was awakened by the sound of wolves howling, except these wolves were also calling out her name. Soo-Ja rubbed her eyes, still red from crying, and quickly rose from the floor, pushing aside the heavy, quilted blankets. She reached into her dresser and grabbed the first thick garment she could find—a long brown coat with fish-hook buttons that came down to her knees. She put it on and rushed out of her room, toward the source of the noise.

Soo-Ja ran through the many wings of the house, her bare feet rapping against the hard cement floors. Her hurried breath echoed through the large, airy rooms, filled with huge armoires, paintings and scrolls against the walls. Her brothers' sliding doors opened and shut as she went by, their sleepy eyes adjusting to her as her nightgown flew in the air, like wings, underneath her coat.

When Soo-Ja reached the courtyard—dark but for a small lamp over the murky lotus pond—she saw her father standing there already. He wore his glasses and was in his pajamas, listening to the ruckus of the college boys outside the gate.

"Show us your face! Show us your face just once!" they called out. "Just one glance!"

Soo-Ja didn't feel flattered. It was embarrassing that her father had to listen to this. She knew the boys were drunk with *soju*, and just being young. They didn't know love; they were only imitating its gestures. Too bashful to even speak to her in class, they couldn't have become courtly lovers overnight.

"Do you know them?" asked her father.

"Not who they are. Only where they came from."

"Your college?"

"I think so."

"Should we invite them in, then, for some green tea?" asked her father, giving her a sardonic look. Soo-Ja knew there was nothing her father would have liked more than to dump a big, cold bucket of water on the boys. He would know how to work out the theatrics of it—how to open the gate slowly, to play up their expectations; how to toss the water from the right angle, to catch more of them; how to deliver the final words, the punchline.

Before he could be tempted to do that, Soo-Ja asked him to wait. She ran inside, toward her mother's room. When she returned, a minute or so later, Soo-Ja had her face covered by some kind of mask. She headed straight to the gate and pushed it open, like a general opening the fortress to the enemy.

The young men grew noisy with excitement, and then utterly silent. They saw an apparition in front of them: Soo-Ja wearing a grotesque *tal* mask, carved out of alder wood and painted in red and blue colors. It was the traditional *Hahoe* dance mask, worn in old times by actors performing songs. It had exaggerated facial expressions—half human, half spirit—with gigantic eyebrows; tiny slits for eyes; and three red dots, one on the forehead, and one on each cheek. Until a few minutes ago, the mask had hung as decoration on the wall of Soo-Ja's mother's room.

"Here I am! You asked for me, and here I am!" Soo-Ja said, from behind the tiny horizontal slits of the mask.

None of the young men knew what to say. As the effects of the rice wine started to wear off, they hesitated—some of them laughing awkwardly—while Soo-Ja stood there, daring them.

"You wanted to see me. Well, here I am!" Soo-Ja felt emboldened by the day's events. Her parents had hurt her; now she wanted to hurt others.

It was then, as Soo-Ja watched the boys look away, that she noticed the crowd part a little, and someone in the middle moved forward. She recognized him right away as Min, the young man she'd encountered on the street. She watched as he came closer, smiling his cocky smile, his hair slicked back with Vaseline. She noticed his lip was a bit cut, and his face bruised. She wondered how he'd found out her address. *Were these his friends?* Min wore the same white jacket and white pants, but either they were a different pair or had already been cleaned, and immaculately so. What kind of man, Soo-Ja wondered, had an armoire full of all-white clothes?

Min came close enough to reach her face. For a moment, she thought he'd try to rip the mask away from her. But instead, in a quick gesture, like a military man, he bowed deeply to her. When his head snapped back, he stared at her again, with great respect. Then he turned to his companions and spoke as if they'd been the ones bothering Soo-Ja.

"Everyone go home. You've bothered her enough for tonight."

The young men hesitated—some hissing—but eventually began to disperse, walking in different directions. They did so slowly, curious to hear the words Soo-Ja and Min were to exchange. Like children—who wondered what adults did after they put them to bed—they imagined some magical alchemy might take place.

"What do you want from me?" asked Soo-Ja, once they were completely alone.

"I already told you. A date."

Soo-Ja sighed and took her mask off. So this is what it came down to—a lovesick boy, caught in some fever, like the youngest member of a tribe long inured to such malaise. Soo-Ja didn't know what to say. All she knew was that it was an ungodly late hour, and the moment could not be any less romantic. Soo-Ja stepped back and leaned her head against the gate, her body parallel to his, and she liked that they didn't have to look directly at each other. She stared at her street through Min's eyes: the rose of Sharon blooming on the ground, stubbornly bursting forth from between rocks and concrete; the rows of acacia trees resting after a long day of giving shade, branches swaying quietly with the wind.

"I'm sorry, I don't think that's possible," said Soo-Ja, turning away from him. She longed to be back in her room, but as she opened the gate, she hesitated. Standing still, her face under a lamp, Soo-Ja watched as dragonflies danced around her. "Please go now. I don't want my father to come out and see you here."

Min placed his hand against the gate, not letting her open it. "Does he like to beat up your suitors?"

"No, he prefers to torture them with long stories about French missionaries."

Then, as if on cue, Soo-Ja heard her father's unmistakable footsteps walking toward the gate. Soo-Ja thought about hiding Min behind one of the trees, but just as she grabbed his hand to lead him, her father came out and saw them. Soo-Ja immediately let go of Min. She felt her father's disapproving eyes corrode her skin, looking straight at her.

Soo-Ja could sense the anger her father felt, but she knew he would not admonish her—not after all the forbidding he'd already done that day. He'd have to forgive this indiscretion the way lords allow peasants a single day of festivity, so they won't mind the return to the fields the rest of the year.

"Come back inside," he said sharply, before he turned around and left.

Soo-Ja stood in the same spot, her heart pumping fast. She wondered if she would ever see Min again. He looked at her, the whites of his eyes shining in the dark. Soo-Ja stared back at him. If she had been the man, she might have kissed him. He stood there, silent, unsure what to do with a river to cross, or a sea dragon to get past. He looked like a boy who's been brought over to the adults' table and asked to sing. For all his swagger, he was no Romeo. He was barely Mercutio.

"Good night," Soo-Ja finally said.

"Good night," Min repeated, suddenly coming to life, as if she'd broken a spell. He turned around and, for some reason, began to run. Never looking back, Min ran as if someone were chasing him.

Seollal, the celebration of the Lunar New Year, began early in the morning, and Soo-Ja woke to the lively sound of relatives being greeted by her father in the main house. They had been arriving since six o'clock, aunts and uncles Soo-Ja rarely saw and didn't really think of as family except twice a year, when everyone would gather for the two major holidays— *Chuseok*, the day of giving thanks, was the other.

Soo-Ja thought for a moment of staying in bed, but she did not want to disappoint her dead ancestors—Seollal was the day of honoring them. She pushed aside the heavy quilted blankets, got up from the floor, and staggered to her armoire, where her collection of hanbok dresses waited for her.

Hanbok was the traditional formal dress, made up of a short jacket top, fastened together with a large ribbonlike *ot-ga-reom*, and a long wraparound skirt. The bottom, with the top held tightly over the breasts, funneled outward until it was as wide as a wedding gown. Unlike an outfit made of cotton or nylon, hanbok did not hang limply—the thick hand-woven silk gave the cloth so much body, it looked as if the fabric floated over her.

After methodically getting dressed—working through the many knots and layers of the hanbok—Soo-Ja decided to stop by the outhouse in the back of the compound. The cubicle next to it had running water, and Soo-Ja thought it best to splash some on her face, still a bit swollen from the previous night's tears.

Soo-Ja walked swiftly outside, holding up the hem of her long hanbok so it wouldn't brush against the ground. The day, devoid of sun and color, felt like an only slightly less punitive extension of night, its chill blowing against her bare neck and ankles.

Soo-Ja was in a hurry; she could hear in the distance the start of the prayers, and she knew everyone would already be gathered in the main house. But as she was about to turn the corner, she heard something that made her stop in her tracks. It was her name, spoken in the high-pitched trill of her cousin Ae-Cha.

"She really must think she's something special," said Ae-Cha, coming off a bit muted, as if inside the outhouse. Soo-Ja leaned against the wall, keeping her breath still so she wouldn't be noticed. "She wants everyone's attention, and that's why she's creating so much commotion."

"So you don't think she really wants to be a diplomat?" Soo-Ja heard someone else ask. Her voice sounded more clear, and Soo-Ja figured it must be another one of her cousins.

"Of course not! She's just making a big show of this to get attention. The sorrow she's causing Aunt and Uncle! How can she be such an ungrateful daughter?" Ae-Cha continued.

"I think you're being hard on Soo-Ja. Maybe she really wants to do it."

Soo-Ja peeked from the corner and recognized her cousin Chun-Hee's short, boyish haircut, heavy glasses, and royal blue hanbok. Chun-Hee sat on a tree stump next to the outhouse, holding a roll of toilet paper. The door—worn out from the wood constantly expanding and contracting in the rain—was left an inch ajar, and Soo-Ja guessed Ae-Cha was inside. Soo-Ja glanced behind her own shoulder, to see if anyone was coming, but there was no one, and she turned her attention back to the conversation.

"Soo-Ja really wants to travel so she can find and marry a brown man!"

"Are you sure you're not just jealous, Ae-Cha?" Chun-Hee teased her. "Because you're not as pretty as she is?"

"I'd be pretty, too, if I never did a day's work in my life. Who ferments her *kimchee*? Who distills her soy sauce? Her servants! It must be very tiresome to have to do all that shopping!"

Chun-Hee chuckled for a while. Soo-Ja listened, in disbelief.

"Diplomat? What a lie! *Secretary* is more like it. She claims she got into the Foreign Service. I'd like to see that letter," Ae-Cha continued, her voice growing louder and more animated. "Although I don't blame her for lying. She's such an old maid—she needs to start looking into other options."

Soo-Ja could not put up with this any longer. She turned the corner and walked to the outhouse. Chun-Hee saw her first, and immediately her face turned white. She froze to her spot, dropping the toilet paper on the floor. Ae-Cha could see her, too, as the door to the outhouse creaked further open on its own. She squatted uncomfortably, holding up her skirt. Her previous look of confidence disappeared.

"You two are right," said Soo-Ja, in a sarcastic tone. "I *am* an old maid.

I'm twenty-two years old, after all. And no matter how hard I try, I cannot get men to look at me."

Chun-Hee fluttered her hands in disagreement. "No, no, *eonni*! You must've misheard us! We weren't criticizing you!"

Soo-Ja stared at her evenly. "I appreciate your being concerned about my parents and me. You two being guests here, I won't say any more. But in the future, if you're curious about my life, feel free to ask me directly. You won't have to wonder or guess. It'll save you time."

With that, Soo-Ja turned away from them and walked to the main house. When she arrived, she saw that the ceremony had already started. All of the men were gathered by a large wooden altar filled with plates of food—offerings to the dead. Two tall candles were lit and placed at each end of the altar, which stood in front of a large folding screen with five panels. The screen covered the entire wall and was filled with *hanja*, Chinese ideograms. Below the altar, incense burned from a small table.

Soo-Ja joined her mother and the other women, who sat against the wall, while the men performed the rites. She watched as her father slowly poured a glass of wine, and then placed it on the altar as the first offering. Soo-Ja gazed at her father's face. She stared at his soft cotton-white hair, and the thick lines on the sides of his cheeks. He had a few days' stubble on his chin, and bags under his eyes. She realized that because of her, he had not slept well the previous night, either.

"Soo-Ja," whispered her mother, after waiting for the men's chants to grow louder and drown out her voice. "It is fortunate that Seollal is today. It'll remind you of the three Confucian obediences that must rule a woman's life."

"Don't worry, Mother. It has been drilled into me from the day I was born. Obedience to father, obedience to husband, obedience to male child."

But Confucius was wrong, thought Soo-Ja.

Soo-Ja's mother watched as the men bowed on the floor, lowering their knees, followed by their hands, and then their heads—all in one continuous, seamless motion. They folded themselves small like human paper dolls, going from adult, to child, to newborn, and then upright again. Soo-Ja's mother narrowed her eyes and spoke softly to her daughter.

"Don't think you can fool me. I know how much you want to go. You've always been rebellious like that. Once you put an idea in your head, you go after it like an arrow to its target."

"If Father really loved me, he'd let me go."

"You clearly know nothing about love. And I didn't realize your life here was so terrible. Most girls your age are breaking their backs farming rice paddies. You sit at home and read poetry."

Soo-Ja looked at her mother. She wanted to tell her, *Mother, you speak as if you've never known what it's like to want something.* Instead, Soo-Ja bit her lips lest she speak out of place. She watched as the men—all the sons—bowed and chanted to the ancestors, while the women stood back. They were all crammed in one room, and Soo-Ja had to fight the desire to run away.

"I thought parents wanted what was best for their children."

"That is a myth. We want what is best for *us.*"

"I know. You want me to get married. But I'd rather go to diplomat school."

"Those two things are not mutually exclusive," said Soo-Ja's mother. She turned to her daughter and looked at her not as her child, but as a fellow woman. "If you find someone weak—a man different from your father—somebody who will let you make decisions; of course, you'll have to let him think he's the one in charge. You're eager to go to Seoul. I'm eager for you to get married. Perhaps there can be a compromise."

"I thought you were against me going to Seoul."

"I'm against you going there as a single woman. There is a difference."

Soo-Ja took in her mother's words and realized she was not so alone, after all.

Someone weak. Who will let me make decisions.

The answer came to her instantly: she'd have to trick her future husband.

chapter two

"*Hana, dul, set!* One, two, three! One, two, three!" The instructor barked out drills at the young men filling the outdoor gymnasium.

The students were in their late teens and early twenties, all of them roughly the same height and build, wearing identically serious expressions. They moved in perfect unison—jumping up and down, squatting, and lifting their arms in the air. Soo-Ja sat on the bleachers a few yards away from them, watching. She did not know if Min had noticed her, so intent he seemed on the exercises. She wondered if the laws of gravity applied to sight, so that a look of interest—however weighty—would not land any quicker than an uninterested one.

When they finally finished, Min ran toward the bleachers, where Soo-Ja sat, and plopped himself down. His breath was still heavy from the effort, sweat covering his face and body. "I don't have much time. I have to go back there."

"Well, you don't have to sit here with me. Why do you even assume I came here to see *you*?" teased Soo-Ja. *Keep this up*, thought Soo-Ja, *and I won't choose you. Some other boy will get me to Seoul.*

"Did you come here to say good-bye?"

"Good-bye?" asked Soo-Ja, worried her plan would be over before it even began.

"I'm heading out to Seoul next week, with some of the other boys from my class. Didn't you hear? Everyone's talking about it. The students there are planning massive demonstrations on the streets."

"In Masan, I heard."

"Everywhere. Masan, Daegu, Seoul. I hope there'll be fights with the police. If the pigs come after me, I'll be ready," said Min, pulling out an imaginary gun and pointing it at an invisible assailant.

"I hope you're wrong. I hope there's no violence. President Rhee should step down on his own."

"I don't understand why everyone hates him so much, by the way," said Min, pretending to put his invisible gun away in its holster.

"Maybe because he takes foreign aid money meant for the reconstruction and lavishes it upon his cronies. Or because he throws people in jail for no reason, especially if they oppose him," said Soo-Ja.

"Does that really sound that bad? I'd probably do the same."

"How long will you be in Seoul?" asked Soo-Ja, trying to hide the envy in her voice.

"For as long as the excitement lasts."

"Isn't it going to be dangerous? Is your magic gun going to protect you?"

"No. But your thoughts of me will," said Min cheekily, glancing at her askew as if to see how she would react.

Soo-Ja smiled at his flirtatious tone. "Just be safe."

"I can't. I'm going to march in the very first row."

The wind grew stronger, blowing Soo-Ja's hair in the air. She held it down with her hand, rearranging her headband. "Don't be a fool. What if something happens to you?"

"Well, it's not like my life is even worth that much," he said ruefully. Min lowered his head heavily and stared at the bleacher below him, tracking its cold silver contours with his fingers. "Although, if you gave me a date, that'd give me a reason to stay here . . ."

Soo-Ja gave him a sideways glance. "I'll think of you while you're gone."

"Well, that's a beginning." He got up excitedly and pretended to hug her. "And maybe if I do something impressive, you'll marry me."

"It would have to be *very* impressive," she said, joking along, amused that he really had no clue that she'd been putting on an act.

You're clearly in love with me. Would it be fair to you, though, if I married you? And used you to get me out of my father's house, and on my way to Seoul? You, who seem to have no career prospects, would you let me earn money for us as a diplomat? You, who seem to flounder and meander, would you have any choice but to let me make decisions?

Min noticed the instructor making his way back to the court outside, gathering the men one last time before dismissing them. "I have to run back. What did you come here to talk about?"

"Nothing. I just came to see you," said Soo-Ja, hoping to sound convincing.

As she walked away from the gym, leaving behind the voices of the men chanting, Soo-Ja wondered which one was Min's. And the thought struck her then—she didn't really know anything about the man she was planning to spend the rest of her life with.

My dear Soo-Ja,

My first week as a revolutionary fighter—how do you like the sound of that?—is over, and while the other students are upstairs on the rooftop, exchanging oaths of loyalty, I write here in the basement, with a bottle of makgeolli by my side.

What a long week it has been! We have gone on several protests already, and each of them is a miracle of logistical planning and precision. Have you ever yelled the same words loudly with a group of a thousand people? Try it sometime; it sends quite a burst of oxygen to the brain. I have never felt so connected to people I feel such disdain for. When we demonstrate, the police stand at a barricade, blocking our way, and there's always a tense moment when neither party knows whose turn it is to push forward. The trick is to have both strong lungs and legs; I've been hit more times now than I can count, but luckily always manage to get away.

It's hard not to come back for the next protest, however. The feeling is quite addictive. Afterward we go to secret meeting places. Yesterday we met at a political science professor's house for drinks. This is, of course, the part that keeps me here. The others begin a long litany of criticisms of the regime. I pay lip service to all that, waiting for the bottle of soju to make its way back to me. I have to say I'm a bit of an outcast here. The others do not entirely trust me.

At times, I feel silly holding up some of the placards. They have such poetry as "Down with Fraudulent Elections!" and "Can Freedom Gained Through Blood Be Taken Away by Bayonets?" The other students have rejected some of my ideas for chants, as well as my suggestion that we simply wait for the President to die of old age. He is, after all, 85 years old. I cannot imagine he'll live that long. If we've waited millenniums for democracy—as ours is such an old nation—I figure we can wait another year or two.

Sometimes I wish to tell my friends here about you, but I fear they would not believe me. I think of your beautiful, silky long hair. Your porcelain complexion. Your high cheekbones. Your big, pendant-shaped eyes. Your long-bridged nose. Your gorgeous smile, warm and wicked all at once. Your face, shaped like those mysterious stone statues on the ground in Cheju Island. We do not know how they came to be there, or who carved them, but we can wonder, and I wonder, at you.

Perhaps if you sent me a picture I could prove to everyone here that you are real—and prove to myself, too, that you weren't just something I invented in my head. May your days be good, and they must be, if they're filled with half the hope and joy you give me.

Min Lee

Soo-Ja sighed and closed her eyes. She was happy, but envious. She wanted to be the one far away, writing letters about her own adventures to some virginal bride who would ooh and aah at her courage. She wanted to be the one telling Min how much she was fighting to keep up her strength. If getting this letter was so sweet, imagine being able to be the one to write it.

But maybe I should just be grateful for what I have, Soo-Ja told herself. There was much to enjoy about living in Daegu. Yes, half the time it was either raining or snowing, but during the glorious fall and spring, she'd lose herself in the hilltops behind her house. There, she'd race past the gingko, pine, maple, bamboo, and persimmon trees, and count constellations of lilacs, tiger lilies, moonflowers, cherry blossoms, and red peonies. She breathed in wisteria and walked on chestnut leaves. She traced trellised grapevines and caressed silkworms in the mulberry groves. Soo-Ja drew imaginary rings around the ubiquitous mountains in the distance, and pretended to be in the Scotland she'd read so much about. And when the monsoon rains came, for days at a time, creating miniature pools on the ground, Soo-Ja and her brothers splashed around, kicking water into one another's faces.

If Soo-Ja ever left Daegu, she knew she would miss its lavender skies and peach-colored sunsets; the fresh red bean cakes from the bakery, still warm from the wood-burning oven; the Saturday afternoons spent soaking with her mother at the bathhouse, the heat as comforting as the sound of gossip all around her; and above all, the innocence of her childhood, still free of secrets, lovers, and ambitions.

It is no good to want to stay. Getting these kinds of letters only made Soo-Ja want to leave more. She prayed for Min to come back safe and come back soon, so he could help her with her plans. And in the meantime, she had to make sure to keep her father from finding out about him.

Soo-Ja put the letter away. There were few places to hide it, since her room was entirely bare except for the large *nong* armoire where she kept her coverlets and comforters and clothes. She decided to go to the kitchen, where her mother stored empty earthenware kimchee jars. But when she got there and opened some of them, she found that they were already filled—with money. This was an old habit of theirs. Her father gave her mother a large allowance every week for household expenses, and her mother, not knowing what to do with the extra money, often placed it in jars, where the hwan bills took on the smell of spices.

Soo-Ja went back to her room, frustrated, and took her clothes off to go to bed. She considered simply leaving the letter inside her jewel box—a small treasure chest inlaid with shiny mother-of-pearl—but it seemed too obvious a hiding place. Then, as she folded her woolen shirt, she decided to place her letter inside it, wrapped between the folds of fabric of its sleeves. She'd have to find some other place before Tuesday, when the servants did the washing. But for now it seemed to make perfect sense to leave it there, ensconced between the clothes she had been inside all day and had just cast off.

Soo-Ja's father sounded angry when he called her into his room. He sat cross-legged on the floor facing her. He did not speak right away, and she found herself staring at the screens behind him—four large ink paintings, one for each of the four mythical animals: blue dragon, white tiger, red phoenix, and black tortoise. She imagined her father as the dragon, and herself as the tiger. She wondered which would win in the end.

"This time you've gone too far," he said.

"What did I do now?" asked Soo-Ja, her eyes rolling to the back of her head.

Soo-Ja's father reached for a stack of letters and tossed them on the writing table in front of him. Soo-Ja opened her mouth, surprised. *How had he found them?*

"Is this the same young man who showed up at our door that night?"

"What night?" asked Soo-Ja innocently. She avoided his gaze, looking instead at the white tiger in the painting on the screen, its mouth open in a roar, one paw in front of the other. It looked as if about to charge, and only self-control held it back.

"You must have him come and introduce himself, so I can officially tell him how inappropriate he is for you."

"He's not in Daegu. He's in Seoul. You shouldn't have read my—"

"I didn't. And what's he doing in Seoul? He hasn't finished college yet? Is he younger than you are? You cannot consider someone who isn't at least a year older than you."

"He's in Seoul for something else. And *appa*, don't make a scandal out of this. He's barely an acquaintance."

Her father flashed her a grim look. "Is he a member of a student group? One of those lazy bums, living in boardinghouses, who can't get a job, and so wastes his time getting into fights with the police? Some fool dying for democracy?"

"He's not dying for democracy," she said, looking away. "Maybe getting bruised, but not dying for it. He's there more for the social aspect."

"How do you know so much about him? I thought you said he was barely an acquaintance."

It was no use trying to lie to her father. Soo-Ja threw her hands up in the air.

"I can't imagine anything I say is going to satisfy you, so maybe I should just sit here like a mute."

"At least you no longer fight with me about diplomat school. I have *that* to be thankful for. You seem to have taken that decision rather well."

"I have, haven't I?" said Soo-Ja, using the back of her hand to wipe off the serene, mysterious smile taking residence on her lips.

My dear Soo-Ja,

I hesitate before writing you this letter, as I do not wish to involve you in anything dangerous. But the protests are moving beyond Seoul and are making their way to our own hometown of Daegu. You may have heard about this—or maybe not, as the government has been trying to keep this away from the newspapers—but a neighbor of ours has gone missing. He's a young boy—a twelve-year-old middle school student— from our very own town of Won-dae-don. His name is Chu-Sook Yang, and he attended a demonstration in Daegu; in Jungantong, we believe. Group records show he called himself a member of our organization. Apparently, he never made it home after the demonstration. All of us here suspect some kind of foul play.

The leader of the Daegu chapter of our group, a rather smart medical student named Yul-Bok Kim, has tried to contact the boy's mother, but she refuses to provide any information, and won't speak to any of us. (Have the President's men gotten to her already, maybe?) Yul has asked me if I know her, and I laughed at him, since I don't exactly spend my weekends with teenage boys from the slums. But then I thought, I may not know the boy's family, but maybe Soo-Ja does. I know your father's factory employs a lot of people in town—even if the boy's mother doesn't know you, I'm guessing she'd be willing to talk to someone of your stature. Yul lives in the Mangwon district, not too far from you. I'm attaching his phone number and address—he'll await contact from you—should you decide to get involved in this.

Min Lee

"Excuse me, excuse me," said Soo-Ja, making her way to the back of the bus. She wore a pink embroidered coat with a high collar, a red silk chemise with a bow over her chest, and a long cream polyester skirt. She also had a yellow headband on top of her head, accentuating her bangs. She looked as if she were simply heading for an afternoon stroll.

According to the instructions she'd been given, she was to take the Dalseo-gu bus at the Won-dae-don stop and sit on one of the last seats in the last row, making sure to keep the one next to her empty. As the bus sputtered forward on the unpaved asphalt, driving over stones on the road, its constant bumps made Soo-Ja lose balance several times, grabbing the metal handrail repeatedly to keep steady. Outside, wreaths of smoke covered the ground behind them, tinting everything she saw out the windows in shades of brown.

When Soo-Ja finally reached the last row, she sank into one of the hard cloth-covered seats, drawing the attention of an old man in a broad-rimmed black horsehair hat, the kind that had gone out of fashion in the twenties. He turned to glance at her, and Soo-Ja glowered at him until he went back to talking to his friends. They were a group of about four white-haired men in their sixties, sitting on the two rows in front and across from Soo-Ja. They talked like teenagers, touching one another's arms and teasing one another over the supposed aphrodisiac quality of ginseng tea. Their laughter was raucous, almost ricocheting against the sides of the bus.

As Soo-Ja watched them, she was reminded of a Swiss teacher she'd had in high school, who had told her how surprised he was to see the physical expressiveness of Korean people. Indeed they moved their bodies extravagantly, used them like punctuation marks, with arms rising, and fingers freely pointing in the air for emphasis; they were like a country full of excitable preachers gesticulating to congregations of one or two listeners at a time. They weren't quiet at all; in fact the opposite: temperamental, given to passions, sentimental to a fault. Their feelings and emotions flashed on their faces with the intensity of a close-up projected on a giant screen, and they weren't afraid to weep or laugh in front of other people.

"Good. Their laughter will drown out our conversation," she heard a young man say as he took the seat next to her. He had appeared out of nowhere, as efficient and unobtrusive as a comma. Soo-Ja swallowed nervously; she knew this was the leader of the student group.

They rode for a few minutes in silence, with Soo-Ja stealing occasional glimpses of him. Yul had on black rectangular glasses and a brown corduroy jacket. He was dressed casually, with no tie. His hair looked slightly unkempt, not in a disheveled way, but in the manner of someone who did not bother with mirrors or Vaseline. He wore it a bit long, like a European beatnik.

"I'm glad you came. I was afraid you might change your mind," said Yul, looking straight ahead. "This is more than we have the right to ask of you."

"You're right," said Soo-Ja, also staring straight ahead. She decided not to tell him how much she had enjoyed being asked to help. Everywhere she went, there was talk of the student movement. Now, she could carry with pride her own sudden, unexpected role in it. "Nevertheless, I'm just a woman riding the bus. You're the one being chased by the police."

"Good point," he said. "But don't worry about me. The police aren't going to do anything to me. The last thing they need is to create a martyr; give a face to the movement." He then lowered his head and spoke in the direction of her neck. "So, have you met Chu-Sook's mother? Do you know her?"

"No, but Min was right. Her husband used to work for my father. She thinks I'm coming to talk to her about some back pay."

"Very inventive of you to add that detail."

"I brought some money, as well as a list of questions I want to ask her," said Soo-Ja, looking into her purse.

"Don't worry about the questions. I'll handle that."

"Damn it," said Soo-Ja, going through her belongings.

"What's wrong?" asked Yul, immediately looking around him.

"Once I memorized the questions, I reached in to throw away the crumpled piece of paper, but instead of the paper with the questions, I threw away the thousand-hwan bill," said Soo-Ja, still digging through her purse.

Yul could not resist cracking a smile. He glanced at her directly for the first time in their conversation. "Maybe it's still in there."

"No, I tossed it out the window," said Soo-Ja, returning his look. "Boy, that's a lot of money to just throw away like that. I suppose I wouldn't make a very good revolutionary, would I?"

"We'll just make sure we never trust you with our secret plans," said Yul, smiling.

He was handsome when he did that, thought Soo-Ja. She let her eyes rest over him for a moment, and she noticed his high cheekbones, alabaster skin, and eyes shaped like laurel leaves. She was surprised by how *solid* he seemed, and also by the fact that he smelled a little bit like cocoa. She felt the impulse to linger near his collar and breathe in his scent, though of course she held back.

Soo-Ja smiled to herself, the earlier tension now gone. The bus made a stop, and the group of old men rose to leave, as another group of people made their way in. Soo-Ja looked over at Yul again, noticing how the sun filtered in lightly through a half-opened window behind him, casting a warm glow on the back of his head.

"So, Min said you studied literature, but that you want to be a diplomat?" asked Yul, gazing out the window, paying attention to who got on and off the bus. Soo-Ja couldn't tell if he felt a genuine interest, or if he was just trying to create an aura of casualness around them.

"The two are not so different," said Soo-Ja, surprised that Min had shared that with Yul. She'd mentioned it to Min almost in passing, and was glad to see that he remembered. "With literature, you learn how people behave, and you learn empathy, a good trait to have as a diplomat."

"Did you always want to be a diplomat?" Yul asked, still looking around.

"No, not always. When I was little, I wanted to be a waitress." Yul laughed at this, and Soo-Ja smiled at him before she continued. The bus began to move again. "I liked the uniforms, and the idea of feeding people all day. Then I wanted to be a journalist. I liked arranging words on a page. It changed, though, with the war."

Soo-Ja looked out the window, and she remembered the view from the car on the day they fled the city—the seemingly endless lines of refugees, walking the narrow roads above the rice paddies, carrying their belongings on their backs; some split their loads by each holding one end of a stick, their bags in the middle. They walked in a long line, Indian file, like prisoners in a chain gang, eyes looking down into the ground. Occasionally, someone would look up at her as the car went by, and she would nod slightly, as if she knew the person. If it was a girl, she'd even smile, as if to say, *I'll see you when we get there, I'll meet you by the seaside. It'll all be fine.*

"My parents and I had to evacuate, like everyone else, and go to Pusan, at the seaside. We stayed with an aunt of ours, by Haundae Beach, and all through the fall and winter, we watched as the refugees came. I remember it very vividly, the guards squeezing all these women and children into these crowded camps. Their clothes were made out of recycled army uniforms, and a lot of them slept and went to the bathroom on the streets. There were rats everywhere. I remember little boys with shaved heads and tin cans in their hands running after army jeeps, begging for food. My family was lucky. My father had retrofitted his shoe factory into an army uniform maker, and the President was very grateful to him. We stayed in my aunt's big house, and never went hungry during the war. In fact, we ate pineapples."

"You shouldn't feel badly about that," said Yul. "Your father probably saved the lives of a lot of soldiers."

"Well, every day I heard stories of people being killed, and bodies mangled, and found on the roads. It was terrifying. I was fourteen at the time."

"Did anyone in your family get hurt?"

"No. No one. It felt like a miracle. I remember when it all ended, the day we came back home. It felt like everything was gone—buildings bombed, roads filled with debris. Only our house, still standing. There were some people living in it, mostly men—war deserters, vagabonds, idlers. They napped on the floors. Some played *hato* cards. They had these bored looks on their faces, like they didn't care that the South had won Daegu back."

"What happened then?"

"Well, my father started telling people to get out. He used his factory-owner voice—very firm, but also kindly. Like he was saying, *Go now, before the real owner, who's much meaner, catches you here.* Nobody protested, the men just got up and started leaving. My mother gave each of them some money, enough for a hot meal, I think, and I remember everyone took the money, but nobody thanked her, or even looked her in the eye. When they left, I wondered where they'd go." Soo-Ja paused and looked at Yul again. "Are you really sure you want to hear this?"

"Yes. Go on," he said, his gaze encouraging her. The bus began to move faster now, over paved asphalt, and Soo-Ja could see the Geumho River rise beyond the windows; the sun's rays rested languidly over its waters—as still as a lover's outstretched arms.

"That night, we slept in the bare rooms. Everything we had was gone—they'd taken all our furniture, every single jar in the kitchen, every dresser and bookcase, all the lamps and writing desks. And what they couldn't carry out, like the doors, they'd pulled out parts of with screwdrivers. The only things left were the floors and the ceiling.

"So the next day, we went to the open-air market to buy new clothes and furniture. It didn't take very long until we noticed something funny about all the items on sale. I recognized a comforter I used to sleep under, yellow on top, with patchwork-like squares of different colors. I saw the armoire that used to sit in my brother's room. The silver dagger that used to hang by the mirror in my mother's room. They were selling our things! My books, from the fourth to eighth grade, the silverware we used at dinner.

"I looked at my father and he just smiled back at me and said, 'Now we find out how much our things are truly worth.' He gave my brothers and me money to go buy back our things. My mother wanted us to call the police and have all the merchants arrested, but my father shook his head and said, 'These people need to earn a living, too.' I'll never forget that. I remember going from merchant to merchant, buying back my old clothes and ornaments, and each time I was amazed that I could do that, that I could welcome back my possessions. I felt so grateful to be alive, and to be safe, and to have all my things back."

Soo-Ja smiled at the memory. She then wondered for a moment why she trusted this stranger so much. Maybe because he looked concrete, self-sufficient; he wanted nothing from her. Two, he simply let her speak, and never interrupted her.

"So that's why you want to become a diplomat. You think diplomacy alone can prevent nations from going to war?" asked Yul.

The bus reached a rough patch, driving over potholes and rocks. As Soo-Ja lurched forward slightly, Yul caught her arm and steadied her. His grip felt electric, his fingers denting her flesh. He took her hand and guided it to the handrail in front of them. Soo-Ja swallowed, embarrassed, but as she sat back again, she let her body fit snugly next to his, shoulder to shoulder.

"You think I'm naive?" asked Soo-Ja, easing back into the conversation.

"Maybe."

"Fine, so I'm naive. But I'd like to make a small difference. A small difference may not change anything, but it could also be just enough. I mean, you must have believed that as well, when you chose to become—well, what you are."

Yul did not reply. Instead, he looked at her thoughtfully. Soo-Ja felt a bit foolish for opening up so much to him. *How had he pulled it out of her?* With him, she felt the ease of being around a friend who'd neither judge nor criticize.

He was older than she was; certainly he must have fought in the war? He must have been fifteen or sixteen at the time; how had he survived, when men older and meaner had perished? Soo-Ja liked this, liked that he made her wonder about him; made her want to make up stories about him, and pick at his serene smile as if it were a lock in the wall. She had not felt this with Min—Min won her over with flattery, wearing her down with his insistence. Yul, on the other hand, made her want to flatter *him*.

"I think we're here," said Yul, as the bus began to slow down. His face became very serious, and Soo-Ja was reminded of the reason for their bus trip. The missing twelve-year-old boy. "Wait till I'm halfway through the bus, then start making your way out. If you see me run, do not run after me. Instead, duck and take cover." Yul rose, and Soo-Ja felt her body tense up. Seeing him stand, Soo-Ja noticed that Yul had the muscular build of a soldier, and an ex-soldier's careful movements. Yul must have fought for sure, either volunteering or drafted against his will. The bus came to a full stop, and Yul began to make his way out. It felt like forever, waiting. As Yul reached the midpoint, the passage seemed clear, and he turned his head slightly and glanced over at Soo-Ja, signaling for her to follow him. She rose and began heading out. She noticed that the bus seemed a little quiet to her ears, almost too much, as if the other passengers could sense something was off. Soo-Ja watched as Yul continued to make his way out in front of her. But when he was almost by the door, a passenger in a row ahead of him suddenly rose, his back blocking Yul's way. He wore a police officer's uniform.

Soo-Ja gasped, then put her hand to her mouth, to hide her reaction. The seconds seemed to stretch into infinity, as the policeman stood in front of Yul, with his back to him, and Yul remained still. Yul did not hint at this as cause for panic, and did not make a sound, but Soo-Ja noticed that he'd discreetly placed his hand near his belt. She wondered if he had a gun; if he'd need to use it. It felt like a century, when only two, three seconds passed. Finally, the officer, who took a moment to gather his things from his seat, simply walked on, and left the bus, as if it were nothing more than just his own stop.

Soo-Ja let out a sigh of relief, and she could see Yul's body release its tautness, too.

Yul started walking out. By the time he emerged, Soo-Ja had almost caught up with him, and the two of them found themselves out on the street at the same time. They did not speak, but when Soo-Ja glanced at the sign in front of the bus, she realized it had been heading not to Dalseo-gu but to Dalseong-gu; he'd made them take the long way to their destination, and made her talk the entire time while he studied her eyes and her voice. *Why?* It didn't matter, thought Soo-Ja. By now he trusted her, but more than that, she trusted him, too.

Soo-Ja and Yul walked along a long row of shacks, all with the same thatched roofs and walls made out of stones of uneven sizes stacked together. They were perched precariously atop a hill, on a narrow, wind-ing path inaccessible to cars, and only wide enough for oxcarts. Soo-Ja noticed that Yul let her set the pace, and he would slow when she did. Near the top of the hill, a man with a broken wheelbarrow attempted to pass them, and Yul subtly placed his body between Soo-Ja and the stranger. Soo-Ja glanced at him, trying to acknowledge the gesture, but he looked straight ahead as if he'd done nothing.

When they finally reached the address they had, Soo-Ja and Yul found a woman squatting by the straw door, pounding on clothes with rods, the way Soo-Ja had seen her servants do a thousand times. She wore a gray rolled-up long-sleeved shirt and a charcoal knee-length skirt; her hands were deep in dirty water, which ran in an uneven line from the tin washboard to the gutter.

"Mrs. Yang, hello. I'm Soo-Ja Choi," said Soo-Ja, bowing to the woman.

Chu-Sook's mother bowed back gravely. Hers was a moon-shaped face with no edges. Her skin was darkly tanned, her short black hair thick and wiry.

Soo-Ja tried to smile at her, then pointed at Yul. "And this is Mr. Kim."

Yul bowed to her.

Chu-Sook's mother began to bow back, placing both hands behind her, and remaining with her head down for a few seconds. In Soo-Ja's eyes, the gesture seemed excessively submissive. She herself never chose to bow very long, making it almost a nod, a quick acknowledgment. When Chu-Sook's mother finished her bow, Soo-Ja noticed a change on the woman's face. She had finally gotten a good look at Yul and seemed to recognize him. Soo-Ja watched as the expression in her eyes changed from interest to fear.

"No, I cannot speak to him," said Chu-Sook's mother, shaking her head. "And for anyone who's watching, you can see that I'm not speaking to him!"

"Mrs. Yang, it's all right. He's a friend," said Soo-Ja, holding her arm.

But Chu-Sook's mother could not stop waving her hands in front of her face, looking around for spies—real or imaginary.

Soo-Ja glanced at Yul, who seemed to stay calm. She wondered if he realized how much of a target he had become for the police. But Yul did not seem concerned about that. He came closer to Soo-Ja, and she drew her body in as well—theirs was an easy, unforced intimacy—closing the circle so they could confer quietly with each other.

"They must have shown her my picture," Yul whispered. "Told her not to speak to me." Soo-Ja nodded in agreement. She guessed that, if something had happened to the boy, the police and the government must have understood at once the importance of the situation. "If we can show they have the blood of a twelve-year-old on their hands, it'll turn the tide of the demonstrations. It'll prove the brutality of their regime." Yul turned to Chu-Sook's mother again, to try to make another plea. "I'm here to help you find your son. I want to help you. Don't believe what the police told you. I'm not here to harm you."

"I can't, I can't. Please go. I can't speak to you. I can't speak to anyone who participates in acts of rebellion against the lawful and righteous government!" said Chu-Sook's mother, with her eyes closed, as if trying to remember the words she was supposed to recite. She started to wave more and more vehemently.

Soo-Ja began to fear that the woman would not speak to them at all.

She stood closer to her and held down both her arms. When Chu-Sook's mother calmed down a little, Soo-Ja looked straight into her eyes and spoke.

"Mrs. Yang, you know *me*. I'm not a member of a student group. You can speak to *me*." Soo-Ja reached for her hand and pointed toward the house. "Let's go in, Mrs. Yang. Let's go in and have a chat."

"Why would I speak to you? You lied to me."

Soo-Ja grabbed her hand a bit more forcefully than she'd intended to and directed her inside. "I want to help you, Mrs. Yang. Please, let's go in. Let's go in before your neighbors see us out here and tell on you to the police."

Soo-Ja glanced at Yul for help, but he seemed distracted, looking intently in the direction of the woman's shack. His eyes were squinting, as if he was trying to guess its contents. He had to know it had no windows, and probably no running water or electricity either, with the only light coming in through tiny slivers on the edges of the straw door, keeping the place dark and stuffy. Soo-Ja was about to follow Chu-Sook's mother into her house when Yul stopped her, reaching for her arm.

"Wait," he said. Yul's nostrils widened, as if he were sniffing something foul. He blocked Soo-Ja's way with his arm, in the firm manner of a traffic officer. He pulled her back, away from the woman's house. "What's that smell?"

Chu-Sook's mother looked away, staring down at the ground. Her body seemed emptied out of tears, with no more blood left to run through her veins. When she spoke, she did so matter-of-factly: "That's my son."

They held the boy's body up in the air, and from a distance, it looked as if it were floating, though it was propped by a dozen hands. They had first wrapped him in a blanket, tucked in from head to toe, like a newborn, but somewhere along the march the blanket fell—his cold, decomposing skin rejecting the human comfort. It felt heavy, almost unbearably so, though in life the boy had been light, and not very tall. Chu-Sook would, in fact, have been surprised to see the effort it took to carry him; similar to the effort it took to find him, after a long search in the river. Were it not for the school uniform he wore, they would not have recognized him—with his face smashed out, bits of grenade still lodged in his skull.

They'd been marching from his mother's shack toward Daegu city hall, starting with a group of about a hundred people, led by Yul in front, and Soo-Ja and Chu-Sook's mother next to him. Yul had been expected in Seoul hours earlier, but he'd stayed behind to lead this extemporaneous protest. Night fell somewhere along the way, and the chants grew less angry and more mournful, turning the walk into a funeral procession.

Word spread quickly of the discovery of the body, and the crowd seemed to grow with each block; first the students from the nearby high schools and universities, then everybody else, until almost all the denizens of the town seemed to have left their homes and joined the demonstration. Along the way, Soo-Ja had to help Chu-Sook's mother remain steady a few times. Her spirit appeared to leave her body, becoming a mere bag of tissue and bones, unable to walk or remain upright. Soo-Ja had to hold her with her arms around her back, until her strength returned. The other protestors glanced occasionally at them. Word had spread about Chu-Sook's mother, but no one knew who Soo-Ja was, which made her glad; she did not want the presence of a woman of her social class to serve as a distraction.

Once in a while, Soo-Ja would glance over at Yul and wonder how his lungs never got tired. He chanted with enormous conviction, and part of Soo-Ja felt self-conscious, watching him. It reminded her of being in church, in the middle of a group prayer, and opening her eyes before the others did. It seemed terribly intimate, to see the parishioners like that, with their lips still moving. Here was Yul, too, unaware of Soo-Ja's gaze lingering over him.

Soo-Ja wondered if he sensed the same thing she did—that in spite of their momentary closeness, they would probably never see each other again after that night. There were boys being killed, and generals authorizing massacres, but all she wanted was to grab Yul's hand and have him turn around and look at her. Would the night, with all that still had to happen, stop for her?

By the time they reached city hall, there were more than a thousand people behind them. Up on the steps of the building, rows of policemen wearing helmets and body armor stood with their rifles pointed at the protestors. Behind them, soldiers stood guard with their own guns. With their outlines traced faintly by the light of the lampposts behind them, they looked like perfectly still marble statues—an impenetrable line surrounding the entire perimeter of the building.

"Join us," said Yul, speaking to them as if they were all brothers. "Be on our side. We have room for you. This is a cause worth dying for, but it's not worth killing for. Drop your guns. This march is for everyone, including you."

The police officers pointed their guns at Yul, who started walking up the steps toward them.

He smiled, shaking his head, as if bewildered that they were at this standstill, when they could be playing hato cards together in a bar. Soo-Ja's heart began to beat faster. She wanted him to turn around and come back. But instead she saw him emerge farther and farther into the light, his body drawn like a magnet to the steel and metal of the rifles.

"You are our friends. You want the same things we do. You want freedom and democracy. This boy—he could've been your brother. Your son."

Most of the officers looked impervious to his words, though one or two of them—the youngest-looking ones, the ones in closest proximity to Yul—seemed to waver, and Soo-Ja could see how hard they were trying not to look at Yul, not let him inside their bodies. His words had already shaken some of their conviction.

But then, a sudden yell came from the crowd. Soo-Ja could not make out the words, until others joined in the chant, and it became clear they were screaming, "Killers! Killers, all of them!" Yul turned and tried to stop the shouting, but the crowd had suddenly taken on a life of its own. In a matter of seconds, the men and women grew bold and powerful, like the ravenous foxes of folk tales, unaware that they were ravenous for the entrails of their own brothers and sisters. Soo-Ja had never seen such force descend upon a crowd before, and she began to fear it.

"You killed an innocent boy! You spilled the blood of our children!" they shouted.

Yul started shaking his head at them, waving his arms in front of him for them to stop.

The officers pointed their guns in the direction of the voices, and Soo-Ja saw what sounded like an order coming from the lips of one of the officers. Amid the chaos, she could not tell whose mouths the yelling was coming from, and she knew the officers could not, either. In a matter of seconds, Soo-Ja watched as the officers pointed into the night and looked about to pull their triggers. Yul signaled to her a fraction of a second before the officers started firing, and Soo-Ja fell to the ground at the same time he did, pulling Chu-Sook's mother down with her. The three of them hit the ground as the rain of bullets flew around them.

Soo-Ja looked up in shock to see the bodies of the other protestors being shot. Seconds before, they had been alive, standing next to her, chanting in unison.

The police were firing indiscriminately at them, and they crumpled down, lifeless, arms and hands waving in the air one last time before coming to rest. Men, women, students—some of them with their backs turned away, trying to run—paralyzed by bullets, pools of blood gushing from their mouths. Soo-Ja remained on the ground, almost being trampled, as people around her tried to flee.

The sound of loud screaming pierced the air, and Soo-Ja tried to keep her head covered with her arms. Next to her, Chu-Sook's mother wailed in horror, letting out all the sorrow that had been trapped in her lungs before.

Soo-Ja then saw that the men who had been holding Chu-Sook's body began to fall, too, like the legs of a table being knocked off one by one. For a moment, Chu-Sook's frame seemed to hang in the air, on its own, and Soo-Ja imagined that it would fly to heaven. The moment suddenly felt very quiet and still—the body rising a few inches, as the last of its pallbearers pushed it upward toward the sky—but then its weight broke through the air again, and Soo-Ja watched as the boy's body fell to the ground, making a thunderous noise. Chu-Sook would not make his way to his savior that night; he chose to stay with the others, becoming one more in a sea of bodies.

chapter three

"**N**ow, more than ever, I long for my life to have more heft," wrote Soo-Ja to Min. It was the first letter she'd ever sent him. "And yes, that's the word I mean—heft. I have tasted what it means to have days packed with urgency and meaning, and I cannot go back to living an unimportant life. I find my routines so dull and tranquil. I know I have everything a young woman of my class could ask for—attentive servants, hand-stitched clothes, a temple-like home—but it all feels like a gilded cage. I can see what will happen if I stay in Daegu. I'll never have to answer the call of my own highest potential. I *must* become a diplomat."

Lying restless on the ground, Soo-Ja thought about Min, and how much she'd misjudged him. Why had she been so quick to dismiss him? He had risked his life at the protests, just like she had. They had experienced the same—only miles apart. Had he thought of her as he evaded bullets, or as he knocked about against the body armor of the police? All he'd asked for was a date. If she'd simply said yes, he could have been out of harm's way.

Come back, Soo-Ja found herself whispering. If he did, they could go on that date he had so desperately wanted. They could take a walk along the river at night and name different constellations. If it got cold, he'd lend her his argyle sweater. Or maybe he'd ask Soo-Ja for hers. But what she realized was that she wouldn't mind that, if she had to be the strong one. She'd like to swoop in and care for Min, who sometimes had the air of an orphan. How had he managed to survive all his life without her to protect him? He was the opposite of Yul, who seemed to need nothing and no one. *Not even a wife*, thought Soo-Ja poignantly.

Min had been lucky. He'd marched in the large protest outside the National Assembly, the one where, according to the radio, more than a hundred people had been killed, and a thousand injured. But he had not been wounded. He'd told her so when he wrote her back. He also mentioned he'd be coming home to Daegu very soon. "My work here is done," he wrote in a grandiose way. "Syngman Rhee has been deposed. Our country's struggle for freedom, which began when we freed ourselves from the Japanese colonizers, then continued with the war against the communists, has finally come to an end with the end of the dictatorship. I was talking about this to the people in the crowd, as we watched the slow procession of the President's motorcade through the streets of Seoul. And you know what the amazing thing was? Some people were crying. I don't know if it's because they were thinking of the terrible things he'd done, or because they felt sorry for him and his wife. But what matters is that he's gone now, and this is a beautiful day for democracy."

Min had left as an idler, but he would return as a hero.

Soo-Ja sat on the front steps of her house, watching the servants do the week's laundry in the courtyard. One of them worked the lever of the water pump, her heavy arms pushing up and down, until a clean stream spurted out. Another sat on top of a stone, scrubbing wet, soapy clothes on top of a washboard. Finally, a third one rinsed the clothes in the pump and shook them before hanging them up to dry with clothespins. Soo-Ja stared at their plump bodies, hidden away underneath their old hanboks. Soo-Ja felt self-conscious about the weight she'd recently lost, shed from her already thin frame.

Soo-Ja enjoyed the rhythms of their talk, the way they spoke like folks from the countryside, dispensing with the more formal -*io* at the end of the sentences. Sometimes their words overlapped, like a chorus, and Soo-Ja envied the easy, casual way they'd tease or scold one another.

If she lost the ability to speak, and needed to learn again, she could simply listen to them. They often spent hours telling stories. The house chores—cooking, cleaning, washing—seemed to be incidental. In Soo-Ja's mind, their real job was to gossip, giving their opinions about the others' lives. Soo-Ja wondered if they talked about *her* behind her back, and she realized that they must, of course.

Soo-Ja closed her eyes. She often became sleepy when melancholia hit her. She could feel her head grow heavy when she suddenly heard the servants' talking stop. She opened her eyes and glanced at them—their eyes were directed at an intruder. A man had arrived at the house unannounced, slipping past the gate, and making his way into the court-yard. He looked tired and beaten down, wearing an army camouflage jacket cut off at the forearms, and pants rolled up to his knees. He held a satchel behind his back, and for a moment Soo-Ja thought it was one of her brothers, returning home from some war she hadn't been told about.

It took a few seconds to realize it was Min, and when she did, Soo-Ja leapt out of her seat and ran to him. He'd been to her house before, but she hadn't been ready then. This time, with no concern for modesty or propriety, Soo-Ja jumped into his arms, and the two of them held each other, burying their noses in each other's shoulders. Their bodies made shapes together—her chin on his sternum, her temple against his cheek—until theirs were interlocking parts. He had not been lost; he'd been returned to her.

"Is your father here?" asked Min, once they finally let go of each other.

"Yes. Why?" asked Soo-Ja, glancing into his eyes.

Min looked shyly at her. "There's something I want to ask him."

"What is it?" asked Soo-Ja, staring at his cherry-sized nose, and his downcast gaze.

"I want to ask him for your hand in marriage."

"You want to marry Soo-Ja?" asked her father, looking startled.

"Yes, I do," said Min, with his satchel by his side, sitting across from him on the floor.

"Isn't this a little sudden?" asked Soo-Ja's father, trying to maintain his self-control.

"The protests—the violence in Seoul—made me realize how fragile our lives are. It could all be over in a second," said Min.

Soo-Ja moved closer to Min and instinctively held his arm. He'd come up with the idea himself, independently of her, and she wondered if he suspected her wish of going to Seoul to join the Foreign Service. She'd always spoken vaguely about her dreams, and never discussed her specific plans with Min, for fear he'd feel used. But perhaps he knew. Perhaps he'd read her mind, when the thought first crossed her head, that day at the gymnasium bleachers. Perhaps her thoughts were obvious to others, and it was only out of politeness that they did not remark upon them, when they could read them as clearly as print on paper.

"But marriage . . . it's not something you bring up lightly," said Soo-Ja's father, suddenly at a loss for words. "No, there has to be a go-between, a matchmaker, someone to make formal introductions, to tell me about your family, and to tell *your* family about ours. Followed by me and Soo-Ja's mother meeting your parents, and getting out our ancestral rolls to check which lineages you each come from. A marriage isn't a union between two young people, as you seem to think. A marriage is a union between two families."

Soo-Ja and Min kept their heads bent down, facing the floor.

"Abeoji, Min comes from a very good family," said Soo-Ja.

"My father manufactures textiles," said Min. "Silk, cotton, rayon. He is an industrialist, like yourself."

Soo-Ja noticed that this did not seem to impress her father. In fact, it seemed to make him more concerned.

"If your father owns a factory, then why aren't you working for him?" he asked, furrowing his brow.

"My father didn't want me to. My brother works for him."

"Your older brother?"

"No, I'm the oldest."

"You're the oldest?" Soo-Ja's father seemed startled by this. "If you're the oldest, then everything belongs to you—including the responsibility. Why would your father not trust you with the business?"

"Well, he didn't want me hanging around the factory," said Min, his voice taking on a self-satisfied drawl. "The girls who work there kept flirting with me. These working-class girls see the owner's son, start getting ideas. You have to be careful with women. I don't have to worry about Soo-Ja, though, she and I are of the same class."

"How lucky for you," said her father gruffly. "Now let me ask you, when these factory girls were—say, coming on to you—was there any girl in particular? Anyone particularly aggressive?"

Min hesitated, his nostrils flaring a bit. "They're obedient girls. But they're trouble."

"Your brother doesn't seem to have a problem ignoring them," said Soo-Ja's father, staring into Min's eyes. "You didn't answer my question."

"Abeoji, please stop grilling him," Soo-Ja interjected. "Min is a guest in our home. Do you want him to leave and tell everyone about how you treat people?"

Soo-Ja's father suddenly banged on the floor with his hand. "Yes, spread the word. Tell everyone."

"Abeoji, please," she said. "Give Min another chance to—"

"You should go now," her father cut in, looking at Min.

Min remained on his spot, his head lowered to the elder.

"I said you can go now," Soo-Ja's father repeated.

Soo-Ja did not look up as Min stood up and, after bowing to her father, started making his way out of the room. He rushed out, as if the departure had been his idea, as if *he'd* been the one who'd decided they weren't good enough for him.

After Min was gone, Soo-Ja ran outside to the courtyard. It had started to rain, and Soo-Ja could feel the drops prickling against her, and the puddles on the ground making her steps slippery. Unsteady, she rested her hand against a pine tree, its battered branches almost breaking. She was on her way to her room, on the other side of the courtyard, when her father—who had followed her—tried to get her back into the main house. They remained between rooms, at an impasse.

"What makes him think that he can marry you? Was he first in his class? Is he a doctor or an engineer? He didn't even finish college!" yelled her father. His eyelids struggled to stay open, and his clothes quickly became wet.

"I don't care about that," Soo-Ja said, trying hard not to shiver. Her long, wet hair covered her entire face, with clumps sticking to her mouth, and strands creating lines over her eyes.

"Don't care about that? A boy like him—with no education or professional skills—he would be laughed out of a matchmaker's meeting!"

"But he comes from a good family! They own a factory," said Soo-Ja, her breath catching in her throat.

"For a firstborn to be sent away from the family business, he must have done something very bad," said her father.

Soo-Ja looked over to her mother's room and saw the lights come on. "We woke up Mother."

"He is unacceptable in every way. And he is the oldest son. Do you know what it means to be the wife of the oldest son?" asked her father, coming closer to her. "You would have to be responsible for the entire family. Do you know how much work that is, having to serve your in-laws? Does he have brothers or sisters?"

"He has one brother and a sister."

"Well, at least he doesn't have a lot of siblings, but the ones that he has you'd be expected to help raise, and this in addition to your own children. Soo-Ja, being married to an oldest son is a lot of work."

"Appa, I know you only want the best for me, but there is nothing to worry about. I have always made good decisions, haven't I?"

Soo-Ja's father stood still for a moment, his clothes growing heavier, soaked by the rain. "It is a losing proposition to always be right when it comes to little things, but then be wrong on the big things."

Soo-Ja knew her father was right. Marriage was serious business. The choice of a husband was the only time a woman could exert her will. Choose wisely and have a chance at a decent life. Choose wrong and have endless time to regret it. Her husband would dictate the rest of her life—her social class, her daily routines, her very happiness. And yet, knowing her father might be right only made her dig her heels further into the ground.

"Well, at least this is one decision that I *can* make, and I don't depend on your approval for it."

Soo-Ja saw by the stricken look on her father's face how much her words had hurt him—he seemed to age five years in five seconds. What is the statute of limitations on resenting those we love? she wondered. Could past wrongs be wielded so easily, pulled out of a back pocket, like a silver knife, and used to tear, rip, slice through an argument?

"Is that why you want to marry him? To *punish* me? For Seoul?"

"Of course not," she said, a little too quickly. Soo-Ja's father looked at her askew, squinting his eyes. She wondered if he suspected her plans to move there after her wedding. For what felt like a long while, Soo-Ja's father did not speak, as if trying to guess at Soo-Ja's reasons. The prisoner is always thinking about escape, but she wondered what the jailer always thought about. Suddenly, Soo-Ja's father seemed to feel the cold and shivered once or twice. They looked at each other awkwardly.

"It's raining," her father said, as if he'd only just noticed it. "Go to your room."

Soo-Ja nodded, terrified to think that she'd won the fight. She turned away from him and walked a few steps until she found herself outside her room. She stood still for a moment, fighting the temptation to run back to her father.

Soo-Ja finally took her shoes off and crossed over the elevated step. Once inside her room, she turned on her lamp and sat on the warm floor, taking the time to catch her breath. Leaning against a corner, she let her long arms and legs droop, weak and disorderly, like broken matchsticks. Soo-Ja felt the tears forming in her eyes. After a while, she could no longer hold her feelings back, and she began to cry. Soo-Ja felt her body shiver with emotion, and quick, guttural noises began to slip out of her lips. Why is it, she wondered, that an enemy or a stranger would leave no mark, but her father—her adored father—could wound her so deeply?

She'd never cry out of pain alone, but pain and love together—especially the love—could inspire her to sob to the point of gasping for air.

Soo-Ja was in the middle of taking a long breath when she suddenly heard her door slide open. She turned around, ready to yell at her brother or a servant or whoever it was who'd come in without knocking first. But when she saw that it was Min, no words came out of her mouth.

"I told your maid she didn't need to show me out in the rain, and I could find my way out by myself. But when I got to your gate, I just rattled the latch and slammed it shut."

Soo-Ja stopped crying. She turned the knob on the lamp until it was dark again. Min took that as a sign that he could come closer. He walked toward her and then kneeled on the floor, facing her. They sat there, speaking barely above a whisper, their bodies open to each other, looking like two people at prayer. She could feel vibrations running up and down her body.

"So you heard everything my father said."

"Yes."

"Is he right?"

"No."

"Was there a girl at the factory? Did you get someone pregnant?"

"No! Of course not!"

Soo-Ja nodded. "I was right. My father doesn't know you."

"But I agree that I am an unlucky kkang-pae, a very poor prospect for marriage," said Min matter-of-factly.

"Don't say that. Have more esteem for yourself."

"Nobody can see the good in me, Soo-Ja. Except for you."

"Don't talk like that. Please," she said, fighting the emotion caught in her throat. Though he did not know it, Min had said the magic words. She found it irresistible—the idea that she alone could see his value, and that he would remain indebted to her for doing so.

"Didn't you hear your father's words? I have nothing to offer anyone," said Min.

Soo-Ja ran her fingers through his hair. "But you're good at heart, I know you are."

Min gave a start, hearing a noise outside. "What was that?"

"It's nothing. Don't worry. Everyone's asleep. They can't hear us in the main house," said Soo-Ja.

"Why are you so good to me, Soo-Ja? When everyone else has been so bad?" He closed his eyes, as she felt the shape of his face with her fingers, tracing his cheeks, the stubble on his chin.

"Do you want me to stop? Does it bother you?" she asked him, smiling.

"It'll just make it all the more painful when you leave me at last," he said, opening his eyes again. She traced his eyebrows with her fingers. She knew he meant this as a question, and she had to answer it.

"Min, I don't know if I can marry you. Not after what happened tonight."

Min shook his head. "If you disobey your father, he'll be angry at you, but over time, he'll see that you made the right decision."

"But he wouldn't like losing me, if you took me away from here. Especially if you let me become a diplomat, and we left the country," said Soo-Ja, using those particular words on purpose, trying him out to see how he would respond.

"I don't care where we go, as long as we're together."

Soo-Ja, gladdened by his answer, peered into Min's beautiful eyes, shining down on her like the Seven North Stars. She traced his dark eyebrows, which stood in such contrast to his pale skin. She smiled, thinking about the freedom she would earn if she married him. Min took her smile as an invitation, and he kissed her, his creamy lips touching hers, his hand grazing her neck.

"Do you love me?" he asked when he let go.

Soo-Ja was tempted to lie and say that she did, but the truth was that she hardly knew him. It wasn't love; it was the promise of a new life. It was the Namdaemun—the gate in the heart of Seoul—awaiting her; visas to foreign countries, and exotic-sounding languages. At the thought, Soo-Ja beamed, which Min mistook for an answer, and he smiled back even more intensely.

"I love you," he said, in his sweet, almost adolescent voice. "I love you so much, I feel like my insides could explode. If you don't love me, then don't marry me out of love, marry me out of pity. I have nothing to live for without you. Give me something to live for. My parents don't care about me. I have no future. I have no reason to go on. But you can save me. Marry me. Marry me and save me. My life is in your hands."

At that moment, Soo-Ja felt like her own life had never mattered more, her body jolted by the rush that must be the addict's first thrill. She'd never felt more powerful. Her father was wrong. Min might not have the education or the prospects, but right that second, those things meant nothing. She would never find someone with so much passion for her—a lovesick boy who'd rather die than live without her. He needed her, and his need felt intoxicating. It was even stronger than love. Min swooned in a fever, and she worried he might faint at any moment. She was going to save him, yes—rescue him from himself and the world that hurt him.

Soo-Ja began to gently massage Min's head, full of affection. Min took it as an opening of sorts, and he began to kiss her again. Soo-Ja kissed him back, and Min enveloped her in an embrace. They lay on the floor, and Soo-Ja could feel parts of them locking together, arm against arm, hip against hip, until it felt like no air could pass between them. His tongue felt wet against hers, like biting a juicy mango, its nectar running down her chin. Though she had her eyes closed, every part of her body felt awake, telegraphing sensations from pore to pore. When she opened her eyes, she could see Min's pleasure in his pupils, and she felt proud of being responsible for it.

Min was now lying with his legs clasped around hers, his hands caressing the sides of her face. Soo-Ja wrapped her arms around his back and squeezed his body against hers. Touching him felt as natural as breathing and was done with the same ease. They were, physically, a natural match. Each kiss led into another, their mouths opening and closing to let in breaths, and each other.

Min began to undo the buttons of his pants, but when he hiked up her skirt, Soo-Ja instinctively stopped him. She knew she couldn't make love to him; *shouldn't, mustn't.* But she also felt a sudden rush of gratitude that made her want to touch and be touched. This felt good, just like thinking about her future felt good. Besides, if they made love, it was as good as signing a marriage certificate. No man in his right mind would dare deflower a woman and then refuse to take her as his wife, thought Soo-Ja. Otherwise, he would be destroying her life. So this could work to her advantage . . .

Finally, when Min tried to lift up her skirt for a second time, Soo-Ja did not stop him. Min held her arms up over her head, against the floor, as if stretching her, and let his fingers interlace with hers. They continued kissing, and as the kisses grew more intense, Soo-Ja closed her eyes and felt herself floating. Their bodies were moving to the same rhythm, him pressing up and down against her, and she enjoyed a lulling sensation, as if the two of them were rising from the earth and swirling in the air, toward the rain beating down on their flesh.

Bang, bang, bang, sounded the wooden drums.

Min and his friends, chanting loudly and playing music, could be heard for miles as they carried the wedding chest down the street. Soo-Ja watched as the men came closer, though still a block away. They all wore male hanboks—loose-fitting gray pantaloons on the bottom, and blue jackets with wide sleeves on top, fastened at the chest with ribbons. They walked proudly, in step, chanting. One of them held up a *jwa-go* drum with the symbol of the flag drawn on it, and he'd beat at it with a stick at the end of each chant.

"Buy the *hahm*! Buy the *hahm*!" they called out.

Min followed right behind them, also wearing a hanbok—it was the first time Soo-Ja had seen him don traditional costume. Min favored Western suits, always neatly tailored and freshly iron-pressed. But the hanbok, with its vibrant blue and yellow colors, fit him well, and as he marched toward her house, she felt a sudden glee, as if this were a complete surprise, and not something she already knew about and had prepared for.

"What's this ruckus?" a neighbor across the street called out, looking sleepy and confused. "Did somebody die?"

"No, somebody's getting married soon," Soo-Ja said, smiling.

"You're getting married?" the neighbor asked. "To which one of them?"

"To all of them!" said Soo-Ja.

Soo-Ja saw another woman come out from the same house, an old lady with wizened lines on her tired-looking face, wearing a light blue hanbok with red *chogori* jacket. "The groom sings out loud and strong. That is a good sign. It means he will have vigor and stamina for the first night!" she said, and then began clapping and nodding her head.

"Good," Soo-Ja replied. "I plan on making him do a lot of work around the house that night."

Soo-Ja ran back inside and went into the kitchen, careful to go down one step, since the kitchen was a foot lower than the rest of the house. There, the servants were putting the final touches on the rice cake they would present the men with once they reached their house. The confection, covered with adzuki beans, was meant to symbolize luck and harmony. Soo-Ja was not particularly fond of *tteok*—it was not sweet enough, and too powdery and sticky for her taste. But a celebration wasn't a celebration without them.

As the servants walked the tteok to the middle hallway—which wasn't really a hallway but a large, empty room connecting the other ones—Soo-Ja and her mother positioned themselves on the yellow floor, along with two of her aunts. At that moment, Soo-Ja felt her father's absence, as well as Jae-Hwa's. Jae-Hwa, who'd been surprised to hear news of the engagement, had said she would come, but had not, in the end. Soo-Ja could still remember the sting of her friend's words the last time she'd spoken to her, when Jae-Hwa accused Soo-Ja of not really being in love with Min. Soo-Ja hadn't told Jae-Hwa about her night of passion— Jae-Hwa would have been shocked.

As they came close to the house, the men's loud, hungry voices vibrated through the thin walls, shaking the floor beneath them. But when the servants opened the sliding doors, revealing the men to the women, all became silence.

The men lowered the wedding chest onto the ground and bowed ceremoniously. The women, already sitting, bowed, too. Then, the men took their upturned, boat-shaped rubber shoes off and walked the wedding chest up the two steps toward the room. They placed it immediately before her mother.

In exchange for the wedding chest, Soo-Ja's mother handed the groomsmen a white envelope filled with cash. Going against custom, Min's friends did not negotiate—they had been instructed by Min not to try. And Soo-Ja's mother did not negotiate, either—she had been instructed by Soo-Ja not to do so.

Knowing that everyone's eyes fell on her, Soo-Ja's mother reached for the long, heavy white cotton coils around the chest. She dug deep into the knots with her nails and fingers and unwrapped them, revealing the beautiful red chest underneath, encrusted with gleaming white mother-of-pearl and adorned with gold-colored fittings and hinges. She did all this with an ease and expertise that suggested she'd been waiting her whole life to perform this task for her daughter.

Once she opened the chest, Soo-Ja's mother pulled out the marriage scroll sent by the groom's family. Written in elegant calligraphy, it announced the upcoming nuptials and listed the four pillars of the groom—his year, month, day, and time of birth—all of which were supposed to indicate his good fortune. Soo-Ja's mother read those dates out loud, and the others nodded back in approval.

After that, Soo-Ja's mother reached for the gifts, revealing them one by one—a pink nightgown, a jade bracelet, and a new hanbok. Soo-Ja's mother held those items in the air, smiling. It was a smile Soo-Ja saw so rarely on her face, it made her realize this was a triumph to her, having managed to marry off a daughter. She had fulfilled a mother's duty, at last. Soo-Ja caught herself smiling, too, as everything that day felt contagious—the men's jubilation, the neighbors' excitement, her mother's approval. She would be the sky for a day, emotions passing through her like clouds, her being changing colors in a matter of minutes.

chapter four

The large square classroom emptied itself out quickly, its wooden walls growing darker with the waning sun, and its concrete floors feeling cooler to the touch. The young women collected their bags and coats, while Soo-Ja alone remained sitting on her embroidered mat on the floor. She could hear the silence filling up the room as she waited for Yul's arrival.

He had sent her a note two days earlier, asking if he could see her. She'd wondered why the sudden communication. He hadn't been in contact with her for weeks. Yul had no less than saved her life that night outside the city hall, yet he had given her no opportunity to show him her gratitude. She wondered why he had been avoiding her.

Soo-Ja had hesitated before writing back, knowing it might not be appropriate for her to receive him at her house, now that she was engaged. But he could walk her home from her weekly drawing class at the local arts school, and that's what she had told him. At that moment, as she waited for him, Soo-Ja tried to ignore the nervousness gliding down her spine. She hoped to concentrate instead on the drawings she'd been working on. They were rice paper paintings of the four gentlemen flowers and plant—orchid, chrysanthemum, plum blossom, and bamboo.

As a little girl, her father had taught her about the importance of the flowers; how in precolonial times, a *yangban*—aristocratic—boy's initiation started by learning how to draw them, and his brushstrokes both revealed and created character. Though those four flowers may seem delicate, they had great force, too—they could teach a gentleman how to absorb a moral value, like inner strength or courage.

"What a perfect choice of setting," said Yul, breaking Soo-Ja's reverie. She watched as he lingered by the steps of the room for a minute, removing his black leather shoes. He placed them on the ground, on the same step as Soo-Ja's—next to hers, in fact—creating two pairs of perfect lines.

Soo-Ja rose, and the two of them exchanged bows. Soo-Ja thought about collecting her things, since the original plan was for him to escort her home. But instead, she found herself sitting back on her mat, eager to keep him there—keep him *still*. Yul sat down next to her, on another mat, facing the persimmon-glazed table in front of her.

"I was surprised to hear from you," said Soo-Ja.

"I was surprised to hear about your wedding," said Yul, a look of concern on his face.

"Are you here to congratulate me?" asked Soo-Ja, avoiding his gaze, and looking at her half-finished painting instead.

Yul moved his head to the side. "I don't mean to be rude, but I'm not sure 'congratulations' is the first word that comes to mind. I haven't spent much time at all with Min, but I can tell you this: he's the kind of person you date, not the kind you marry."

Soo-Ja reached for a blank piece of rice paper and laid it on the table in front of her, buying time as she tried to think of a response. She thought of explaining to Yul her reasons for getting married to Min. Would he understand? she wondered. Or would he judge her?

Instead, Soo-Ja kept her eyes averted and dipped her brush into the inkstone. She was about to make her first stroke when Yul surprised her by moving his body closer to hers. She thought he would try to take the brush away from her hands. Instead, in a gesture that startled her, Yul took her right hand into his, holding the brush with her.

"What are you doing?" she asked, looking at the way his hand made a shell on top of her own.

"Teach me. I'll follow your lead," said Yul.

Soo-Ja hesitated. "I didn't know you drew."

"I don't. But I've always wanted to try."

Soo-Ja nodded. This would be better than talking about Min. Soo-Ja made their hands trade places and had his fingers hold the brush. She then placed her hand over his. Slowly, they began to draw their first stroke together, starting from the base, and forming a thin, black arc. They crossed the arc with their second stroke, again from the base.

Soo-Ja gripped Yul's hand tighter and noticed he'd kept his arm loose, so she could guide him freely. She continued, drawing black leaves—six or seven of them—crisscrossing each other. For some of the strokes, Soo-Ja had them lift the brush for a second before continuing the stroke, creating an inch or so of white space right in the middle of a leaf. It looked like someone had erased that part of the orchid, splitting it in half.

"I know I should have come earlier. I debated seeing you, but I wasn't sure it would be appropriate," said Yul as they drew.

"You saved my life that night. I wouldn't have known about the gunfire if you hadn't warned me," said Soo-Ja.

"But you also wouldn't have been there to begin with if you hadn't met me."

"I am *very* glad I was there, Yul," said Soo-Ja firmly. "Don't ever worry about that."

"Maybe if I'd come to see you, you could have avoided this engagement."

Soo-Ja quickly reached for another blank piece of paper, eager to change the subject. "Do you want to do the chrysanthemums next? You see how in the painting of orchids, we emphasized the leaves? For the chrysanthemums, we have to do the opposite and highlight the flowers. And the flowers are trickier to draw. The petals at the heart have to be drawn with a darker ink than the petals at the edges."

Soo-Ja and Yul—their hands still moving together—painted the flowers; their petals grew diagonally upward, creating the illusion that they kept moving beyond the frame of the long, rectangular sheet of paper.

"What do you think a gentleman can learn from a chrysanthemum?" asked Yul.

"Well, the chrysanthemum blooms even in the winds, rains, and snow of late autumn and early winter. It follows its nature and is not afraid of danger or death. I might venture that those are the values that a gentleman should have: courage, loyalty, and commitment to ideals."

As their hands moved together, Soo-Ja felt enveloped by Yul's warmth. After a while, she started to let go, letting him fill in a dark leaf by himself; then she'd guide his hand along again, to create distance between the stems. Each time she held his hand felt like the first time—letting go of it for a few seconds only made her long for it more.

"Now, I'd like to draw something for you," said Soo-Ja. "For you to take home."

Soo-Ja smiled at Yul as he sat back and watched her. She began to mix the ink in the inkstone. Then, Soo-Ja drew a gnarled branch, going in four directions—one to the right, one to the left, one moving into the background, one coming forward. She occasionally lifted her brush in the air in the middle of a stroke, once again creating "breaks" in the branches, white space that would be left empty, and "filled" in by the mind of the person looking at the painting. Then, she mixed some water in the inkstone to get a lighter shade for the delicate round flowers, and she sprinkled them on top of the branches.

"See, there must be harmony between the *yin*—the female—and the *yang*—the male," said Soo-Ja. "That's why there must be a balance between the empty space and the painted area."

When Soo-Ja was done, she handed Yul the painting of the plum blossoms. Yul leaned closer and stared at it. Though he did not speak, his eyes looked full of admiration. He rolled the rice paper with great care and placed it inside his bag.

"I sense my advice is unwelcome. Maybe I should go now," said Yul, a hint of sadness on his face.

Soo-Ja did not want him to go just yet, and watched with disappointment as he headed out of the classroom and into the chatter of the street, now bustling with night students and teachers about to go home.

But as Yul made his way out, Soo-Ja quickly realized that his expensive leather shoes—which he'd left by the steps immediately outside the door, as per custom—were gone. Soo-Ja's were still there, but Yul's had been replaced with a cheap pair of random sandals.

Soo-Ja was mortified. If Yul's shoes had been stolen, then, in the eyes of an observer, it was her fault. For that hour, while she had been with him, she'd been responsible for his well-being. She'd been the host, and therefore was accorded some privileges, but also responsibilities. Besides, she was the one who had suggested meeting at her school and initially had them stay in the empty, unguarded classroom. Soo-Ja knew he knew all this, and that, right at that moment, she was about to lose face.

But much to Soo-Ja's surprise, Yul simply smiled and placed the sandals on his feet, as if nothing had happened and those were really his own shoes. When he saw Soo-Ja staring at him, he told her, "Oh, I just ran out of the house late this morning and didn't notice what I wore on my feet. Anyway, thank you for the drawing lesson. I'm very glad I got to see you again."

Soo-Ja nodded, touched by his kindness. He had not wanted to embarrass her. Standing up, Soo-Ja gathered her art materials and made her way out of the classroom.

Just as she was about to go home, however, Soo-Ja felt Yul place his hand on her left arm. He touched her lightly, as if she were a flower. Soo-Ja's body turned back in his direction, and her senses felt sharper, keenly aware of the region of her arm that Yul had just touched. She felt the air grow warmer as he drew closer to her, his breath soon almost within her reach. Yul gazed at her with his lips apart, but no words came out of his mouth. He looked as if he had practiced a million things to say, but he was now discarding them one by one. Soo-Ja could tell, as his face changed expressions, what each of those opening lines were—she could see as they fell to the ground—a confession, an apology, a request. She wanted to pick them up, one by one, and cradle them in her arms, lest they be the last thing she had from him again.

"Don't marry Min," he whispered, his lips brushing against her ears. "Marry me instead."

Soo-Ja felt the entire world grow silent, and the only thing she could hear was her own heart, beating fast. She looked at Yul, startled, feeling the warmth emanating from his body. Soo-Ja felt as if she had gone mute. Words failed her like broken clocks, trains without rails. Here it was, happiness, offering to dance with her, calling her nicknames, jaunty and giddy, leading her to a bed of hyacinths.

As if pained by her silence, Yul pressed his forehead against hers and took her hand into his.

"Let me build a house for you near the mountains, nestled in a valley filled with groves of mulberry trees." Yul spoke so tenderly that Soo-Ja could not help but close her eyes. "I will make sure it rests on fertile and healthy soil, so we can plant a garden and watch the azaleas rise in the spring, and pluck the red dates from the branches. I will have the house face south, so it'll get plenty of light year-round, even in winter, and while everyone else in town shivers, you will stay warm in your room, reading a book, wrapped in a blanket made of the finest lambskin. The house will always smell of jasmine tea and beds of chrysanthemums, and every room will be decorated according to your own whims. We will have a room for you to spend in serious contemplation, another one where you could craft very long, elaborate jokes shared only with me, and a third one where you could draw and paint and practice calligraphy."

The vision made her smile. Yul moved closer, and it felt like the entire world enveloping her. He grazed his lips against hers. But just as Soo-Ja was about to kiss him, a powerful feeling of guilt tugged at her, telling her to be ashamed to picture such a life when she was already as good as married. The preparations for the wedding had been lengthy, and had involved not just Min and her, but their two sets of parents, who had to meet, talk, and be sure to trust one another. Elaborate negotiations had taken place regarding the dowry, the honeymoon, and their futures.

But what if none of those things mattered? What if I simply ran off with Yul?

And then, a sudden image arose of Soo-Ja's body under Min's as they made love. Min's face, sweat dripping on his forehead, and his eyes almost rolling backward in pleasure. All the noise on the street returned—chatter from the students walking by, cars honking in the distance, a bell ringing as a front door opened. The memory shamed Soo-Ja, and she pulled away from Yul. Even if she lied and kept that night a secret, Yul would find out on their wedding night, just by looking at their sheets. What did the heroine say in that novel she'd been reading? Soo-Ja tried to recall, as the words suddenly felt very urgent. "Men—they have minds like moral flypaper," or something to that effect. She had not understood what the author had meant until right that second.

"I have to go home now," said Soo-Ja, almost in a panic.

"Soo-Ja, please!" said Yul, dreadful sadness painted on his face.

Soo-Ja swallowed. This was the moment, she knew, to which she would go back to in memory and say, *You fool, you simple-minded fool.* This was the moment she would think back to and decide, *That was the night my life began, and I stopped being my father's daughter, and earned my own name.*

Soo-Ja shook her head. When she spoke, she could not tell if the apology was directed to Yul or to herself. "I'm sorry. It's just . . . impossible."

chapter five

Outside the temple, the sun began to set, as Soo-Ja's yin, her night, crept onto Min's yang, his day. They arrived in their own traditional palanquin—Soo-Ja's an enclosed carriage hiding her body from the world, Min's an exposed wooden chair held by four bearers. Soo-Ja wore a traditional green and yellow silk hanbok dress with billowing sleeves, keeping her arms bent in front of her, one on top of the other. She had her long black hair tied tightly at the back and fastened by a long pin with a dragon head at one end. Min wore a high black hat with flat sides resembling wings, and a maroon jacket embroidered with the picture of two red-crested white cranes. At the bottom, his flowing silk pants were cut off at the calf area, revealing black boots made of cloth.

As the bearers rested the palanquins on the floor, Soo-Ja and Min emerged, facing the two hundred or so invited guests sitting on long rows of white foldout chairs. Guided by their attendants, Soo-Ja and Min took their initial places, standing a few feet apart from each other. With the sound of a twelve-string zither underlining their movements, Soo-Ja's and Min's respective attendants gently guided them so that they would face each other. Soo-Ja and Min performed their first bow—long and slow, in perfect unison.

Then, Soo-Ja alone began a second bow, as her attendant filled a gourd with rice wine and handed it to her. Taking it with both hands and her head down, Soo-Ja kneeled on the ground and stretched out her arms, offering Min the drink. Min made sure to also hold it with both hands, his elbows out, and drank slowly, before handing the empty gourd back to his bride.

After that, it was Min's turn to receive a gourd of wine from his attendant and offer it to Soo-Ja. Once the two of them had performed a quarter bow, not as deep and long as their initial one, Min handed her the drink. According to custom, Soo-Ja was supposed to take only a sip, express her embarrassment, and hand it back to Min. But much to his surprise, and that of the guests, Soo-Ja drank it all, in a single gulp, making a point of enjoying it.

At this point, like seasoned actors, Min's parents took their places on the ground. Soo-Ja and Min turned to them and performed a long, elaborate bow, one in which they folded their entire bodies, hands touching the floor, and heads lowered in respect. Then, Soo-Ja walked to them in small steps, her head slightly lowered, as customary, and offered them wine. Min's father bowed back lightly and took the wine from her. The attendant then refilled the gourd, so Soo-Ja could offer it to Mother-in-law, who took a small sip in a solemn manner.

Her offerings done, Soo-Ja rose, as Min's father threw jujube fruits into the air. Soo-Ja had some trouble navigating the way out, having to maintain her arms in a difficult position, and keeping aloft the costume's heavy silk fabrics. Min, walking slightly ahead, seemed only dimly aware of her presence, almost leaving her behind.

During the meal afterward, Soo-Ja mentioned the awkwardness of the moment to Jae-Hwa, who told her not to be paranoid about such silly things, and that from the outside, she looked glorious, and it was one of the best ceremonies she'd ever been to.

When a young woman finally marries, the custom rules that she spend three days with her own parents, and then go live with her husband and his parents at their house. But as she stepped past the gates of Min's home, Soo-Ja felt like she was trespassing. Her arrival there was marked by the fact that neither of her in-laws had stayed up to greet her, and both the main house and the adjacent quarters were completely dark. All of the lights were off, including those outside in the courtyard, and she had to walk carefully so as not to trip. Min made his way easily, clearly accustomed to this, but he never looked back to check on her, and she finally had to ask him to slow down.

Soo-Ja followed Min into the compound, walking past a small garden and toward the back. There, Soo-Ja saw where the main house ended and Min's own adjacent, one-story house began, as humble and unassuming as a distant cousin. Min and Soo-Ja had two rooms to themselves, one for him to receive visitors, another for them to sleep in. They would be sharing the kitchen in the main house, where she was expected to cook and eat with the rest of the family. The single outhouse, on the other side of the courtyard, would also be shared with the others.

They went into Min's quarters, and Soo-Ja waited for him to turn on a light to illuminate her way, but he didn't. Finally, she reached for the lamp herself and turned the knob. Min looked at her as if she had violated a rule.

"You're not supposed to do that," he said.

"What? Light the lamp?"

"My mother doesn't like us to waste electricity," he said, pointing to the lamp.

"But it's dark."

"I know. We should be asleep. Turn that off."

"I can't see anything. How am I supposed to find the blankets?"

"They're in the back there, on top of the armoire. Now turn that off. My mother will see the light," said Min, pointing at the lamp again.

"Is she still up?"

"She's in the house, praying."

"Praying for what?" asked Soo-Ja, confused.

"What do you think?" Min retorted dismissively.

A grandson, of course. Already. And every night, until Soo-Ja delivered the expected news, her mother-in-law would pray, sometimes loudly outside, rocking her body back and forth with her eyes closed. During their honeymoon, which was to begin the next day—a trip to Cheju Island—Soo-Ja was expected to conceive. It was not unromantic; it was practical. Two days away from home, they could be noisy if they wished.

Soo-Ja reluctantly turned the light off, but only after she quickly memorized the position of everything in the room. There was not much furniture to speak of, only the armoire with mother-of-pearl for their clothes and blankets, and a small oak table resting against the back of the wall. As she began to make her preparations, Soo-Ja remembered something she had noticed a while back, during their wedding reception.

"Who were those three boys standing near your parents all the time at our wedding?" It was dark, and Soo-Ja could not see Min, just hear him breathing. She felt her way among the unfamiliar comforters, measuring through touch their thickness. The thinnest one went on the floor, and they'd sleep over it; then, they would place the thicker one over their own bodies. It would be unclean to sleep directly on the laminate and, no matter how hot it was, it would go against custom to sleep without something covering them. Soo-Ja began to spread the mats and comforters on the ground, waiting for Min's answer.

"They're my brothers," he finally said.

"I thought you said you only had one brother and one sister."

"You must've heard wrong."

Suddenly, she heard the flick of a match, illuminating Min's face for a second as he lit his cigarette.

"How old are they?" she asked.

"Chung-Ho is seventeen, Du-Ho is ten, and In-Ho is eight. And then there's Na-yeong, my sister, and she's fourteen."

"So you have three brothers and a sister," noted Soo-Ja, surprised.

"*Two* sisters. Seon-ae left when she turned eighteen."

"Where is she?"

"Who knows."

"Why didn't you tell me you had such a big family?" she asked, without moving.

"Are you getting the blankets ready?"

"Almost. You should have told me, Min."

"I couldn't risk it. I didn't want you to slip away from my hands."

"Like a bird, you mean?" Soo-Ja asked, half joking. She was on the floor now, unfolding the blanket and spreading it out to four corners.

"I can't believe it. It's done. I got you here," said Min to himself, as he lit another match and watched it burn. His voice sounded completely foreign, as if he'd been using an accent and had finally dropped it. His features, too, seemed to rearrange themselves, returning to some earlier, previously unseen mold.

"What's done?"

"My parents didn't think I could find a wife. Because of my . . . poor economic prospects. But they underestimated the power of looks. Parents do that. They never know when their kid's handsome."

"I didn't marry you for your looks," said Soo-Ja sternly.

"Did you see my friends' faces? Did you see how envious they were? Nobody thought I could do it. Nobody believed in me."

Soo-Ja was done arranging the mats and pillows on the floor. Though she could not see Min well, she could tell from his movements that he'd taken his shirt and pants off before he slipped under the comforter in his undershirt and long pajama bottoms. She did not join him.

Instead, she leaned her back against the wall and stayed there, listening to the hum of his inhaling and exhaling the cigarette smoke. Min did not call for her or demand that she join him, as if he were already spent, as if the important act had already taken place, and all he wanted to do was rest and revel in its aftermath.

"I did it. I got you."

"And I got you," said Soo-Ja, trying to sound casual.

Min laughed, as if she were a fool. "Yes. That's what you got."

Soo-Ja was still bothered by Min lying to her about how many siblings he had. "Was there anything else you lied to me about?" She realized this might sound harsh, but Min did not seem to notice. Strange talk for one's wedding night.

"I couldn't take the risk of you bolting. If you knew I had five siblings, you'd never have agreed to marry me."

"I never thought about your family much. I always knew we'd leave them and go to Seoul, just the two of us," said Soo-Ja, tasting the anticipation in her lips.

"I don't know what gave you that idea," said Min, his voice sounding like metal. "We belong here, with my parents. It is our job to serve them."

Soo-Ja felt as if the air were being squeezed out of her lungs. "But you said you're going with me to Seoul," she said, narrowing her eyes at him. "To start my training as a diplomat. You said you'd let me—"

"I never said anything like that," said Min, a little too quickly, almost snapping at her. "Why would I?"

"I thought . . . You told me . . ." said Soo-Ja, her heart sinking.

"Are you talking about that letter your father gave me?" asked Min.

"My father?" asked Soo-Ja, her jaw dropping. "He gave you that—"

"Yes, but I threw it away. Pieces of paper like that are dangerous. They give you paper cuts."

Soo-Ja felt the room begin to whirl around her, and she had to reach against the wall to remain steady. Soo-Ja realized how badly she had misjudged Min. He would never let her go to diplomat school. He would never support her goals. She had imagined she could live outside her own time and place, free from the same gravity that bound everyone else. But she'd been wrong.

"What did my father tell you when he gave you that letter?" asked Soo-Ja.

"Your father is not like mine," said Min, not answering her question. "Once my father makes a decision, he sticks with it. Is this how it's always been for you? He says no to you, and then he feels sorry and says yes? I bet you don't even know what it's like. To not get what you want. You have been spoiled all your life, Soo-Ja. I could tell when I first met you." Min let out another big cloud of smoke. Soo-Ja knew the unfairness of his words. "You also have a habit of not wanting to admit defeat. I'm not sure yet if it's a good or a bad quality."

"I didn't realize I was defeated," said Soo-Ja, feeling bruised. Her mind wandered to the night they had first made love. Lights flashed in her head, blinding her.

"Have you ever *not* come out on top?" asked Min.

"You didn't get much in the bargain, Min," said Soo-Ja, trying to re-cover some of her footing. "I'm not exactly a princess."

"No, but you're not a factory girl or a farmer's daughter, and those were the kinds of girls I was courting before I met you."

Soo-Ja closed her eyes. She could not bear to look at her husband. "I think we should try to go to sleep. We have a long trip ahead of us tomor-row. I would say good night and turn off the lamp, but it's dead already."

"All right, I'm sorry," said Min, sounding disingenuous. "What I said, just strike it from the record."

In the dark, Soo-Ja changed from her street clothes into her pajamas. She slipped under the blankets and lay next to Min. Tears began to fall. She could not fall asleep, and she sensed that neither could he. Then she heard a small voice say something. It barely registered, like a sound squeezed out of an animal's throat. She turned to Min and heard him repeat it, louder this time.

"Thank you," he said.

"For what?" Soo-Ja whispered back.

Min turned his back to her. "You'll find out soon enough."

PART TWO

Orchid

Three Years Later
Daegu, South Korea
1963

Soo-Ja thought of herself as a mother first, but for the rest of the world, she was a daughter-in-law. And as such, she was expected to take care of all the Lee children, especially her teenage sister-in-law Na-yeong. Her parents lavished upon Na-yeong all kinds of expensive sweets and treats, though Soo-Ja wasn't sure why they had chosen her as the single object of their attention and love. Perhaps they favored Na-yeong because she was one of the youngest, thought Soo-Ja, and thus least damaged, or the one with the shortest list of grudges. Maybe the chosen one had originally been Min, until her in-laws finally realized they couldn't rely on him—Min was too erratic and rebellious, quitting activism one day, then taking up boxing the next, only to quit it, too, and return to his father's factory, though not as a manager but as a packer. Soo-Ja wondered if maybe her in-laws, in private discussions, had gone down the list of names of their children one by one and ran out of options—Min's sister Seon-ae, the second oldest, had left home and never come back; Chung-Ho, the third eldest, resented being forced to leave school and work; Du-Ho was not very smart and therefore written off; and In-Ho, the youngest boy, was too prone to sickness.

So when Na-yeong turned eighteen, it was a momentous occasion, and her in-laws set up a meeting with a matchmaker to find her a husband. When Soo-Ja heard about this, she began to look at Na-yeong with a suitor's eyes. Tall, long-limbed Na-yeong wasn't beautiful, but she also wasn't homely. Na-yeong had fine, almost patrician features, her face not round like her parents', but a long oval. Her eyes were also bigger, and sometimes luminous. Na-yeong did not look like Mother-in-law, who was tanned and robust, but when Soo-Ja looked through an old photo album of the family, she saw she looked just like her grandmother. Na-yeong's features had skipped one generation, and she had been plucked straight from the past, maybe from a long line of women who looked just like she did.

But Na-yeong was clearly her parents' daughter, in that she had almost all the same facial expressions and, like her father, hardly ever smiled. You could tell right away they were father and daughter. Soo-Ja imagined that what was inside Father-in-law had managed to manifest itself on the surface of Na-yeong's body, as if what's inside a parent could show up on the child's appearance. Father-in-law had a general's build and moved like a tree trunk, but in Na-yeong's thin frame, Soo-Ja could see the emptiness inside Father-in-law; in Na-yeong's bony arms and legs, his exquisite avarice.

If she were the matchmaker, what kind of man would she bring for Na-yeong? Soo-Ja wondered. For there must be someone for her, since everyone has a match. Only in books is marriage reserved exclusively for heroines. In real life, her cousin and her cousin's cousin must get married, too. Soo-Ja pictured boy after boy for Na-yeong—slender, chubby, young, old, rich, poor—until Na-yeong caught Soo-Ja staring at her, and she looked away. But when Na-yeong focused her attention back on a magpie outside the window, Soo-Ja stared at her again, wondering what makes two people right for each other. Was it invisible, like gas, or open to the eye, like sparks in wiring?

Weeks went by without news from the matchmaker, until finally she said she'd bring a suitor for Na-yeong. Mother-in-law clapped her hands once, in excitement, as if catching a fly, and when Na-yeong shyly looked up from her romance novel, Soo-Ja could hear her young heart beating from across the room. So they were like her, Soo-Ja realized; unable to temper their emotions with caution, jumping at a new possibility like a mad diver off a cliff. How is it that they were not exhausted and spent at the end of the day, when the mere promise of love, of a partner, could whip them all into a state of frenzy?

The day the suitor was to arrive, the entire house was in a whirl, for they rarely had guests, and never any of consequence. They all felt invested in this, as if they'd been movie extras previously forgotten in a greenroom, and had finally been asked to report to the soundstage for their scene. The boys all dressed up in their best, and Father-in-law and Mother-in-law put on their hanboks. Soo-Ja herself spent the morning making sweet rice cakes. She steamed the grain until it became sticky and pounded it on the mortar until it hardened. She then covered the white cake with mashed red beans, cutting it into square pieces.

Soo-Ja did not complain as she prepared the confection. In the years since her wedding, Soo-Ja had mastered what she called her outside Hahoe face—serious, though not serious enough to the point of being a frown. She put that mask on, preventing others from looking in and seeing her unhappiness. With it, she could hide her anger and frustration, and expertly play the part of the obedient daughter-in-law. For Soo-Ja, that was a job like any other, and if she couldn't be a diplomat, then she would take all her energy and discipline and channel it to the household. While her sister-in-law frequently feigned being ill to avoid doing chores, Soo-Ja rose without complaint early every morning, and did the work that kept things running.

Around the time the suitor was supposed to arrive, Soo-Ja ran back toward her room to change. She wanted to make her daughter and herself look more presentable. She was about to go in when she saw Mother-in-law walking urgently in her direction.

"The rice cakes are on the plate. I'm just getting changed," Soo-Ja told her.

But Mother-in-law—her hanbok gown sweeping the floor—kept walking until she reached her. She looked worried.

"Hana's mother, go for a walk with your daughter and stay outside for a few hours."

"Go out? Why?" Soo-Ja stood on the small walkway between the main house and her own quarters. Her daughter leaned against her legs playfully.

"Just until he's gone."

Soo-Ja looked at her, stung. "Why? Why can't I stay?"

"Because of the way you look."

"The way I look?" asked Soo-Ja, more confused than offended.

"Like a poor relation."

Soo-Ja looked down at her old pink cotton shirt, faded after many washings; her indigo skirt passé now, but fashionable a few years back. It had been months, too, since she'd had a proper haircut, and now she wore her hair held back all the time.

"It's cold outside," said Soo-Ja curtly, holding her daughter closer to her. "I don't want Hana to get sick."

"You're always dying to go out, to do this, to do that. Now I ask you, for a good reason, and you're reluctant. You're like the stubborn frog in the folk tale, always doing the opposite of what he's asked."

"I'll just wait in my room until he's gone."

"No! The child's going to make a racket and disturb the guest!"

"*Child?* You mean, your granddaughter," said Soo-Ja, indignation scorching her body.

"Yes, grand*daughter*, not grand*son*. You have a big mouth for someone who's failed at her *only* duty in life. Now go. You remember what happened last time you disobeyed me?"

"You took Hana away from me for a day," said Soo-Ja, the memory still branded into her brain.

"Yes. Let's see how you'd like it if I made that a week. But the problem isn't her, it's you. You can leave her behind if you want," said Mother-in-law, turning around and rushing back to the main house.

Soo-Ja wouldn't leave Hana behind any more than she would leave behind an arm or a hand. Hana went everywhere with her. How unfortunate that mothers didn't have pouches on their bellies, like kangaroo mothers did! Instead you saw them as Quasimodo creatures on the street, women with babies (and sometimes toddlers as old as three) strapped to their backs, hunched forward like two-headed animals, one face to the past, the other to the future.

Hana, who'd been listening to this conversation carefully and who loved leaving the house, glanced at her, waiting for her decision. Saying nothing, Soo-Ja put a coat on her daughter and placed a warm woolen cap over the child's head. Hana spontaneously danced, as she always knew when Soo-Ja gave her the cap that she'd get to go for a walk.

"I like *eomma* when eomma take me out!" said Hana, the words roundly slipping out of her lips.

"I know, but it's cold, Hana."

"I don't like eomma!" Hana protested, thinking that her mother had changed her mind.

"But you just said you did," Soo-Ja teasingly replied.

"Only when eomma take me out!"

"Oh—so only when eomma take Hana out?" asked Soo-Ja, kneeling in front of her, smiling. "You don't like eomma all the time?"

Hana shook her head. "No!"

"Eomma likes Hana all the time, though. Does Hana like eomma when I give her sweet potatoes?"

"I like eomma!"

"How about when I sing a song for Hana?"

"I like eomma!"

"Then I guess I'm going to have to take you out all the time, and give you sweet potatoes, and sing to you, huh?"

"Yes! Do that!"

"Do that?" Soo-Ja could not hide her delight. "All right, I'll do that."

How could her daughter entertain her so? Soo-Ja wondered. In her little girl, she had found her greatest ally. Hana made her laugh, made her feel light. Even though Soo-Ja spent so much time taking care of her, she still felt like she was the one getting the better part of the bargain.

Soo-Ja could not imagine her life without Hana. From the moment she was born, Hana had delighted her. On each birthday, Soo-Ja thought, with a tinge of regret, *Oh, don't get older. You'll never be as adorable.* She didn't want her child to lose her baby fat. She would miss the plumpness of the girl's arms, the rotund, soft belly. She wanted to keep Hana a baby forever.

But babies had a way of surprising their parents, and each year, Soo-Ja found her daughter even more lovable. Around Hana, Soo-Ja felt like she could do and say anything. Her daughter, now almost three years old, gave her a magic lasso, and inside this circle—large enough only for the two of them—Soo-Ja felt freer than ever.

"All right, Hana, let's go," said Soo-Ja.

On her way out, Soo-Ja saw everyone nervously and excitedly gathering in the main room. Nobody noticed her, the whole family caught up in the roles they were to play. Only Du-Ho, who was now fourteen, and who appreciated her help with his *sugje*—his homework—stopped her and asked her where she was going. When she told him she had an urgent errand, he smiled mischievously and said not to worry, as he'd fill her in later and let her know if the suitor was ugly or handsome, and what kind of clothes he wore. If he wore flannel pants, Du-Ho said, he'd make faces at him. She smiled back at him and continued walking to the door.

As she made her way into the courtyard, Soo-Ja noticed the fish swimming in the murky lotus pond. There were four or five of them, and they seemed as excited as the people inside, rushing off in all directions. Soo-Ja smiled, admiring their intense colors and odd shapes—a yellow koi with a long tail; some goldfish with protruding mouths; twin orfes with silvery fins. The fish were about to disappear from her line of vision when she noticed the first specks of snow of the season landing on the stone edges of the pond.

Soo-Ja looked around, hoping to find Du-Ho or one of the boys, but they were all inside, adjusting their outfits and combing their hair. She could not find a servant, either. There had been many forecasts of snow; Soo-Ja wondered why no one had had the forethought to remove the fish from the pond and put them indoors. As Hana cooed at her beloved pets, her little fingers tracing their zigzags, Soo-Ja realized that the fish had been simply left to die.

With no further thought, Soo-Ja reached for a pot and tried to use it to scoop up the fish. She failed the first few times, with the fish too alert to her, anticipating her movements. Soo-Ja grew frustrated, aware that the suitor could be arriving at the house at any moment. Mother-in-law would be furious if she caught her still at home.

But the more eagerly Soo-Ja approached the fish, the quicker they seemed to evade her, swimming out of the pot each time she tried to lift it out of the water. *Oh, you dumb, dumb fish*, Soo-Ja muttered under her breath. *Can't you see I'm trying to save you? What do you think is going to happen if you stay in that pond?*

Soo-Ja placed the pot by the side of the pond. She decided she would have to catch the fish by hand. Trying to ignore the glacially cold water, Soo-Ja lowered her outstretched palms into the pond and waited for one of the fish to linger over them. She could barely keep her hands still, as the cold seemed to travel directly to her brain. She fought the temptation to free her hands, watching as they trembled.

When a goldfish that had been lying sluggish at the bottom of the pond finally rested above her palms, Soo-Ja snapped her hands shut. She could feel the fish beating against her flesh wildly, obviously unaware that she was trying to save it. As if reading her mother's mind, Hana quickly raised the half-empty pot in her mother's direction, spilling much of the water. Soo-Ja opened her hands into it. The tiny fish flopped in the air for a second, and then seemed to take a dive, careening wildly back and forth before it finally settled down. Soo-Ja repeated this with the others, one by one. By the time she'd finished, her hands had turned a ghostly white, and she could no longer feel any sensation in them.

Soo-Ja sighed with relief, glad that she was done before the suitor's arrival, and before the snowstorm started. But just as she was about to finally make her way out of the courtyard, Soo-Ja heard the gate open and saw a handsome man in his thirties, wearing a Western-style suit, walk hurriedly toward her. He had surprisingly long hair, with bangs that fell slightly over one eye and a healthy tan that spoke of far away, of long retreats in the mountains. He smiled overexcitedly and delivered a deep, heartfelt bow. Soo-Ja bowed back and knew right away that this was the suitor, Iseul.

"Did I get the time wrong? I thought I was early, but maybe I'm late, as I see you've gotten impatient and decided to leave," said Iseul.

Soo-Ja saw that he had mistaken her for Na-yeong. She glanced over to see the matchmaker still at the front gate, haggling with the taxi driver who'd brought them there in his Senara.

"You're mistaking me for Nam's daughter," Soo-Ja told him, trying to think of an excuse to leave. "I'm his daughter-in-law."

"I don't believe you. I think you saw my ugly mug and changed your mind," teased Iseul. "You're going to ask some ugly cousin to pass herself off as you."

"Who do you think this is, then?" asked Soo-Ja impatiently, pointing at Hana, who'd been hiding her face against her mother's hips.

"Some child you're babysitting!" Iseul said, scratching his arms.

Around this time, Mother-in-law and Na-yeong appeared next to them, and both looked horrified to see Soo-Ja and Iseul together. Soo-Ja tried to think of something to say so she could leave without appearing rude.

Before she could speak, however, Soo-Ja was interrupted by the matchmaker. The old woman had finally joined them, pocketing the extra coins she'd saved through the haggling.

"I see you've already met Min's mother, and her lovely daughter, Na-yeong," said the matchmaker, ignoring Soo-Ja completely. "Min's mother, Na-yeong, this is the suitor I spoke so highly about. He comes from a wonderful family that owns property in Seoul, and he is a very successful engineer!"

The matchmaker stopped once she noticed the frown on Mother-in-law's face. The suitor turned to look at Na-yeong, the true intended, and his smile immediately vanished. Na-yeong saw this, and she looked as if she was on the verge of tears. Soo-Ja wanted to disappear.

The suitor turned to Mother-in-law and bowed, all his enthusiasm gone.

"I'm sorry. I made a foolish mistake. I'm honored to meet you, Min's mother."

Not knowing what to say or do, Soo-Ja nodded her head slightly to the others and began to walk away. But before she could take a single step, the suitor turned to her.

"Where are you going?" Iseul asked, confused.

"I have to go. I really have to," said Soo-Ja, picking up the bucket of fish.

"No, you must stay for tea," said Iseul, taking the bucket from her hands and putting it back on the ground.

"She has to go! Let her go!" snapped Mother-in-law. "Come inside, before the apples turn sour and dark."

But the suitor would not budge. "I expect the whole family to be there," Iseul said sternly. "What kind of a first meeting is this, where not everyone is there? Are you trying to hide something?"

"No, of course not," said Mother-in-law, offering him a strained smile.

"Then let's all go in," he said.

Soo-Ja tried to escape one more time, but the suitor reached for her arm and then pointed the way with his right hand, as if he were the host and she the guest. He walked next to her the entire way to the house, ignoring Mother-in-law and never looking at Na-yeong. Soo-Ja glanced behind for Hana, and saw that she had picked up the pot with the fish inside and was carrying it into the house.

In the main room, two serving trays with tea, rice cakes, and sliced pears had been set up on the floor—one for the adults, and one for the children. Soo-Ja saw the look of surprise on her father-in-law's face when he saw her coming back in. He clearly had to hide his reaction, however, as he received the suitor. The boys, too, looked confused to see Soo-Ja and Hana still there, though Du-Ho smiled, quietly cheering their presence.

After a series of bows between the guests and the hosts, Iseul finally sat down on a mat, asking Soo-Ja to remain next to him. Soo-Ja reluctantly agreed, knowing that if she refused, she'd simply be drawing more attention to his request. Soo-Ja sat down, telling Hana to join the boys at the small table. Mother-in-law plopped down on the other side of the suitor, with Father-in-law sitting across from Soo-Ja. Na-yeong and the matchmaker remained the farthest from the suitor, completing the square.

"Iseul, you haven't spoken a word yet to Na-yeong," said the matchmaker in an animated manner. "Have you ever seen such a beauty? I knew at once that you two would make a fashionable pair."

"Don't call her a 'beauty,' matchmaker. It's too much for her to live up to. Who can stand so much pressure?" asked Iseul. He looked quite pleased with himself, as if he'd just said something very wise. He didn't notice the look of annoyance on Mother-in-law's face, or the embarrassment registering in Na-yeong's eyes.

"Did I mention already that your zodiac signs are very compatible?" asked the matchmaker, ignoring Iseul's comment. "You being a horse, and Na-yeong a dog."

"What sign are you, Hana's mother?" asked Iseul, turning to Soo-Ja. As the suitor glanced adoringly at her, Soo-Ja understood why Mother-in-law had wanted her gone during his visit.

"I'm a tiger, and my husband's a rabbit," said Soo-Ja, quickly but patiently. She prayed that Na-yeong would not notice the way Iseul stared at her. But when Soo-Ja looked in the direction of her sister-in-law, her heart sank. Na-yeong seemed to be fighting back tears, and trying to hide her face.

Iseul eventually noticed the subtle dance of gazes between Soo-Ja and Na-yeong. He shook his head, as if chastising himself, and took Mother-in-law's hand into his. "With all this talk of animals, I'm forgetting the real purpose of my visit."

Mother-in-law's face brightened. "There's no real purpose for this visit. My only concern is that you enjoy yourself."

"If I'm not paying enough attention to Na-yeong," Iseul continued, "it isn't because I don't find her enchanting. It's just that the bride is only half the matter. The other half is the family."

The matchmaker nodded. "It is very smart of you to know that. And I can assure you the Lee family is a truly extraordinary one."

Iseul gave her a skeptical glance. "You *have* to say that. They're paying you."

The matchmaker let out a loud snort. It registered as a girlish chuckle, but was really more of a rebuke. Mother-in-law laughed as well, as if trying to pass his comment off as a joke.

"I should ask someone more objective. Someone who has nothing to gain from this," said Iseul. He then turned to Soo-Ja in a theatrical manner. "Not long ago, you were in the same boat that I am. What do you think of this family? Are you glad you married into it?"

"I'm not sure what you mean by that," said Soo-Ja, trying to buy time. She knew that everyone's eyes suddenly fell on her. She also knew what lies they expected her to say: *This is a wonderful family.*

"I'm asking a simple question," said Iseul, his manner growing a little more impatient. "I'm asking if you recommend that I take your in-laws as *my* in-laws."

Soo-Ja looked around her. She could see her mother-in-law piercing daggers into her with her eyes, and Na-yeong looking as if she was about to faint. But Soo-Ja had never been able to lie when asked a direct question.

"I'm sorry, Iseul, but I cannot answer that."

With that, Soo-Ja excused herself and rose to leave. She reached for Hana and the bucket of fish, and then made her way out. She knew the suitor would not stay much longer and, in spite of Mother-in-law's efforts, would probably never return.

The punishment came swiftly.

That same night, Soo-Ja came to her room to discover that someone had gone through her things. As Soo-Ja opened her drawers and looked through them, she realized her bag of cosmetics was gone. She wondered if one of the boys had taken it, as a prank.

After she put Hana to bed, Soo-Ja decided to find Mother-in-law and ask her if she had her makeup kit. Soo-Ja found her in her quarters, sitting on the floor with Na-yeong in front of her, brushing her daughter's long, silken hair. Mother-in-law's room was one of the largest in the house, and the only one with a mirror. Egg-shaped, with a cherry frame around it, the mirror sat atop a large chest decorated with a painting of long-tailed dragons. The chest, which was Mother-in-law's pride and joy, had been inlaid with paper-thin layers of bull's horn that were attached to the oak wood, and the horn plate had the odd effect of making the chest look as if it were made entirely of translucent bull's horn, when in fact it was only the outer layer.

"*Eomeonim*, I wonder if I may have your attention for a second?" Soo-Ja asked after her initial bow. She sat in front of her mother-in-law, with her knees touching the floor and her bottom resting on her ankles, her body feeling awkward but in the proper position for a well-bred young lady.

"You can have it for a moment. I'm going to bed soon. It has been an exhausting day," said Mother-in-law, never taking her eyes off her own daughter.

"I just wanted to know if you borrowed my makeup kit," Soo-Ja asked in a restrained voice.

"Makeup kit? Why are you bothering me about a makeup kit?" asked Mother-in-law, still facing her own daughter. "A single girl, I can see why she'd own a makeup kit. She needs to make herself attractive for her suitors. But a married woman? Why would a married woman need a makeup kit?"

Soo-Ja held her tongue at this, arching her eyebrows. "Just so you know, I wasn't wearing any makeup today," she said.

"Oh? Is it because you think you are so beautiful that you don't need it?" asked Mother-in-law, looking away from the mirror for the first time.

Soo-Ja rested her bottom on the floor, trying to remain calm.

"What did you do with my makeup kit? Did you do something to it?"

"And if I did?"

"That was *my* kit, purchased with *my* money, from before I was married to Min," said Soo-Ja, her blood starting to boil. "It was a kit from Europe, from Paris. *Very* expensive. I used it sparingly, to make it last longer, since I knew I wouldn't be able to get a new one for a long time to come. Please, give it back."

Mother-in-law looked at her with disgust. "For as long as you live in my house, you're not to wear any makeup. Keep your face the way God made it."

Mother-in-law reached inside her *bandaji* and produced Soo-Ja's makeup kit. She tossed it at her daughter-in-law.

"I'm sorry about what happened with Iseul," said Soo-Ja, trying to speak evenly. "But that does not give you an excuse to take my things."

Mother-in-law looked angrily at Soo-Ja, while Na-yeong watched quietly. "You're not scared of me. Why are you not scared of me? I talk to my friends. Their daughters-in-law are *terrified* of them. But you, you're not afraid of me at all."

"Why would I be? You're not a mountain bear."

"And how can you not be afraid of Father-in-law? The way you talk to him . . . it's so informal. It's almost brazen."

"I don't see why I should treat him like some god just because he was born a man."

"I knew you'd make a bad daughter-in-law, but I didn't expect you to be *this* bad."

Suddenly, Mother-in-law grabbed the kit back from Soo-Ja's hand and pulled some of the cosmetics out of the bag. She then proceeded to break the lipstick off at the base, snap the cover off the foundation case, and tear off the tips of the mascara brushes. She did this with the quick movements of a child, completely focused on the task, glancing over at Soo-Ja occasionally, daring her to stop this. Na-yeong watched this, too, with a look of surprise on her face, and a tinge of regret, as if all these items could have—should have—been hers. Finally, Soo-Ja reached over and took away some of the pencils and lipsticks that her mother-in-law hadn't yet gotten to. While Soo-Ja leaned forward, her mother-in-law tried to pry her fingers open, slapping at her arm.

"Stop that!" Soo-Ja told her.

But her mother-in-law kept hitting her, and she leaned forward clumsily, so that her arms and hands fell over Soo-Ja for support. When Soo-Ja moved to get away from her slaps, Mother-in-law lost her balance, fell back, and hit her head on the floor. She gave a great cry of pain.

The commotion brought Father-in-law and the boys to the room, along with Min, who appeared a few seconds later. Soo-Ja pictured the tableau through their eyes: Mother-in-law rubbing her head with her hand, squinting her eyes in obvious pain; Soo-Ja—enemy, attacker, villain—standing over her with no apparent weapon but her strong hands.

"She hit me! She hit me!" Mother-in-law cried out.

"I didn't!" Soo-Ja called out. "She fell on the floor by accident."

"I fell because of you! Because you hit me!" She began to bang on the floor, like a woman whose body has been overtaken by a spirit. *"Aigo meah! Oh my Lord!"*

Everyone's eyes turned not to Soo-Ja but to Min, to see how he would respond to this. Soo-Ja looked at him a little complicitly, expecting him to ask his mother if she wasn't sure she'd fallen by accident. He was, after all, her husband, and she expected him to side with her. But instead, he turned to his wife, hate flashing in his eyes.

"Why are you so mean to my mother?" Min cried out. He reached for Soo-Ja's arm and shook her. "I know what goes on behind closed doors! You act nice to her in front of me, but I know when it's just the two of you, you're abusive to her! Well, you've been caught this time."

Soo-Ja looked back at him in disbelief, and then she turned to Na-yeong, waiting for her to tell them it had been an accident, and that she had never laid a finger on Mother-in-law, even while she was slapping her. But Na-yeong said nothing, and the men stared down at Soo-Ja in fury.

"Hana's father, you don't believe her, do you?" asked Soo-Ja. "I didn't hit her."

Min did not answer. Instead, he spied a pair of scissors on the floor near a sewing kit and dove to grab them. In a second's flash, he was waving those scissors in front of Soo-Ja, not saying anything coherent. Soo-Ja watched the sharp blades as they punctured the air. All the others stepped back, afraid of getting hit by accident.

If you stab me, my death will be slow and agonizing, thought Soo-Ja.

It was Du-Ho who quickly grabbed Min's hands from behind and took the scissors away from him. Soo-Ja noticed that Min gave them up freely, as if he had been waiting for someone to do precisely that.

His hands now free, Min used them to grab Soo-Ja. He dragged her all the way to their room, where he finally let go of her arm. He did it with such force that Soo-Ja almost fell to the floor.

Sitting down, Soo-Ja massaged her bruised skin and looked at Min with anger in her eyes. "Don't you have any desire to hear my side of the story?"

Min paced the room in a half circle, his fist tapping against the walls. "Why did you have to flirt with Na-yeong's suitor? If you're not satisfied with me, why don't you go after the milkman, or the gardener's son?"

Soo-Ja felt the frustration tighten around her neck. "Because I'm not you, Min. I don't believe in sleeping with the help."

Min made his hand into a fist and he held it above Soo-Ja's face. He glared at her, trembling a little, as if trying to gather the courage to hit her.

"You lay a hand on me, Min, and I will kill you. I will take a knife from the kitchen and I will stick it in your heart."

Min's eyes grew bigger, and he punched the wall instead. The thud was so loud it made Soo-Ja flinch. She waited to hear if Hana woke in the next room. The impact, however, had not been loud enough to disrupt her daughter's slumber.

Min, as if tired from the punch, sat down on the floor next to Soo-Ja. He looked like a man ill with fever.

"I'm not going to hit you, Soo-Ja. I'm not my father."

Soo-Ja looked at him sideways, cautiously, her words prodding him like a stick. "Your father used to hit your mother?"

Min laughed. "He had a room especially for that." Min rested his head against the wall. "He had us empty it out, take out the furniture. Then he'd put Mother in there and he'd beat her. He'd chase after her in a circle, and she'd try to get away. When he caught up with her, he'd hit her. She'd fall, then get up, and keep running in the circle, until Father's knuckles gave out. Even when I stayed away from the room, I could still hear them, and I could see their shadows on the paper doors."

"Is that what you wanted to do to me tonight?" asked Soo-Ja. Outside their door, she could hear the wind howling as the snow dove onto the ground. By morning, they'd all be buried in layers of crystals and powder. "Trust me, I didn't flirt with Iseul."

"No, you did something much worse." Min's voice gained a sureness that bothered Soo-Ja. She wondered if something else had happened.

"If you'd met Iseul, you wouldn't be saying that."

"I *met* Iseul," said Min, cutting her off. "I ran into him as he was leaving. He pulled me to the side and told me to take better care of you."

"Why would he say that?" asked Soo-Ja, confused, turning to him.

Min met her gaze. "He said he saw you pulling fish out of our pond. He said it looked like your hands were freezing."

Soo-Ja placed her hand on her forehead and squeezed her temples. So the suitor hadn't been late, after all. He'd been at the gate, watching her that entire time. Soo-Ja wondered why he hadn't come to help her.

"Why do you do things like that? To make people feel sorry for you?" asked Min.

"I didn't know he was there."

"He said that you must have married badly. Did you, Soo-Ja? Did you marry badly?" asked Min.

In his voice, Soo-Ja heard a kind of desperation she had never thought him capable of feeling. She figured he wanted her to say *Yes, I did*, so he could continue to fight with her, and yell at her, and accuse her of being ungrateful. In his words, Soo-Ja heard a bottomless guilt, frustration the size of an ocean. He did not provide for her, and did not take care of her. He did not know how to.

Soo-Ja felt the tears form in her eyes. She closed her eyelids, trying to trap them inside. "My life is good, Min. Don't worry about me."

It had not been so bad in the beginning. During the first week of the marriage, Soo-Ja's in-laws bragged about their new daughter-in-law, whose enterprising father, they liked to remind others, had started one of Korea's first modern shoe factories. Mother-in-law took Soo-Ja to the market with her and introduced her to all the shopkeepers she did business with. When she met them, Soo-Ja saw that her mother-in-law had already spoken to them about her, and brought her because they'd asked so often to meet her.

But even then, Min's mother would give her daughter-in-law a hard time. She'd comment on Soo-Ja, saying, "Your hips are very narrow. That is not good for birthing babies." Or she'd sneer, "Your hands are so smooth. Have you ever done a day's work in your life?" Like other women of her generation, Mother-in-law did not welcome a comely daughter-in-law. Beauty meant trouble, and mothers whose sons married attractive girls often cursed the union. The ideal daughter-in-law had rough hands, large hips, and a homely face.

During the months of Soo-Ja's pregnancy, Mother-in-law prayed every night to her ancestors at a small shrine she had built in the backyard, asking for a grandson. She observed all the traditional restrictions that were believed to encourage the birth of a boy. She did not let her daughter-in-law run, read, or walk up too many stairs. She did not let her have visitors, or talk about serious matters. She did not let her wear clingy clothes, or get near rotten or raw meat. Interestingly, thought Soo-Ja, her restrictions did not extend to her chores as a daughter-in-law. She still had to scrub the laminated floors of the house every day—floors that had to be clean enough for them to sit, eat, and sleep on—as well as wash everyone's clothes, many of which were white and also had to be cleaned daily. Those activities were not thought to affect the sex of a baby, her mother-in-law explained.

When Hana was born, Soo-Ja's in-laws were deeply disappointed. Mother-in-law tore off the chili peppers she'd hung on the entrance to the house, and disassembled the small shrine in the backyard. Girls were like grass—to be stepped on. As the oldest, Min was expected to give birth to a son and continue the family line. In his eyes, and in the eyes of the family, Soo-Ja had failed at her duty.

From that day on, her new family began to treat her differently. Occasionally, they'd remind her that if she were to get pregnant again, and give birth to a boy, her status in the household would improve. But Soo-Ja could not bring herself to have another child with Min. One was enough, she decided. In her mind, children had to be born out of love, not out of necessity. Besides, she already had her daughter, and even though no one ascribed the child any value, Soo-Ja believed that Hana was a blessing, and a thousand times better than any boy.

• • •

Soo-Ja had been ironing clothes when Father-in-law unexpectedly came to her room. She was a little startled by his presence there, since he'd never been there before. He slid the paper door shut behind him and sat down in front of her, without asking first if he could see her. He made it clear that this room, too, belonged to him. As usual, he never smiled or shifted his gaze. She had realized early on that he derived his authority from the fact that he did not care if others liked him. He'd given up the need to be loved—in the same way some monks gave up sex or rich food or nice weather—and it had made him invulnerable. While the rest of the world would stumble and trip in their quest for kindness, he remained impervious, never bothered by needing or wanting anything from anyone. Watching him made you think of love as a kind of weakness; without it, you were able to operate in as precise and calculated a manner as you wished.

"To what do I owe the honor of your visit, *abeonim*?" Soo-Ja asked. She placed the iron down, so that it wouldn't face Hana, who was folding the clothes next to her.

Father-in-law glanced at his granddaughter but did not smile, as if wondering what she was doing there. "I'm concerned about you. I've been watching what's been happening lately, and I can tell you're not happy here."

"No, I'm perfectly content. This is married life. It's not meant to be a playground."

"But you and I both know your days here could be much more pleasant."

Soo-Ja turned her face away. "I'm not going to get pregnant again. Let one of your other boys marry and have a son."

"That's not what I'm here to talk about. I don't care so much about the future generation. I care more about bills, and heating costs, and no one living off my sweat."

"I'm not sure I understand."

"Let me put it this way. If you were a guest in a boardinghouse, would you expect to live there without paying?" asked Father-in-law.

Soo-Ja stared at his leathery, dark skin, noticing how the folds around his eyes and his chin lent him the appearance of a bulldog. "You think I'm living off you?" asked Soo-Ja, furrowing her brow.

"I see for all the studying you have done, you don't know much at all. In fact, you may know even less than the beggar on the street. At least the beggar knows he must beg, or he will not eat. You, on the other hand, seem to be under the impression you need not do anything, and a roof will always be over your head, and rice will magically appear."

"I think no such thing," she said. "That is why my father gave my husband a dowry, so I would not be a burden to my in-laws."

Father-in-law scoffed. "Your dowry is gone. It has been spent."

Soo-Ja gasped. "Gone? How can such a large sum be gone?"

"Don't argue with me. If I say it's gone, it's gone."

Oh, how she wanted to lash out at him. But one word, and he could have thrown her out. And if he did, word would get around town and shame her father. No, she had to endure this. She had to succeed here, as a wife and a daughter-in-law. A good report must go to her parents. Above all, they must think that she was happy. Her duty to them was the harshest taskmaster, making her bear pain and put up with matters she had not thought she could. Her days were fueled by hate for her in-laws, but that was insignificant next to the need to make her own parents proud.

"What would you like me to do?" Soo-Ja finally asked, hoping to quell the growing frustration building inside her.

Father-in-law looked pleased. The question, she realized, was what he'd been hoping to hear from the beginning of this conversation. "You must ask your father for money. And that money you must bring to me."

Soo-Ja looked at Father-in-law, dumbfounded. She realized, in that moment, how much they had misled her about their supposed fortune. Soo-Ja had thought about this first when she noticed the armoires in their sparsely furnished rooms. Unlike the antique nong and bandaji in her own father's house, which were made of dark, decorative grains like zelkova and persimmon, the dressers and chests in Min's home had rusty fittings and were made of wood with undistinguished grain, like chestnut and pearwood. Even the clothes they wore seemed cheaply made.

Mother-in-law's and Na-yeong's hanboks were made not of shimmering silk, but of dull ramie. They also lacked details, with no bindings along the hem or cuffs.

"How can I ask him for more money?" Soo-Ja asked, frowning. "Hasn't he already given you enough?"

"Know that I can kick you out of here any day, for any reason," barked Father-in-law. "No one will question me, and if they ask, I can say you were lazy, or dirty, or drank too much. They would side with me, you know that." Soo-Ja's eyes burned with anger, thinking about the shame that would bring to her parents. "Either way, know that from this day on, everything you eat, every piece of clothing on your back, is there thanks to my charity. I will keep strict accounts, and every day that passes, you will owe me more and more. And I will be able to ask more and more of your father."

Some mornings, when Soo-Ja had to go food shopping at the market, she would stop by a newspaper stand and scan the headlines of the *Chosun Ilbo*. The military, which had seized power two years earlier, had finally agreed to transfer rule to a civilian government. Conveniently, the candidate chosen by the people turned out to be the same man who had staged that earlier coup d'état, Chung-Hee Park. His inauguration would take place shortly.

As she filled her basket with barley and dried laver, Soo-Ja often wondered what she would be doing, right at that moment, if she had indeed become a diplomat. She might be sitting opposite the ambassador from Uganda, wearing a light blue seersucker jacket with big buttons over a white silk blouse, and a freshly ironed navy pencil skirt tight at the waist. She might be explaining the election results' relevance to the international community: "While not ideal, this shows our country moving in the direction of freedom, and proves that it deserves to be accepted into the United Nations. South Korea has established diplomatic relations with thirty-five countries in only the last two years, and will not abide by Russia's attempts to block it."

On the way back, with a pensive smile on her face, Soo-Ja would make a detour and stop by her father's house to visit her family. Soo-Ja never told Mother-in-law about these trips, as she would have been furious. Mother-in-law thought she spent too much time there. "*This* is your new home. You don't live there anymore. Stop visiting them so much. Do you like them better than you like us?" she would ask her.

Ignoring her mother-in-law's words, Soo-Ja took the bus with Hana by her side, and then walked to the house in Won-dae-don. Her heart grew lighter with joy the closer she got. This was her true home, she knew. As soon as she walked past the gate, she could hear her brothers' loud screams of delight, followed by her mother coming out, complaining that she'd have to pull out the good china.

Soo-Ja's mother took Hana by the hand and guided her to the house, where Father sat in the main room, waiting. He had softened since Soo-Ja had left home. Not having to see his daughter every day was a good thing—perhaps the secret to many a harmonious father-daughter relationship.

Soo-Ja told Hana to peck him on the cheeks, and Hana and her grandfather traded turns showering each other with kisses.

"Hana, who is this?" asked Soo-Ja, in an animated voice.

"It's Grandpa!" Hana replied.

"Hana love Grandpa?"

"Yes!"

"How much does Hana love Grandpa?"

Hana frowned, very serious all of a sudden. "Too much!"

Soo-Ja laughed at her daughter's seriousness. "Too much? That's a lot if it's too much. Hana love Grandpa more than candy?"

The toddler looked thoughtful for a moment, as if weighing an enormously important decision. Finally, she nodded her head momentously. "Grandpa *is* candy!"

Soo-Ja laughed. "Grandpa *is* candy? Are you going to eat him? *Yan, yan, yan?*"

"Yes!" Hana smiled sheepishly, and then pretended to chew, mimicking her mother. "*Yan, yan, yan.*"

Soo-Ja's mother cut up a melon and served its slices with tea, a gesture that made Soo-Ja feel sad—Mother-in-law was right, she had become a guest in her own house.

"And to think I almost missed out on all this by moving to the West," said Soo-Ja.

"You could still become a diplomat, you know," said Soo-Ja's father with a hint of guilt in his voice. Soo-Ja thought about making a biting remark, but decided not to. This would be as close to an apology as she'd ever get from him, she knew. She watched as he lifted one leg and rested his arms on his knee. "Your mother and I could watch Hana during the day."

"Oh, appa, you know Min and his parents wouldn't let me do that."

"Then why don't you separate from him?"

Soo-Ja's mother glared at her husband. "Don't put such ideas in her head! Not even in jest."

"Yes, Father, you heard Mother: *Not even in jest!*" mocked Soo-Ja.

Soo-Ja's mother began smoking one of her cigarettes. Hana, seeing this, walked toward her grandmother, trying to wrest the lighter away from her.

"Your father misses you a lot," her mother continued. "You should see him crying at night, getting all your pictures wet with his tears."

"You're softening with old age, appa," said Soo-Ja quietly. "But it's not as if I died or moved away. I'm not that far, and I always come visit."

"I don't cry just because I miss you. I cry out of worry for you," said her father, trying to fill Soo-Ja's sudden, contemplative silence. "If you had married well, I'd rest, in relief. But you . . . in that house . . . with those people."

"It's about time she matured," said Soo-Ja's mother. "A woman changes when she has a child."

Soo-Ja's father shook his head, his face that of an artist who has toiled night and day at his creation, only to see it ruined. "I fought with you so many times to make sure you'd have a good life. Maybe I should have just let you be."

"It's fine, appa. There's nothing perfect in this world. It could be much worse." Soo-Ja thought about Father-in-law's request. Of course her father would give her the money. Should she ask for it?

But before she could even broach the subject, her mother cut in again. "She's right. Just look at your friend Jae-Hwa. Look what she has to live with."

"What do you mean by that?" Soo-Ja turned to her mother.

"Jae-Hwa hasn't said anything?" asked her father.

Soo-Ja felt guilty for a moment. She hadn't spoken to Jae-Hwa in months, busy as she was with housework and Hana. Jae-Hwa had called on her once, but Soo-Ja hadn't been home. After Mother-in-law told her about it, Soo-Ja said to herself that she should return the visit. But she had never done it.

"Sang-Kyu's mother lives across the street from them. She says . . ." Her mother's voice trailed off.

"What does she say?" Soo-Ja asked. "Is Jae-Hwa not happy with her husband?"

"He beats her," her father blurted out.

"What? How long has this been happening?" Soo-Ja asked.

"Since they returned from the honeymoon. He's always getting drunk, calling her names. *Babo. Byeongsin,*" said Soo-Ja's mother. She inhaled deeply from her cigarette and let out a big cloud of smoke. She then turned the radio on, and the plaintive voice of an old woman singing a ballad began to fill the room.

> *My brother, the musician, is so mean to me!*
> *Always peevish, always in a hurry, always lying.*
> *Why do you have to steal my food?*
> *You take the meats, and leave me only soybeans!*
> *Why do you leave me alone for hours?*
> *It's like living with a vagrant.*

Soo-Ja pictured Jae-Hwa as an eight-year-old, her age the first time she'd met her. Plump Jae-Hwa was a new girl in her school, and had been eating her lunches alone in a stall in the bathroom. When Soo-Ja found out about this, she insisted that Jae-Hwa sit with her at her table. They'd become inseparable, and Soo-Ja's father had jokingly nicknamed her *Duljjae Ttal*, Daughter No. 2.

"I have to help Jae-Hwa," Soo-Ja said distractedly, trying to think of a plan.

"No. Stay out of it, Soo-Ja," said her mother sharply. "Her life is her life."

"We have to tell Jae-Hwa's parents."

"They know," said Mother.

"And what are they going to do?" asked Soo-Ja.

"What all parents do. Bury their heads in the sand and never speak of it." And as if reading her daughter's thoughts, she added, "And it would be monstrously impolite if someone brought it up to them. They would lose face for the rest of their lives."

"What about the police?"

"The police would never interfere in a private matter."

"Something has to be done!" cried out Soo-Ja.

Soo-Ja's mother shook her head at her, putting out the cigarette on a round silver ashtray. "Look at you getting all worked up. And where were you when Jae-Hwa went to your house that day? What do you think she went there for? To borrow some chili peppers?"

"I can't, Soo-Ja. I already spoke to my parents. They think I should stay here," said Jae-Hwa, her voice practically quivering. Soo-Ja sat next to her on the floor, in the middle of the small, windowless room. Although everything in it was similar to where Soo-Ja herself slept—pink mats and cushions, the black ink calligraphy scrolls hanging on the walls, the huge armoire with mother-of-pearl and pictures of cranes and blackbirds—the place felt oppressive, as if it had soaked up Jae-Hwa's unhappiness during the night, only to exhale it during the day.

"Stay here with a lunatic? What kind of advice is that?" Soo-Ja asked, unable to hide her anger.

"I talked to my brothers and sisters, too. They're afraid of offending my parents if I stay with them. So I have nowhere to go," said Jae-Hwa.

"Stay with *my* parents, then."

Jae-Hwa shook her head. "Soo-Ja, you know how people treat a separated woman. Nobody will have tea with me or meet my eyes when I walk by them. I would hate to become some kind of pariah."

Soo-Ja edged closer to Jae-Hwa and reached for her friend's arms. She had her stretch them out in front of her, and then she pulled the sweater back so she could see her skin. When she did so, Jae-Hwa flinched a little. Her body was covered with purple and green bruises.

"What time does Chul-Moo come back?" Soo-Ja asked.

Before Jae-Hwa could answer, the front gate slammed, and their bodies became instantly taut, like coiled wires. Jae-Hwa's husband had arrived. He soon slid open the doors to the room and looked at them, still wearing his white cotton mask over his mouth. Soo-Ja saw the frightening might in his eyes, but she wouldn't let herself be intimidated.

"Say good-bye to your wife. She's going to stay with my parents for a few days," said Soo-Ja, speaking politely, but making it clear this would not be a matter of debate.

Behind her, Jae-Hwa reached for a padded comforter and spread it on the floor. She began to put her clothes in the middle of it, leaving enough room so she could later tie up all the edges together.

"Jae-Hwa, come over here and massage my neck," said Chul-Moo, ignoring Soo-Ja. "It'll help me go to sleep." He then began undressing in front of her, pulling off layers until he had on only the sleeping long johns he wore underneath his day clothes.

"Please don't pretend you didn't hear me," said Soo-Ja. She ignored the effrontery of his changing in front of her—she knew he was just trying to unnerve her.

"Go take care of your own husband, *ajumma*," barked Chul-Moo. "Before he starts wandering around seeding other women's babies."

He spread a mat on the floor and lay down, ignoring Jae-Hwa as she packed her things.

"I can assure you she'll be treated very well at my parents'," said Soo-Ja drily, unable to hide her contempt as she stared at him. "Since I'm sure you're very concerned about your wife's well-being."

"Jae-Hwa, quit this nonsense and come over here," said Chul-Moo, ignoring Soo-Ja.

Jae-Hwa shook her head defiantly. But she also began to hesitate as she knotted the edges of the comforter together, her clothes packed inside but almost too heavy for her to lift. Jae-Hwa rested her hands over the silk cover. She could see an area where the fabric had ripped, revealing the thick, curdled dust fibers that served as padding.

"Jae-Hwa!" Chul-Moo growled again, and Soo-Ja could see the fear rising in Jae-Hwa. His voice sounded like a lion's, low and guttural. "Wherever you're thinking of going, they'll grow tired of you after a while, boring woman that you are who can't cook, and then you'll come back here on your knees, begging for me to take you back, and by then I'll have had such a long rest, my hands will be ready for a spectacularly vicious beating. Better not leave at all and spread out the beating over time, so you can take it little by little instead of a big beating all at once."

Soo-Ja was ready to tear the few remaining hairs out of his head. "Jae-Hwa deserves better than you. How can you speak to her like that?"

Chul-Moo got up from the mat and pointed a finger at her. "Be careful now. You may be a guest in my house, but guests in my house, they have no rights!"

"And what are you going to do? Are you going to hit me?" asked Soo-Ja as sharply as the edge of a knife, her voice rising with every syllable. "See what the police will say, you hitting another man's wife!"

Chul-Moo hesitated, though the anger still gleamed in his eyes, and Soo-Ja could feel it sting her like a hot fork.

"Jae-Hwa, can't you see your friend is envious of what you have?" asked Chul-Moo, sounding much more gentle now. "Yes, I may get angry with you sometimes, but what happens afterward? What happens after you stop crying and I comfort you? Nobody sees that part of things, when you open up to me like a happy flower and giggle. You can tell just by looking at your friend that she doesn't get the same kind of love from her own husband. She doesn't want you to be happy, so she comes here to meddle and take you away from the only man you have."

Jae-Hwa, whose head had been bent down while her husband said this, finally looked up. She seemed wan, weightless, colorless. Soo-Ja knew what would happen if her friend stayed there. She would become one of those ghost women in the village with dead eyes and hunched shoulders.

"Jae-Hwa," said Soo-Ja, holding her hand. "There *is* a better life for you. I can't prove it, you just have to believe me. But there *is* a better life for you. Not everyone is mean. I've seen enough beauty and kindness in the world to know that not every man is awful to his wife. I believe there *are* good men out there. Please believe me when I say this."

Soo-Ja watched Jae-Hwa drop her bundle, and she knew then that her friend wouldn't be coming to her parents' house with her. She had failed. She could see from the corners of her eyes Jae-Hwa's husband's quiet jubilation, along with a hint of fear, as if he knew how close he'd been to losing his wife that night. But such nuances didn't matter. Jae-Hwa was staying, and that was the end of it. All Soo-Ja could do was pick up Hana, waiting at her parents' house, and return home.

Soo-Ja held Jae-Hwa in her arms for one last time, and as their cheeks brushed past each other's, she could feel the moistness under her own eyes. She wiped them quickly and then nodded, resigned to leaving Jae-Hwa behind. Why did she feel so much sadness for her, when her own life was in shambles, when she herself was not that much better off? Soo-Ja wondered.

Is that the real reason I wanted to save her? So that in saving her, I could see if I could save myself, too? And what did it mean, then, that I have failed?

Soo-Ja rose, her back aching a little from sitting on the floor so long. When she slid open the door and went over to the porch looking for her shoes, she was struck by the coldness of the air, lashing at her from all sides. She realized it was even later than she thought, and the feeling of being out at this hour made the whole moment feel oddly surreal, as if the real Soo-Ja were still sitting at home with Min's parents, at the house in central Won-dae-don, while this other Soo-Ja wandered around aimlessly, knocking about from place to place.

Soo-Ja had not walked very far when she heard her name being called. It felt unfamiliar to hear it like this, at night, in an anguished voice. She turned around and saw Jae-Hwa standing on the steps of her house. She stood as still as a pillar, like Lot's wife, who'd dared to look back. She did not have her coat and seemed to shiver slightly.

"He won't let me take my clothes with me," Jae-Hwa finally said, the syllables seeming to escape from her lips one at a time. "He said it's a waste of energy, since I'm coming back."

Soo-Ja felt the relief lift her up, and she smiled, extending her hand to Jae-Hwa. Jae-Hwa hesitated, and then slowly began to walk toward her. When Jae-Hwa finally reached her, Soo-Ja took off her own coat and placed it over Jae-Hwa. It would still be a while before they got to Soo-Ja's parents' house.

Soo-Ja arrived home to find Min's silhouette waiting by the door. It struck her then, how boyish and skinny he looked. If she wore a mini-skirt and held her hair back with her signature headband, would she look like a teenager, too? Is that what they were, teenagers playing at being adults? Would one day someone—a real couple, wearing heavy coats and wool scarves—come by, thank them for taking care of their child, and haul away Hana and their clothes and marriage license, and would she and Min nod and leave that house and walk in separate directions, like contestants in some radio show who didn't know each other? Would she be relieved and look back on the whole adventure with fondness, but enjoy her safe, welcome distance from it? Or would she find life without Min and her in-laws unbearably easy, meaningless almost, as her sacrifices had made it possible for her to appreciate the smallest of gifts—like the beloved quiet for a half hour or so in the morning before the house woke and the day lay rich with promise. Or the sight of Hana sleeping peacefully, or any one of a thousand surprises that shook the day—like being able to help a friend who weeps in your arms with gratitude, whispering, "A better life . . . Yes, a better life for me."

"You were gone so long," said Min. "What happened?"

"A lot," Soo-Ja said simply, slipping past him like a draft of wind, with Hana sleeping in her arms.

"Did you talk to your father?"

It took her a second to realize what he meant. Of course,

Father-in-law must have told Min about his plans. She wondered what Min's reaction had been. She assumed he had simply gone along with his father's wishes, as he always did.

"No, I didn't," said Soo-Ja curtly. "I didn't ask for the loan. I didn't get a chance to. And that's for the best. I shouldn't even have considered asking my father for more money."

Min followed her into their room. He seemed lost in thought. Close like this, he looked different, thought Soo-Ja, wearing a blue sweater with a light yellow vest over it, and pants that ended slightly too short at the ankle, showing his long johns underneath.

"We have to pay back our creditors, Soo-Ja. The situation is very dire. If we don't pay them back, they'll take the factory from us," he said.

Soo-Ja busied herself getting their mats and comforters ready for bed. She avoided Min's eyes, but she could feel them on her skin, following her around.

"Your father would have plenty of money to pay those creditors if he didn't mismanage the factory," she said.

"Yes, my father is horrible and your father is perfect. Are we in a children's playground? Don't you get tired of playing this childish game? My father is your father now," said Min, starting to pace.

"If the factory goes down, you can find a job somewhere else. I can go work in a store, or a restaurant, and ask my mother to watch Hana during the day," Soo-Ja said matter-of-factly, brushing some stray fibers off a comforter.

"No, Soo-Ja. If we have to shut down the factory, things will be much more serious than my needing money or another job. Do you know what happens to men who default on their loans?" He paused, waiting to catch her gaze. "They go to jail."

Soo-Ja took this in. "Your father's been essentially stealing from others, to keep the factory operating. I know he never intended in good faith to pay anyone back."

It was then that she saw a shadow fall over Min's face, and she realized something was truly wrong. When he spoke, she could hear the fear in his voice. "Soo-Ja, last month, when the troubles got serious, my father changed the ownership of the factory . . . to me. If someone has to go to jail, it's going to be me."

Soo-Ja looked at Min, shocked. She thought she didn't love him, but maybe she was wrong. How else to explain the punch in the gut she felt, the sudden overload of emotions grabbing at her? How could he do this to his own son? And why wasn't Min fighting him, yelling at him? "Your father is a disgusting man."

"I'd go to jail for him anyway," said Min, full of bravado.

Soo-Ja dropped the comforters on the ground. "No, no, you can't be defending him!"

"What he did makes perfect sense. I'm the oldest; so whatever is his, is mine, too. The good things *and* the bad."

"But that's not what he's done," Soo-Ja said, shaking her head. "Can't you see what he's done?"

"Yes, but I'm trying very hard not to see. He's my father. I'd rather think what I think and be a fool, than be a man—"

"With a *bastard* for a father," she said, cutting in.

They were standing face to face, Min fidgeting and Soo-Ja frozen, staring at him. Min did not jump to his father's defense, and she could see how even he—the most devout of sons—would have trouble explaining this away to his own heart. Min's father treated Min as if his life belonged to him, to be used or discarded as necessary. And Min never disputed this. She wondered if he, too, believed, deep down, that he was a mere appendage to his father, and his life worth only as much as was of service to the elder.

"Do you want me to ask my father for money?" asked Soo-Ja.

Min looked at her and she saw the hope dance across his eyes. But then only a few seconds later, she saw his pupils darken, and his jaw tighten a little. To her surprise, he shook his head, and in that moment, she saw the most extraordinary event in nature—that of a human being changing. She wondered if a few seconds was all it took to shake up one's habits and impulses, unearth them like hardened soil, and replace them with the trickling drops of choice and whim, and all those things that made life unbearably complicated. She could see the strain in her husband, leaving behind one thought and reaching for a new one. She could see him become a different person—or try, at least, as he unstitched his father's shadow from his back, and checked to see if his own could grow.

"I don't want you to talk to your father," said Min. "Before, I wanted you to. I waited for you all night to ask you if you had. But now I don't want you to anymore. I can't put you in that position. I can't use you like that."

Soo-Ja nodded, feeling waves of tenderness rush at her. "Maybe if you explained to a judge . . ."

"I can't challenge my father's decision. I don't know how to explain, but . . . It would be disrespectful." He looked at her to see if she understood, and she nodded. "See, he can't know that I know what he's doing. Because he would lose face. I would be making him look bad, and that would be worse than any jail time. I can't do that to him."

Soo-Ja wondered if Min secretly wanted her to speak to her father, but do so out of her own volition, and not at his request. She searched his face for signs of this, but found none, much to her relief. She couldn't ask her father to do this for her. Father-in-law had lied; it wasn't a small loan he wanted. As Min explained the details of the bankruptcy, she realized that Father-in-law wanted Soo-Ja's own father to take up the burden of all the costs of his operations, paying a sum of money so big she was taken aback at first when Min told her.

That night as they lay on their own mats to sleep (though sleep would not come till much later), she felt for the first time that they were husband and wife. More so than the day of their wedding, or the night of their honeymoon, this was when it felt like they were truly spouses: they were on the same side; they shared a decision; they were in this as one. They had decided together not to speak to her father—not as a compromise but as an agreement—and the meaning of that weighed upon them both. In that moment, Min may have lost his freedom, but he earned her gratitude, and perhaps even her love; she could see the equation being one he could live with. Besides, he wasn't in jail yet. All was not lost. They had watched enough movies to know rescue could come; it would be delayed just long enough for the hero and heroine to learn something about each other.

"So where were you tonight? What happened?" There was no recrimination in Min's voice as he lay next to her.

Soo-Ja stared straight ahead, at the ceiling. If the roof blew away, she could see stars. "I went to help a friend. I tried to help her get out of a bad marriage."

"What makes it a bad marriage?"

"Her husband isn't nice to her. But she's afraid to leave, so I tried to help her."

"Do you think the husband knows she wants to leave?"

"I think husbands always know, don't they? They know everything that is taking place," said Soo-Ja.

"And wives, too? Do wives know what their husbands are thinking?"

"Yes, they do. They both know. But sometimes they choose not to say anything. Because they think things can change."

"But they're wrong?" asked Min. "Things *can't* change?"

"I think if both people try . . ."

Min was silent for a moment, and she could hear his chest heaving. Finally, when he spoke, his words landed as quietly as a single drop of dew on a leaf. "I'm sorry," he said, and he did not need to say anything more.

She realized, much to her surprise, that she had already forgiven him.

chapter seven

By December of that year, Soo-Ja had a new president, a new constitution, and a missing husband. The police had come by several times by then, and each time they told them Min had fled to Japan, and they had no contact with him. The officers, of course, did not believe them, and searched the house every time. Flashlights made circles in the kitchen furnace, and turned visible the excrement in the outhouse. Gloved hands dug through the armoires in every room, clothes flying in the air like grasshoppers. Standing behind them with her hands locked, Soo-Ja imagined Min as an invisible man, rushing from room to room, only steps ahead of the investigators, in narrow misses. She rooted for him, though she knew, of course, exactly where he was: hiding with a relative in the port town of Pusan, in case he had to hop into a boat and flee, in fact, to Japan. Soo-Ja had offered to go with him, but Min insisted that he hide alone—it would be easier, he said, though she suspected he simply did not want to inconvenience his parents by depriving them of their daughter-in-law.

Over time, Soo-Ja grew tired of the police's constant visits, as if they were mad guests who liked to play at scavenger hunts, undoing the stone paths she had so painstakingly arranged, or stepping on floors wearing shoes, much to her horror. Her fear of them quickly became annoyance, especially one time when the lead officer (a new one, when the case was reassigned) dared to reach for Hana, and asked her if she had seen her daddy. She thought it was cruel to ask a three-year-old that, though later she wondered if she'd been simply covering up for her own guilt at seeing Hana deprived of her father.

Soo-Ja didn't know exactly where Min was, though one of his letters mentioned a house with a thatched roof, slightly belowground, in a remote village, and that to get there one had to cross a potato field, some rice paddies, and a river. He was terribly bored, he said, unable to work or leave the house. There was no radio there, and the only time he saw someone was once or twice a week when his old uncle would come by with pots full of watery rice and a little banchan: cubed turnips laced with grains of sand, and pickled cabbage more sour than spicy. She felt like writing back, *Can't they boil an egg for you? Or kill a chicken?* Soo-Ja wondered if this was any better than jail, but as she lay in bed alone at night, thinking about it, she figured it was. At least he could breathe in some fresh air, and watch the sun rise and fall. And she knew Min was safe. Her only worry for the moment was that Min would alienate his uncle. She could see the uncle start out feeling sorry or protective of Min, but then growing tired of him. Maybe the uncle would not come by as often, or not be as nice to Min, frustrating and frustrated as he was, living the life of a dog tied to a post.

Around Christmas, Soo-Ja decided she should visit Min. It had been almost two months, and Soo-Ja felt that it would be safe. She wanted to check on his state, and to have him see Hana, as she knew the separation was tough on both of them. How do you explain to a three-year-old that the police are after her father, and he has to hide for the time being? Soo-Ja knew how much Hana wanted to sit on her father's familiar lap, and how much Min wanted to kiss his daughter's cheeks, turning her upside down and making her giggle.

When Soo-Ja told Father-in-law of her plans, he nodded and said that he would come, too, along with Mother-in-law and the others, as if this were someone's strange idea of a family vacation. Soo-Ja told him she should go on her own, and this was just so Hana could see her father. But Father-in-law looked terribly hurt, and said he missed Min much more than Hana missed her daddy. Soo-Ja at first couldn't believe he was comparing his feelings to those of a toddler, but finally she relented, amazed that he'd already forgotten the very reason Min had to hide in the first place. Father-in-law felt no guilt for sacrificing his son, nor—her second hope—any gratitude toward him. She wondered if he wrestled with those demons on his own, in the dark, until she figured that was wishful thinking on her part. Regret and pangs of conscience are feelings we assign to others to make the world seem a little more fair, to even things out a little and provide consolation. In reality, those who do wrong to us never think about us as much as we think about them, and that is the ultimate irony: their deeds live inside us, festering, while they live out in the world, plucking peaches off trees, biting juicily into them, their minds on things lovely and sweet.

Min looked much changed—his almost adolescent gait gone, his old swagger replaced by an older man's contemplative stillness. He'd started smoking more often, he informed her within minutes of her arrival, and each drag of his cigarette seemed like a reproach to her. Min had lost weight, and his clothes—a light brown pullover sweater with crew neck and dark brown pleated gabardine pants—hung over him like an older brother's hand-me-downs. He seemed to her like someone who had come to life only upon her wish, but in doing so made her aware of her initial impulse—to long for him, endlessly, rather than actually have this awkward, foreign body inches away from her.

Father-in-law and the others had stayed behind in his brother's house near the harbor; Soo-Ja and Hana alone had made the crossing in the middle of the night, knees deep into freezing lakes, past wet marshes and muddy banks, before arriving at the secluded one-room house by an abandoned potato field. The house was miles away from the main roads, in a mostly unpopulated area, and the few people who did live nearby—farmers and rice paddy workers—did not think to bother Min. Although, he told Soo-Ja in a paranoid manner, those who did pass by him acted as if they knew he was there hiding, and were careful not to get too close, keeping the river and the night between them.

Soo-Ja figured this was the worst kind of solitude, but she could see how it might become comfortable after a while. She had a vague feeling that less than an hour after their arrival, Min already wanted her and Hana to go—even though he had waited two months for this visit; even though this was the first time since getting there that he got to speak to a human being other than his uncle; even though as soon as they left, he would no doubt start missing them again. Soo-Ja felt like the two of them were bothering him, reminding him of all the things he couldn't do. Whatever his little routines were now—counting cans by the window, doing push-ups against the floor, reading the same books over and over—they had probably become his reality, and maybe more reliable to him than this mirage of wife and daughter appearing just so it could grow fainter and disappear again.

Soo-Ja watched Min play with Hana, as she sat on his lap, her little back resting against his belly as she played with a pair of dice she'd found on the floor. Hana had a habit of biting her lower lip in intense concentration, and when she'd notice him staring at her, she'd look up and smile briefly, as if thankful for the attention, before going back to busying her hands.

The two of them did this for a while, until Hana noticed Min's plate of food, filled with the fruits and fried meats that Soo-Ja had brought him. Hana reached for a sweet potato; it was, Soo-Ja knew, one of her daughter's favorite things to eat. Hana dug her fingers into it clumsily, mashing it when she tried to peel the skin off. Soo-Ja thought of helping her, but she liked watching her daughter do things on her own. Hana loved to mimic. She'd pretend, for instance, to do laundry, and when her mother sat Indian-style by the water pump, Hana would do the same, rolling up her shirt to her upper arms, and wiping the imaginary sweat off her forehead.

When Hana finished peeling the sweet potato, Soo-Ja thought her daughter would eat it, but instead Hana split it into three parts. She held one piece toward her mother, one toward her father, and a small chunk for herself.

"Thank you, Hana," said Soo-Ja, touched by her daughter's gesture.

"Thank you, Hana," said Min, taking his portion. He did not put the potato in his mouth; instead, he stared at it, as if staring at his daughter's love.

Soo-Ja held back a tear, as she realized how much father and daughter missed each other. All three of them ate in silence, Soo-Ja and Min watching Hana. They appreciated the illusion of normalcy, eager to forget that they were miles and miles away from their home, in a tiny room scarcely bigger than an outhouse. Soo-Ja realized at that moment that the biggest luxury in life was the ability to make plans, to count on the future as if it were something pinned down on a map. She wanted to speak in terms of years, not days; know exactly when Min would return, when they could resume their lives. How strange, she thought, that she longed, desperately, for old routines that once drove her to tears—tiresome and dull as her days had been, their certainty had made them bearable. This was like holding your breath in a bad dream, and when you woke up, you found out you still could not breathe out.

During their days in Pusan, Min's family stayed at Min's uncle's house, about a good hour away from the hiding place. Because they were cherished guests, they were given the best and largest room in the house. Soo-Ja had no idea where the uncle and his family—a wife and a five-year-old boy—slept, since she saw only two other small rooms in the house, both of which were cluttered with old furniture, worn-out bicycles, dusty boxes of rice and noodles, and a surprisingly large collection of vinyl records, along with an old Victrola.

This meant all of them—Father-in-law, Mother-in-law, Na-yeong, Chung-Ho, Du-Ho, In-Ho, Hana, and Soo-Ja—slept on the floor in one room, one next to the other, in a row of horizontal lines. This wasn't something to argue over, or to be discussed. It was simply accepted, and many families, who could not afford to rent houses with more than one room, did this routinely, with couples and their relatives cooking and living and sleeping in the same room.

While everyone else seemed to thrive in this arrangement, Soo-Ja found the lack of privacy and solitude unbearable. It was too cold to stay outside for very long, and in other rooms, Soo-Ja felt like she got in her uncle's way. So she had to be in the same space with Father-in-law and Mother-in-law for hours on end, and she found herself unable to hide her irritation at them. This tableau would be her life if something, *God forbid*, she thought, happened to Min.

As Soo-Ja played with Hana on her lap, she watched her family. In one corner, the boys played a game of *baduk*. In another, Mother-in-law clipped Na-yeong's fingernails. Across from them, Father-in-law sat by himself under a window. Soo-Ja noticed that he had a strange ability to be doing nothing but making himself look busy, in the same way emperors and kings—who were just sitting most of the time—managed to as well.

"It would be a waste to come all the way here and not do some sightseeing. Tomorrow we'll go to the Haundae Tourist Hotel. We'll pretend to be guests, and bathe in some of their medicinal hot spring water," said Father-in-law.

Soo-Ja looked at him in disbelief. "What about your son? You should go visit him while you're here."

Father-in-law waved his backscratcher at her. "Don't tell me what I should do."

"What you should do is go to the police and tell them what you did," said Soo-Ja. "Tell them how you let him take the blame for you."

"Min's lucky he never got arrested for something or other before," said Father-in-law. "He's been getting in trouble since he was seven years old. I had to grease a lot of palms to keep him out of jail."

Soo-Ja could see how much he wanted to yell at her, but something held him back. She realized then that he still had hopes that she would get her father's money for him.

"He's your son. You can't put him through this," Soo-Ja said, directing this to the others, hoping to elicit their rebellion.

"You're trying to undo something that already happened. I go to the police and turn myself in, things would turn out ugly very quick. Why do you think the police have been so lackadaisical looking for Min? Why do you think Min is still free? They *know*, Soo-Ja. They know because sons have sacrificed themselves for their fathers for centuries. If anyone's at fault here, it isn't me, for exercising my parental privileges, but Min, for not offering himself first."

The world, as explained by her father-in-law, felt like the narrow mazelike streets near her house that Soo-Ja used to run through as a child. You had to know where to turn, or you could get lost for days, steeped in their unspoken secrets.

"Then I will stay here with Min," said Soo-Ja. "It's not fair for him to endure this alone. He needs Hana and me."

"No. You're coming back to Daegu with us," said Father-in-law. "And you're going to get your father to help us."

Soo-Ja noticed that Mother-in-law had been silent through this. She had stopped dyeing her hair with henna, and the gray now crowded out the black. Her eyes—usually knowing and canny—seemed foggy and distant. So she missed Min after all, thought Soo-Ja. In her fantasies, Soo-Ja could see Min's mother making Father-in-law magically disappear, trading him for the son she loved.

"Be sensible, Soo-Ja," said Father-in-law gently, almost kindly. "Go talk to your father." She finally understood his pull. After all his angry and harsh words, the mere hint of his approval could be irresistible. For all her mistrust of him, it was amazing how much she still wanted him to like her.

Nevertheless, Soo-Ja decided to stand firm. "No, I won't bring my father into this. You'll have to find some other way."

Pusan reminded Soo-Ja of the years during the war, when her family had fled there to escape the communists. It also made her think of Yul, who had moved there a few months after his graduation from medical school. They hadn't seen each other in almost four years, but for a while, he had sent her letters—not to her house, but to her parents' house. An investor had agreed to back Yul's medical facility, and he'd opened an office, along with another partner, in the ever-growing port city. Soo-Ja pictured him practicing medicine behind a window in a square box of a room, with a wooden plaque the size of a mailbox out front, his name carved and colored in black ink.

Soo-Ja desperately wanted to see Yul. It would be foolish to be in Pusan and not look for him. So the day before she was supposed to return to Daegu, she decided to track down his address. She got it rather quickly, just by asking the telephone operator, who told her of a Dr. Yul-Bok Kim practicing in the Suyeong-gu district, near the city's busiest marketplace. The woman also gave Soo-Ja directions, telling her which bus stop to get off at. ("On the way back, you should try the fish market. Squid like you've never tasted it.") Soo-Ja wrote down the street name on a piece of paper and stared at it for a long time.

She knew she didn't have much time, and that she couldn't bring Hana. She couldn't subject her child to the ride on the bus and the walk in the cold wind. But Soo-Ja feared asking Mother-in-law to watch her, as she'd bombard her with questions. The boys she couldn't trust, since they were rowdy and unreliable and would probably leave Hana forgotten by the side of the road, while they threw snowballs at one another. That left Na-yeong, a poised eighteen-year-old, old enough to have her own daughter now. She'd never shown much interest in Hana, preferring her Bible and hymnal books, but Soo-Ja figured she'd do her this favor.

"Where are you going?" Na-yeong asked, taking Hana's hand as Soo-Ja offered it to her. They were standing by the front steps of the house, with everybody else scattered about.

"I have to get some of my shirts mended, I left my good ones in Daegu," said Soo-Ja, looking down at her clothes.

"Can't this wait until we get back? And why can't you take Hana with you?"

"If you don't want to watch her, just tell me, and I'll ask Du-Ho. He seems to have more maternal feelings than you," said Soo-Ja. She reached back for Hana, as if she were an exotic gift from abroad and Na-yeong simply too uncultured to appreciate her.

Na-yeong held on to the child. "It's fine. Go, eonni. I'll watch over her," she said, calling her "older sister."

Soo-Ja turned to Hana and kissed her head, feeling enormously guilty. It was rare for Soo-Ja to leave her behind; Hana was always beside her or strapped to her back, wherever she went. Soo-Ja looked at her daughter and waited for her to tell her not to go, to ask for her to spend the day playing with her. But of course, Hana just said, "Bye, eomma," and focused back on the doll she had in her hands. Soo-Ja wavered a bit. Was she on a fool's errand? But things had been set in motion now. She knew that if she didn't go—even if it was just to see what Yul looked like now, even if it was just to gather one more memory of him to last her another four years—she would regret it, and taste that regret on the rim of every glass she drank from thereafter. Then, as Soo-Ja put on her heavy winter coat, something in Na-yeong's demeanor made her hesitate. A sadness fell over her, like sudden hail, and Na-yeong suddenly seemed as old as Mother-in-law herself.

"Iseul never asked for a second meeting." Na-yeong was talking, of course, about her suitor. The only one she'd ever had. Soo-Ja wasn't sure whether she was asking her a question or stating a fact, so she simply nodded. "He barely spoke to me that day. He was too busy admiring you."

"There'll be other suitors, Na-yeong. You're still very young," Soo-Ja said gently.

"The first time is the only one that counts. Were you afraid I'd make a better match than you?"

"I can't imagine a better match than your brother," Soo-Ja said, not hiding her sarcasm.

"I've been so mad at you. And you haven't even noticed. Could you tell I've been giving you the silent treatment?" Na-yeong looked terribly sad, more sad than angry, and Soo-Ja felt as if she were seeing her for the first time. Na-yeong was always so quiet that Soo-Ja had made the mistake of assuming her silence indicated a kind of nothingness, when inside her there must actually be drums and waves and peaks.

"I didn't mean to ruin that day for you, Na-yeong."

"Why didn't you sing my praises to him? I'm sure he was impressed that you chose to marry into our family. Your words would have counted for a lot."

"I'm not sure if I'm the right person to be selling other people on your family."

"Of course not. You look down on us. You don't think I noticed the look of disdain on your face when I met you for the first time? I'm sorry we're not as educated as you," said Na-yeong.

"Maybe I should stay," Soo-Ja said. "It's so cold, anyway."

"No. Go," urged Na-yeong, speaking normally again. She looked a little embarrassed by her earlier burst of emotion. She forced a smile and began toying with Hana's hair. "I'll take her for a walk. I saw some kids playing outside, maybe I'll introduce her. It'll be good for her to meet kids her own age, instead of being with adults all the time."

Soo-Ja hesitated, and almost reached back for Hana, but she decided she'd just make the situation worse if she changed her mind. Hana, distracted by her doll, did not pay attention to their conversation. She was like a figure in the corner of a painting, placed there amid the scenery. Soo-Ja stepped back, feeling an odd sensation of being exiled. For a second, she hoped something would keep her from going to see Yul—an emergency or some urgent news—but no, the road was clear, nothing on the way, nothing to prevent her from doing this.

The doctor's office smelled of lye and cleaning supplies. In the middle of the room, a boiler gave out heat; the few waiting patients clustered around it, all still wearing their heavy coats and jackets. Soo-Ja sat down in one of the small metal foldout chairs. She wondered if the others could read on her face her reasons for being there, and hoped that they would take her for another sick person.

Not too much later, Soo-Ja saw a nurse come out. She wore no uniform, only a red windbreaker and a mask over her mouth. Soo-Ja signaled to her, asking if the doctor would be long.

"No," she said. "It looks like a heavy snowstorm is on its way. Even the sick are staying indoors. You said you had business with the doctor? You can speak to him as soon as this patient comes out."

At that moment, Soo-Ja heard the door to the inner room open, and the sound of talking filled the air behind them. She looked at the nurse, who nodded brightly and said *Yes, that's the doctor.* Soo-Ja turned, full of hope, her heart beating fast, expecting to see Yul, but instead she saw a man much older and shorter than him, wearing thick glasses and a long white uniform.

"Excuse me, miss." Soo-Ja reached toward the nurse again. "But that is not Dr. Yul-Bok Kim."

"Ah, Dr. Kim is not in today," said the nurse, a little too loudly. "He and his wife are vacationing in the mountains. They ski. Do you know what skiing is?"

"Skiing?" Soo-Ja repeated weakly.

The nurse's words echoed in her head: *He and his wife* . . . So Yul was married now. Why was it that she'd never considered that as a possibility?

"He'll be back tomorrow, though. Are you a patient of his? What is your name?"

Soo-Ja looked at her and panicked, feeling ill.

How foolish I've been! What did I think was going to happen? That Yul would rescue me from my marriage? He'd probably think I was crazy for coming here.

"It's all right. I—I'll come back tomorrow," said Soo-Ja, knowing she would be back in Daegu by then.

"Where were you?" Mother-in-law asked her as soon as Soo-Ja came into the courtyard. Behind her, Soo-Ja could see the sun erasing itself.

Soo-Ja looked at her, confused, noticing how Mother-in-law's voice seemed too strident, almost hysterical. For a moment, Soo-Ja felt the odd sensation that her mother-in-law stood in her way, not letting her go find Hana.

"I was just running an errand. Didn't Na-yeong tell you?" Soo-Ja tried to walk past her mother-in-law.

"Leaving your child with another child, what kind of thinking is that?"

Soo-Ja could hear it clearly now, the panic in Mother-in-law's voice. Soo-Ja swallowed, feeling something hard sprout inside her lungs.

"Na-yeong is hardly a child. Where is she? Where is Hana?"

Mother-in-law didn't answer but looked at Soo-Ja with pity and fear in her eyes. The lump inside Soo-Ja's lungs felt like a massive growth now, and it began to pulsate.

"Where's Hana? Tell me, where's Hana?" Soo-Ja walked past her and went into the house. As she opened the door to the main room, Soo-Ja found Father-in-law and the boys gathered there. When they looked up at her, she witnessed the graveness in their eyes. Then, she saw something that chilled her blood: in the back of the room, as if hiding, Na-yeong ate from a bowl of rice by herself, *without* Hana. Trying to keep her rising panic in check, Soo-Ja walked slowly toward her.

"Where's Hana?" Soo-Ja asked, hearing the dread in her own voice.

Na-yeong made no answer, using her chopsticks instead to hide part of her face.

Soo-Ja did not see Mother-in-law appear behind her.

"Na-yeong, go to your uncle's room and wait there."

"No, stay here," said Soo-Ja. "Tell me. *Where. Is. Hana?*" She knew by then something bad had happened.

"I don't know!" Na-yeong blurted out. "I lost her!"

"What do you mean, lost her?" yelled Soo-Ja.

Mother-in-law grabbed Soo-Ja by the arm. "There's no sense in getting hysterical. She didn't do it on purpose."

Soo-Ja shook her arm away from her. "What happened, Na-yeong? Where did you leave Hana?"

"Outside," said Na-yeong, quivering, the chopsticks in her hand beating against the sides of the bowl of rice.

Turning her back on all of them, Soo-Ja ran outside, calling out her daughter's name. "Hana! Hana! Where are you?" she screamed into the twilight. Almost immediately, Na-yeong followed, her little body shaking with fear. Soo-Ja looked at her with a madwoman's eyes and began to squeeze her sister-in-law's arms. "Tell me exactly where you left her. Tell me *exactly.*"

"I . . . I followed you," said Na-yeong, trembling, looking back toward the house, as if to make sure no one could hear them. "Today . . . I took Hana with me and I followed you. I knew you weren't going to the seamstress. I wanted to know if you were doing something bad, so I could tell on you. Oh, if I'd known you were just going to the doctor I never would've—"

"You followed me? You followed me all the way to the marketplace? You mean, you didn't lose Hana here, you lost her in the busy marketplace?"

Na-yeong nodded. "I wanted to make sure it was a doctor's office, and I had to cross the street to read the sign properly. I told Hana to stay quiet, and away from the curb. I thought it'd be all right if I left her there for just a few seconds. I was coming right back! So I went over to get closer, and tried to peek in through the window glass. I saw the back of your head in the waiting room, and knew for sure it was you. When I saw you, I got this panicked feeling that maybe you'd turn around and see me, so I hid, and ran back to Hana, as fast as I could. But when I got there, she was gone. I kept calling her name and looked for her everywhere, but it was like she was never there in the first place! I did this for a while, until a policeman came to me and I got scared. I told him I wasn't looking for anything and I ran back home. I was so afraid he was going to put me in jail if he knew what I'd done."

Soo-Ja grabbed Na-yeong by her bone-thin arm; it reminded her of a wooden ladle, almost slipping away from her. Soo-Ja made her walk with her, and as she did so, she could see her own Fury-like gaze reflected back in the girl's eyes.

"What are you doing?" asked Na-yeong, whimpering. "Let me go, eonni."

"We're going back to the marketplace. You're going to show me exactly where you left her."

"Eonni, it's getting dark now. It's not safe. We can't go back there."

"Yes, we can. And we are," said Soo-Ja. Soo-Ja grasped harder at Na-yeong's arm, almost snapping it in half. If it bruised, fine. Let it be a reminder of what she'd done.

Soo-Ja had to block out her fears for Hana, otherwise her heart would stop beating. All she could hear was her own voice inside her calling out for her child, *Wait for me, Hana. I'm coming for you.* She needed her daughter more than she needed any of her own limbs. She had only one thought, running through her head in a single loop: *Bring Hana back. Bring Hana back.* If somebody had told her that her child was in Mongolia, she would not have stopped to pack a bag or change clothes, but simply started walking in the direction of Mongolia.

Na-yeong looked back toward the house. "I should tell appa. They don't really know what happened. Appa!" Na-yeong called out, hoping to alert her father. But Soo-Ja pulled her forward as she bent her body back like a rag doll. "Appa!"

Soo-Ja kept dragging Na-yeong with her, until the others were too far away to hear them. They passed block after block, on their way to the central marketplace. The streets were empty, some unpaved, and they could feel the dried-up mud on the ground softening the blow of their heavy steps. The sky grew darker by the minute, and they saw people in the distance scurry home, to their warm floors and family dinners. It was only she, it seemed, who stalked forth in the night, like the sole woman awake in a town of sleeping souls. Soo-Ja had never moved with such sense of purpose before. For she knew, as long as she kept walking, kept moving, kept looking, Hana would be closer to safety. It was only if she gave up, and stopped trying, that she knew Hana would be in danger. A few minutes later, Soo-Ja imagined, Mother-in-law would come out looking for them, but all she'd find would be the memory of their bodies, their shapes left behind like the outline of a ghost.

When Soo-Ja and Na-yeong arrived at the marketplace, Soo-Ja experienced not déjà vu but the strange feeling that she had never been there before, as if the town were simply a diorama, and it had been rearranged only a minute before by its restless owner. The streets were still vibrantly alive, now filled with food stands on every corner, their little red plastic curtains cordoning off the sizzling kimchee pancakes and vegetable-filled sausages being served with glasses of soju. You could barely see the hardy stand owners buried inside their heavy jackets and hats, cheeks glowing red from the alternating cold and heat, working the three-burner stoves only inches away from their customers—tired-looking fishermen who ate heartily by the counters.

Though night had fallen, the streets were not dark. Some of the closed businesses kept their windows lit for another few hours, along with the small revolving sausage-shaped signs above their doors, with their rotating strips of colors. Soo-Ja felt as if she'd left the countryside and was now in the big city, full of faces that seemed familiar but belonged to strangers. She could not imagine Hana here on her own, although she did see some children standing behind boxes of apples, trying to sell them, jumping back and forth and blowing into their own bare hands to keep warm.

"It was here," Na-yeong said, pointing to a small patch of grass below a maple tree, two or three steps away from a closed tobacco shop.

"Are you sure?" Soo-Ja asked her, still holding her arm.

Na-yeong looked as if on the verge of tears. Soo-Ja was not bothered by the fact that she had, in essence, kidnapped her sister-in-law. She squinted her eyes, looking at the area Na-yeong pointed at, as if she could see not just the people in front of her right then, but everyone who had walked by or stood there earlier in the day, including Hana.

After Na-yeong nodded again and pointed to the spot, Soo-Ja let go of her. She began to canvass the area, looking absurd, she knew, with her long hair falling over her face. Her brown scarf, initially wrapped around her shoulders, now almost swept the ground, and her white blouse, once impeccably ironed, was now wrinkled and spotted. The day's mishaps, it seemed, had chosen to leave marks all over her. She was not dressed for this cold weather, and she froze a little bit each time the bitter wind blew in her direction.

Soo-Ja felt as if the way to find her daughter was to provide the right answer to a riddle. *I know you are here somewhere. You couldn't have gone very far. I can find you. If I look in the right place, I can find you. I will look the way a mother does. I will bring purity of heart to this search.*

Soo-Ja started to call out her daughter's name again. "Hana!" She looked all around her, at all the little girls, one of whom might turn and reward her with a look of recognition. Soo-Ja waved at the adults, one of whom maybe had found her Hana earlier and was waiting for her mother to come claim her. It was that simple, Soo-Ja imagined. Any minute now, she would hear her daughter's voice call out to her and this would end. "Hana!"

Soo-Ja's cries became more and more panicked. She started to walk around the marketplace, circling it a few times, stopping people and asking if they had seen a lost child. Strangers sitting by the food stands started to look in her direction and point, and soon she realized it was not sympathy in their eyes, but irritation and disgust. As she approached them, they would immediately shake their heads and bury their noses in their steaming bowls of soup. Some of the women, mistaking Soo-Ja for a beggar, grabbed on to their own children, wanting to protect them from her. She was made to feel like a woman sick with some terrible malady, one that could be easily contracted. One misguided look and her fate could become theirs. But she could not stop; she had to ask every single person in that square if they'd seen her daughter.

Soo-Ja could not stand the growing panic she felt as she gathered more and more nos, each shake of their heads getting her farther and farther away from Hana. As she approached men walking toward her, they would avoid eye contact and sidestep, quickly striding past her. Some of the women listened, especially the older grandmas, their eyes full of kindness. A couple of them offered her a glass of water and warm wheat dumplings, which she refused.

Na-yeong reached for her, looking spent and worn out. "I'm going home," she said, her voice cracking a little.

"Good." Soo-Ja nodded. "You go home and tell your father to let Min know what happened. Min can come help me look for our daughter. They will take it more seriously, at the police station, if it's the father who's there to talk to them."

"Now you've really gone insane," said Na-yeong, her voice rising. She sounded so much like Mother-in-law, thought Soo-Ja. That was a favorite word of hers—insane. *Michyeoss-eo.* "You want my brother to go to the police? They'll arrest him right then and there. He can't leave his hiding place!"

"Then am I supposed to look for Hana alone? And why aren't your mother and father here to help me? She's not just my daughter, she's also their *sonjattal!*" Soo-Ja knew the only people who'd help her were her own parents and her brothers, but they were three hours away by train, and it was night already.

"I want to go home! I don't think you're going to find her!"

Soo-Ja grabbed Na-yeong by the arms again and shook her. "I *am* going to find Hana. What you just said, I'm going to forget it ever came out of your mouth. Because if I don't watch myself, I might just kill you with my bare hands."

Na-yeong cowered, averting her gaze. Two or three people stopped to watch their argument. Upon seeing them, Soo-Ja let go of Na-yeong and asked them if they had seen a little girl on her own. They shook their heads. Soo-Ja did not notice Na-yeong running away. She felt as if her sight had narrowed into a circle, and everything outside it had turned into a blur.

All night, Soo-Ja kept wandering through the streets, reaching for strangers who were like buoys in the cold sea, only to be tossed back by them every time, her body growing more and more unsteady as the imaginary waves beat against her. She was in such agony she could hardly stand. And the more desperate she became, the more cruel and cold the people around her grew, until boys began laughing at her and the food stand keepers started to shoo her away from customers. She was like the lowliest of beggars, pleading with no dignity or self-respect, but with tears streaming down her face and questions that were not questions but cries. She needed to tell everyone that her daughter was missing; the pain inside her was so big, the only way to bear it was to give a slice of it to every single person in the world.

Piercing cold air, cold enough to break.

An hour or so after midnight, the town square started to become more and more deserted—noodle stand owners packing red tents, fruit peddlers putting away bruised pears, drunks staggering elsewhere—until not a soul walked the streets other than Soo-Ja, shivering in the wind. Snow began to fall little by little, dancing in front of her. Initially, it acted like a friend, glad to see her. Then, more like a spurned lover, quickly covering the ground, and turning it thick and slippery. She had nowhere to go, not a *won* in her pockets. Soo-Ja could not go back to her in-laws'. She could not add to the distance between her daughter and herself. But she also could not stay in a single spot for very long, as the lashing cold made every drawn breath feel like swallowing ice. So Soo-Ja kept walking in circles, going nowhere, helpless. Eventually, she felt her hands and feet freeze up, and had the distinct feeling she might topple over, stiff, like a statue.

When Soo-Ja had only five more steps left in her, she took those halting steps to the front of the medical office at the end of the street. She had felt such guilt earlier that now she did not think she'd dare come back to the place where this nightmare had begun. But, hoping that there might be a night nurse on call, Soo-Ja made her way there and knocked on the door, tasting the bitter ice in her mouth. She waited a few seconds, but no one came. The nurses, too, must have gone home. She banged on the door until her knuckles were almost stripped raw. Whatever hope she had left in her vanished instantly. Soo-Ja had been saving that door as a last alternative, but it had never been an alternative to begin with. With not an ounce of energy left in her body, Soo-Ja collapsed and fell to the ground. She pushed against the cold glass of the window, trying to pull herself up, but to no avail. She opened her mouth wide, having trouble breathing. She sucked in the air hungrily, but nothing happened. She closed her eyes, unconscious, as the snow began to bury her.

chapter eight

Soo-Ja opened her eyes, waking to find a tall, plump, upside-down nurse looking at her. The woman reached for her and lifted her up, as strong as a rhino. Putting Soo-Ja's arm over her shoulder, she led her into the unbelievably warm office. Soo-Ja could still barely breathe, but she knew she would not die of frostbite and that certainty thawed her lungs. To see kindness—someone looking down and helping you—may be the world's best placebo. Over the course of the next few minutes, as the nurse sat her down on a chair, placed her feet in a basin of hot water, and rubbed her cold hands with her warm ones, Soo-Ja felt her temperature start to return to normal. She didn't know what did it—the warm water or simply the look on that woman's face, smiling at her as if she were her long-lost sister.

"I'm sorry I didn't answer the door sooner! I was practically falling asleep, and didn't know if the knocking was real or only a dream," said the nurse. Soo-Ja smiled at her, to say it didn't matter and she was just grateful she was there. "I'm here all alone at night and usually there's a patient or two, but with the bad snowstorm, it seems even the medical emergencies have decided to wait."

Soo-Ja drank green tea from the cup the nurse poured for her. She could feel her fingers again. The pain in her chest began to dissipate.

"Looks like our new President is making a lot of promises," said the nurse, settling into a chair, with the newspaper before her face. "He says he's going to start plans for reunification, give us a self-supporting economy, and turn horse dung into paper money! Imagine that. Personally, I voted for the other fella. I think Chung Hee Park is just a greedy powermonger, like the rest of them. He's an autocrat, another Syngman Rhee, just minus the stupid Austrian wife. I wouldn't be surprised if he was a puppet of the North Koreans. Did you hear he went to the funeral of the American president? Now, that man didn't like Park alive, and I can't imagine he likes him any better dead."

"Nurse . . ."

"What is it?" asked the nurse, lowering the newspaper and glancing over at Soo-Ja.

"I need to leave *before* the doctor comes," said Soo-Ja, still in too much pain to move from her chair.

The nurse misunderstood her. "Dr. Yul-Bok Kim will be here early in the morning, in just a few hours, in fact, and he'll be able to examine you. He went on a trip, but is back now. What you have, you think it can wait?"

"No, no. What I mean is, I need to be gone *before* he arrives. I have to go. I have to leave. Even if it's still snowing. Please warn me if he's on his way."

The nurse seemed confused, and Soo-Ja could tell she was looking at her for signs of dementia. She could see the question forming on the nurse's lips: *What were you doing walking around the snow-covered streets at one in the morning?* But the nurse simply nodded and said, "Don't worry, I'll make sure you're gone before he gets here."

"Soo-Ja . . ."

Soo-Ja woke with a start, stunned to hear Yul's voice. He switched the light on, and the ceiling turned into white dotted mazes. Soo-Ja looked down and spotted her green hospital gown peeking from under a blanket. She was lying on one of three small beds, each facing a different wall.

"Yul . . ." Soo-Ja mumbled.

He wore his civilian clothes, but with a doctor's robe over them. He didn't look much different from the last time she'd seen him. Except now he wore his hair longer, and his clothes looked almost European in their cut. He still had the same serious eyes, the dimples on his cheeks, and the tall, muscular frame of a fighter.

"Your clothes are drying by the boiler," said Yul. "I had the nurse wash them. I'll have her bring them back to you."

"I need to go," said Soo-Ja.

"Listen . . . I heard what happened," said Yul.

"How?"

"There's a waiting room outside. People talk."

Soo-Ja looked around her. "Please. Tell the nurse to bring back my clothes. I need to go look for my daughter."

"Have you gone to the village police yet?"

"No, I haven't."

"That's the first thing we'll do then."

Soo-Ja looked at him, surprised. "*We?* Are you going to help me?"

"Yes, I am," said Yul forcefully.

"My husband will be here at any moment now . . . And my in-laws, too."

"Yes, I'm sure they will," said Yul kindly. "I don't doubt that."

Soo-Ja took a deep breath, dropping her act. She couldn't lie to Yul, as if at one point in the past she had made an oath to him. "It's not Min's fault. He doesn't know. He's in hiding. We all are, in a way, my in-laws and I. Debts." Soo-Ja was surprised to hear herself telling that to Yul. She had never told anyone of their circumstances, not even her father.

"Don't be embarrassed about that. There are a lot of people in debt these days. You have all this paper money in your hands, and the next day, the government says it's worth nothing," said Yul.

The nurse, who'd overheard their voices, came in with Soo-Ja's clothes, and left as quickly as she had appeared. Yul turned around so Soo-Ja could get dressed. Soo-Ja walked behind a screen and began removing the hospital gown.

"Someone must have seen Hana. I don't know if I can find Hana herself straightaway, but I can find someone who saw her playing, or walking by. Like the fruit peddlers on the street. They sit there all day, they must do their share of people-watching." Soo-Ja put on her black cardigan sweater, embroidered with white trim along the edges, then took her big brown scarf and wrapped it around her shoulders and her arms. When she finished dressing, she did not tell Yul to turn around. Instead, she walked to him, tapping him lightly on the arm. Yul turned quickly, almost bumping into her. The sudden proximity of his body made Soo-Ja feel nervous, and she stepped back. When Soo-Ja looked at his face, she saw the intense look in his ink-black eyes. He hadn't changed much. Still the same serious gaze, the melancholy air.

"We'll get to her," said Yul.

Soo-Ja believed him. She followed him out, past the waiting room and its many eyes looking up at them. When they came out onto the street, with its sudden, harsh morning light, Soo-Ja silently thanked him for his help, in a prayer.

Between puffs of his cigarette, the village police officer halfheartedly took down Hana's description onto a palm-sized notebook. Behind him, fishermen carried nets and boxes packed with mackerel, hairtail, cuttlefish, and sea mussels from their trawlers onto the dock. Every breath took in scales and gills. Small ice islands, from the previous night's snow, floated and cracked as they hit the boats. When he was done, the officer smiled suggestively at Soo-Ja. "It's just that we're so busy these days. I wish we had more resources, some money perhaps . . ."

Soo-Ja looked confused, but Yul seemed to understand his gist right away. He pulled some bills from his pocket and placed them in the officer's hands. The man smiled, nodding slightly.

"I will see what I can do," said the officer, walking away. Based on the way he spoke, it seemed clear he would do nothing. Soo-Ja put her arm out in his direction, but he was gone.

"I'm sorry, Soo-Ja," said Yul. "But the only people the police want to find these days are North Korean spies."

"Let's go back to the market square," she said. "I have to find a mother. A mother will want to help. They notice children, and they notice very subtle things. They can tell when a child is with someone she doesn't belong to." Soo-Ja was amazed at her own coolness, after the previous night's desperation. But it was a precarious coolness; a single word, and she could be undone.

Besides, she had something inside her pocket that gave her confidence, an odd kind of security. Before Yul and Soo-Ja had left his office, she had stolen something from him—his prescription pad. If she could not find Hana—odious thought!—she knew exactly what kind of pills she'd have to swallow.

"When was the last time you ate?" Yul asked her.

They had been working through the market square for hours, as Soo-Ja spoke to every living being about her daughter. She even asked the children, who were the most curious about her, and who shook their heads vigorously. Soo-Ja overheard one or two people saying she was crazy, that this daughter of hers didn't exist.

Oh, but she does, she does, thought Soo-Ja. How could she explain to them that hers was the most beautiful and precious child, one who laughed so easily when you tickled her, and who shrieked with joy when you lifted her into the air? She loved her daughter, and in that love she had once expected to live forever, the rest of her days.

"Soo-Ja, you have to eat. You can't go on like this," Yul continued. Soo-Ja ignored him, approaching another woman with a description of her child. Soo-Ja cursed herself for not having a picture of Hana, for having left everything back in Daegu. "You haven't had breakfast, *or* lunch. We're going to stop by that noodle stand, and you're going to eat."

Soo-Ja looked at Yul as if he were the most unreasonable being she'd ever met, and she shook her head. It had been more than twenty-four hours since she had eaten anything, but she had no appetite. "You go eat. I'll be here."

"No, please." Yul reached for her arm.

Soo-Ja looked at him and saw the concern on his face. She was not

a superhero, like in the radio shows; she was a human person, she had
to remind herself. Without saying anything, Soo-Ja let him guide her to
the noodle stand, which was only a couple of yards from them. It quickly
drew them in, with the smell of bean-curd paste rising from the pots.

They sat at one of the two tiny tables at an arm's reach from the cook,
and next to a teenage couple. They were so crowded in, elbow to elbow,
they could be a single party. Soo-Ja did not speak to Yul. Instead, she
listened to the hissing of the griddle and the whistling of the kettle. She
watched the dumplings turn brown and jump from the pan to the plates.
The cook, who did not smile, placed their food in front of them and then
his daughter—Soo-Ja heard her call him appa earlier—as if to compen-
sate, smiled brightly as she filled their cups with water.

"For you, *ajeossi,*" she said, respectfully, handing Yul his glass. Soo-Ja
already had a full glass in front of her, but the waitress still wanted to
acknowledge her. "Ajumma, you have a very pretty scarf."

Soo-Ja nodded weakly, quietly signaling that she did not want to talk.
The girl, who must have been thirteen or fourteen, did not see this and
remained standing next to her, her hands casually resting against her
hips. She played the host a little too well, acting like the cook's wife
instead of his daughter, almost a parody of an older woman. Soo-Ja
wondered if the girl was replacing her sick mother for the day, and had
been repeating what the elder woman usually said to the customers. But
maybe she wasn't imitating anyone at all. Maybe there was no mother—
dead or separated—and she had always played this part herself, helping
her father, serving customers by his side, never knowing what it was to
play like a child.

"Did your husband get it for you as a gift?" the waitress asked, smiling
at Soo-Ja. When she said *husband*, the girl glanced over at Yul for a second, before turning her gaze back to Soo-Ja. Soo-Ja knew instantly that
she should correct her, but to say he wasn't her husband also felt wrong.
Yul might take her correction—if offered too quickly, in protest—as a
slight.

"We're not husband and wife. We're not married," said Yul, before
Soo-Ja could speak.

The waitress looked confused. "*Ay*, you sure do look like husband and wife," she said, her smile now gone. She returned to her father's side, occasionally stealing glances at the two of them. Her words hung heavy in the air.

"I want to go back to looking," Soo-Ja said, rising from her seat. "You can stay here and eat your soup."

Yul reached for her, as if to pull her down. But once his hand felt her arm—real, made of flesh and bone, not just an image across from him—he seemed to lose courage and did not protest. "I'll come with you," he said, also rising.

Back in the market square, Soo-Ja felt as if she'd lived there forever, recognizing the fruit peddlers camping out on the ground, and the old men sitting on boxes turned upside down, playing *janggi*. At the stalls, women wearing head scarves wielded knives with acrobatic precision, cleaning fish on top of wooden crates, while men with bloody aprons around their waists yelled out prices. On the counters, piles of catch—kandari, saury pike, whip ray, and sea bream—glowed in the afternoon sun.

Weary-looking customers carrying straw baskets ignored Soo-Ja, walking briskly past her in the overcrowded plaza. Yul alone stayed with her, looking solemn as she asked strangers about her daughter. With him there, the locals appeared more responsive. They actually seemed to think before finally delivering a no, now offered with regret rather than as a dismissal. With each no, Yul seemed as disappointed as Soo-Ja, and for that, she loved him—that he could feel what she felt; as if by doing so, he could lessen her load.

The sun began to set, and Soo-Ja prepared to make her way back to the other side of the marketplace. While taking a minute to catch her breath, she noticed an old woman standing in front of a tobacco shop, blowing smoke in the air exuberantly. She wore her gray hair tightly held back, exposing her deeply tanned face, which appeared to have as many lines as the surface of a leaf. Soo-Ja tried not to stare, but the old woman kept looking over at her.

"Who is she?" Soo-Ja overheard the old woman ask her friend. "Why is she walking around like that?"

"She lost her daughter," her friend replied.

"When did this happen?"

"I saw her first last night."

"What does her daughter look like?"

The tobacconist had heard Soo-Ja describe Hana so many times, she had memorized her words. "She sounds like a rich man's kid. Nice red jacket with a hood; pretty, embroidered gloves; heavy, sturdy leather shoes; a gold-colored ribbon on her head. Three years old."

"Three years old," the old woman echoed thoughtfully.

So this is what I've become, a story. She'd have to spend the rest of her life wandering those streets, while strangers newly arrived in town would point, curious. They'd be filled in and look at her with pity, secretly glad that her fate wasn't their own. She had become a part of this plaza, like the nicks on the wooden benches, or the rusty stains on the lampposts.

Soo-Ja looked at the old woman one last time before she started walking again, and this time their eyes met. She gave her that faint flicker of recognition you give when you know a face but can't place it. Soo-Ja didn't know why, but she began moving toward the old woman, as if obeying an order, and the old woman walked toward her, too. As they drew near each other, Soo-Ja felt a light frisson of anticipation, knowing she was about to meet someone who would be important to her.

"You're a very lucky woman," the old woman said, when they got close enough to talk. She did not offer her name, nor did she ask for Soo-Ja's.

"Why do you say that?" Soo-Ja asked.

Left behind, Yul watched them from a distance, without joining them.

"You're lucky . . . that I smoke," the old woman said, scattering some ash onto the floor.

"Please explain, *halmeoni*," said Soo-Ja, calling her "grandmother." Her voice quivered a little. "I'm a very distraught woman. And I know that you know because I heard you talk to the shopkeeper. So if you have something to tell me, do so. But don't waste my time. Please." Soo-Ja made as if to move away, but she knew the old woman could tell she was bluffing. Soo-Ja was riveted to her spot.

"Yesterday, I felt the urge for a cigarette," the old woman began. "This is where I usually come to get them." She pointed behind her to the tobacco shop. Soo-Ja noticed for the first time how small it was, the shelves only half filled, a poster with a picture of an American cowboy. "But for some reason, I decided to go to a different tobacco shop, one that's a little farther from my house. I didn't know why I decided to do that. But *now* I know why." At this, she grinned, revealing her yellow teeth, slightly broken in spots.

"What did you see?" Soo-Ja asked her.

"I'm a very observant woman. I see more than I see . . . Other women my age may need glasses to see just what's in front of them. But I would need them so I could see *less*. I don't just look. I notice."

"And what did you notice?" asked Soo-Ja, almost trembling.

"A man walking with a toddler. Now, lots of men walk with toddlers, but this pair stood out to me. You see, I was sitting on the curb, enjoying my cigarette, and so I got a very good look at them. And I noticed the man wore really shabby clothes, just a plain jacket with heavy lining. But the girl—she looked new, like a doll. Whoever dressed her took pains to do so. I remember her jacket had little bird patterns embroidered on it"—Soo-Ja's heart leapt hearing the detail of the birds, which she hadn't mentioned to anyone, because she'd forgotten—"and there was something else, too. She just didn't look like she was from around here. And so I knew these two people—this fortysomething man, he must be, and this little girl—didn't go together. And there were other things, too, like, why was he carrying her in his arms? The girl was big enough to walk. So with all these things to pique my interest, you can see why I watched them as they went inside the *sul-jib* next to the tobacco shop.

"Now, I didn't go into the sul-jib but I could hear him talking to the barmaid, who seemed to be his wife. I couldn't see very well, but when he opened a door, I noticed there were more rooms there, and that must be where they slept. I then heard the sound of the woman fighting with the man, and it was over the child, who had started crying. At that moment I knew, for sure, that the baby wasn't his. It was such a loud wail, so full of spirit, demanding to be heard. That cry was for me, you see. She knew I was outside, invisible to everyone but her, and she was talking to me. So I left. And I began my wait. Very patiently. Because I knew that eventually, the child's mother would come to me. *You* would come to me. So all day, I sat outside and wandered around, waiting. And finally, you came. I saw you and I knew, right away, even before Joon-Ho's mother described the girl to me. Even before she told me who you were. So maybe it's not luck. It's seeing. You saw that I was more than just an old woman smoking a cigarette. And I saw you for what you are: a woman in love with her own child."

By now Soo-Ja was heaving with pain, fighting back tears. "Where is this sul-jib? Tell me where it is."

"Don't worry, child," the old woman said, reaching for her. Soo-Ja was surprised by how warm her touch was. "I will draw a map for you. But where? On your arm? How about here, in the palm of your hand? That way you'll never lose this map, and you'll just have to follow the lines you see."

"Thank you," said Soo-Ja, nodding slightly.

"Now, the only thing is, you'll have to be careful. The man showed the baby to his wife like she was a gift. Not something he might let go easily. And the way he hurried her to the back. Like he was hiding her. Like he knew exactly what he was doing."

Soo-Ja and Yul set out toward the sul-jib, trekking up and down the narrow, serpentine streets. They moved quickly, even though it was quite dark, and the ground was slippery with melted snow. Next to them, thickets of dried branches dotted the road with sharp pins and edges. A car or a bicycle would pass them once in a while, but for the most part, the hour belonged to them.

Soon it would be all over. It would be morning; Soo-Ja loved mornings. When she was little, on hot summer days, her father would come into her room while she slept and open the windows. Like the god of wind, he'd let in the cool breeze, its fresh touch enveloping her as she dreamt of cherry blossoms. Yes, soon she could be home with her daughter again, and all this would be just a memory.

It never occurred to Soo-Ja that she wouldn't find Hana at the address the old woman had given her. She felt complete certitude. For the first time in two days, she cracked a smile. Yul, on the other hand, had fallen into a new sorrow, and it seemed ironic that just as Soo-Ja was about to regain her daughter, she was about to lose Yul. For although she had stumbled around like a madwoman for the last twenty-four hours, she had been grateful for every second of Yul's company. The firm way he held her arm, supporting her, as she walked unsteadily; never calling too much attention to himself, but always there, like the baseboard of a wall.

"How can I ever repay you for helping me today?" Soo-Ja asked him, as they walked past a stretch of closed shops.

"I've already been paid back. Your finding Hana is payment enough."

Soo-Ja sighed. "I'm touched that you helped me. More than that, the fact that you believed we'd find her."

"You know, if things are so terrible back home . . ."

"They are. But I'm not going to give up just because I'm not happy there. I have Hana to think of. She needs her father."

"A father who didn't even look for her."

"I told you already . . . he doesn't know. If he knew, he would have run out of his hiding place."

Yul nodded. They didn't have much farther to go before reaching their destination. Both knew this might be the last chance they'd have to talk.

"So what is your wife like?" asked Soo-Ja, trying to hide the interest in her voice.

Yul hesitated before answering. Soo-Ja knew he was wondering how she had found out about her. "She's not you," he finally said.

"What do you mean by that?" asked Soo-Ja.

"What do you think?"

Soo-Ja felt her face grow warm. "I didn't realize you still had feelings for me."

"Of course I do, Soo-Ja. That should have been obvious to you when I left Daegu."

"What do you mean? Why did you leave Daegu?"

"Because of you, of course," said Yul.

"Because of *me?*"

"I didn't want to run into you at the farmers' market, see you happy with another man. I came to Pusan to run away from the memory of you. To leave you and that part of my life behind. To try to bury it."

"If that's the reason you left Daegu, you shouldn't have."

"Why did you marry Min instead of me?" Yul suddenly blurted out.

Soo-Ja thought for a second, shaking her head. "I don't know. Probably because you told me the truth and you were honest with me. You were supposed to lie to me, to deceive me. Don't you know that's how you end up marrying someone?"

Soo-Ja was about to say more when she realized they had reached the right street. She looked at the signs outside the shops, and saw the one for Gai-Tan sul-jib. The lights were off. They were already closed for the night. But then she remembered what the old woman said. She looked toward the side and noticed the door to the actual house. It was behind a gate, hard to see. The people inside must be asleep.

Soo-Ja's heart began to do somersaults inside her chest, and she wondered what to do next. Yul moved toward the gate, to rattle it, but Soo-Ja stopped him. That would be giving them a warning. She knew if she did things the wrong way, she might never see Hana again. If she called out for the sul-jib's owner, he could come out and simply tell her, *I have no idea what you're talking about, leave us alone.* Then he could run away, move somewhere far away, and give Hana a new last name. The thought chilled Soo-Ja's spine. It rested in her hands to do this right.

At that moment, it occurred to her what to do. It was the simplest option.

Soo-Ja gathered all the strength she had in her body, and she screamed, louder than the loudest blast from a train whistle: "HANA!" And then again, "HANA! HANA!"

Soo-Ja heard back the sound of her own child yelling back, "Eomma! Eomma!"

Within seconds, Soo-Ja saw her daughter burst out of the door and run toward the gate. The toddler was completely naked, like a newborn, her eyes bloodshot with tears and her cheeks swollen red. Yul quickly lifted the latch from the outside and tried to open the metal gate, but it did not give way. Soo-Ja thrust her arms in the direction of her child, only a foot away but impossibly far, as Hana wailed and screamed, piercing Soo-Ja's heart with the sound. Hana kept stomping her bare feet on the ground. She shook her arms in the air, in utter despair.

"Get the gate open! Get it open, Yul!" Soo-Ja cried out.

Hana's entire face was wet with tears, and her mouth was wide open, dribble slipping from her chin. Yul finally got the gate to release, and as soon as he did so, Soo-Ja swooped in and lifted Hana into her arms. Hana practically fled into her mother's grasp, climbing onto her, horribly frightened. Her cries grew even louder once she reached Soo-Ja, and her little round body began to shake. Soo-Ja quickly wrapped her scarf around Hana. Yul also hurriedly took off his jacket and placed it over her like a blanket.

As Soo-Ja held the child in her arms, she felt her own cheeks quickly become wet with tears. Her heart beat against her insides like a fist. She could not believe it. She had Hana back. She began to quiver, all the emotion finally coming out of her.

"Eomma! Eomma!" the child cried, between big, hungry gulps of breath. Her little fingers were tearing at her mother's neck and shoulders, afraid of losing her once again. Hana grabbed at Soo-Ja's blouse, gluing herself to her. Her tiny hands were clenched so tightly they shook. Even though Soo-Ja held her firmly, Hana still kept reaching madly for her, her fingers clutching her arms, digging into her mother's skin.

"I'm sorry, baby, eomma's here, eomma's here!" said Soo-Ja, almost gasping for air. She looked at her daughter's face—the mouth howling in anguish, the nose overrun with snot. But what almost destroyed her was seeing the look of fear in her eyes—Hana looked terrified that her mother might leave her again. Soo-Ja covered her own face with her free hand, so full of shame was she for not having protected her daughter.

It was then that the man came outside, followed by two boys, one around age six, the other a little older, maybe ten. Wearing a windbreaker over his beige long johns, he did not look like a kidnapper. He was the most ordinary-looking person Soo-Ja had ever seen. He looked at her with confusion on his face, as if he couldn't imagine who she was, or what she was doing at his doorstep at midnight.

Yul moved forward toward him, making his presence known. Soo-Ja saw the two little boys cower, and she moved between Yul and the man. Soo-Ja turned to face Yul and shook her head. This was *her* fight. Hana was *her* daughter. If someone was to have the satisfaction of questioning this man, it would be she.

"Who are you? What are you doing here? You know what time it is?" the man asked, pointing at them.

Soo-Ja could see him better now: he was tall, in his early forties, with beady eyes and a hangdog expression on his face. His name, she found out later, was Dae-Jung. "I am this child's mother!" Soo-Ja barked at him. "And why is she naked? If I find out that you hurt her, I swear I'll kill you!"

"You're her mother? I don't believe you. Look at the way you're making her cry." Dae-Jung made as if to take her back, but Soo-Ja immediately turned her body to the side, shielding Hana.

"You have no business believing or not believing. She is my daughter. And you, you are a kkang-pae, kkang-pae. We have to call the police. Right now!" Soo-Ja was yelling at him. If Hana had not been in her arms, she would have punched him in the face.

"Call them. Call them. All I've done is rescue this child who was dumped on the street," he said, looking at Soo-Ja with contempt, his head slightly raised.

"Dumped?" Soo-Ja spat the word out, stung by it. She would have expected Dae-Jung to either run away or bow in shame. Never this.

"Yes. Dumped. You said you're the girl's mother? What kind of mother leaves her child alone in a busy market?"

"Don't you dare speak to her that way," said Yul. "Let's get the police here, see what they say." He started looking around for an officer, and Soo-Ja could see Dae-Jung panic a little.

"Call them! Who do you think they're going to side with? Me, who serves them drinks every night, or you, from God knows where, who's disturbing the peace? Everyone knows I have a kindly disposition. I was taken in by this abandoned girl's smile and decided to give her a home.

If there's a victim in all this, it's me, who tried to help a child and instead of thanks, I get a crazy woman yelling at me."

Yul advanced toward him and grabbed him by the top of his shirt. "You're not allowed to talk to her like that, you understand?"

Soo-Ja couldn't stop him, and Dae-Jung struggled to break free.

"And who are you?" asked Dae-Jung. "Because you're definitely not the child's father. I could tell that from a mile away. But I guess you can explain to the police when they come here. I'm sure everybody in town will want to know what you two were doing running around at night like this." Dae-Jung turned his head to his son. "Bae, go call the police."

The boy hesitated, and it was a studied hesitation, as deliberate as a gesture by an actor in a bad play. But at least it gave Soo-Ja the chance to step in.

"I *have* Hana, Yul. And I want to take her home now. I don't want to spend hours in a police station explaining what happened. Let's just go home."

Yul weighed her words and she could see his reluctance as he gradually let go of Dae-Jung, finally tossing him back like a dirty towel.

Hana's crying had subsided a little now, and she buried her head on her mother's shoulder. Soo-Ja felt disappointed in herself for not taking revenge. How could she not put this man behind bars for what he'd done? How could she simply walk away? But this was Pusan. This was how things were done. If a man took your daughter and then gave her back, you said thank you and bowed your head as you left. If she took him to court, the judge would say, *Isn't it enough you have your daughter back? What more do you want?* They might even ask her to give him some money, for the food and lodging he had provided.

"Let's go, Yul," Soo-Ja repeated, and turned toward the street. But as they started to make their way out, she heard Dae-Jung's voice behind them.

"And where do you think you're going with her?" he asked, his voice tinged with an odd sense of conviction. "You didn't prove that you're the girl's mother. You think I'm going to let a stranger just take this little girl?"

Soo-Ja looked at him in utter disbelief. She had never felt more anger toward another human being. As she drew near, her fist about to punch him, one of his boys—the one who looked to be about ten—stepped forward, standing between them. He had a shaved head, to prevent lice, and a jacket that was a couple of sizes too big for him.

"Appa, I will go with her. I will go see where they take Hyo-Joo."

It took Soo-Ja a second to realize "Hyo-Joo" meant her daughter. So they had already given her a new name! What else had they taught her, Soo-Ja wondered, in those twenty-four hours? Maybe to stay away from windows and not long for your mother, who will never come . . .

"All right," said Dae-Jung, too quickly, glad for the "compromise," glad to let his version of events come to a logical end.

How amazing that even in matters of child kidnapping, one still had to let the other person find a way to save face.

"Your father, is he good to you?" asked Yul.

The ten-year-old looked thoughtfully at him and nodded. They were walking, the four of them, back to Soo-Ja's uncle's house. As they moved through the night, Soo-Ja could feel a familial closeness—the boy, at least for now, was clearly on their side.

"Yes, he treats me well. But not my brother," Bae replied. In his tattered clothes, he resembled a street urchin.

"Is your brother naughty?" asked Yul.

He would be a good father one day, thought Soo-Ja. He had a natural ability to talk to children.

"He's not. He's the same as me," said Bae.

"So he's a father who takes the rod out on one boy, but spares the other. Why do you think he doesn't beat you?" asked Yul.

"I don't know, sir."

At this point Soo-Ja felt as if Yul had given her enough of an opening so she could ask the boy some questions. "Why did your father take Hana? What did he tell you?"

Bae contorted his neck, weighing his loyalties, and took a while before he finally began to speak. "My father is not a bad man. But sometimes he does strange things. Things that we don't understand, but in his head it all makes sense."

"Why did he take Hana to your house?" asked Soo-Ja.

Hana lay in her mother's arms, afraid to let go. She grew heavier with every block they passed, but Soo-Ja swallowed the pain. In spite of Yul's offers to carry her, she knew it was best for her daughter to stay with her.

"You see, ma'am, we're all boys in the house. Me and my brother. And my father always wanted a girl. So he said this was God's way of giving us our wish. But I think he did it because of the way she was dressed. He kept saying, 'Look how nice her clothes are, she must come from a good family!' He was excited to have a girl from a good family."

Soo-Ja looked over at Hana, wondering how much of this entire ordeal she understood. Bae stopped talking and watched her as she watched Hana. Soo-Ja turned to him again. "Go on, Bae."

"He told us to be very careful with her. That a girl isn't like a boy, you can't be rough with her. He also told us if anybody asked, to say she was our sister, but that her mother wasn't our mother, which I didn't understand. If my mother isn't her mother, then how can she be my sister? But I suppose it makes sense, since you're Hana's mother and you're not my mother."

"Would you *like* her to be your mother?" teased Yul.

So this is how you talk to boys, thought Soo-Ja. You tease them about girls, even if that girl is your mother.

"Yul! Please," Soo-Ja admonished him, though she did not really mean it. It was the first smile she'd seen on Yul's face this entire time, and it made her glad.

The boy immediately nodded. "Yes! Yes, I would. You're very pretty, *agassi*."

"It's ajumma. I'm not too vain to say it. I may be young enough to still be agassi, but I'm a mother now, and ajumma and eomma sound the same to me," said Soo-Ja. "But Bae, go on. What else happened?"

"We all gathered around Hana. I know boys are not supposed to like girls, but she was very entertaining, we couldn't stop watching her! It was like having a rabbit in the house. And she cried. Oh, she cried so much in the beginning. And then my father said, if you keep crying, your mother is going to get really mad, and she won't take you back. That's when I knew something was wrong. But I couldn't say anything."

"And where was your mother through all this?" Soo-Ja asked as they kept walking, the streets completely deserted in front of them.

"She was serving customers. I think she was mad at my father, and was avoiding him. She looked horrified when Father brought Hyo-Joo, I mean Hana, home. She said, 'Why would you bring me one more mouth to feed?' And my father said, 'She'll earn her keep. She can work at the counter and serve customers when she's older.'"

Soo-Ja tightened her grip on Hana when she heard this. Did her little girl know the life she had been spared? Of course she did, thought Soo-Ja, the way children always know everything.

"She's a very clever girl, your daughter," said Bae, smiling and show-ing his teeth for the first time. It seemed that he was enjoying being the center of attention. "This morning, she finally stopped crying. She said she liked it with us, and that the house was good. But could she please get some air? She said that it was stuffy in the room. So my father said all right and let her go outside.

"But then as soon as she got outside, she tried to run away. She reached to undo the latch on the gate, but it was too high for her. My father ran back out to get her, this look of panic on his face. He couldn't believe that a three-year-old could be so clever. That's why he made my mother take off all her clothes. So she couldn't go outside. There was nobody to watch her, so we had to leave her alone at times, you know? My father just stuffed her under some blankets and she stayed there the whole day. And he was right. She didn't try to escape with no clothes on. But I swear, I could see in her face that she still hoped to figure out a way to escape."

So that's why she was naked when she came out of the house, thought Soo-Ja. She breathed a sigh of relief. She knew this boy was tell-ing the truth. Besides, if this man's intentions had been bad, there just hadn't been enough time, what with a small house full of boys and his wife and the customers drinking next door.

Soo-Ja looked at Hana again, who looked back at her with a pained expression on her face, as if to say, *Eomma, how could you leave me? Do you not know what I went through?* The tears had stopped, but her face was still wet.

I know, baby. Eomma knows everything. And eomma was bad, to let this happen to you. But now you can sleep. Eomma is here. You can sleep like a child again.

When they arrived in front of her uncle's house, Soo-Ja lingered for a moment to give either of these two men the chance to leave. Was she being considerate, sparing Yul from bad company? Or was she afraid they would ask him questions, maybe adding two and two? The boy looked at them awkwardly, and she saw in his eyes that he didn't want to go yet. He wanted to trade as part of some parent-child swap program and come live with them. *But, child,* she would have to say to him, *Yul doesn't live here with me. I live with some other people. This makeshift family you experienced on our way here, with the four of us, it was as new to me as it was to you.*

Yul also seemed to sense the boy's hesitation. "It's time for you to go home," he said, and his firmness came as easily as his teasing earlier, and was just as effective, as the boy bowed to them and started to leave. But before he was gone, Yul reached into his pocket and gave Bae some money. "This is for you. Don't show it to your father."

The boy bowed again and—this is how Soo-Ja knew that what he'd told her earlier had been true—he smiled at Hana and said, "Good-bye, little sister. Be nice to your mother."

Soo-Ja and Yul watched Bae run home, into a dark she found very foreign. After Soo-Ja and Yul could no longer make out the boy's shape in the distance, they finally turned to each other. So this is that scene in the movie, thought Soo-Ja—the good-bye, first to the less consequential character, then to the important one.

Soo-Ja had felt this before, and she felt it again: that she was always saying good-bye to the only man she truly cared about. But she was wrong. For each time she said good-bye to Yul, he was a different man—one she knew even better, and for whom her feelings had grown deeper. Now she loved him the way a wife might love a husband after a few years—love him after watching him perform an act of kindness, love him after seeing the way he is with other people, love him for the quality of his heart. But he was not her husband; she was not his wife. It was wrong to even think that way. But what was it that counted in the end, the life you lived in front of other people, for their benefit, or the life you lived in your own heart—where she loved him and he loved her back. And could she help it if that life just felt so much more real? Yet whatever happened in that other version of her life—kisses, sighs, joy—in this one he was just a friend, standing in front of her, unsure if he should go in or not, maybe suddenly remembering he had patients, a wife, a life to step back into as soon as he stepped out of hers.

"I don't know if I'll ever be able to thank you enough," said Soo-Ja, speaking softly. Blankets of fog shifted around them, and she felt as if they were wading through clouds. She could see sliced sections of tree branches and the gates of houses, but nothing whole; they seemed to float, all light and watery, without their usual density.

"You don't need to. We're friends. Friends take care of each other," said Yul, as he reached for her and rearranged the wrinkled collar around her neck. He then gently patted Hana's head; she lay asleep, wrapped in his windbreaker. Soo-Ja made as if to give it back to him, but he shook his head.

"Do you want to come in and meet my in-laws?" asked Soo-Ja. Even in the dark, she could see the sadness ebb and flow on Yul's face, like the waves in the sea.

"What would you introduce me as?"

"It depends," Soo-Ja said softly, looking into his eyes. "If I want to lie, or if I want to tell the truth."

He stared back into her eyes. "I think one should always tell the truth. Except in situations like this."

Soo-Ja's heart leapt and then sunk. But she knew that she had no right to be disappointed. She was the one who turned away from him when he asked her to marry him, who refused when he first held out his hand and said, *Try me, and be happy.*

"*Chamara*, Soo-Ja. *Chamara*," said Yul. *Chamara*. What is the word that comes closest to it? Soo-Ja wondered. To stand it, to bear it, to grit your teeth and not cry out? To hold on, to wait until the worst is over? There is no other word for it, no way to translate it. It is not a word. It is a way to console yourself. He is not just telling her to stand the pain, but giving her comfort, the power to do so. *Chamara* is an incantation, and if she listens to its sound, she believes that she can do it, that she will push through this sadness. And if she is strong about it, she'll be rewarded in the end. It is a way of saying, *I know, I feel it, too. This burns my heart, too.*

chapter nine

When Soo-Ja opened the door triumphant, with Hana in her arms, feeling like Admiral Yi Sun-Shin back from his campaigns, the house awoke and Mother-in-law scrambled to turn the lights on. Soo-Ja knew they must have been in a state of suspense for the last two days. And then she saw him: Min on the floor, at first half asleep, then wide awake, leaping to reach for his daughter. Everyone gathered around them, with Mother-in-law clapping her hands, and the boys smiling and waiting for their turn to pet Hana. How odd to see them like this, thought Soo-Ja. Did they, in the end, love Hana more than she gave them credit for? Father-in-law was the only one not there, though her wondering about him didn't last very long, caught up as she was in the warmth and excitement of Hana's reception. This was truly a family, after all.

Soo-Ja knew Hana was tired and should be put to bed. She was tired, too. She had spent the last twenty hours on her feet, and she felt ready to topple over any second now. But she could not stop this scene, so rare and wonderful it was: everyone fussing over Hana, kissing her cheeks and taking turns holding and hugging her. Theirs was not an affectionate extended family. For all she knew, this might be the last time Hana experienced this kind of love from them.

Finally, after many hallelujahs from Mother-in-law and a thousand cheers from the boys, Soo-Ja told them they should all go to bed. Hana herself could barely keep her eyes open. In a matter of minutes, all the noise gave way to a placid quiet, as if all of them had been given a potion from an apothecary. Their eyelids grew heavy, and they fell asleep in one swoop, all at once, their bodies covering the floor in all kinds of shapes, looking like one giant figure with many limbs.

In the middle of the night, Soo-Ja woke to use the chamber pot and found Na-yeong still awake. Soo-Ja told her to go to sleep, but Na-yeong said she could not. Soo-Ja decided to use the outhouse instead, in spite of the cold. As she rose to leave, she heard Na-yeong call out for her. Soo-Ja made a *shhh* sound and lowered herself back, coming to sit next to where she lay.

"What is it?" Soo-Ja asked.

"Are you going to tell them that I lost Hana in the market?" Na-yeong asked sheepishly.

"You didn't tell them that?" Soo-Ja had wondered why no one had come to help her look for Hana. So that was why.

Na-yeong inhaled a deep breath. "No. I didn't want them to know I followed you. That was wrong of me."

"Na-yeong, I don't really feel like speaking to you right now."

But Na-yeong continued. "They were looking for Hana all over the neighborhood. I felt a little silly, watching them call out for her, when I knew she was nowhere near."

"Don't worry, I'm not going to tell anyone that you followed me, or that you lost Hana in the market," said Soo-Ja frostily. It wasn't all for-giveness—she simply doubted that her in-laws would punish Na-yeong. But it didn't matter—she had Hana back.

"Thank you."

Na-yeong turned, as if to sleep, but Soo-Ja was wide awake now. Na-yeong had passed on her restlessness to her. "When did Min come back?" asked Soo-Ja.

"Right after you left. My mother told Du-Ho and Chung-Ho to go to the hiding place and tell *oppa* what happened. The three of them were looking everywhere for you and Hana. Oppa was very sad. He thought he'd lost both of you."

Soo-Ja thought about Min having to go back to the hiding place tomorrow. So that's how long the happy ending lasted—only a few hours.

"And where's your father?"

"He's in Daegu."

"Why did he go back early?"

Na-yeong shrugged. "I don't know. But I guess we'll see him tomorrow when we get back home."

"I guess so. You should sleep now, Na-yeong."

"Eonni . . ."

"What?"

"I'm sorry," said Na-yeong, and Soo-Ja could hear the anguish in her voice.

"Go to sleep."

"Do you forgive me?"

"Go to sleep."

When they arrived back in Daegu, Soo-Ja immediately headed with Hana to her father's, so she could tell him what happened. But when she got there, Soo-Ja's mother greeted her very coldly. She offered her something to eat, but with a strain in her voice. She seemed angry at Soo-Ja, but also appeared to be trying to hide her anger. Soo-Ja wondered what she had done this time. She assumed that her mother was still annoyed at having to host Jae-Hwa for so long. Jae-Hwa had taken her time getting her bearings, and had only recently left their house, to take a job at a factory that manufactured electric fans.

Soo-Ja and her mother sat in awkward silence, waiting for her father in the main room. Hana alone ate the rice cakes on the tray, smiling each time she put one in her mouth.

"I hope your husband's family enjoys the second dowry," Soo-Ja's mother finally said.

Soo-Ja looked at her, confused. "Second dowry?"

"Your father worked very hard to build that factory. He can't keep sell-ing off parts of it. Things have not been easy since President Park took office," said her mother sharply.

"Does Father need money?"

Her mother's face suddenly changed, as if she'd just realized some-thing. "You don't know? They didn't tell you?"

Soo-Ja started to worry. "Did something happen to Father? Is he all right?"

Soo-Ja's mother put her right hand over her mouth and began to laugh. "Oh, this is too, too precious. They didn't say anything to you, did they?"

"Eomma, please, what happened?"

Soo-Ja's mother then told her that Father-in-law had come to see her father, and had told him about his debt, and about Min facing possible jail time. Father-in-law had explained that he needed 50 million *won*.

"He didn't say straight out that he had come at your request. He just let your father assume," said Soo-Ja's mother. "And your father thought you were at home, too worried and ashamed to come yourself, to ask him for the money. The thought of you, feeling so badly, really got to your father. He felt like he had to rescue you. He was happy, I think, to almost ruin himself so he could help you. He went back to an old friend, who had been asking for years if your father would sell him the branch in Jungangtong. You can imagine how happy this man was when your father, out of the blue, told him he'd do it if he could get the money right away. Fifty million *won*. Into the hands of your father-in-law."

Soo-Ja looked at her mother, stunned. "Did abeoji—did abeoji give Min's father all that money?"

"He said whatever belongs to me belongs to Soo-Ja," said her mother, her eyes growing big. "But what about your brothers? Or your father? He's getting old, he can't work like he used to. So I hope your husband enjoys his liberty, because it has come at a dear price."

Soo-Ja fought the panic rising in her. "Eomma, I swear I didn't know about this! Father-in-law had no right to come here and pretend to speak for me!"

"Don't let your father see you like this," said Mother, with sorrow in her eyes. "He was so happy to help you. I think he did it so he could see the look of gratitude on your face. What kind of a father is this, who throws so much away just for one look?"

"This doesn't change anything," said her father, when Soo-Ja told him how they'd kept her in the dark. "By helping your husband, I'm helping you. They're your family now. Your fate and their fate are inextricably linked, till the day you die."

They were sitting in his room, drinking warm cups of *yulmucha* tea. Outside, Soo-Ja could hear the cold wind howling. She watched as her father lit some incense, and its delicate smell filled the room.

"He should have told me," said Soo-Ja, her body filled with anguish. "I would have stopped him."

"Then I would have given him the money behind your back. Anything to keep your husband out of jail. Now, you know I don't like Nam. But he's Min's father. And being wanted by the police in suspicion of a crime is one thing, actually being arrested for it is something else entirely. This would ruin his future. And *your* future. And think of Hana's prospects, too. It's not Min's fault that he has a father like that."

"So you know everything," said Soo-Ja, her body slumped, as if her ankles and elbows were weighed down with stones.

"I guessed it the second Min's father opened his mouth that the debt was really his, and not his son's."

"He must think he's so clever," said Soo-Ja, sighing.

Her father nodded, smiling. "I hate that you have to live with them."

So he knew all about that, too. Soo-Ja wondered if all of her efforts to look happy were in vain, and people acted as if they believed her just to be polite, when deep down they could clearly hear her heart breaking.

"If I had let you go to Seoul to study diplomacy, you would never have married him," said Soo-Ja's father.

"You can't blame yourself for my mistakes," said Soo-Ja.

"But isn't it true? Would you still have married him if I had let you go to Seoul?" he asked. Soo-Ja did not reply, and her father began to nod, taking her silence for an answer.

"Is that why you gave him the money?"

"You were a rebellious daughter. But what were you rebelling against? Me. Why should I enjoy my money when my daughter lives in misery?"

"Please don't lose sleep over me. It's not so bad."

"You're lying," he said.

Her father held his cup of tea with both his hands and drank from it. When he put it down, Soo-Ja saw that it was not tea in his cup—it was soju. She'd been so distraught by the news, she hadn't noticed how out of sorts he looked. How long and how much had he been drinking? she wondered.

"It is the worst feeling in the world, to know that your child is unhappy."

"It's not that bad," said Soo-Ja. "It's just strange, to think of my life here and my life there. It's not worse, it's just different."

"And how is Hana?"

Soo-Ja then told him all that happened. Her father looked stunned the entire time, and he kept looking out toward the hallway, where Hana was helping her grandmother pick off the ends of soybean sprouts. He stared at her with longing, as if in the telling of the story, Hana was once again lost, and once again recovered.

"You should have called for me!" he cried out. "I would have taken the first train to Pusan. To think of what you went through!"

"I didn't want to worry you."

"Worrying is what a father does. Take that away from him and he has nothing to live for. How can I trust you, if you don't reach out for me in a moment of need?"

"Please, Father, after all I've been through, I don't need your chiding."

"All I want in this world is to see you happy."

Oh, and what a terrible burden that is for me, thought Soo-Ja, glancing at his tired-looking eyes.

"I can't take that money. I can't take so much from you."

Her father shook his head, and he looked terribly sad, as if disappointed in her. And then, finally, a burst of emotion came out of him. "Use me up. Use me up to the bone. Take all my strength, my energy, my will. When you let me be your father and let me worry about you, care for you, and even suffer for you, you're not doing a favor to yourself, you're doing a favor to *me*. When you need me, I am alive." His words felt like a lasso, reaching for her, wrapping itself over her skin. "What you felt, wandering through those streets, looking for Hana, that is the same thing I feel for you. How can you not understand?"

"I do. Father, I do."

"It runs in your veins, this love. It goes from me to you, and from you to your daughter. You should never worry about causing me pain. It's the opposite that I'm afraid of. Because that pain is the love, too, and how can you separate the two?"

"Yes, Father," said Soo-Ja, wiping away her tears.

Soo-Ja found Father-in-law sitting in his room, his eyes closed, leaning back on a chair. Du-Ho stood over him, shaving Father-in-law's face with paranoid care, as if hair by hair. He dipped the razor—large, more like a knife—occasionally into a bowl of hot water sitting on a tray next to him. He glanced at his father's chin as if it were a mountain. Du-Ho almost shook with nervousness.

Soo-Ja came in unnoticed, leaving the sliding paper door open so as not to make noise. When Du-Ho saw her, he was about to acknowledge her when she shook her head and put her finger to her lips. He did not speak, confused, but then understood when she signaled to him to hand her the razor. He realized she meant to take his place without Father-in-law knowing.

Du-Ho, who at fourteen was no stranger to harmless pranks, handed her the razor. Soo-Ja then motioned her head toward the door, signaling for him to leave. He smiled and started heading out. For a moment, he stopped and hesitated, as if he could read her mind, as if he knew she might do something terrible. He left, though his look lingered.

Father-in-law opened his eyes and saw Soo-Ja standing where Du-Ho should be. He gave a start, but did not move. He gazed into the mirror Du-Ho had propped up against the wall, and the look he gave her confirmed everything to Soo-Ja. Now she knew the secret that was not a secret.

Soo-Ja held the razor in the air.

"Put that razor down," he demanded.

"Did you think I wasn't going to find out?" asked Soo-Ja. Instead of doing as he asked, Soo-Ja lowered her hand and pressed the razor against his neck.

"This is between your father and me," said Father-in-law, tightening the veins on his neck. He made no pretense of not knowing what she was talking about.

"So I have nothing to do with this?"

"Nothing."

"That's funny, since last I knew, I was his daughter," said Soo-Ja. She began to shave the soap off his neck, keeping the blade tight against his skin. One quick move and she'd hit his jugular.

"In business, we deal with resources. Like your father. It would have been stupid of me not to take advantage of it," said Father-in-law, sitting very still. His eyes were glued to Soo-Ja in the mirror as she stood behind him.

"You took advantage of my father's love for me."

"You're not mad at me, you're mad at your father, for being a fool," said Father-in-law.

"My father is not a fool," said Soo-Ja, bursting with anger. Her hand began to shake and accidentally nicked his leathery skin. Drops of blood began to coat the blade. When she saw what she had done, Soo-Ja stepped away. "You have no right to talk like that. He saved you! You should be kneeling on the ground, singing his praises!"

"Fool. Yes, fool," said Father-in-law rapidly, like a machine. He reached for a towel and wiped off the blood. "For giving money away like that. If I were him, I would not have given me the money. But he did, and I, unlike him, am no fool. So I took it. It's not my fault that he's a bad businessman."

Soo-Ja reached for Father-in-law and came face-to-face with him. She held the razor in the air, her face full of desperation. "He gave you the money to save Min. Your own son. And you show no gratitude?"

"Gratitude doesn't put food in your stomach. Business savvy does, and I have a lot of it. I saw a situation, and I went in for the kill. It took smarts for me to know your father's weakness. Do you think I didn't know what I was doing when I got my son to marry into your family?" Soo-Ja looked at him, shocked. She had always thought they had been against the marriage, considering the way they treated her. Father-in-law shook his head. "You think Min is smart enough to figure out who to marry on his own? Of course I helped him, of course I steered him in the right direction. I knew your father's money would come in handy someday. And I knew your father's affection for you would come in even handier."

Shaking, Soo-Ja looked at the razor in her hand. It would take a quick second or two to sink it into his right wrist. She couldn't reach for his throat, but his hands were only inches from her.

"But before you hate me too much, think about this," said Father-in-law, his words slow and calculated. "Don't you think I'm going to do *everything* I can to make sure you're all provided for, and that we have a roof over our heads? You think it's easy making a living? Half our country is still in shambles from the war, everywhere you look you see peasants eating grass porridge for dinner and banana peels for dessert. Orphans and paraplegics and sick old people with no homes. You think this house is free? And you think it's easy, having an eldest son who can't hold a job anywhere? If a fool's giving away money, I'm a bigger fool not to take it."

"That 'fool' is my father," she muttered, in disbelief. She placed the razor on the table, turning away from him, as if he were a hallucination. "From my first day in this house, you have treated me badly. Why is that?"

Father-in-law grunted. "From your first day in this house, you have tried to turn my son against me. Do you think I don't know that when you go to sleep at night, you whisper lies in his ear?"

Soo-Ja wanted to laugh at his paranoia, but held back. Father-in-law had nothing to worry about. Min loved his parents, almost desperately. But still they were concerned. Soo-Ja thought of their daughter Seon-ae, the missing girl, the sister Min and the others never talked about. She had never met her. All she knew was that she had left home one day and never returned. Did Father-in-law fear, deep down, that his other children would leave, too, one by one?

"We're not going to talk about this anymore," said Father-in-law, dropping the bloody towel on the ground on his way out. "Our lives go back to normal. It's all in the past."

Soo-Ja, left alone, stared at the tiny pieces of hair floating on the bowl of water.

Soo-Ja sat in the restaurant waiting for Min, occasionally glancing at the steam rising from gigantic pots of bubbling *jjigae* on the open kitchen. The menu in front of her had been written in chalk on a worn-out blackboard, and below it a tiny radio noisily broadcast a Seoul news station.

Soo-Ja had told Min to meet her there. He'd been back from hiding for a couple of days now, but she'd gone into hiding herself, staying with Hana at her parents' house. She wasn't sure what to do. She couldn't stay there forever, but she also couldn't imagine going back to life with her in-laws. Too much had happened recently. Her in-laws' betrayal, and before that, seeing Yul again. Yul had reminded her of her old self—the old Soo-Ja she now longed to reconnect with. And Soo-Ja knew she could never do that as long as she stayed with Min.

If Jae-Hwa can leave her husband, why can't I leave mine as well?

Min came in and found her quickly, as she was the only person there, sitting at one of four low wooden tables, pots of cactus flowers behind her. He said nothing as he sat down.

"Did you know about your father's plans?" Soo-Ja asked him.

"I didn't know until three days ago," he said ruefully. "And when I heard about the money, I was glad—I thought you had gotten it for us."

Soo-Ja looked at him, surprised. "No, it was your father."

"After so long in that awful place, I started to dream of you coming to save me," said Min. "But in the end it wasn't you, it was my father."

"So you're not mad at my father, you're mad at me," said Soo-Ja, tasting the irony. "You don't think he did anything wrong. In fact, he's your hero now."

"He got me out, didn't he?" Min asked matter-of-factly.

Min would always be his father's son, and side with him always, thought Soo-Ja. It was a battle she had lost. He would never be hers, and it was foolish to think she could be his.

"We shouldn't be together anymore," Soo-Ja said, letting the words hang in the air. "You know what I'm asking, right?"

Min took the napkin in front of him and started folding and unfolding it. He'd then smooth it out, looking at the creases. He never set his eyes on her, but she could sense his sadness, and it was black as tar. "After everything I've been through, you tell me this?" he asked.

"What about what *I've* been through?"

"You have another man?"

"No," she said.

"You have another man," said Min, looking at her for the first time. He tore the napkin into pieces, and he threw them aside, like confetti. "Maybe not in your arms. But in your heart."

"There is no one," said Soo-Ja firmly. "That's not the reason I want us to separate. Maybe if we didn't live with your parents, maybe then we could have a chance, but not like this. I can't, Min. Our time together is over."

"Why do you want to leave me?" asked Min, staring at her sternly.

Soo-Ja knew she had to tread carefully. Wives were rarely permitted to divorce their husbands without consent, and even if a judge allowed it, the terms—especially regarding the custody of children—were always in the husbands' favor.

"Why do you want to stay with me?" Soo-Ja retorted, though she already knew the answer. She knew how much Min needed her. She was his lifeline. She had, however reluctantly or accidentally, given him love, and because he had never known it before, he could not let go, much like a baby who holds on tight to his mother with his strong fingers. Soo-Ja thought they were both unhappy—and they were—but she'd been naive to expect Min to want to get out of this unhappiness when for him, the other option was worse. But for a moment, as Min nodded, Soo-Ja softened, thinking perhaps this kind nod would be what she remembered him by, years later. She rose from her chair, ready to leave the restaurant, Min, and her marriage. "Good-bye."

Suddenly, Soo-Ja felt Min grab her arm. The whistle of a kettle cut through the air, and the cook's curses could be heard, as she swept away the boiling water overflowing onto the stovetop. "You can go, Soo-Ja. But you can't take Hana with you," said Min, rising slowly so he stood next to her.

Soo-Ja froze, and when she gazed into Min's eyes, she saw a blank.

Min continued, their bodies almost glued together, the intimacy of lovers. "You know the law, don't you?"

"The law?" Soo-Ja asked quietly. She almost couldn't hear the words come out of her lips.

"The husband keeps the children," said Min. He looked at her with the daunting gaze of a judge sentencing a prisoner, as if he knew he could create different destinies for her, and it was up to him to decide which one to give her.

"You have never once changed Hana's diapers. You have never bathed her," said Soo-Ja, trying to quiet the anger building inside her. Min still had his hands on her arm.

"My mother can raise her," said Min casually, as if making arrangements for a weekend trip.

She fought back tears, and could feel her hands shaking slightly. "You wouldn't do that to me," said Soo-Ja, as her breathing grew more labored.

"I will never, ever let you keep Hana," said Min. "You will never see her again."

"Min, you can marry another woman. You can father another child, a boy."

Min shook his head. "I don't think I can do better than you. So unless you want to lose custody of Hana, you'd better stay with me."

Soo-Ja felt as if she were falling into an abyss. "You'd really take Hana from me?" She could hear the desperation in her own voice.

"If that's the only way I can keep you, then yes."

Soo-Ja nodded. The pain in her stomach hurt so much, she almost doubled over. She felt a slight shudder as he put his arms around her and led her out of the restaurant. Back at their house, her in-laws would be waiting for her.

PART THREE

Plum Blossoms

Nine Years Later

Seoul

1972

chapter ten

All of this nothingness could be mine, thought Soo-Ja, as she walked through the empty fields in the neighborhood of Gangnam, south of the River Hangang, with Min and Hana following her. It was a cold Friday morning in early winter, and Soo-Ja was on her way to a meeting with a real estate developer who knew her father. Gi-yong Im sold plots of land in undeveloped parts of Seoul, and speculators (or *aspiring* speculators, like her) bought and sold those lands for profit. The appointment she had with Gi-yong was her first real business meeting, and though she should be nervous, Soo-Ja was in fact elated. Min was the one sweating; he had repeatedly asked if he could stay with Hana at home. Soo-Ja, too, would have liked to have gone on her own, but she knew the developer would never do business with her. She had to pretend she was simply tagging along, and that Min was really the one interested in investing.

Soo-Ja dressed Min in an elegant brown suit, with a form-fitting, flattering cut that gave him square shoulders and a slim frame. She herself wore a yellow silk blouse with ruffled trim along the buttons, and a long beaded necklace hanging down to her waist, just above her red polyester pants. She didn't wear hanbok anymore—she thought only maids and old people stuck to it. Western fashions seemed to be all the rage, especially American and French—miniskirts, bright colors, and even things like gold spangles and folk-music-inspired patterns.

Gi-yong had them meet at the plot of land itself, a barren desert of rocks and parched soil, a sea of brown and faint yellow, as lifeless as straw, framed by the clear blue sky above and the cerulean water from the adjacent river. She spotted Gi-yong in a heavy woolen trenchcoat, wearing black leather gloves and a white mask over his mouth to keep his face warm. He looked to be in his late forties, though his hair was still a lustrous black. It was hard for her to tell a man's age, since their faces often had few lines; she could tell much quicker a man's status, since powerful men in Seoul never acted humble.

The land was more desolate than she expected, and the closest buildings were kilometers away. Nobody had any interest in constructing here, and so the land was worthless. All the building was being done on the other side of the river, in Gangbuk. As far as everyone knew, that's the direction in which Seoul would continue to grow. In addition, no one knew if the city had reached capacity, or if it would grow more. The President had been very keen on stimulating the countryside, making those areas more livable, and if he succeeded, the constant move to the capital could soon stabilize. But that, of course, was the beauty of investing. In five, ten years, this land could be worth either ten thousand *won* or ten *million won*.

As Soo-Ja stepped forward to walk to Gi-yong, Min reached for her arm and stopped her. For a moment, she thought that he wanted to check her appearance, and she remembered to take her red scarf off her head and wrap it around her neck—she didn't want to look like she was fresh off the bus from *sigol*. But Min instead flashed a stern look at her, and he shook his head softly.

"Let's go home, Soo-Ja," said Min. "This kind of thing is not for us. *Meoggo-salja.*"

Soo-Ja looked back at him, stifling her frustration. Min's motto literally meant "eat and live," or in other words, if you have enough to eat, be content, for it's enough. It was an old saying, and many people lived and died by that notion. But just being fed wasn't enough for Soo-Ja. She saw all around her people becoming rich overnight, like the owners and managers of the large electronic export manufacturer *chaebols*.

Her country was changing. Some folks lived like peasants, toiling in rice paddies all day and coming home to huts with thatched roofs at night, while the men and women of the city (and in her own home-town of Daegu for that matter) bought into Western-style apartment buildings with—and this would have been unimaginable a decade ago—playgrounds for the children, and well-lit, air-conditioned, indoor shopping centers nearby.

"This doesn't look like a good investment," he continued. "Who'd want to build here? It's too close to the river, and there's nothing for ki-lometers." Min pointed to the vast open space around them, at the fields of dried-up, barren soil.

Soo-Ja noticed Gi-yong looking in their direction, waiting for them, but she knew she had to have this conversation with Min. She stood closer to her husband and spoke quietly, so Hana would not hear. "Even if I brought someone from the future who said we'd become rich, even if I showed you a lab report saying there's gold under the ground, you would still deny me this, and say no. Isn't that right?"

Hana, who had been quietly watching them, pointed to someone behind them, and they realized Gi-yong was making his way down, ap-parently tired of waiting. Soo-Ja turned away from Min and took a deep breath. She tried to wipe the anger off her face.

"*Annyeong-ha-seyo,*" Gi-yong greeted them, a crescent moon smile on his face. He bowed deeply, and then shook their hands. He also tried to pat Hana's head, but she moved out of his reach.

"She's not a child. She's almost a teenager," Soo-Ja said, smiling.

To Soo-Ja's surprise, Gi-yong did not look offended or embarrassed. He simply laughed heartily, nodding, and Soo-Ja could tell he didn't laugh out of some social obligation, but rather because he seemed amused by his own mistake. She liked this—she liked people who had a sense of humor about themselves.

"Mr. Lee," said Gi-yong, looking at Min. "This is the land you are interested in buying. It is eighty percent sold. I hope to have it one hun-dred percent sold by the end of the month."

Min gave him a scornful look. "Your land doesn't look like much."

At that moment, a young woman who looked like an assistant of sorts came to Gi-yong and spoke to him for a second. Gi-yong made some hand gestures to them—part apology, part request for them to stay and wait, and he followed the woman back to a makeshift office erected a few meters away.

"Let's go now, let's go before he comes back," said Min, eager to continue with Soo-Ja the conversation Gi-yong had interrupted.

"No! Let me do this," said Soo-Ja, pulling away from him as he tried to reach for her arm.

"You can give the money back to your brother," said Min.

Soo-Ja walked a few steps away from Min and kept her back turned to him. She had told Min that the money to invest had been loaned to her by her younger brother, who now worked as an architect. In reality, Soo-Ja had been saving the money from her job as a hotel manager. Whenever Min asked her how much money she had made, she would show him only half. The other half she'd stuff in the pockets of her clothes in the dresser. She had managed to save 200,000 *won*.

"The investment is risky, yes, but I believe in this city. Everyone is moving here. I run into old acquaintances from Daegu and Pusan all the time—women with children I knew as babies. The future is in Seoul."

"You sound like President Park. You know he tortures people," said Min.

"Well, if you spruce up your old skills with the student revolutionaries, you can fight him back. Although I think fighting me is enough," Soo-Ja said, turning around and facing him again, with her hands in her pockets.

"That's very funny," said Min, not smiling. He then turned to Hana. "You have a very funny mother. Tell that to your prospective husbands; they'll be sure to ask for your hand."

"I have already decided on this. We're not going to live hand to mouth. We are going to invest, and buy some of this land," said Soo-Ja, walking away from Min. No one could mistake the seriousness in her voice.

"'I already decided.' What do you think you do to your husband when you say things like that?" asked Min. "Isn't it *my* job to decide? It's bad enough I have to ask my wife for money."

"And I always give it to you," Soo-Ja calmly replied. "I have never complained or made you feel self-conscious about anything. If you have issues with that, there's nothing I can do about it."

This was a sensitive topic, the fact that for the last few years, Min had not had a job. It was understood that the reason wasn't because he was lazy or unintelligent, but because of his bad back. Seven years ago, Min's parents had decided to immigrate to the United States, and they had asked Min to come with them and bring his family, so they could work together in a factory there. Soo-Ja refused to go—unable to live with them after the way they had deceived her—and Min had to decide between obeying his parents and staying in Korea with his own family.

At the time, Min was walking by a mini–grocery store near their home in Daegu when an old woman—a distant acquaintance—asked him to help her carry boxes of apples into her store. She did not mention how heavy they were, and when Min lifted the first one, he heard a loud crack—it was his back. At this point, Min should have dropped the box on the ground, but, afraid to embarrass himself in front of the old woman—for she might think he was weak—he carried it all the way into the store, taking one long, excruciating step after another, and cracking his back even more.

Min suffered great pain for days, and his back never fully healed. He could not, he told his parents, move to America, and they left without him. By the time he could again move normally, Min also decided that the bad back would become the official reason why he couldn't work. It had become an essential part of how they constructed their lives—it explained to Hana why, unlike other men his age, her father didn't have a job, and it helped explain to others why Soo-Ja was the one earning their bread.

"I'm so sorry to keep you waiting!" Gi-yong waved his hands in front of him, animated.

"It's no problem at all," said Soo-Ja, after realizing that Min, now sulking, would not reply to Gi-yong, even though he was the one being addressed. "My husband is very excited about this investment opportunity. There are those who say our country will not grow, but I disagree. I think this is all just the beginning."

Gi-yong nodded. "There's one thing I want to alert you to, before we move any further." She noticed that though he kept looking at both of them, Gi-yong was now really addressing her.

"What is it?" she asked.

"When we spoke before, it was almost a year ago, and I said I was selling the land for three hundred *won* per *pyeong*. Because interest in the land has been so high, the prices have gone up since then. If you change your mind, I will understand." He looked embarrassed as he said this.

"How much more?" Soo-Ja asked.

"Five hundred *won* per pyeong, and I'm selling a minimum of a thousand pyeong."

Five hundred thousand *won*. And she had only 200,000.

Soo-Ja nodded silently. "I expected the price to be higher, with inflation and all, just not that much higher."

Gi-yong looked directly at her. They both dropped the pretense that he was doing business with Min.

"You look like a good person, and I want you to be able to buy the land. But I have to think of myself and the other investors. I can't make an exception for you."

"You won't have to. I may not have all the money right now, but I will. When do I have to put down my share by?"

Gi-yong sighed. "The end of the month."

Soo-Ja tried to hide her hesitation. "I'll have the money by the end of the month. Don't sell my share of the land to anyone else."

"I can't hold them for very long."

"Don't worry, I'll have the money. When I see you again, Mr. Im, I'll have the payment and those acres of land will be mine."

Soo-Ja could see in his eyes that he did not believe her, but the friendly smile on his lips told her that he'd do her the favor of waiting. As they parted, she decided to memorize the look of doubt on his face, as she knew she would need that look to encourage her in the long, hard weeks ahead.

Since Soo-Ja and Min had moved to Seoul seven years earlier, they had watched as the city stubbornly rose from the ground, crushing the earth on its way up, with hundreds of new buildings built on slums and empty lots. Walking around the streets of downtown Seoul, Soo-Ja could see bulldozers and trucks digging through the hard soil every day, the landscape filled with scaffolding and brickwork. Thousands of new businesses and industries sprouted around the city, manufacturing goods that could be exported to rich countries. Rickshaws gave way to Kias, and streetcars surrendered to trains. President Chung Hee Park had been borrowing money heavily from the Americans and was using it to open factories, modernize shipyards, and build highways. Soo-Ja had not expected to see her country change so much in the course of less than a decade.

But, as Soo-Ja quickly realized, modernity seemed to require an endless amount of labor and sacrifice. Everyone around her appeared to be working sixty-hour weeks, from the factory assemblymen to the shoe shiners. Students like Hana, from first to twelfth grade, had to rise in the early morning and make their own breakfast before spending the entire day doing their rote memorizations and math exercises. No one spoke about happiness, or enjoying the day. Their entire lives they'd been taught to sacrifice, either for their parents or for their children, and now they were asked to extend those feelings to their bosses and their jobs. So they worked, and watched, as the buildings began to reach the sky, and money started to flow.

President Park ruled like a dictator, everyone knew. With the adoption of a new constitution—one that he drafted himself—he had made it impossible for anyone to remove him from office (or be dethroned, as some snickered). But he'd been effective in raising everyone's standards of living, and his occasional show of populism—prosecuting corrupt businessmen, or replacing the straw roofs of rural homes with cement—gladdened the hearts of the poor. Park had become his countrymen's father and mother, and established capitalism as their new religion.

Soo-Ja worked twelve-hour days at the hotel, but she found nothing extraordinary in this, since everyone else worked similar hours. To be productive was to be honorable, and to raise capital was one's duty. Confucianism had taught them to be dutiful, and capitalism had given them something to be dutiful to—the laws of economic prosperity. It didn't matter what happened behind closed doors, in bedrooms, and in private—what tears were shed or desires suppressed. Feelings, emotions, aspirations—all that had to be set aside, as there were no individuals, only a collective will to succeed.

And Soo-Ja planned to be a part of that success. She rejected the notion of meoggo-salja; for her, it wasn't enough just to "live and eat." She wanted her family to reside in one of the impressive new gated houses being built in Seoul for the nouveaux riches sons and daughters of electronic export manufacturers. She wanted to buy her daughter clothes in the elegant ateliers and boutiques sprouting around the city, selling Paris-inspired fashions. And above all, Soo-Ja wanted the money to pay back her father. In her fantasies, Soo-Ja found some way of getting her father-in-law to return the money. But in reality, she knew that wasn't likely, and that if she was to pay her father back, she'd have to earn the money herself. The land in Gangnam was the key.

Ever since they had moved to Seoul, Soo-Ja and Min had been supporting themselves by managing a hotel. As in most small businesses in Seoul, Soo-Ja lived with her family there as well, in two small rooms near the entrance. This work, which included demanding patrons and required long hours, did not pay very well, and Soo-Ja knew there was no future in it. What Soo-Ja liked even less was that the idea to do this had come from a friend of her father-in-law, and she hated being indebted to him for the introduction.

Soo-Ja also disliked the male customers who showed up late at night, without a reservation, in need of a room to sleep off the alcohol, or with a girl by their side, or both. Often, they'd ask her to send a girl to their rooms. At first, Soo-Ja ignored the requests. But then women started to come on their own, asking if there were lonely men in the hotel. They did not wear fox furs or miniskirts. They did not curse or leer. They looked like ordinary women, some with children in tow. They were hungry, with tired eyes. Soo-Ja began to tell them what doors to knock on, and sometimes, she'd warn them about a particularly nasty guest.

When Soo-Ja listened on the radio to the President talking about his five-year plan to modernize the economy, and his lofty goal of turning what he called a "backward" country into a great superpower, Soo-Ja thought about these women. She wondered what their roles would be— the women abandoned by their husbands or disowned by their families. They reminded her of the rose of Sharon, the national flower of Korea. White with purple throats and hardy petals, it had been chosen for its ability to survive droughts, heat, and poor soil. They were lovely in bloom, though that required patience, as they tended to arrive late in the spring. Once they bloomed, however, they lasted all through summer, long after other flowers had perished.

When they returned to the hotel from their visit to Gangnam, Soo-Ja forgot her usual worries and, though she was still short on money, she felt a rush of excitement—like a child on the eve of summer break, the future looming warm and inviting. In fact, it was Hana who took her out of her reverie when she handed her a note. Soo-Ja was still taking off her coat and scarf when Hana's soft fingers placed the folded-up paper on the counter. Min had gone inside to take his daily afternoon nap by then.

"What's this?" Soo-Ja asked.

They were standing in the front desk area, where Soo-Ja spent most of her hours greeting guests. A modest affair, it featured a white wooden counter, some worn-out oak chairs, and a glass table with out-of-date magazines. In the far corner, some bamboo plants covered the back wall, and a bulletin board featured deals on tourist attractions and nearby restaurants. There wasn't much space, and when guests came in from outside, they were almost immediately face to face with Soo-Ja.

"That man slipped it to me as we were leaving. He said to hand it to you when you were alone," said Hana.

"You mean Gi-yong Im? The man we just met with?" Soo-Ja reached for the note and quickly opened it, intrigued.

I would consider giving you a break in the price if you went on a date with me. You're very pretty, and your husband can wear a blindfold for now.

Soo-Ja stifled a curse word, amazed that he thought she'd agree to such a thing. She felt the bile rise, and the frustration, too. She hated that she couldn't phone him and give him a piece of her mind, but she needed him more than he needed her. Trying to contain the humiliation she felt, Soo-Ja crumpled the paper into a small ball. She placed it in her pocket lest the hotel maid found it in the wastebasket or, God forbid, Min himself ran across it.

"Hana, you didn't open this, did you?" Soo-Ja asked her daughter, trying to sound casual.

"No," said Hana. "Why?"

"No reason. Now help your mother and tell Miss Hong to do another once-over in room 312. The woman who called to book it seemed very particular, and won't appreciate a dirty room."

"Oh, I know, I spoke to her," said Hana. "She called again this morning. She couldn't believe we don't have showers in the hotel. What does she think the bathhouse across the street is for? And then she asked if she could have an extra room free, for her to leave her clothes. Sure, but are those clothes going to earn money by themselves and pay for their own room? Some *ukineon* women out there."

"Hana, please don't use that expression," Soo-Ja said.

"But she *is* out of her mind! What is she thinking? And she asked if we have rats in the hotel! Can you imagine? What kind of a question is that?"

"Hana, go speak to Miss Hong, please."

Hana made to leave, and she had her back to her mother when she asked, "You're not going to accept Mr. Im's offer?"

Soo-Ja detected some disappointment in her daughter's voice. "You read the note?"

"Are you going to?" Hana asked again.

"Hana, if you knew what you were asking, you wouldn't be asking it."

"Why don't you?"

Was Hana betraying her adored father in this moment? Or was she simply voicing what he himself might say, her husband who was at once insanely jealous of other men and completely casual as to Soo-Ja's worth to him?

"Hana, he's not just asking me to go get some jelly cakes with him at the grocery store. When grown men say 'dates,' they mean much more."

"I know. He wants whatever it is that happens in the movies after a man and a woman kiss and the screen goes black," said Hana.

It occurred to Soo-Ja that Hana herself was using euphemisms, that she was well aware of what happened after the screen went black. Soo-Ja looked at her daughter's smooth teenage face, her hair in two tiny pigtails in the back, her pink angora sweater with a white collar and buttons in the front. Hana was twelve, and looked twelve, but she was the oldest twelve-year-old Soo-Ja knew.

"Hana, I know it can be frustrating for you to see your friends ride in taxis and buy new clothes every season at the *baeg-hwa-jeom*, but listen to me, they are absolutely no better than you. Now go to your room and do your homework. And for sure do not tell your father about the note. It'll hurt him." Soo-Ja added the last part because it was the only way she'd keep her daughter from sharing its contents with him. Hana doted on her father, loved him more than she did her mother; mostly, Soo-Ja suspected, because he let her get away with more.

When Hana left, Soo-Ja pictured her daughter going to their bedroom, where Hana and Min would sit on the floor and eat tiny oranges together. Min would diligently peel off the skin and remove the white pith from each slice before popping them in Hana's mouth, one by one. Hana loved how her father always had time for her, more time than any other adult his age. Min said yes to her every whim, agreed to the most outrageous demands, and bought her records, comic books, and fan magazines. He treated her more like a small, about-to-be-deposed queen than a daughter.

At times, Soo-Ja caught the showiness of his love for Hana, and she noticed how it was more for her benefit than their daughter's, as if to say, *Look, I'm not a bad father, I have redeeming qualities, and I am, after all, capable of love—just not capable of loving you, as you're not capable of loving me.*

Meanwhile Soo-Ja told Hana no all the time. She was always too busy checking in guests to talk to her daughter about her crushes on the singer Jung Hyeon Shin and the actor Sung-Il Shin. She refused to buy Hana new dresses when it was so cold and she'd be covered by a winter coat all the time anyway. (Soo-Ja was of the school that you didn't spend too much on things other people couldn't see, which explained the sorry state of her own undergarments.)

When Hana was six and seven, Soo-Ja had to spank her just to get her to do the simplest things, like put on her pajamas or eat her meals. When she did so, Hana would yell out, "It doesn't hurt at all!" This brazenness amazed her mother, and only made her want to hit her harder (which she didn't). Hana never backed down, and Soo-Ja was, by turn, infuriated and impressed by her willfulness.

Hana had grown a bit calmer lately and was too busy with school to really give her any troubles. Occasionally Hana would catch her mother staring at her and she'd ask, "What are you looking at?" And Soo-Ja would smile mysteriously and say, "I'm looking at *you*." For yes, Soo-Ja was still amazed by this porcelain-skinned beauty who had been given to her twice—once at birth, and once in Pusan—and was therefore twice loved, twice adored.

Hana, do you know that I love you? I envy the mothers in American movies, able to say that out loud.

I know I can't say it, but I say it when I tell you to put on your jacket and your hoodie. I can't say it, but I say it when I make seaweed soup for your birthday, and also get you coconut cake, your favorite. Your father and I compete for your love, never openly admitting this, but instead simply reminding you to be respectful and obedient. Be obedient, my daughter. Be obedient.

"Did you have a good stay?" asked Soo-Ja, smiling at the two guests in front of her. They were women roughly her own age, and they did not respond, as if Soo-Ja were a machine of sorts, there simply to check them out. From their nice clothes, Soo-Ja guessed these were married ladies enjoying a vacation away from children and husbands. While Soo-Ja added up their bill, she noticed that the two of them were staring intently at her, and whispering to each other. "Is everything all right?"

"Yes," said one of the women. "My friend thinks she recognizes you, but I think she's wrong."

"Oh," said Soo-Ja, looking at her with curiosity, trying to place their faces as well.

One woman was tall, and had a perm, with curls chasing down her cheeks. The other was short, and looked to be about sixteen, though she was probably twice as old. Soo-Ja didn't know either of them, but didn't rule out the possibility that the woman was right. In her college years, especially, many people had known her—by name or by sight.

"My friend here thinks you're Soo-Ja Choi, from Won-dae-don." Soo-Ja smiled, about to confirm that, but could not get a word in as the woman continued, "But I'm telling her she's wrong. That Soo-Ja was, well, rich. What would she be doing working as a hotel hostess?"

"I'm not a hostess," said Soo-Ja, instantly losing her smile.

"It's her!" the other woman interrupted. She leaned forward, inspecting Soo-Ja's face. She spoke as if Soo-Ja weren't there. "She doesn't look anything like her, I know. She's not as pretty, and the Soo-Ja I remember wouldn't be caught dead in those bargain-bin clothes, but it's her!"

"You're wrong, Bok-Hee. Do you really think Woon-Gyu Choi's daughter would be working in a place like this? She's probably in France now, redecorating her château."

They were talking to each other, acting as if Soo-Ja couldn't hear them. They stared openly at her, scrutinizing her clothes, her posture, her looks.

"It's her, I know it's her," said Bok-Hee. "It's you, isn't it?" Bok-Hee finally addressed Soo-Ja. "You're Soo-Ja Choi."

Bok-Hee spoke dripping with self-satisfaction, and looked at Soo-Ja as if she had unmasked her. Bok-Hee had a broad smile on her face, clearly thinking she had won in the game of life, and couldn't wait to share her discovery with her old classmates. Soo-Ja looked away from her and presented them with the bill.

"I have no idea who you're talking about," said Soo-Ja curtly. "That's not me."

"Of course not," said Bok-Hee, her smile hinting at the glee she'd feel when she started spreading the news.

You will never guess who I just saw working the front desk of a one-star hotel . . .

After the two women left, Soo-Ja thought about closing for the day—and maybe even for the rest of her life. But she knew she couldn't do that. Unlike the guests who had just left, she didn't have a husband to support her. Only the land in Gangnam could buy her freedom.

At that moment, Soo-Ja wondered if that was the real reason she had moved to Seoul—to get away from her old classmates, who would have run into her frequently had she stayed in Daegu. The irony was not lost on her—more than ten years ago, she had longed to come to Seoul to attend diplomat school, but when she had finally arrived, it was to work as a hotel clerk. With so many bills to pay and the weight of real life on her shoulders, the mere idea of just being a student sounded like a far-off fantasy.

Soo-Ja looked at the list of guests who were supposed to check in, and she thought once again of the woman she had spoken with on the phone the day before. Eun-Mee Kim. Did she know her? Had she gone to school with her, too? It would not surprise her if Eun-Mee Kim turned out to be an old elementary school classmate who wanted to see for herself what fate had befallen Soo-Ja Choi, the once famous beauty of Won-dae-don. *Eun-Mee Kim, Eun-Mee Kim.*

Soo-Ja spoke the name quietly, under her breath, and tried to see if it evoked any memories. It was barely a few seconds after she had realized who the woman was that she saw her materialize in front of her. She did not need to be introduced. The woman's identity was unmistakable as she came into the hotel and was followed by her beloved Yul himself. Soo-Ja felt the earth stop spinning as she found herself face to face, for the first time, with Yul's wife.

chapter eleven

"This has to be some kind of joke," Eun-Mee said as soon as she came in. Soo-Ja suddenly felt keenly aware of the simplicity of her hotel—the two table ferns flanking the counter, the lack of windows, the bright fluorescent lights, the dismally generic painting behind her of a python and a deer facing off in a forest.

Yul's wife seemed so out of place there, with her long, black hair done up in elaborate French tresses in the back. She was a stunning beauty, with her milky complexion, long-bridged nose, and big eyes made even bigger by the black mascara. She wore a jacket top with a gaudy gold circular print, and a bright yellow skirt with a white line on the sides that fell just below her knees. Her enormous purse had a rough surface, and seemed to be made of lizard skin. Yul, standing behind Eun-Mee, tried to avoid looking at Soo-Ja directly, and kept shifting his eyes from her to the floor, then back again. He wore a heavy gray trenchcoat, wrapped in front with a belt and a long row of silver-colored buttons. He never took his hands out of his large pockets.

Yul did not look that much older than the last time she saw him, eight years earlier, though she knew he must be in his late thirties now. His hair was a little long, which lent him a boyish quality, and he still had the same serious, handsome face that seemed to her more appropriate for a student leader than a doctor. Soo-Ja couldn't pretend she hadn't thought of him in the years since she had seen him last. Of course she had, and it was amazing to see he did not look much different in person than he had in her dreams. He still had those deep eyes that seemed to contain mountains of sorrows. But when he smiled, his entire face followed the lead of his lips, expression lines forming on the sides and around his eyes.

Soo-Ja hoped that upon seeing him again, she'd simply feel the expected warmth and surprise you feel when reunited with an old friend—for that's what he was in the eyes of the world, a distant friend, the kind you run into at weddings and funerals, once every decade or so. But instead, she felt a piercing sensation in her heart, and her breathing became shallow. Soo-Ja could not run to him—if she couldn't do that before, why did she think she could do that now?

"This can't be the place where we're staying! Was there some kind of mix-up?" Eun-Mee asked Yul, ignoring Soo-Ja. "Whoever suggested this hotel must've been pulling a prank."

Yul bowed to Soo-Ja, and she bowed back to him. Then he asked after her health and the health of her daughter. His wife, watching this, suddenly made a big show of making a realization. She started pointing at Soo-Ja.

"Ah! Your husband must be a friend of my husband's," Eun-Mee said, suddenly bowing warmly and smiling, full of affection. She then turned to Yul. "You want to help your friend's business, that's why we're staying here! Why didn't you tell me that's why you picked this place?"

Yul did not reply, and Soo-Ja realized it was because he did not want to lie.

"Our husbands were in a youth group together, back in the sixties," Soo-Ja cut in.

Eun-Mee smiled at Soo-Ja, seemingly satisfied. "Oh, I see! I was wondering why we were here. I thought it was a prank. No offense, but we're used to better accommodations. But now I understand! My husband is a friend, and you will give us a good rate. In fact, friends being friends, it wouldn't be out of place to let us stay here for free!"

Soo-Ja wasn't entirely unused to this—the richer the guest, the more they expected, and for the least amount of money. Yul stepped forward. "Of course we're paying full price. Just because we know each other, it doesn't mean we can take advantage."

"Oh, honey, let's leave it up to her, shall we?" cooed Eun-Mee.

Soo-Ja pulled out her guest book and her calculator, seemingly to check them in, but more to hide her nervousness. "For how many nights?" she asked, not looking up.

Soo-Ja had asked Yul this, but it was Eun-Mee who answered. "We don't know. At least two weeks, but it may be more."

Soo-Ja looked at her, confused. Yul smiled at his wife weakly, then turned to Soo-Ja. "We'll be here for two nights." Soo-Ja realized at that moment that Yul did not really want to stay at the hotel. She couldn't decide what had led to them showing up there, but it was clear that Yul was trying to figure out how to shorten the stay without making it seem like he was hiding something.

"Two nights? It'll be much longer than that, for sure! At least until the house is ready." Eun-Mee turned to face Soo-Ja. "Do you know about this? We've just bought a big house here in Seoul. I've been asking Yul for years to get us out of that fish sinkhole of Pusan and he finally relented. Seoul is so much more my style, and the house is beautiful. As soon as we're done building and painting the last bathroom, we can move in. It's a *modern* bathroom. With a toilet. And tiles on the floor."

Soo-Ja tried to hide all of the emotions that hit her at once. Time had not dulled her feelings for Yul—she still loved him, and felt both petrified and elated that he was there to stay. And not just stay in the city, but in her own hotel! For a moment she didn't care that he was there with his wife, or that her own husband waited for her inside. Of course they wouldn't do anything senseless. There would be no action, no doing; but he'd *be* there. He'd *be*, and that could be the world. Sometimes it is nice just to see the face of the beloved—the excruciating pain comes later. And she could see him, maybe every day. *Fine*, she thought, as if she had made a pact with the devil and came out on the losing end—*here's love, but it's attached to a string and a hook, and if you try to grab it, I will yank it back again and again.*

"Listen, since we're all friends, do you mind if I look around and pick a room that I like?" Eun-Mee seemed to completely forget how unsuitable she had found the place. The fact that she might essentially be staying for free seemed to mitigate all worries.

"Yes. Miss Hong will show you which rooms are empty, as well as the one I originally planned to give you," said Soo-Ja.

Miss Hong, the chambermaid, had been drawn to the front by the noise, and was standing just beyond the front area. She stepped forward, bowed to Eun-Mee, and signaled for her to follow her, which Eun-Mee did, smiling happily, as if she had just won the hotel in a contest and wanted to check its contents.

When Eun-Mee was gone, Soo-Ja and Yul did not speak at first, though she could only pretend for so long to be engrossed by her calculations, and he clearly had something stuck in his throat.

"She—Eun-Mee—she found a note on my desk with your name and the phone number of the hotel. She became very suspicious, seeing a woman's name, and I didn't have a lie ready, so I told her it was just the hotel where we'd be staying in Seoul. I don't know if she called because she didn't believe me—"

"Why did you have my phone number on your desk?" Soo-Ja asked, cutting him off, aware that Eun-Mee could be back any second.

Yul did not answer her question.

"Soo-Ja, I promise I will check out of the hotel as soon as I can. I know that this is awkward."

Yul looked right into her eyes, and his hand suddenly came up. Soo-Ja thought he was going to touch her face, but his hand merely stopped in midair, as if lost. It finally came down, to rest on the counter.

"No, stay," said Soo-Ja. "I'd like for you two to stay here. But you still haven't answered my question. Why did you have my phone number?"

Yul was looking straight into her eyes when he finally spoke, and it was then that she knew. "Because I'm still in love with you."

"I don't see why he thinks he can stay at the hotel for cheap. I hardly know the fella," said Min, lying next to Soo-Ja on the laminated floor.

They'd often talk before falling asleep, with Min bringing up some trivial event from earlier in the day: a fish seller who had mistakenly charged him twice for a pound of abalone; an acquaintance with a cold who sneezed into his hand and then offered it to shake.

"He didn't ask for it. His wife did," said Soo-Ja, her hands resting on top of her stomach, eyes looking up at the ceiling.

Min ignored her and continued. "When we were in the student group together, he hardly ever spoke to me. And now he thinks we're friends? He'll be lucky if I nod to him while he's here."

"What was—what was he like when you met him?" asked Soo-Ja, trying to hide the interest in her voice. It was a luxury, to be able to talk about Yul. Nobody in her life knew him, or knew of his importance to her.

"I never actually met him. We just spoke on the phone a couple of times," said Min. "You probably spent more time with him than I did. You remember him from back then, don't you?"

"Barely. It was a long time ago."

"Didn't you two go together to that woman's house—the woman whose son got killed? That must've been difficult."

"Not really. We didn't know at that point that the boy had died."

"Yes. So much tragedy out there in the world. But we're the lucky ones, aren't we?"

"I suppose so. Good night, Min."

"Good night. And make sure Yul doesn't check out without leaving a sizable tip."

Eun-Mee's things arrived in the morning, and then continued to arrive throughout the day. Eun-Mee had so much luggage that some of it rested in the hallway outside her door. For much of the day, Eun-Mee sat there on the floor, wearing a shower cap and a robe, looking for items, smiling at the occasional guest. She unpacked what looked like dozens of coats and dresses, of all colors and for all seasons, arranging them in the room like the limbs of an adored child. But what Soo-Ja noticed most were her shoes, some of which looked imported from Italy.

Ever since she had started saving money for the land, Soo-Ja had stopped buying things for herself; she got used to wearing her shoes until they fell apart. Around Eun-Mee, she could not help trying to hide her feet under her dress. *Shoes matter*, she remembered her father telling her when she was little. *What you stand on is what you are.*

Yul stayed in a separate room, and while Soo-Ja found this odd, she thought it best not to comment on it. Soon, Soo-Ja found herself drawn to his end of the hallway almost magnetically, and if she could have seen her thoughts through some kind of magical X-ray, she might have been alarmed by the buzzing lines and ricocheting sparks leading directly to his door.

Yul's character hadn't changed much over the years; Soo-Ja had realized this during their check-in, the day before. In front of Eun-Mee, and much to her smiling approval, Yul had signed a guest bill featuring a substantial discount. But when she hadn't been looking, Yul added 1,000 *won* to the sum, which was more than Soo-Ja normally charged for the rooms.

Soo-Ja kept the extra money in an envelope and set it aside. She planned on returning it to Yul on the day he checked out. Of course, she couldn't simply hand it back to him, or he'd refuse; she figured she might need to perform a delicate sleight of hand, using distraction and trickery to slip it into the pocket of his trenchcoat on his way out.

Occasionally, guests called the front desk, and Soo-Ja sent Miss Hong to attend to them. But when she heard a buzz come from room 311, Soo-Ja decided to go herself. She took a deep breath and dried her damp hands by pressing them against the front of her dress. The door to the room had been left ajar, and Soo-Ja came in, her steps tentative. Yul stood with his back to her, and he did not meet her eyes right away. The room, like all the others, had no windows, only wallpaper featuring brown half squares meant to suggest traditional wood lattices. A small straw basket, weighed down by cotton blankets, sat against a corner; it was the only piece of furniture there.

"Did you call for me? Everything all right with the room?" asked Soo-Ja.

"Yes. I like the room very much. I wasn't sure if I should ask you here or not. It seems a little demeaning to ring a buzzer, but I couldn't think of another way to be alone with you."

"Don't worry. You're not only a guest, but a friend, too. I want you to enjoy your stay."

"I've been thinking about what I said to you yesterday. I didn't mean for it to come out quite that way. It's just that—the last ten years have been difficult, and I don't want the next ten to be like that."

Soo-Ja heard the sound of voices vibrating through the walls from the room next door. For a moment, she worried that others might hear them, too, and she found herself walking farther into the room, standing closer to Yul. "Are you ill?"

Yul let out a rueful laugh. "Soo-Ja, there's nobody listening in. You're with me now. And I know you." Yul walked past her, to the door, and closed it, bringing silence into the room. He then returned and stood in front of Soo-Ja. "Do you remember the first time we met? The long ride in the bus? Do you remember when I came to your art class, and we drew those paintings together? Why don't you talk to me the way you talked to me back then?"

"That might as well have happened to somebody else. It's not my life now." Soo-Ja produced a stained dishrag from her pocket, the way a gentleman might produce a silk handkerchief. "Look at this. Can you imagine me scrubbing floors back then? My body seems to have a lower center of gravity now."

To her surprise, Yul took the rag from her hands and pressed it against the back of his own hand. The gesture felt warm, tender, and she imagined how gently he'd hold her, if only he could. "Why do you think Fate keeps putting us in the same room?"

"It's not Fate. *I* came to you in Pusan, and now *you've* come to me. It's definitely not Fate. It's will."

"I've never given up hope that I could be with you."

"I love my husband," said Soo-Ja, reaching back for the rag. Yul did not return it to her immediately, and Soo-Ja had to pry it out of his hands using her own weight. In that second, their bodies felt connected, as the pressure from one pulled against the other.

"You're lying. You only stay with him because you're afraid he'll take Hana away from you. I know the divorce laws."

Soo-Ja avoided his eyes, pulling harder for the rag. "Things around here are not perfect, but I'm trying to make do with them," said Soo-Ja. She had been getting better and better over the years at keeping up a stoic facade.

"I'll leave you alone, but only if you say to me that you no longer have feelings for me."

"I no longer have feelings for you," said Soo-Ja, and she immediately felt the tears welling in her eyes. Right at that moment, Yul's fingers finally let go of the rag, and Soo-Ja found herself wrapping the harsh cotton against her knuckles. Why had he let go of it, and of her? Why had he not held on to it in the palm of his hand?

"Does this mean you forgot about me? I remember the last time we saw each other. I could swear, from the look on your face that night, you would have run away with me."

"And why didn't we, then?" asked Soo-Ja, and she felt her yearning break through the surface and gasp for air. "All right, you want me to tell you if I still—*love*—you? Is that the word you think I'm so afraid of saying? Love? I could do that. I could tell you that. But what does it do? Nothing except make us feel bad. It doesn't change anything."

"Is that how you feel?"

"I'm a married woman. I'm not free to tell you how I feel." It was true, but only because she feared that once she started, she would not be able to stop. "Your wife is just across the hall."

"I know. But I thought I'd forget you with time, and I haven't. When I was younger, I thought there was only room for one person at a time in your heart. And each time you met someone new, you evicted the one who was there before. But now I realize that there are multiple rooms, and your old love doesn't leave. It sits there, waiting."

It occurred to Soo-Ja that if she gave him permission, he'd kiss her right then and there. But she realized that all along, what she really wanted wasn't to have him in the present—how could she, married woman that she was, married man that he was—but to rewrite the past, have him go back in time and create a version that allowed them to kiss. To be able to kiss him did not seem to take much—a step forward, the angling of her face. But, in fact, it required rearranging the molecules of every interaction they had ever had, from the very first day that they met.

"Forget me, Yul. As long as you're here, you're just a guest."

How could I have chosen Min over you? Soo-Ja asked herself, facing the past in the cold light of the present. *I made a terrible mistake.*

When Soo-Ja could no longer remain steady, she left the room. As she emerged, she was thankful that no one was out in the hallway. Otherwise, they would have seen her burst into tears, her breathing sharp and difficult, and they might have wondered what had just happened to her.

chapter twelve

Over the next few days, Soo-Ja began to pick up more and more details about Eun-Mee. She learned that in the course of her life, Eun-Mee had had several brushes with fame. The first time, when Eun-Mee was ten years old, she had participated in the ribbon-cutting ceremony for the reopening of the Namdaemun Market after the war. The dress she wore—a pink velvet one-piece with puffed-up shoulders and ruffled hemming—became something of a sensation once it appeared on a photo on the front page of the *Chosun Ilbo*, with little girls from as far away as Pyongyang copying that style.

Happy with the publicity, the organizers of the market offered Eun-Mee a gift—a glass duck. Eun-Mee, however, turned it down and asked for something else instead. They bated their breaths, hoping it wouldn't be cash. Instead, Eun-Mee asked that she be given free rein to come in and out of every single one of the shops and stalls in the market, and to let it be known that she was "Queen of Namdaemun Market." For a year, after school, Eun-Mee wandered around the maze of open-air alleyways. She'd go into stores to chat with the owners and play board games, knowing they could not kick her out. However busy they were, they had to stop what they were doing and entertain her.

In high school, Soo-Ja also learned, Eun-Mee had participated in several beauty-pageant contests and had tried out for Miss Seoul. At one of the early rounds, during a photo session—a rather modest one, Eun-Mee complained, taken with an old, antiquated Brownie box camera—one of the contestants had accidentally tripped and stepped forward in one of the shots. When the photo was later released, Eun-Mee had expected the woman to look disastrous and clumsy, but instead she had managed to look beautiful and to stand out, being a foot or so in front of the group.

At the next photo shoot, for a promotion connected to the renaming of the Shinsegae Department Store, Eun-Mee decided to "accidentally" trip and step forward in every one of the shots. When Eun-Mee saw that the photographer's flash was about to come on, she'd propel herself forward, as if she were so excited, she couldn't just wait for the film to come capture her—she had to meet it halfway.

In the final competition, Eun-Mee came in seventh. The disappointment over that ranking, however, did not last very long. After all, Eun-Mee was the kind of person who'd win even when she lost, and what she had won was something precious indeed—the interest of her future husband.

Because Eun-Mee spent so much time in the hallway, it was probably no accident that she spotted Soo-Ja one evening as Soo-Ja came out of her room wearing a dress and makeup. Soo-Ja and Hana were going to a *gye* meeting. When Eun-Mee found out about this, she invited herself to come along.

"I love gye! I was wondering how I could join one in Seoul, and I suppose I have the answer right in front of my face!" said Eun-Mee.

"I'm not sure if that's such a good idea, I don't think my gye is accepting any new members," said Soo-Ja, trying to make her way past her.

"If they're not, I'm sure they'd make an exception for a doctor's wife," said Eun-Mee, smiling. "Just give me one second and I'll put a dress on. Don't you dare leave without me!"

"What about your husband?" Soo-Ja asked, making another attempt at discouraging her.

"Oh, he's working late. We'll probably be back before he is," said Eun-Mee, disappearing into her room.

Once a month, the women members of Soo-Ja's gye gathered for an informal dinner at a restaurant. While they ate the *sundubu* and *japchae* and *seolleongtang* in the banquet-hall-style room, at long, continuous tables set up like picnic benches, lit by white and red Chinese lamps, a volunteer went around each table and collected dues from all of them. By the evening's end, one of the members of the gye would go home with all the money collected. The next month, somebody else took home the money.

Everyone contributed to the pot religiously, and you did not dare miss a payment, otherwise you'd never be eligible to be a recipient. There was, of course, the risk that somebody who'd been a receiver in an earlier round might disappear, or refuse to continue contributing (in which case they'd say the gye was "broken"), but those cases were rare, and people did in fact pay back their loans. For that's what they were—loans. You couldn't rely on banks, with their excessive collateral requirements and high interest rates, but you could rely on your friends and other members of the gye.

It was a more formal extension of a common practice in extended families—Soo-Ja's own relatives were always giving money to one another, to help cousins start businesses, to finance a niece's education, to pay for weddings and funerals. You gave, yes, but you always got back, and some of Soo-Ja's aunts even kept notebooks, recording how much they had received and from whom, so they'd know who deserved their loyalty and help later on. The gye simply expanded this spirit of helping one another on a larger scale, following the notion that money should always be flowing, and friends should help other friends.

When they arrived at the restaurant, Eun-Mee had Soo-Ja introduce her to everyone she knew, and Soo-Ja discovered the first of Eun-Mee's many magical charms: the ability to make strangers instantaneously fond of her. In a matter of seconds, Eun-Mee became closer friends with some of these women than Soo-Ja had been for years. Initially, Soo-Ja was a bit annoyed by this. But then the feeling was replaced by a sense of relief, as she realized she would not have to spend the entire evening by her side. She was sure Eun-Mee did not know about the history between her and Yul, but Soo-Ja still felt awkward on her end.

So Soo-Ja ate her *bibimbap*, a medley of beef and vegetables mixed with hot chili paste, still cooking in the pot it was served in, while attentively watching the volunteer, an old woman whose face never shifted expressions as she collected one white envelope after another. If Soo-Ja were chosen as the gye recipient, she could take home all the money, and she'd be able to buy the land she wanted. She hoped that the members of the gye would choose her. (This was one way their gye differed from others—instead of randomly selecting winners through a random drawing, they were able to vote for someone each month, until no one was left. This meant if you were well liked and considered trustworthy, you'd probably get selected early on. If you rubbed others the wrong way, you might be dead last. At the end of the day, they chose character over chance, though Soo-Ja wasn't sure what that said about them, that they put so little stock in luck.)

Soo-Ja was waiting for the evening's business to start when she heard a roar of laughter coming from the front of the restaurant, followed by smaller chortles, like a wave's ripples. She thought she heard Eun-Mee's voice, and she turned around to see a group of women gathered in a circle. Soo-Ja could not see the source of the activity, since their backs were to her. Curious, she rose from her seat and walked in their direction, the laughter drawing her in like a siren's song.

When she reached the group, Soo-Ja peeked in among them in almost childlike excitement, as if about to enjoy a street performer. Soo-Ja smiled. These were peers; she liked them; she longed to share a laugh with friends. The circle broadened slightly, to let her in.

Indeed, it was Eun-Mee, standing near the area where everyone took their shoes off before coming into the restaurant. Eun-Mee stood there alone, as if on a stage, and held in her hands an old pair of women's shoes. She had them as far from her as possible, her arms stretched out, her fingers becoming imaginary forceps.

"Have you seen anything like this before? It's like something out of the war! Look around, everyone, we have a refugee from the North among us!" said Eun-Mee, with the timing and delivery of a comedian. Eun-Mee waved the sandals in the air for all to see—it was a sorry sight, with the straps falling off slightly, and the soles barely hanging there. They looked as if they had been patched up repeatedly, their owner insistently prolonging their life.

Soo-Ja was about to join in the laughter of the crowd when she suddenly recognized the shoes being held up. It was strange, to see them up in the air, used as a prop, instead of on her feet, but there was no doubt about it—they were Soo-Ja's own shoes. Her smile slowly dissipated as she felt the mortification rise in her body.

"We don't need to take a vote anymore, we'll just give whoever this belongs to all the money! Since clearly, she needs it more than any of us!" Eun-Mee continued, drawing another thunderstorm of laughter from the group. "I mean, have you seen anything like this? Look at this strap, it's crying out for dear life!" Eun-Mee touched it lightly, and the strap, in her hands, seemed to quiver back. "Somebody put this out of its misery!"

The crowd laughed again, and this time the roar was so heartfelt, it almost crested into applause. Eun-Mee smiled and shrugged her shoulders, prompting more chuckles from the audience. Soo-Ja looked around at the laughing faces, their glee prickling at her ears.

Eun-Mee curtsied. She had a performer's uncanny ability to draw everyone's attention to her. You could be walking through a crowd and you'd notice her. Soo-Ja thought about how at one time, she, too, had that quality; but that had been a long time ago.

She slowly retreated from the crowd. She wanted to get away before someone pointed at her, or discovered that the shoes were hers.

"What's happening over there?" asked Hana, when Soo-Ja sat down next to her. "Can I go look?"

"No. It's nothing," said Soo-Ja, digging into her plate with her fork, and trying to maintain her composure. "I wish they'd put more chili pepper paste in my bibimbap. I'm not sure it's spicy enough."

There was about an hour or so delay from the start of the meal to the end, at which point everyone would write their choices down on tiny pieces of marked paper. About halfway through the meal, Soo-Ja noticed that Eun-Mee, who had chosen not to sit with them, had changed seats again and gone to eat at a different table from the one she started at.

Eun-Mee fit into the restaurant about as well as a mermaid, with her long, curve-hugging white gown, much more expensive than anything the other women were wearing. She also carried a fan with her, decorated with the peony rose, one of the three flowers of ambition. Eun-Mee fluttered the fan in front of her, concealing half her face, and she seemed to make a point of avoiding women her own age, talking only to older members of the gye, which was what she was doing right now, sitting next to a grandmother.

Soo-Ja turned to Hana and, speaking quietly so as not to attract the attention of the other two families near them at their table, told her to walk by Eun-Mee and see if she could find out what she was doing. A little too theatrically for Soo-Ja's taste, Hana cleared her throat, put down her chopsticks, and leaned forward, asking the woman seated across from her if she knew where the bathroom was.

Soo-Ja watched as Hana lingered next to Eun-Mee's table, with her back to its occupants. Hana positioned her body so that she was right behind Eun-Mee and the other women didn't notice her. She remained in her spot for a few minutes, until she drew the attention of one of the waitresses, who told her to return to her seat.

Soo-Ja turned to her expectantly, but Hana said nothing as she sat down, shaking her head. According to Hana, Eun-Mee was simply socializing. They continued their meal in silence, with Soo-Ja feeling foolish that she had asked Hana to spy on Eun-Mee. But then, a few minutes later, as a waitress began to go from table to table serving small plates of sliced tangerines, Soo-Ja saw Eun-Mee get up once again, and instead of heading back to her original table, she went to yet another one, her third of the night, where she sat next to a senile-looking old woman, presumably to enjoy dessert with her. Soo-Ja was about to ask Hana to go stand near her again when, much to her surprise, Hana leapt out of her chair without her prompting, again feigning a need to go to the bathroom.

"It looks like I've had too much tea. That *boricha* goes right through your system, doesn't it?"

Soo-Ja followed with her eyes as Hana walked toward Eun-Mee's new table, not too close lest she be noticed. Hana did not know what to do with her own body, and she stood there awkwardly at first, until a friendly ajumma emerged, and Hana engaged her in brief conversation. After a few minutes, the ajumma finally disengaged herself and Hana had no choice but to return. This time, however, Eun-Mee noticed her, and she shot her a strained smile, aggressively flaring her nostrils. Hana stared back at her with uncharacteristic fear, as if confronted with Medusa. As Hana almost ran back to her table, Soo-Ja could see Eun-Mee watching her, too, her lips shaped into a disdainful frown.

When Hana sat down, Soo-Ja took advantage of the fact that the woman across from them had the entire table engrossed in a tirade of hers—about how the widows of Cheju Island had no business diving for shellfish naked—and she asked her what she had overheard.

"I couldn't really tell at first," whispered Hana, "but it sounded to me like Eun-Mee offered Yoon-Shin Kang, the pharmacist's mother, to put her name down next month in the ballot if she put *her* name down this month."

"Some kind of backroom deal—that's exactly what I thought she was doing," Soo-Ja whispered back.

"I'm a little confused, though. I heard her offer Ae-Rin Bae, the bathhouse manager, the exact same thing. She told her if she put her name down in the ballot this month, she'd do the same for her next month. How can she do that if she's going to put down the pharmacist's mother's name?"

So she had been going from table to table making deals with different women, and keeping each of them in the dark about the others! Soo-Ja tensed up. The voting would begin in less than fifteen minutes. There was no time to do anything about this. Eun-Mee was going to take home the pot.

"I wouldn't be surprised if she disappears next month and breaks the gye," Soo-Ja said.

"What happens if the gye breaks?"

"Then all the money we've put into it over the past year is gone, pfft."

"Say something," said Hana. "Do something!"

Soo-Ja thought about her options. She could go speak to Hyung-Soon Oh, the organizer of the gye, and tell her what Eun-Mee was doing. But the thing was, she didn't want to be a tattletale, and, more practically, if Hyung-Soon confronted Eun-Mee and the others, she knew they would all deny it and say it was just a slanderous rumor. Soo-Ja could go to each of them separately and reveal Eun-Mee's plans, but there was no guarantee they'd believe her. Eun-Mee struck her as a smart improviser who could charm her way out of any situation. Finally, Soo-Ja could speak to Eun-Mee directly, and demand that she withdraw from the gye, or else she'd expose her. Would she believe her bluff?

Soo-Ja did not have a chance to make a decision, as out of nowhere Eun-Mee herself appeared in front of her. She pulled up a chair and sat next to her. She was fuming, her face pinched like a small ball, her gaze burning into Soo-Ja's skin. She placed her hand on top of hers, like a lover, and she spoke with the clarity of stones being dropped into a river.

"Awfully sneaky of you to send your daughter to spy on me," said Eun-Mee.

Hana pretended not to hear her, though she could not help occasionally shooting daggers at Eun-Mee with her eyes.

"I don't know what you're talking about," said Soo-Ja.

"What did she tell you, Soo-Ja?" asked Eun-Mee, with a sharp edge in her voice. "What did she hear?"

"You already know the answer to that, or you wouldn't have come here to speak to me," Soo-Ja replied, nonchalant.

"I'm oversensitive, that's all, that your daughter—with her adorable ears—may have misunderstood what I said to Mrs. Kang. I simply wished my sincerest hopes that she should be blessed soon with the gye. She's very deserving, you know."

"Not as deserving as quite a few other people here," Soo-Ja said, unswayed by Eun-Mee's charm. "Like the woman whose shoes you were mocking earlier. Or Bog-yan Lim, whose tailor shop caught fire last month when her clerk left some candles unattended. If I don't get the money myself, I'm hoping she will." Soo-Ja pointed discreetly at Mrs. Lim, a serious-looking woman with long, permed hair sitting a few tables away. Mrs. Lim had not told anyone about the fire; Soo-Ja was one of the few people who knew.

Eun-Mee rolled her eyes. "She doesn't dress very well for a tailor. I can't imagine she has that many clients." Then, Eun-Mee fixed her gaze upon Soo-Ja again, speaking barely above a whisper: "Don't even think of saying *anything* about this to anyone, especially my husband. If you have to gossip, then do it *after* they count all the votes and hand out the money."

Soo-Ja moved her hand away from hers and sat with her back very straight. Eun-Mee, however, remained leaning forward toward her awkwardly, as if she were frozen in the middle of a bow.

"Eun-Mee, you're going to go to Mrs. Oh and tell her you're withdrawing yourself for consideration this month. And then next month, you'll compete fair and square, without making any deals."

Eun-Mee stifled a laugh. "Hana's mother, you'll never get anywhere with that mentality. Half the room is making deals, and the other half are suckers."

This made Soo-Ja snap. Was *she* one of the suckers?

"This is your first time at our gye! How can you expect to win the pot? Why don't you just sit and watch for the first few meetings?"

"That's not my style. I like to make a big first impression, and grab everyone's attention all at once," cooed Eun-Mee.

"And why do you even want the money? Your husband makes a lot, I'm sure, as a doctor."

Eun-Mee sighed. "He does make a lot of money, but he likes to spend it on practical things, like furniture and appliances." To Soo-Ja, Eun-Mee looked about as practical as a peacock. Even her way of speaking seemed luxuriant, the cadences dripping lazily, stretching out like spoonfuls of syrup.

"He also buys you nice clothes and jewelry," said Soo-Ja. "I can't think there's much he'd deny you."

"But a woman likes to have her own money," said Eun-Mee, her eyes betraying a weariness Soo-Ja hadn't detected before. "And I'm not cut out to work part-time as a perfume clerk or a secretary. In fact, I find women who work outside the home to be rather sad spirits." Eun-Mee quickly added, "No offense intended."

"None taken," said Soo-Ja.

"The thing is, I need money and I need it desperately. I need money more than you do. Or anyone else in this room." Eun-Mee stared straight ahead, as if hypnotized.

"Why is that?"

"I owe money. A lot of it," said Eun-Mee. She did not sound like herself, and for a moment, Soo-Ja felt sorry for her. "I joined a women's savings club in Pusan, and I, like always, enjoyed taking charge. I promptly became the leader—well, actually, I staged a bit of a coup d'état. I mean, if that's good enough for President Park, then it's good enough for me—and in my role as leader, I decided on the first investment for us: imported Western goods, mostly cosmetics and perfumes from France. Alas, it turned out to be a scam, and I lost everyone's money. The worst part is that a lot of the wives and their husbands were patients of Yul's, and things became very awkward for him. I was so embarrassed!" Eun-Mee looked at Soo-Ja as if they were old confidantes, holding nothing back. She reached for Soo-Ja's hands again, and this time Soo-Ja let her. "That's why I insisted that we move to Seoul, even though our friends and our lives, really, are back in Pusan. In fact, I was surprised when Yul so readily agreed to move here. I thought he'd fight me on this. He's so fond of the families he works with in Pusan."

Soo-Ja bit her lower lip, thinking of her name and phone number on Yul's desk. She urged Eun-Mee to go on, though she realized pretty quickly Eun-Mee did not need much prompting to tell her stories.

"So, if I can get money, I can pay back all the other wives, and show my face around Pusan again." Eun-Mee smiled, glowing, and Soo-Ja understood why Yul had fallen in love with her: Eun-Mee had the gaiety of a child, and, like a child, she could make your anger for her turn into pity, or even affection, in the flash of a second. Soo-Ja tried to hate her, but she couldn't. Eun-Mee kept you too busy trying to protect her from herself.

"Eun-Mee, I'm sure it wouldn't take very long for your husband to earn the money to pay them back," Soo-Ja said to her, trying to be re-assuring. "And even if you never did, an investment is an investment. Those women can't be mad at you for losing their money. There's always a risk. It's not your fault; you didn't know you were dealing with con art-ists."

Eun-Mee laughed again. "Hana's mother, I can tell we're going to be friends, since you're so naive, and I find you amusing. Of course I knew the investment was shady. How else did I expect it to return double the amount? I just wasn't counting on the man to run off with all that cash. Hana's mother, this is a new society. Everyone looks for an angle, cuts a corner here, gives out a bribe there—"

"Of course I've heard that before, but I don't believe it," said Soo-Ja sharply, letting go of Eun-Mee's hands. Their sudden, instantaneous friendship dissipated as quickly as it had materialized.

"I'll tell you what, if I get the pot today, I'll share some of it with you—"

"Eun-Mee!" Soo-Ja cut her off. "It's like a compulsion. You just can't stop making deals, can you?"

But it was too late. Soo-Ja knew already that she wouldn't expose Eun-Mee. As sorry as she felt for Mrs. Kang and Mrs. Bae, Soo-Ja couldn't afford to draw too much attention to Eun-Mee, who had come as her guest. Everyone associated her with Soo-Ja at this point. A vote against Eun-Mee would never be a vote *for* Soo-Ja. And there was the potential humiliation for Yul, who had just arrived in Seoul and would need new patients. If people heard of his wife's behavior, it would make him look bad. Seoul, for all its size, could sometimes feel like a small community, and Soo-Ja couldn't risk tainting people's first impressions of his name.

Still, Soo-Ja was no saint, and for a moment she felt the urge to tell everyone about Eun-Mee's deeds, just for the sake of shaming her. For a second she fantasized leaving an anonymous note under Yul's door:

"Know your wife!" Soo-Ja pictured Yul throwing Eun-Mee out, his right arm stretched out, pointing to the door. Eun-Mee, her coat on, her bags under her arms, walking to the exit. But the fantasy died as quickly as it arose. The only thing that lasted was a smile on her face, which Eun-Mee must have seen and misread, for she hugged Soo-Ja tightly and whispered, "So we *are* sisters, after all! Thank you, eonni."

Soo-Ja had gained her trust. She didn't mean to win it. Eun-Mee's trust seemed superfluous, or even, frankly, disposable, and if it were a gift, she'd have returned it unopened—an empty box full of air.

In the end, neither of the women won. Nobody knew Eun-Mee well enough to vote for her, and she received only three votes. Soo-Ja, much to her surprise, received five (which did not include her own—she thought it would be tacky to vote for herself). The person who won the pot, with twenty votes, was the person she had voted for—Mrs. Lim, the woman whose shop had caught fire. Mrs. Lim immediately began weeping and praying, in gratitude, as seemingly countless hands touched her to congratulate her.

Soo-Ja did not feel bad that she did not get the money; she was too busy enjoying the fact that Eun-Mee hadn't, either. If it seemed petty on her part, fine, thought Soo-Ja, but this was the woman Yul had married, and in that choice lay a thousand questions. For Soo-Ja, Eun-Mee was as fascinating as some old religion, and that was the reason she hadn't exposed Eun-Mee: it was to keep her own self cloaked, as she lay exploring her love's truth, in this stranger's face.

chapter thirteen

The next day, Soo-Ja could not concentrate at work. It hit her then that she hadn't won the money at the gye, and was still 300,000 *won* short of what she needed to invest in the land. To make matters worse, construction workers had begun work across the street on a new building. It was to be a new electronics shopping mart—the first of its kind—and for the next few months, it would mean constant dust, drilling, and hammering.

She tried to speak to Min about her worries, but he waved her away as he went out to a bar for some lunch and *sul.* She knew he was still terrified at the idea of investing, though she wasn't sure which outcome scared him more: losing the money or doubling it.

Distracted, Soo-Ja did not notice that her most recent group of guests, teenage girls from Inchon, had managed to evade their hotel bills. They were here to see a pop concert by the Pearl Sisters, who were not twins but always wore the exact same matching hairstyle and clothing on their shows and album covers—a recipe for disaster, in Soo-Ja's opinion. Their fans were like a cult, dressing like they did, memorizing their songs, and following them on their tours.

The girls—three squeezed in one room, two in another—had checked in two nights earlier, but showed no intention of paying. So when Soo-Ja saw them emerge that afternoon (to go to lunch, she overheard them say, though it was two o'clock already, and they still looked sleepy) she told them they had to take care of their bills. They looked at her annoyed and one of them—a seventeen-year-old wearing a psychedelic shirt, a short skirt, and long boots—began to attack Soo-Ja.

"You need to coordinate better with the manager! He already told us we didn't have to pay," the girl snapped. She was the one who had signed for the room, and Soo-Ja remembered her name as Nami.

"*I'm* the manager, and I didn't tell you my rooms were free," said Soo-Ja.

"You're not the manager, you're just the attendant at the front desk. We spoke to Mr. Lee, the handsome guy with the little girl, Hana, is that her name?" Nami continued.

Min, thought Soo-Ja, *what did you tell them?*

One of the girl's friends, a round-faced bulldog with giant fake eyelashes and harsh bangs, piped in, thrusting her face in between them like a child playing peekaboo: "We told him we didn't have the money, and he said don't worry about it! He has a handsome smile, that man! It's good to know there are still good people out there like him."

"We're just here to have fun," said Nami, looking at Soo-Ja incredulously. "Now be a good sport and follow the boss's orders."

Before Soo-Ja could reply, the girls swiftly disappeared out the door, giggling. But they were not the ones Soo-Ja was really mad at. She picked up the phone and called the sul-jib Min always went to. The bar manager, who knew her by now, had no trouble finding Min. Soo-Ja soon had him on the other end of the line.

"Why are you calling me here?" Min asked.

"Did you tell a group of teenage girls yesterday that they could skip on their bills?" Soo-Ja could tell she sounded like a machine gun, the words snapping out rat-tat-tat-tat.

"They're just children, Soo-Ja, and they don't have the money. What are we going to do, send them to jail?" asked Min.

Soo-Ja pictured him looking around the half-empty bar, eager to return to his leatherette booth. "You had no right to do that! I'm trying very hard to earn money here, and at the same time, here you are, giving rooms away. The least you could do is ask me before doing that."

Min seemed offended. "Ask my wife for permission? That's a new low you want me to go to, isn't it?"

"I hope it made you feel good, letting them stay without paying, because that good *gibun* cost us three hundred *won*."

"I'm a very generous man," he said, and his voice sounded to Soo-Ja a bit distant, as if he had moved his head away from the receiver and said this to someone else, at the bar.

"Yes, that's what these girls think. You are so nice to them, giving them things for free. I don't see you offering any generosity or niceness toward me, though. I could use your help around here."

"A hotel is woman's work. And what's so hard about standing around, saying 'Welcome to the Hotel Seine'?"

Soo-Ja sensed a bit of cruelty in his voice that had not been there in a while, but she bit her tongue. "I have to go now, there's something I need to do before the girls return."

Soo-Ja bade Min good-bye and hung up the phone. She moved fast, lest she change her mind. She rushed to the girls' rooms and, after glancing down the hallway for a moment, she went inside.

Clothes were strewn everywhere, creating spots of bright pink, orange, and green on the floor. Their silver-hued suitcases, featuring labels like Chanel and Hermès, looked like impressive knock-offs, with shiny fasteners and hard rough black coating. On their beds sat all kinds of expensive Pearl Sisters–related paraphernalia, including LP records still in the original wrapping, smelling like freshly minted vinyl. Soo-Ja glanced at the price tags and saw that they all added up to a pretty penny; if they hadn't spent so much money on souvenirs, they could easily have paid for the rooms.

Soo-Ja opened their bags and began stuffing them with their belongings. When all the suitcases were full, she dragged them to her office and locked them in there. She did notice that the bags looked a bit lonely and sad, left on their own in the cold, blue room, but she stayed strong and told herself that if the girls really valued their things, they'd pay up and *earn* the return of their precious records and clothes.

When Soo-Ja finally came out of the alcove she used as an office, she saw there was someone at the front desk, and though she did not recognize him at first, she realized it was a guest who had checked in earlier that day. Mr. Shim? Or was it Mr. Yoo? And even though it was not even five in the afternoon, the man was clearly drunk. He had a bottle of *maegju* in one hand, and with the other he was undoing his tie. Soo-Ja couldn't tell how drunk he was, as men in Seoul often tended to exaggerate their drunkenness.

They were like drunks in movies, stumbling around, heads spinning, eyes rolling to the back of their heads. Most people in real life, when they were drunk, didn't actually look or act like that (Soo-Ja herself, on the few occasions she drank with her friends, would never have trouble standing up; she'd simply glow, red and happy, enjoying the buzz in her body). But men in Seoul *did* in fact do all those things you saw on-screen, not because their tolerance was any less, but because they enjoyed putting on a show—they were the real *kiesang* geisha girls, singing, dancing, and making spectacles of themselves.

Soo-Ja came back to her station behind the counter and gave Mr. Shim a discouraging look, hoping that he'd go up to his room. Mr. Shim was a short, obese man in his early forties, wearing a gray office shirt and a black blazer with small white dots. He had a large receding hairline, and combed his few hairs to the front, giving the impression that a skinned cat had landed on his head. But the thing she noticed the most was that he could not stop smiling a certain maniacal smile, like someone who had read that people liked to be smiled at, and thus ordered one and slapped it on his face like a prosthesis.

"You're a very pretty agassi," he said, calling her miss and staring at her from the other side of the counter.

"It's not agassi, it's ajumma. I'm a married woman," Soo-Ja sharply replied.

"That can't be the truth. If you had a husband, he wouldn't let you work as a hotel hostess, and let men steal looks at you all day." He frowned at her sternly, in an almost professorial way, as if he had caught her in a lie.

"Don't call me hostess," said Soo-Ja, scowling at him. "I prefer the French term *concierge*, which can refer to either a man or a woman."

"I was right the first time then, agassi, you're a single girl, which means you can go on a date with me."

"Did you see the twelve-year-old girl who was here when you checked in? She is my daughter."

"I don't see her now. And I don't see a husband, either. Is he hiding under the table?" Mr. Shim asked, mocking her. "Should I close my eyes for a second, while you make him magically appear?" He was leaning on the counter now, his head only inches away from her.

"Please go back to your room," said Soo-Ja, very seriously.

"I'll go back, but only if you pour me some maegju first," said Mr. Shim, pointing to the bottle of beer he had placed on the counter.

"This is not a bar, and I'm not a barmaid. I can't pour you a drink."

"Be nice, pour me a drink," he repeated, pointing to the tea set she kept at the end of the counter for her guests. There were three empty celadon cups there, as well as an empty kettle.

"Mr. Shim, why don't you go back to the sul-jib you came from?"

Mr. Shim walked to the end of the counter and picked up the tea set, bringing it closer to them. He placed two cups in front of her, as well as the beer bottle. He pointed at it and waited for her to pour him the drink. When he saw that she would not, he suddenly raised his hand and threw the teacups onto the ground, smashing them into pieces. Soo-Ja was stunned at how quickly his flirtation had turned to anger.

Soo-Ja said nothing at first, startled by the suddenness of his gesture. Her mouth felt dry, ashen, barely able to mouth the words "Go back to your room." Mr. Shim ignored her and remained standing there. Feeling trapped, and wanting to get out from behind the counter, Soo-Ja moved to the left, but Mr. Shim followed suit. Soo-Ja then moved to the right, and Mr. Shim blocked her way once again.

"Let me go," said Soo-Ja.

"All right, I will."

Soo-Ja watched as Mr. Shim stepped back, letting her pass. But when she was about to make her way out, Mr. Shim suddenly ran to the other side of the front desk area and knocked down an oak chair and a plant. Soo-Ja stood back, shocked to see her place of work—her own home, in fact—being vandalized in front of her eyes. She expected some guests to appear, brought out by the noise, but no one did, and she realized, for one very long, sharp moment, that she was all alone with him in the front area, and that the seconds ahead could stretch into minutes. She could feel her heart beating fast, alarms ringing through her body. She needed to get out. But as soon as she made her way to the front door, Mr. Shim rushed toward her and began to grab her, reaching for her arm and pulling at her clothes. Soo-Ja started to yell for help.

A few seconds later, a guest—a white-haired woman wearing a robe—appeared and tried to help Soo-Ja. Mr. Shim pushed her away, and the woman fell to the floor. As soon as she managed with difficulty to get up, the woman rushed to the back and started knocking on people's doors.

Soo-Ja struggled to keep her clothes on, as Mr. Shim tried to overpower her. "Help me!" Soo-Ja yelled. "Help me!"

A male guest rushed out—a thin reed of a man dressed in a white undershirt and nighttime long johns. He tried to come to Soo-Ja's aid, but Mr. Shim lunged drunkenly at him, forcing him to step back. The man appeared afraid of getting hit, and couldn't seem to figure out how to stop Mr. Shim.

"Let go of me!" Soo-Ja yelled when Mr. Shim ripped her shirt, revealing the strap of her white bra underneath. Her hand flew over her exposed shoulder, and she held her arms crossed in front of her chest. Soo-Ja felt the tears form in her eyes.

Suddenly, just as she had given up hope that anyone would be able to help, Soo-Ja felt Mr. Shim being yanked away from her, his body pulled outward as though by powerful suction. She stood confused for a second, until she realized someone had grabbed Mr. Shim and thrown him to the floor. When Soo-Ja looked again she realized it was Yul, still wearing his doctor's green scrubs. Yul started punching Mr. Shim until blood gushed out of the man's face. When Mr. Shim tried to get up, Yul lifted him with his hands and knocked him against the wall.

Yul began yelling at him: "*I-sae-kki! I-sae-kki!* You goddamn son of a bitch!"

As Yul kept punching Mr. Shim, his scrubs became stained with red, and he looked as if he had just emerged from surgery. Mr. Shim kept

spitting blood, as Yul hit his face over and over again. Soo-Ja heard the
gasps from the guests watching. Knowing that she had to do something,
Soo-Ja tried to stop Yul. "Let go of him, Yul. You're killing him!" she
yelled.

Yul grabbed Mr. Shim and tossed him against the opposite wall.
Shim's body made a loud thud and began to slide down toward the floor.
Yul reached for him and pulled him up, and held his body in place, as he
punched him in the stomach and ribs. Shim spat more and more blood.

"Yul, please stop. Let him go!" Soo-Ja pleaded.

Yul's strength seemed almost supernatural. She had never seen it before—the power of his fists—and she wondered if he had kept his anger
hidden, buried beneath hard soil until it could no longer be held down,
finally breaking through as an earthquake.

Knowing she had to act, Soo-Ja pulled Yul away, grabbing him from
behind, a strange kind of hug. His body felt heavy but warm against hers,
and it came to her easily, glued to her, letting her pull him away from
the bloody man, who fell to the ground. Soo-Ja saw that thankfully, Mr.
Shim was still breathing.

Soo-Ja wondered how closely they had gotten to beating him to
death. As she held Yul, her face against his back, her arms clutching
his, she was struck by the realization that this was the first time she had
touched him in years. Both of them breathed heavily. Soo-Ja feared that
she would never have a chance to talk to him about what had just happened, and certainly not get to touch him as she wanted to but in the
middle of this mess—a bloodied man screaming obscenities on the floor,
a crowd looking on in both horror and approval—she was able to whisper
quietly, in Yul's ear (nobody saw it, she was still behind him), "Thank
you." In response, he discreetly squeezed her hand.

Mr. Shim rose slowly, his clothes covered in his own blood. Then,
when he was completely up, he caught Yul's face staring angrily back at
him and, after a second of suspense, Mr. Shim suddenly ran out of the
hotel, each leg practically knocking the other out of the way, arms flail-
ing in disarray.

With Mr. Shim finally gone, and the door slamming behind him,

Soo-Ja let out a sigh of relief. Her eyes took in the front desk area—pieces of glass littered the floor, and soil from the fallen plants had spread everywhere. Next to her, Yul looked like a cracked boulder.

Soo-Ja waited outside the bathroom while Yul dressed his wounds. The hotel was still fairly empty at this time, and she had to turn away only one guest, directing him to the other lavatory, at the end of the hallway. Yul had left the door slightly ajar, so they could talk. Anyone watching them would just think of her as the hotel manager and him as the guest she was helping recover from the earlier fight. But when they spoke, in the cautiousness of their words, they spoke as lovers.

"I pictured your husband when I was hitting him," said Yul. He had his back to her, but she could see his reflection on the wall mirror as she stood just outside the door. He had taken his scrubs and his shirt off, and she could see some marks on his body. His physique was not as muscular as it had been in his younger years, though he still had a well-defined chest and strong arms. There was a certain tiredness to his body that evoked in her a feeling of warmth.

"I wondered where the anger came from." She realized then that he could see her, too, reflected in the mirror. There they resided, side by side, within the cut glass frame: he in his corner, she in hers, only inches apart. She watched as Yul reached into the first aid kit laid open on the sink. He dabbed a cotton swab into alcohol and began to clean off the blood. He then tore up the strips of gauze and the white tape expertly, moving as swiftly as a man getting dressed in the morning. His knuckles were soon covered with small patches of gauze.

"You shouldn't be doing this kind of work, Soo-Ja," said Yul.

"The money's not bad. The owner of the hotel pays me above market rate."

"Why isn't your husband here? Dealing with drunks is better suited for a man than a woman."

"Min wouldn't be good at the front desk. He'd be too afraid to charge people."

"No. I mean it. Seriously. How can your husband let you work here? Where is he? Why isn't he here?"

"It's not always this bad," said Soo-Ja, hoping to sound convincing.

"You could still go to diplomat school. Put Min in charge of things. Think of yourself for a change."

"Yul, that was more than ten years ago. I can't tell Thailand from Timbuktu anymore. And I kind of like hearing people speaking Korean around me, instead of, say, Swahili."

"You could still do it. A lot of people start careers in their thirties."

"Well, that's part of the reason. Women diplomats are common now. There's nothing special about it. If I can't be the first Korean woman diplomat, then I'd like to be the first something else. That's why I've been taking astronaut lessons," said Soo-Ja, smiling.

"You want to go to the moon?" asked Yul, smiling back.

"No, but sometimes I want to send Min to the moon," said Soo-Ja, with a straight face.

Yul smiled at her again. "Promise me you'll find something else. Anything. Promise me you'll quit the hotel."

"I can't do that," said Soo-Ja.

"You cannot work here," he insisted.

"Please don't say anything to Min if you see him."

"Maybe I should introduce him to my wife. Maybe they will like each other and go off together," Yul said ruefully.

Soo-Ja could not tell if he was joking or not. "Don't say things like that. It's not fair to them."

"You've met my wife. Is she anything like me?"

"Why did you marry her, then?"

"I was getting old," said Yul, as he threw away the extra strips of gauze. "And patients find it odd when their doctor is a single man, especially when they bring their children in."

"I noticed you still don't have children."

Yul placed the gauze, the alcohol, and the scissors back in the kit. "Eun-Mee does not want any. She says children, especially babies, are selfish and mean-spirited."

"Well, they're also easily lovable and very naturally kind," said Soo-Ja, smiling.

"What about Hana? Does she remember me?" Yul closed the first aid kit, placing it on the floor. He then reached for a clean shirt hanging from a hook on the wall. He put it on quickly, and she could hear the whooshing sound he made as he thrust his arms into the sleeves.

"I've told her the story many times, but always leaving out the part you played," said Soo-Ja. "Which means I leave out the most important part."

"Well, if I were to tell the story of my life without mentioning *you*, I'd be doing the same."

Yul emerged from the bathroom and stood at the door, looking directly at Soo-Ja's face for the first time. His eyes were as beautiful as she remembered, a light kind of brown. She gazed into them, swam in that lovely shade, rested in the round of his iris.

"How can you go about your days, knowing everything that you do?" he asked very quietly, so that she had to lean forward to hear him, almost folding into him. "It's hard, you know, to find happiness with someone. That becomes more clear to me with every passing year. I can never forget the day I asked you to marry me, before your wedding. That day has been burnt into my brain, and I can recite things you said like lines from a favorite song. I can't say I haven't seen you in eight years, because I have. I'd have pictures of you in my head and I'd ration them out carefully. I wouldn't use them up; I'd savor each sweetly. Because at one point each mental picture would disappear—I'd lose it. I'd have it, I'd see you, then I'd lose it. You were elusive even in my memories." Soo-Ja felt the longing in his voice tear at her. "Am I going to have to spend my whole life running after you? I have so little left now, just that day, you standing in front of me, the ink on your fingers. I always ask myself, What if you had said yes? Our lives would have turned out so differently."

"I think of that day, too," said Soo-Ja. "You're not the only one."

"If I left my wife, would you leave your—"

"Please stop."

Soo-Ja heard a hotel guest coming their way, and she moved Yul to-ward a dark area underneath a stairwell. They stood there quietly for a moment, and she waited for the man to round the corner. When all was silence again, she turned back to look at Yul and saw his impossibly seri-ous face, and his sad, broken eyes, casting a shadow over her mouth.

"Soo-Ja . . . I love you."

Soo-Ja felt his words caress her ears, and when he brushed his lips against hers, she did not resist. For a while, they stood still, exchanging breaths. She could feel the warm air come into her mouth from his, and though they did not kiss, she could feel his tenderness surround her, and she let it fall over her skin, like a silk sheet.

In the old stories her father read to Soo-Ja as a child, once a climactic event took place, the story would stop there for a moment, only to be picked up again the next day, or sometime later. But as she grew up, Soo-Ja realized, of course, that there were no chapter breaks in real life. Something exciting may happen to you, like getting a first kiss, or win-ning a race, but it may be followed by something completely mundane, like remembering to clean the earthenware jars, or to empty the cham-ber pot, or to pick up food at the outdoor market. The day's big event was soon forgotten, and though it became relived in the retelling—all the emotions coming back in the descriptions of what happened—it soon turned into no more than an anecdote, like something that hap-pened not to you, but to somebody you knew.

That is how Soo-Ja felt when Min burst into the hotel a few hours later, his face red as a ripe mango, his body shaking with anger. His but-tons had come undone, revealing his white undershirt, and she could feel energy vibrating from him a meter away. He had just heard what happened, and, for him, it was as if it had just happened. How odd, thought Soo-Ja, that he arrived as drunk as Mr. Shim himself, and for all of his anger at Mr. Shim for trying to hurt her, her husband and Mr. Shim looked and sounded much the same right now; the only difference, it seemed, resting on the fact that she was married to one, and attacked by the other.

"Where is he?" Min asked, furious, almost shouting.

"He's gone," said Soo-Ja, after a brief pause. She knew he meant Mr. Shim, though for a fraction of a second she thought he meant Yul.

Min headed back out the door, toward the street.

"Where are you going?" Soo-Ja asked, running after him.

"To find him!" Min yelled back.

"Stop! You'll never find him. And curfew is only an hour away. I don't want you to get stopped by a policeman in your state." Soo-Ja grabbed him by his arms and pulled him back in. She could hear the loud noise from the street beckoning him through the half-opened door.

"Let me go! I'm going to find him! No son of a bitch gets away with touching my wife!"

"Get hold of yourself!" Soo-Ja said, dragging him to a chair, where he reluctantly sat. Close to him like this, she could smell the chicken and beer on his breath, mixed in with the scent of his body. She could picture the last hour of his life: running from the sul-jib to the hotel, his sandals flapping on the ground, as he bumped into people in the crowded streets, worry sculpted on his face.

"How did you know what happened?" Soo-Ja asked him.

"Miss Hong told me."

Miss Hong, the chambermaid, was a girl of twenty or so, recently arrived from the countryside. She was so shy she never looked Soo-Ja in the eye, preferring to look down at the floor and bowing slightly whenever she spoke to her. Soo-Ja had noticed Min glancing at Miss Hong a few times, and once she overheard him telling her the plot of a movie he had seen—he went to the cinema almost every afternoon—and he described it as if he had written it himself, just for her. *How charming he must seem to her!* thought Soo-Ja. An older man, her employer, the "owner" of the business.

Soo-Ja was about to ask Min how and when Miss Hong told him, when the five Pearl Sisters groupies suddenly burst into the hotel, back from their concert. Their voices came in first, singing "Nima" in unison followed by their teenage bodies falling on one another's, all arms and elbows, necks and hips, moving forward like a single multilegged spider.

Nima—my adored—who went so far away
Nima—my honey, my love—are you coming back?
The full moon rises, then sets again
The day you promised to return is long gone

All five of them wore roughly the same thing: long-sleeved black turtleneck shirts, interlocking metallic belts, knee-high boots, and sleeveless white coats with a red lining. Soo-Ja and Min watched as the girls made their way past them in the front area, keenly aware of the two of them, but without acknowledging their presence. They were not in the same room, the girls and Min and Soo-Ja; they sped by like planets. Their drunk, bouncing joy seemed to feed off the couple's stillness and gain its certainty and power from having them there to witness it. Their happiness was of an aggressive kind, meant to evoke envy. It wanted to take something away from you.

When they were gone, Soo-Ja and Min unfroze, and Min was ready to continue his demonstration of rage. Was she being too cynical? Soo-Ja wondered. Perhaps it was real. But Soo-Ja held off on her own reentry, as she was waiting for the girls to come back in a matter of seconds. Which, with the precision of clockwork, they did.

"Where is our stuff?" Nami yelled out. Nami acted like the leader of the pack, while the others stood behind her like foot soldiers awaiting orders. *Am I a fortress of some kind*, Soo-Ja asked herself, *with guests as invading armies trying to get to the other side? Is today some kind of battle day, as predetermined as the moment a comet hits the sky?*

"Yes, where's our stuff?" echoed her second-in-command, a girl with cat's-eye glasses and an almost bridgeless round nose. This gave rise to the others, too, joining in the chorus, repeating the words, their voices quickly becoming indistinguishable from one another. *Where's our stuff, what kind of a hotel is this, you are low class, and this place is low class.*

Soo-Ja felt adrenaline rush to her veins, her shoulders growing higher, her face becoming tighter and harder. She was not afraid of the girls at all—they were just teenagers, barely older than her own daughter.

"If you want your things back, you need to pay for your rooms," Soo-Ja said.

"We're not paying! The manager said we could stay for free, you dumb *gashinaya*!" Nami yelled. The curse word—*bitch*—hurt double. The word itself, of course, and the fact that it was leveled at Soo-Ja, who was so much older than they were, old enough to be a parent. You simply did not address an older person that way.

Soo-Ja tried to stay calm. "Call your parents. Or your boyfriends, if your parents don't know that you're here. Have them send you money."

When she thought later about her days working as a hotel manager, she'd remember days like this the most, being yelled at by a group of guests. But it wasn't like this all the time, nor were all the guests this bad: some left little gifts on her desk, some had children who smiled and curtsied at her, some bowed almost as low as the floor and thanked her profusely for something as small as a bar of soap.

"Are you deaf? You stupid old hag! We don't have to pay! Now give us our things back. Or we're going to call the police," Nami yelled.

From somewhere down the hallway came another voice, a man's, yelling, "What kind of a hotel is this? All this shouting all the time, keep your noise down!"

Soo-Ja looked straight into Nami's eyes and held her gaze. "You want the police? All right, let me call them. I'll have you all arrested for trying to skip on your bills." Soo-Ja picked up the rotary phone and started dialing random numbers. She could feel the girls' tough facade cracking. Soo-Ja knew how to bluff.

One time, a drunk man took a room to sleep off the alcohol, and the next morning, he told her she should let him go peacefully or else he'd beat her. At the time, another guest—a big, hulking man with almost no eyebrows—had been sitting in the front desk area waiting for his wife to come out. No Eyebrows saw her arguing with the drunk man and gave him a dirty look. Without missing a beat, Soo-Ja told the drunk man in a stage whisper that No Eyebrows was a member of the secret police and was here to protect her. He would take him to a dark room and drown him in bathwater if he didn't settle the bill. She wasn't sure if the drunk man believed her story, but he clearly did not want to take the chance, as he pulled his wallet out and handed her the money he owed her.

"Or would you rather just pay and go?" Soo-Ja paused for effect and put the receiver down. "I think you'd rather just pay and go."

The girls looked defeated and seemed to debate what to do. Meanwhile Soo-Ja wondered, Was it so offensive to them, to have to pay for things? And it wasn't just them, it was people all over the city haggling, hustling, cutting in line, and giving one another a hard time—yes, the men and women of Seoul were "on the move," making more money, but they were so unhappy, too. It was like a virus, spreading over the crowds, every face that of someone trying to take what's yours. They made up for it, sure, by being overly effusive to their own friends and loving to their family members, but life there did take its toll on their souls.

But the girls hadn't used their trump card yet. Nami finally turned to Min, as if she had just noticed him. He had been quiet this entire time. "Mr. Lee, when we told you yesterday that we didn't have money, and we were poor girls from Inchon, and we asked you, 'Couldn't you be nice to us,' didn't you smile and say, 'Don't worry about it, go play, and be children'? Isn't that exactly what you said?"

Min remained silent for a while. Soo-Ja was expecting him to explain to the girls that he had misspoken, but instead Min turned to Soo-Ja and said, "Why don't you let them have the rooms?"

That was it, thought Soo-Ja, that was their marriage right there, in those words. Min leaned closer to her, so the others couldn't hear, though obviously they could. "The thing is, I gave them my word. I already told them something else yesterday—I can't go back on it."

"These girls have the money. They're trying to pull one on us. I know the scam—teenagers with money in their hands make a bet they can get everything for free." Soo-Ja said this for them as much as for Min. And she could tell, by their nervous shifting and glancing at one another, that it was true.

"I'll cover for them. I'll make up the difference," said Min.

Why was he so eager to help them? He didn't even have the money to do so.

"I'm trying like crazy to get enough money to buy that land by the river, and you're here hoping to give it away," she said.

"We don't need to buy that land. Things are fine here," said Min.

Oh, how she wanted to shake him! No, that wasn't enough, thought Soo-Ja, how could that be enough, to just have enough to eat, when elsewhere there were cities in countries she longed to visit, different shades of blue in new skies and oceans, the sound of foreign tongues whistling by—a life where she could be a mother for more hours than she was a hotel manager.

"Is the price of the room worth my honor?" asked Min. "Is it worth going back on my word?"

"You should not have said anything to begin with," Soo-Ja said.

"I don't know of any other wives who treat their husbands like this," said Min.

"Lucky is the wife who never had to argue with her husband about money," she said.

"I want us to do well, too."

"Do you? I hear the words coming out of your mouth. But I hear something else from every other part of your body. Even now, I think, you're saying to these girls, *I tried, but she won't let me. It's not my fault, it's hers, she's the one holding me back.* When all my life I've waited for you to stand up and take charge. It is exhausting to me, all the fighting we have to do, just so you won't feel bad about yourself."

What happened after this happened so fast, Soo-Ja only fully registered it after the fact. And only later did she understand that the bottle was the same one left on the far side of the counter earlier in the day by Mr. Shim—she had been too shaken up to think to get rid of it. Later, with her eyes closed, she could slow the actions down enough to see Min reaching for the bottle and throwing it against the wall, the glass shattering and shards landing on the ground. Only later she could hear the girls shrieking and stepping back and some even putting their hands over their faces as Min was about to break the bottle. They knew what Min was about to do before she did; they had the benefit of seeing him as a stranger, while Soo-Ja's sense of him had been dulled by their being together so long. These schoolgirls knew everything about him just by looking at him; she was used to unlearning him little by little, and she realized she knew him less year after year. Later, also, she saw the clear liquid splashing on the wall, gushing forth from the bottle, spreading out from the center. It made her think of Miss Hong, the chambermaid, of how sure she was that she and Min made love in the afternoons, and how he had come inside her, and how foolish that was. Later, too, she heard the cry Min let out at that moment, an odd, guttural, anguished cry—though she didn't know if the cry came before or after the bottle exploded. She wondered how much pain you had to be in to cry out like that. But when all this happened, she did not see anything, did not think any of this. She simply felt a tug in her heart and thought, *Where is Hana? I don't want her to see this.*

As Min made his way out, Soo-Ja wondered if he was going back to some sul-jib, to the arms of a barmaid. Or maybe he was going to meet Miss Hong at some agreed-upon place, where she would comfort him.

"I don't know what time I'm going to come back," said Min, with his back to her.

"All right," said Soo-Ja, fighting back her tears. "Just one thing . . . Do whatever you want to do, with whomever you want. But don't get any diseases and give them to me later."

Min stood with his body very still, and Soo-Ja thought for a moment that he might turn around and strike her. Instead, he grabbed the front door with such fury she feared he'd yank it from the wall. He went out into the street, the door slamming shut behind him.

Soo-Ja remained still for a moment, collecting herself, and then she went inside the alcove, where she had been keeping the luggage of the Pearl Sisters fans. Without being urged, she brought their bags out, heavy as they were, and placed them in front of the group. She did this noiselessly, without saying anything. By the time she had come out, Nami had already reached into a red envelope in her purse and pulled out a series of 100-*won* bills. She placed the money on the counter—it was the exact amount; they knew exactly how much they owed. Soo-Ja saw Nami put the rest of the money back in her purse, silently, while the others took the bags and headed out of the hotel. She herself stayed in the front area for a while, and waited for the time to come to close for the day.

chapter fourteen

"Aren't the renditions beautiful? Almost like art," said Gi-yong, point-ing at the pictures on his walls. Gi-yong and Soo-Ja were in his office, in Myong-dong, a few miles from her hotel. Behind his desk, Gi-yong had put up two posters of the land south of the Hangang River: one set, marked "Now," were photos of the land as it was in the present—empty, mere fields, grass dried out by the sun and the cold winds; the other set, labeled "The Future," was an artist's drawing showing the land in the way Gi-yong expected it to be eventually—an urban landscape, with gleaming glass surfaces, high-rises, and billboards advertising Coca-Cola. "You came in the nick of time. I don't know how much longer I could have held your spot."

"Actually, I don't have the money yet. I came to ask if I could have more time," Soo-Ja said, clutching her purse, looking at Gi-yong from across his desk.

"Mrs. Choi," said Gi-yong sternly. "You know I have other investors interested in the land, with cash on hand to pay me. I'm waiting for you as a favor. I could sell the last lot tomorrow if I wanted to. Do you want to give up? Should I just go ahead and sell it to someone else?"

"No. I still have two weeks left," said Soo-Ja. "And you gave me your word. I'll get the money. I'll have it for you by the time we agreed upon."

"I don't doubt that. I have a feeling you're the kind of woman who always gets what she wants," said Gi-yong.

"Actually, I hardly ever do, but I can feel my luck changing," she said, faking a smile.

"Yes. It must be frustrating for you to have to work in that hotel. A woman with your beauty needs a man to take care of her."

Soo-Ja did not blink. "Great. I'll tell my husband that."

Gi-yong laughed. "You must think I'm a pig, don't you? I'm not, I'm just direct. Look at your hands. They're beautiful. They're not meant to scrub things. They should simply rest on top of beautiful, very expensive marble countertops. The kind I happen to have in my house."

Soo-Ja shook her head. "Mr. Im, I'm not interested in being a rich man's wife. I don't care about marble, or onyx, or any of that. That's not why I want the land."

"Really? Then what *do* you want?" asked Gi-yong, leaning forward.

Soo-Ja thought for a moment. "For one thing, I would like my daughter to have her own room, in our own house, far away from all the men who stay as guests in the hotel."

Gi-yong nodded slightly. He dropped his leer and gazed at her the way he might a sister or a mother. "I get a feeling, Mrs. Choi, that you'll get that—and more—very soon."

"Thank you, Mr. Im."

After a brief silence, both of them rose from their seats, and Gi-yong and Soo-Ja shook hands. "Two weeks?" he asked.

"Two weeks," she replied.

It seemed petty to pray for *won*, when others might be praying for food, or health, or love even, thought Soo-Ja. But every night that week she prayed, asking God to help her, and it may or may not have been a co-incidence when, on the third day, she received a phone call from her old friend Jae-Hwa, asking if she could visit her at the hotel. Soo-Ja had not seen Jae-Hwa in three years, though she often thought of the night she had helped her leave her husband. Jae-Hwa had married again— miraculously, to the owner of the electric fan factory where she worked. Soo-Ja had not gone to their wedding—she did not have days off at the hotel—but Jae-Hwa forgave her, and often sent letters talking about how Soo-Ja had saved her, and that if she had a good life now, it was only because of Soo-Ja.

Soo-Ja had no doubt that Jae-Hwa would lend her the money. In fact, she imagined them investing together, buying adjacent acres of land, calling each other with news of each year's favorable jump in value. Jae-Hwa would never say no to her. That, in essence, was Soo-Ja's mind-set before she saw her friend, and it may, in the end, have been the thing that got her in trouble.

"You look exactly the same! Not a day older than when we were in college." Jae-Hwa gasped at Soo-Ja, her arms outstretched, coming into the hotel. Soo-Ja quickly moved out from behind the counter and embraced Jae-Hwa.

"You look wonderful, too!" said Soo-Ja, directing her to the chairs in the waiting area, where they sat down.

"How old are you now?" asked Jae-Hwa. "Thirty-six? Thirty-seven?"

"Jae-Hwa, you know we're the same age—thirty-four. But thank you. You look wonderful, too." She did: Jae-Hwa had a well-rested look on her face, pleasantly plump, with that paleness that was in fashion at the time, one that indicated not a day spent laboring under the hot sun. Jae-Hwa wore a light pink suit-jacket with an embroidered white round collar, and a white cashmere hat.

"No, I'm serious. I'm witnessing a miracle. Your skin does not have any lines. You *are* the modern woman. You work hard, you cry, you suffer, but at the end of the day, you always remember to put on Pond's night cream over your face."

Soo-Ja laughed, partly because she found her funny, but partly to tell her how happy she was to be with a friend. Friends seemed like such a luxury these days, to be savored like the rare pieces of chocolate smuggled into the house during the war. "You talk about my so-called beauty more than most men I've known."

"Women always notice these things more than men. Because it

affects us more, I suppose," said Jae-Hwa, sitting close to her, her knees touching Soo-Ja's. "You'll never know what it's like to be me, you've always been the prettiest girl in the room." Jae-Hwa said this matter-of-factly, without resentment.

"You have no reason to envy me. Things turned out so well for you."

"Only because of you, Soo-Ja. If you hadn't dragged me out of that first marriage, out of that vile drunk's house, I would never have met Woo-suk."

Soo-Ja waved her gratitude away. "Don't credit me with that. You would have left him eventually."

"No, I wouldn't have," said Jae-Hwa, and Soo-Ja could tell she meant it. "I didn't have the courage. Lucky for me, Woo-suk doesn't hit me. I don't think he has the energy."

"Jae-Hwa! You're going to shock all my guests. How long are you in town for? Do you have time to go to a coffeehouse?"

Jae-Hwa gave her the broadest of grins. "Only if the time is spent wisely. Let's speak ill of other people!"

"Excellent. Let me just tell Miss Hong to watch the front desk. I'll be back in a minute."

Jae-Hwa smiled, with her lips sucked in, as if holding her breath, then began tapping her purse with her gloved fingers while Soo-Ja went looking for the chambermaid. Miss Hong was not in her station, or in any of the guest rooms, and Soo-Ja did not see her housekeeping cart anywhere. Soo-Ja then realized she had not seen her all morning, and some of the rooms had not been cleaned yet. She was about to walk to the second floor and look there, when she decided, out of some instinct she hoped would be proved wrong, to check her own room instead.

When she neared the door, Soo-Ja could hear her husband's voice. He spoke in a familiar manner, without the honorific -io at the end of each sentence, as if talking to a social inferior.

"I do a lot more around here than people think. Just today, I went to the bank to deposit some checks. And the day before, I ran some errands for Soo-Ja. She acts like it's all on her shoulders, but it's just part of her martyr act. She loves playing the victim."

Soo-Ja abruptly slid the door open. Miss Hong was there, indeed, and looked quite startled to see her. Min sat next to her on the floor; they were playing a game of baduk. It looked like Min was winning, his black pieces surrounding Miss Hong's white ones on the wooden board. Or was it the other way around, and Miss Hong's white pieces were the ones actually encroaching upon the black ones? Soo-Ja could never tell, looking at the game like this, with all the pieces next to one another. Both Min and Miss Hong looked at her like small children, sheepishly.

"Please don't keep Miss Hong away from her duties. She has better things to do than to entertain you," Soo-Ja said to Min, coolly, before turning to Miss Hong and telling her to watch the front desk in her absence.

When Soo-Ja turned the corner, into the hallway, her mask of confidence slipped, and she felt her anger rise to the surface. It was one thing to know in her head, and something else entirely to catch them together like that. She took a deep breath and fought back her tears.

So they really were sleeping together.

Soo-Ja felt humiliated. Had Min done this to get back at her? And to get back at her for what, exactly? Soo-Ja wondered. She supported him financially, gave him money for alcohol and cigarettes. She knew they didn't make love very often—Soo-Ja was terrified of getting pregnant—but if he were to have an affair, did he have to choose someone so close at hand?

As Soo-Ja walked back to the front desk, she tried to put on her best smile and pretend nothing had happened. She wanted to be fun and light, and entertain Jae-Hwa on her only day with her in years. And she didn't want Jae-Hwa to lend her the money because she felt sorry for her.

But when Soo-Ja got back to the front desk, she could feel her face drop with disappointment, and an ominous feeling came over her. Jae-Hwa was talking in an animated manner with, of all people, Eun-Mee. They were holding each other's hands like old friends, though she knew they must have just met, and their heads were thrown back in raucous laughter. When they saw Soo-Ja, they looked almost sorry to be interrupted.

"Soo-Ja, I didn't know you had such charming friends here in Seoul! The wife of a doctor!" Jae-Hwa exclaimed, impressed.

"And you, the wife of a manufacturer!" echoed back Eun-Mee, the two of them establishing an instant sorority.

"And I, the wife of—" Soo-Ja trailed off, smiling sardonically.

Jae-Hwa looked at her, a little embarrassed, while Eun-Mee seemed to be not at all sorry. Soo-Ja reached for her coat and her purse. "Are you ready, Jae-Hwa?"

"Yes. And oh, by the way, do you mind if Eun-Mee comes with us? She said she loves coffeehouses!" said Jae-Hwa.

Soo-Ja was amazed that the two could strike up a friendship so quickly; once again, she had underestimated Eun-Mee's charm. She was like a mugger with a gun, but instead of your wallet, she wanted your affection, and she could get you to drop it in front of her in seconds.

"Eun-Mee, could I please speak to you in private for a moment?" asked Soo-Ja.

Eun-Mee made buggy eyes at Jae-Hwa, to signal her puzzlement, before following Soo-Ja into her office. Once in there, Eun-Mee smiled at Soo-Ja coquettishly, like a bad student trying to avoid her teacher's dressing-down.

"This is not just a friendly outing. I have things to discuss with Jae-Hwa," said Soo-Ja, hoping to reason with her.

Eun-Mee nodded slightly. "Does this have anything to do with the rumor that you're trying to buy land from Gi-yong Im?" asked Eun-Mee innocently.

Soo-Ja tried to hide her surprise. How did Eun-Mee know about that? Had she listened in on one of her phone calls?

"Your friend doesn't seem like the kind who likes risky investments, though," Eun-Mee continued.

"How did you hear about—"

"Oh, I don't care. I'm just bored, and desperate for social activity," Eun-Mee interrupted. "I promise to take long powder-room breaks at the coffeehouse, in order to give you ample time to bore Jae-Hwa with your plans."

"Eun-Mee!" called out Soo-Ja behind her, trying to stop her. But it was useless. Eun-Mee had already sauntered out of the office and rejoined Jae-Hwa in the lobby.

Jae-Hwa rushed toward them. "Are we ready? I'm feeling left out! And you're all right with Eun-Mee coming, of course?"

Soo-Ja could tell from Jae-Hwa's eager eyes that she could not refuse, and if she tried to, Jae-Hwa would bring Eun-Mee anyway.

Soo-Ja was not much of a coffee drinker, nor was she a great fan of tea, though she drank yulmucha, boricha, and ginseng tea sometimes. She liked yulmucha for its thickness—it reminded her of soup, and when she drank it, she enjoyed its warmth tickling her throat. Boricha looked a bit like dirty water, which she sometimes suspected it was—it barely tasted like anything. But if she couldn't sleep, it was what she turned to. She drank a cup and almost dropped to the ground, so fast was its effect on her. She liked ginseng tea the most, and loved stirring the teacup, watching the thin white layers of circles appear and disappear, as if they wanted to hypnotize her.

The three women were sitting in the middle of the coffeehouse, Soo-Ja drinking tea and both Eun-Mee and Jae-Hwa drinking espressos. The coffeehouse, which had an English name, "Room and Rumours," was fairly crowded, either because of all the shoppers from the adjacent shopping mall, or because, like Soo-Ja, all of these men and women had small residences and preferred to meet guests in teahouses or coffee shops. They came for the convenience of a second home, and the establishment in fact looked like your average abode, with long-leaved Chinese happy plants in the corners, wooden-boarded walls, and practical fluorescent lights above. The only differences were the small oak chairs and tables (they did not sit on the floor there), and the sound of *trot* singers crooning their sad ballads from the jukebox.

"I wonder if they have American music in the jukebox," said Jae-Hwa. "I just got back from New York last month, and I love what they play on their radio stations." Jae-Hwa had taken her white hat and gloves off, and Soo-Ja could see she had an emerald ring on her finger. Sitting next to Jae-Hwa, Eun-Mee looked elegant in a form-fitting burgundy dress with a high, upturned collar and sleeveless arms. Soo-Ja found it too formal, but Eun-Mee did not look out of place there—people often stopped in for a drink of coffee before heading to the theater or a party. Now used to seeing her every day, Soo-Ja knew of Eun-Mee's habit of dressing up for no reason. She suspected Eun-Mee's motto might be *Look the part, and you'll win the part.* Soo-Ja wondered if she herself came across as the other two women's maid, in her simple zebra-striped housedress, and her long dark hair held back only by her ears. She could tell it bothered Eun-Mee, though, that as men walked by, it was Soo-Ja's eyes that they tried to catch the attention of.

"I love America!" proclaimed Eun-Mee. "But I don't like Americans. I love shopping in Manhattan and on Rodeo Drive. This purse is from a store there"— she pointed to her Fiorucci bag—"but the people! Especially in California. They have such pink faces, and the men look like the women, and vice versa—long hair and long eyelashes and lazy grins! I hate them!"

"Don't be shocking now. What if there was a serviceman sitting right behind you?" asked Jae-Hwa.

"I'd tell him to go home already! And to stop staring at my neck!" Eun-Mee replied.

Jae-Hwa laughed.

"I'm sure they would love to go home," Soo-Ja interjected, "but they're here to protect us. We should be thankful to them."

"They're not really here for that reason," said Eun-Mee, rolling her eyes. "Why do you think they chose to be stationed in Korea? They have an eye for us Oriental ladies! Yes. That's why they come here, and stay here. I would not be caught dead near an army base. I wouldn't be safe. They would drag me in and caress me, and tear my clothes off, and ravage me, a room full of them, taking turns at me. Those men, they haven't seen a woman—a real woman, not a prostitute—for ages. They have stored up all this passion, all this hunger—they would tug at my breasts like wolves, those blond-haired boys, mouths still wet from suckling mother's milk."

Jae-Hwa smiled at Eun-Mee. "I'm tempted now to kidnap you and leave you by the border, just to see what they'd do with you."

Eun-Mee lightly slapped Jae-Hwa's wrist, and Jae-Hwa turned her palm up and playfully squeezed Eun-Mee's hand. "Don't joke like that. I'm just explaining how I feel about the Americans, who are so different from the Europeans. Have you been to Switzerland?" Eun-Mee asked Jae-Hwa. Jae-Hwa nodded, and Eun-Mee continued. "It's like being home—all those mountains! When the snow covers up all the signs and the streets, I do not know where I am anymore. And I love that first night after the first flurry, when the sky is white and clear, and you can almost read outside. Have *you* been to Switzerland?" Eun-Mee asked Soo-Ja, as if remembering her presence suddenly.

"No, I've never been."

"Have you never been to Europe? No London, no Paris, no Istanbul?"

"No," Soo-Ja said, smiling.

"What about America? New York? Los Angeles? Boston?"

"I've never been there, either," Soo-Ja said, still smiling.

Jae-Hwa placed her hand on Soo-Ja's arm; Jae-Hwa had a warm smile on her face—the kind you reserve only for people you've known for a long time. "When we were in high school, Soo-Ja always wanted to travel. Before any of us did. She almost went to diplomat school in Seoul. She was going to be a diplomat, and travel to every country."

"And did you?" asked Eun-Mee.

"No, it didn't quite work out that way," Soo-Ja replied.

"You must not have wanted it badly enough. You probably gave up too easily," said Eun-Mee.

"Yes, that was probably it," Soo-Ja said, trying to end the conversation.

Jae-Hwa started patting her hand, as if apologizing for Eun-Mee.

"See, if you want something in life, you have to go after it!" Eun-Mee exclaimed to Soo-Ja enthusiastically. Soo-Ja nodded lightly and gave her a half smile. "You can't be tentative. That's how I got married to my husband."

Soo-Ja turned her head toward her. She had to hold herself back, resist the temptation to say, *Go on. Tell us more.*

"I'm sure he proposed on the first day he met you. A woman like you wastes no time," said Jae-Hwa.

"I knew at once when I saw him, standing with a group of men outside Pusan University Hospital," said Eun-Mee, smiling, glad to be holding her audience's attention like fish in a net. "He wore a Western suit and pleated pants, so incredibly handsome and confident, and I thought, *I would like to be your mother!*"

"Eun-Mee!" Jae-Hwa cried out, laughing.

"I want to tuck your shirt in, and feed you soup when you're sick, and help you with your homework!" said Eun-Mee, waving her arms in front of her. "That is when a woman knows she is ready to be a wife—when she decides to mother!"

"I would *strongly* disagree with that, but go on," said Jae-Hwa. Neither of them noticed Soo-Ja's silence.

"Anyway, I invited him to come to a pageant I was in and after that we began to date a little bit, going to music rooms where we'd sit side by side on the soft velvet chairs while we listened to Bach recordings. We didn't do much—he was as chaste as Chunhyang in that fairy tale, and I call it a fairy tale because who would wait so long for a lover who gives no sign of returning?"

"There must've been somebody else. Was he courting another girl at the same time?" asked Jae-Hwa, and for a second Soo-Ja turned to her nervously, wondering if she knew about her and Yul. But she couldn't; Soo-Ja had never told her.

"No, there was nobody else. Just a memory. He'd talk about this girl he met while he was in medical school in Daegu. He talked about her like a country he had been to once and always intended on going back to. He claimed she was just an acquaintance, but I knew better. Whenever we were together, I could feel her presence between us, no matter how gay or loud I became. She was always there." Eun-Mee stopped, her expression uncharacteristically distant. The entire room seemed to grow silent, out of sympathy.

It was strange, for Soo-Ja, to hear her story from Eun-Mee's perspective. She sounded so powerful, when in fact she had been so helpless all along the way. Soo-Ja would have given anything to switch roles with Eun-Mee, just so she could have Yul's body, and be able to feel his weight against her. It was nice, thought Soo-Ja, to hear that she had had Yul's thoughts, but his thoughts alone could not warm her on a cold night, could not fit into her. Now that she knew how extravagantly Eun-Mee had had his touch—every night, for years!—Soo-Ja felt starved for it.

"Did you get him to forget this other woman?" asked Jae-Hwa. She took a sip of her coffee, but put it down immediately. It had grown cold.

"Of course! It was hard, but I did it. It was like fighting the sun—he saw her everywhere."

"What do you mean?" asked Jae-Hwa.

"It's hard to explain. First love leaves a deep mark. Fortunately, I know how to medicate such wounds."

"Did you ever meet her? The woman from Daegu?" asked Jae-Hwa.

Soo-Ja turned her face away, lest her eyes confess for her.

"No, I never met her," said Eun-Mee. "For a long time I couldn't look at the face of beautiful women I walked by on the street because I would always think it was her. It drove me mad. Is that her? Or is *that* her? I felt that any day she'd come to my house in Pusan and take Yul away from me. Pick him up like a lost piece of luggage. Can you imagine what it's like to live like that? That's why in the beginning I hesitated to have children. I didn't want them to have a crazy and neurotic mother. Anyway, I forgot about her eventually, and years went by. And then one day, it was as if I had hopped on a train—things started to happen, they started moving forward fast. We had to leave Pusan suddenly. We had to leave for reasons that, well, I shall share another time—" Eun-Mee trailed off before continuing. "Anyway, I came into his office unannounced, and as soon as I came in, I saw him hide a piece of paper under a notebook on his desk. He didn't think I saw it, but I did. It was a woman's name and phone number. Now, my husband isn't the cheating kind. I figured out at once who it was, and I thought, *All right, it is time for us to go to Seoul. It is time for me to meet this woman.*"

Then Eun-Mee turned to Soo-Ja, and Soo-Ja saw it in her eyes: she knew. She knew it was her. How had she found out? What a naive question, thought Soo-Ja. Lovers always know. Eun-Mee had not said a word, keeping Soo-Ja in the dark, maybe to enjoy that competitive advantage. But how long had she waited to drop a hint, whisper in her ear: *I know who you are.* Soo-Ja felt a chill run through her body—she had seen this kind of chill described before in ghost stories; Eun-Mee's tale turned out to be just that.

Soo-Ja felt trapped in this very large, very public coffeehouse. The last three weeks, when she had practically lived with Eun-Mee, were suddenly taken away from her. Soo-Ja felt like an actor who has been reciting words from the wrong play, and realizes this only in her last line. She had been so caught up with seeing Yul again, she had not noticed Eun-Mee's barely concealed jealous glances at her. But looking back, of course the signs had been there all along. Eun-Mee's hostility and aggressiveness, which Soo-Ja had assumed to be simply part of her personality, were in fact a direct response to her. And yet, Eun-Mee had confided in her, maybe even tried not to hate Soo-Ja. Eun-Mee wanted Soo-Ja to disappear, but she wanted her there, too, in case her absence weighed heavier than her presence. Eun-Mee was as trapped as Soo-Ja, just in a different dark room.

"So what are you going to tell her when you finally see her?" Jae-Hwa asked.

"I will tell her that I will fight to protect what is mine. That she should not get any ideas. Men do not leave their wives to pursue old crushes. She should keep to her own husband, look to her own roof," said Eun-Mee, looking at Soo-Ja, her voice as sharp as the end of a needle.

It was only the second time since they had sat down that Eun-Mee looked directly at Soo-Ja's face. Soo-Ja rose and excused herself to the ladies' room—she could no longer bear the throbbing in her head.

The small ladies' room fit only one person at a time, and Soo-Ja locked the door behind her as she went in. She walked to the sink, ran warm water under her hands for a long time. The mirror above fogged up a little, and as she wiped it with the back of her hand, she imagined she saw Yul reflected there, standing right behind her, looking at her. Tears were rolling down her cheeks, and he wiped them off with the tip of his finger. He held up his hand afterward, as the wetness lingered for a second, and then his skin absorbed her tears, and absorbed *her*.

Soo-Ja pictured Yul hugging her from behind. He buried his head in her hair, and she could feel his nose nuzzling against her neck. She turned around and let him kiss her, his tongue caressing the soft, raw parts of her underlip, then reaching deeper, stroking her tongue with his, until they could not breathe without intruding on the other. He embraced her, with every part of her body coming alive, instantly bound to his. One hand pressed against her neck; another against her waist. His mouth emerged for air and lingered over her ears, his warm breath entering her again. His solid frame melted, bending like clay, molding to her frame like a perfect pillow.

Soo-Ja heard knocking on the door. She was tempted to tell the person to go away, but then she heard Jae-Hwa's voice asking her if she was all right, and telling her she had to go back to her husband soon. Soo-Ja was reminded, amid all this, that she had business to take care of, and that she had never gotten to ask Jae-Hwa about the loan. She didn't have much time left. She splashed some water on her face, turned the faucet off, and told Jae-Hwa she was on her way out.

When Soo-Ja came back to the table, she found Jae-Hwa holding her purse and waiting for her, but Eun-Mee had already left. She had to take care of some business having to do with the new house she was renovating, Jae-Hwa told her. Apparently it was almost finished. Soo-Ja knew, though, the real reason she had left. Things between the two of them would always be uncomfortable from now on.

Today, with Jae-Hwa, Eun-Mee had found the perfect opportunity to confront Soo-Ja. They could never have had that conversation on their own, not if they wanted to keep up the pretense that they didn't know about each other. Jae-Hwa had been essential, an unknowing witness, a midwife of tales, though the tale was not intended for her, but for Soo-Ja. Soo-Ja also noticed that Eun-Mee had taken great pains to draw

Jae-Hwa's sympathy. She cared what Jae-Hwa thought of her. But why?

"Jae-Hwa, before you go, I need to ask you something. You know that I don't like to ask for things, but this is very important." Soo-Ja told her about the loan she needed, emphasizing it was only a loan, and she'd pay her back, and that yes, Jae-Hwa was the only person she knew who could help her. When she finished, Jae-Hwa looked at her strangely.

"Did you two time it? You must've planned it this way. Is that why you were in the bathroom so long? To give Eun-Mee her time? So that's why Eun-Mee left early. So you could have your turn."

Soo-Ja looked at Jae-Hwa, a little surprised by the briskness in her voice. She was so different, this Jae-Hwa, from the diffident girl who had always been glad to be a satellite to her sun; foolish was the one who expected to touch the same river twice. "I'm a little confused," she said. "What do you mean?"

"Eun-Mee asked me for a loan as well, and I already agreed to it. She's a safe bet, being a doctor's wife and all. Oh, Soo-Ja, if only you had asked me before! I can't lend money to *both* of you, my husband would kill me. And I already gave her my word."

"When did she ask you?" Soo-Ja could sense her own face turning ashen. *I can't believe I left Jae-Hwa alone with Eun-Mee.*

"Just now, while you were in the bathroom. Oh, Soo-Ja, I'm sorry. It sounds like a good investment. But come here and give me a hug. It was so wonderful to see you again."

As Jae-Hwa embraced Soo-Ja, Soo-Ja's chin dropped and her body stiffened. It had taken less than a second for Soo-Ja to realize exactly what Eun-Mee had done to her, and what she would continue to do.

That night, the watchman Soo-Ja had hired to stay at the front desk did not show up, and when she went looking for Min in her room, she saw he was already asleep. She did not want to wake him up (she had always been partial to sleep—it was the only time they were truly free, truly without worries—how could she begrudge Min that?), and so she returned to the front desk, to watch it herself. After a couple of hours, around one in the morning, she decided to make herself some coffee. It was then that she saw Yul come to the front desk, wearing a thick dark blue robe over his pajamas. They were the only people awake in the hotel, it seemed, and it felt a bit like having it to themselves.

"You can't sleep?" Soo-Ja asked him.

"I was hoping to catch you alone," he said, leaning over the counter. "Eun-Mee told me what happened with your friend Jae-Hwa today."

Soo-Ja felt her blood boil at the mention of Eun-Mee's name.

"Why would she tell you that? To make me look bad?"

"Why didn't you just ask me for the money?" asked Yul, reaching for a small bonsai tree sitting on the counter. "I could lend it to you."

Soo-Ja glared at Yul, feeling as though he had just stepped on her heart. "Please don't insult me by saying things like that. I don't need your help."

"There's no reason to be proud—"

"If you don't drop it immediately, I'm going to leave," said Soo-Ja, taking the bonsai from his hand and putting it back on the counter. "You can stay and talk to yourself."

Yul nodded gravely, as if to an officer of the law, and put his hand up to signal his acquiescence.

"You can't sleep, and I can't stay awake. Would you like a cup of something?" asked Soo-Ja, changing the subject. "Here, I'll make you a cup of tea. It'll lower your body temperature and help you fall asleep." Soo-Ja led him to the kitchenette in her office. "How are the house renovations?"

"Almost done," he said, following her into the alcove.

"Oh, I see . . ."

So he was about to disappear from her life for the third time. Soo-Ja wondered if this was what they were doomed to do: meet every four or five years for the rest of their lives, launching into the same cycle, like those events in nature that recur under the right atmospheric conditions. Were they like those fissures that open in the ground to release some pressure, only to close again and remain so for a few more thousand turns of the earth around the sun?

Soo-Ja placed the kettle over the gas flame and turned her head a little so Yul couldn't see the disappointment on her face. For the last three weeks, she had enjoyed living so close to him. She saw him sometimes in the morning, as he left for work, and sometimes in the evening, as he came back. It felt normal, their version of normal, and she could forget—for a second or two—that they were not married, and he was just a guest in the hotel.

"When will it be ready?" she asked.

"Next week."

"Oh."

"Yes," said Yul, looking at the floor, as awkward as a child. He might be a respected doctor during the day, but right now he was just a little boy, and Soo-Ja felt her heart swell with love for him.

"Are you happy with how it looks?" Soo-Ja asked.

"Yes. Both the contractor and the decorator stayed very close to what I wanted."

"So Eun-Mee didn't make the decisions?"

"No. I asked them to build the house I always wanted to live in. Well, the house I always wanted to—" he trailed off. *The house I always wanted to live in with you.*

"What? What were you going to say?"

"Nothing."

Soo-Ja poured the hot water in the teacup, and as she did so, she could feel its warmth rise and caress her face, as if it were Yul's own hands touching her.

"What is the house like?" she asked.

"The house is like you, Soo-Ja."

He said nothing more.

"Drink your tea, Yul."

They stood quietly for a while, Yul drinking his tea, she sipping her coffee. They drank the night, too, and all its silences.

"Would you like to go outside for a moment and have a smoke?" Yul finally asked.

"You smoke now? You're a doctor."

"I'm a self-destructive doctor," said Yul, pulling out a packet of Plea-sure Lights.

"You just heal other people."

"Yes, you give those people a place to sleep, and I give them healthy bodies to sleep in."

"Don't you dare romanticize me, Yul. I'm doing this to keep a roof over my head. Before we go, do you want to check on Eun-Mee?"

"She's in her room, and she's asleep. Everyone's asleep. The entire world. We're the only fools who don't get any rest."

They walked outside and felt the night chill envelop them. They stood side by side, incongruous, Soo-Ja wearing her purple windbreaker over her housedress, and Yul in his fine robe, the legs of his flesh-colored pajamas visible underneath. They had lit only one cigarette, and simply passed it back and forth between them. It was past curfew, and there was nobody out. Beyond, neon lights, once flashing, now dormant, advertised coffee shops, noodle houses, music rooms, beauty parlors. Soo-Ja put his cigarette in her mouth, drew in smoke, then placed it back on his lips. When she did so, because the cigarette was so small by then, she ended up touching his lips with her fingers. But she did not move her fingers away as he inhaled. She let him take a drag, then put it back on her lips again.

"Does Eun-Mee like the house?" Soo-Ja asked.

"Yes, especially the refrigerator."

"Yes. It'll make her housework easier, not having to go to the farmers' market every day."

"We have a maid, too. A teenage girl from the countryside."

"Oh."

"Actually, Eun-Mee likes everything but some of the decor. She hates the ink paintings I put up on the wall. She wants Western art, full of color and drama. But I'm not going to put my paintings away."

"Ink paintings? Who's the artist?"

"Actually, it's only one. It's the painting of plum blossoms that you gave me, back in 1960."

"You still have it?"

"You seem surprised."

"I am." Soo-Ja could not hide her delight. "It's been so long. I thought something would have happened to it by now."

"No. It's just as it was then. Intact. Nothing's changed."

Soo-Ja thought of the plum blossoms. The almost tender way the long, dark leaves gave way to the small, round flowers. "The plum blossom is associated with spring, a time for hope. It celebrates perseverance."

"If you'd like, I can give it back to you," said Yul.

"No. Keep it," said Soo-Ja, smiling back. She was looking at the sky, and for a moment, she thought she could see the stars linking, forming the stems, the leaves, and the circles of the flower buds. It was as if she were painting again, and her strokes could link different constellations together. When Soo-Ja glanced back at Yul, she could see him staring intently at her. She immediately guessed what he was thinking.

"No, Yul."

"How do you know what is on my mind?" he asked.

"The way you are staring at my lips," said Soo-Ja.

"Mouths were made for kissing."

"They were also made for talking."

"Maybe if I didn't kiss your mouth. And I just kiss . . . your shoulders," said Yul, his lips pecking her clothed shoulders, and moving up from there, "and your neck, and your ears, and your nose." He kissed each of those parts, and she felt a slight shiver each time. She closed her eyes, letting the soft touch of his lips press her recalcitrant skin. He rested his hand lightly over hers—half hovering, half grazing—and she found its weight to be at turns alarming and reassuring. She knew it was wrong—this closeness—but the night had a dreamlike quality to it, the promise of forgetfulness. With her eyes shut, Soo-Ja pictured Yul kissing her—he'd kiss her like a sigh, his love filling her lungs. But when he tried to do so, she opened her eyes and pulled away. His face remained in midair—homeless, orphaned. It hurt to say no, when there was nothing she wanted more than to hold him and have him hold her, to kiss and be kissed back. Soo-Ja thought he'd head inside after that, but Yul remained on the same spot, standing next to her. They were like teenagers trying to figure out what to do with lips and arms and hips. They stood side by side, with their arms pressing together. Soo-Ja rested her head on Yul's shoulder, and they said nothing more.

The next night, Soo-Ja and Yul met again. This time, the two of them grew adventurous and decided to break curfew. They slipped out of the hotel, again like teenagers, watching for police officers in the distance. At first, they moved a bit surreptitiously, constantly glancing over their shoulders for informants. But then they realized that the streets were empty, and they began their walk, their steps slow and leisurely, looking at their own neighborhood with the interest and curiosity of tourists abroad. They passed by colorful toy stores and candy markets, all built without an inch of free space between them; took in the smell of spicy soups and fried seafood still lingering in the air.

"By the way, have you ever wondered if Hana is yours?" asked Soo-Ja, smiling mischievously.

"How could she be mine? You and I have never made love," said Yul, stealing glances at her as they walked. The night was cold, and they could see their white breaths bending and coiling in front of them.

"Still, I wonder," said Soo-Ja, shrugging her shoulders lightly, her hands inside her pockets.

"I like that you do," said Yul, smiling.

"You know, I never thought I'd see you again after I left you that night in Pusan, and here you are. You are here! I spend so much time thinking of all the different ways I don't have you, but you're right here."

Yul turned to her, his eyes glowing with impishness. "Do you want to list all of the ways that we don't have each other?"

Soo-Ja laughed. "Oh, Yul, you're not good at being vulgar. And trust me, you wouldn't enjoy making love to me. I just lie there." Soo-Ja was surprised to hear the words slip out of her mouth. But the combination of the night being so still and so *theirs*, and being able to enjoy it alone with Yul—all of it had made her a little tipsy.

"It would be different if you were doing it with someone you loved," said Yul.

Soo-Ja laughed again, turning her head sideways. "Really?"

"I'm sorry. I just feel like I can say anything around you. I feel completely free around you," said Yul.

"I feel the same way. That means we're good friends," said Soo-Ja. Even though the temperature seemed to drop with each block they passed, she did not feel cold. She could have walked all night with Yul, waking up to the dawning sun, her body next to his on a bench, the moistness of morning in her breath.

Yul shook his head. "Why is it so hard for you to say that I mean more to you?"

"You're being awfully presumptuous. What makes you think you mean so much? Maybe I can barely stand you," said Soo-Ja, smiling.

"Is there anyone else you talk to this freely?" asked Yul, suddenly stopping.

Soo-Ja kept walking, leaving him behind. She then stopped, too, and waited for him to catch up with her. When they were next to each other again, they resumed walking. All this was done with the precision of a dance, the movements carefully modulated, the counts invisible but steady.

"I used to. With my father."

"Why do you say 'used to'?"

"He and I don't talk much anymore," said Soo-Ja, growing a little forlorn. "Every time I do, I can't help thinking, *I ruined the life of someone I care about.*"

"Why do you think that?"

"Only because he gave me all his money and it went to pay off my father-in-law's debts."

"Then you didn't ruin his life. You gave him the chance to show his love for you."

"That's a nice way of looking at it. But in reality, I just avoid the topic. I avoid *him*, actually," said Soo-Ja, looking straight ahead. The strip of shops had ended, and they could see a walled-in park ahead, the tips of magnolia trees arching over the red brick walls.

"You should talk to your father. Don't let things be awkward between you. He would be glad to have his daughter in his life again. And when you make a fortune from your investments, you can pay him back."

Soo-Ja smiled at him. "How do you always know what to say to me?"

"Because I care too much," he said, with a hint of playfulness in his voice. They were developing quite a repertoire that night, creating an act to take on the road, like the old clowns of yesteryear, who would travel to villages doing mask dances and comic routines.

"And why do you care 'too much'?"

"Because you were my first love," he said, taking the edge off the word by lingering on it. "Don't you know, from the movies you see, that you never forget your first love?"

"It's too bad you were never able to love anyone else," said Soo-Ja teasingly.

"What makes you think I was never able to love anyone else?"

"Are you saying you love Eun-Mee?" asked Soo-Ja, in disbelief.

Yul laughed at Soo-Ja's certainty. "In the beginning. She was a different woman when I met her."

"Then maybe you should be talking to Eun-Mee right now," said Soo-Ja, the sharpness in her voice half contrived, half real. "Should we head back?"

"No, wait," said Yul.

The temperature seemed to drop further, and Soo-Ja could hear the howl of the wind as the cold lashed at her. It would be nice, she thought, if he put his arms around her. It would distract her mind; it would make the cold dissipate.

"Are you ever going to say it? How you feel about me?" asked Yul.

"I don't know what you mean," said Soo-Ja, though she did.

Soo-Ja and Yul stood in front of each other, waiting for the other to speak first, each afraid to break the moment. Then, sirens began to soar in the distance, announcing the end of curfew. Citizens would now be able to leave their homes and go to work, drive in the streets, and eat in restaurants. Soon roads would be filled with cars and pedestrians and smoke billowing out of buses. But for now, for those fleeting minutes, all was quiet, everyone still asleep. If they kissed, or embraced, no one could see, no one would have to know.

"Let's head back," said Soo-Ja.

In the morning, Soo-Ja grew bold and decided to do something she'd always wanted to do. She went into the hotel kitchen and made a lunch bag for Yul to take to work. She cooked her own recipe of *japchae*— mixed vegetable noodles, and fried gyoza—and placed them in a hot steel container. She did not say anything to Yul, but simply left it outside his door, without saying it was from her. At night, the brown bag reappeared outside her own door. She opened it and was happy to see it was completely empty—it meant he had enjoyed it and eaten it well. The next day, she cooked something else—*pokum bab*—fried rice with egg, ham, and peas, topped with some strips of meat. Once again, Soo-Ja left it by his door. Eun-Mee never saw the bags, as she always slept in. At night, they reappeared on her own doorstep, always empty.

Soo-Ja pictured Yul eating in his office, enjoying his food. It would make him glad, not having to ask one of the receptionists to fetch him lunch. *No, not today, I have it,* he'd say, and the receptionist would reply, *Good, Dr. Kim, everyone here always felt so bad for you, we all always have our lunch bags, except for you.*

One morning, as Soo-Ja dropped the bag off in front of Yul's room, she rose from the mat to find a pair of eyes peering at her. Unmistakably curious and full of disapproval, the eyes belonged to Hana. Soo-Ja did not speak, but knew that her own surprised reaction would tell much of the story. Hana said nothing, and Soo-Ja knew instinctively that her daughter wouldn't tell Min. But in the moment that passed between them, Soo-Ja feared that her daughter would swallow up a piece of her mother's ache, and hoped that it would not damage her.

"Hello, this is Hotel Seine," Soo-Ja said into the receiver in the morning, hiding a yawn.

"You sound so tired! You really need to get that husband of yours to help you more." It was Jae-Hwa, with her familiar, singsongy trill.

"Jae-Hwa, did you make it back to Daegu all right?" Soo-Ja asked, glad to hear her friend's voice.

"Yes. Thank you for seeing me while I was in Seoul. I loved it, although now I have so much dust in my lungs! Too bad the vacuum cleaner doesn't reach inside my throat."

Soo-Ja laughed. "It was good to see you, too."

"So you're not mad at me for—"

"Of course not," Soo-Ja cut her off, feeling bad that she had worried her friend. "But let's not talk about that anymore."

"But how're you going to find the money?"

"To be honest with you, Jae-Hwa, I'm beginning to accept the fact that I won't," said Soo-Ja, half sighing. "But maybe that's not such a bad thing. I had money growing up, and it only attracted trouble."

There was silence on the other end of the line.

"Jae-Hwa, what is it?" Soo-Ja asked, concerned.

"It's just—well, I lied to you. I said I couldn't lend you the money, but I could. In fact, the amount you asked for isn't even that much for me."

"Jae-Hwa, you don't need to explain. It was wrong of me to put you on the spot like that."

"No, it wasn't wrong. You always lent me money when we were young. Actually, when we'd go out, you always paid for things. And never asked for anything back."

"I didn't mind helping you back then," Soo-Ja said, playing with the long, beige coiled phone cord. She imagined Jae-Hwa at the other end, sitting in one of the brocaded sofas in her living room, probably dressed in her usual cashmere. "I got pleasure out of giving you things."

"Soo-Ja, the reason I didn't give you the loan was because . . . well, when I came to visit you, and saw the hotel, and saw the little rooms you and your family were living in . . . I thought, she's not asking me for money to make an investment, she's asking it so she can make ends meet."

Soo-Ja felt her face fall. "Jae-Hwa, I'm poor, but I'm not *that* poor. And I wouldn't lie to you."

"I know. But I looked at how you were dressed, and I thought, There's no way she'll be able to pay me back. And that's why I didn't give you the money. Because I was afraid you wouldn't be able to pay me back. I'm sorry."

"Don't be," said Soo-Ja curtly. In that moment, Soo-Ja decided she did not want Jae-Hwa's money. What did she take Soo-Ja for? A beggar? Even if she had called to offer her ten times the sum, Soo-Ja wouldn't have taken it.

"This doesn't change anything, I hope? I mean, money shouldn't come between friends," said Jae-Hwa.

"Of course not," said Soo-Ja, her lips tightly pursed.

They would never be friends again. The difference in class made it impossible.

Soo-Ja held the telephone in her hands, not ready to dial the numbers. In a moment or so, she'd call Gi-yong Im to let him know that she wasn't able to raise the money to buy the land. In a moment or so, she'd thank him for waiting for her, and for giving her the opportunity. In a moment or so, she'd hang up the phone, and then it would be over. And because it would be over—taking her hopes with it, and replacing them with the ring of defeat—she hesitated before calling.

"My favorite investor, Mrs. Soo-Ja Choi," said Gi-yong, in his animated voice, when he answered the phone. He was always selling—a place, an idea, an emotion. "How are you?"

"I am well. I could be better, of course. Which is why I'm calling you," said Soo-Ja, holding the phone close against her face, her hand made into a fist brushing against her cheek.

"If you've changed your mind, it may be too late. The money has already been routed to my account, and once it gets in there, it's awfully hard to pry it out of my fingers," said Gi-yong jokingly.

Soo-Ja thought she could hear him tapping against his desk with a pen. "Yes, the money. I'm sorry I don't have the money. That's why I'm calling you. To let you know that you're free to sell the land to someone else. I did the best I could, but I couldn't get it."

"Mrs. Choi, the land is yours," said Gi-yong calmly, and she could hear him leaning forward on his desk, becoming more attentive. "Your money has been deposited, and the contracts have been drawn. I thought that's why you were calling, to set up a time for the signing."

Soo-Ja stood confused for a moment, as if Gi-yong had been speaking a foreign language, and it took her a few extra seconds to translate the words, one by one. "Did you say, 'your money has been deposited'?"

"From your silent partner," said Gi-yong, a little impatiently.

"My silent partner?"

"Yes, and he's so silent I don't even know who he is. All the arrangements have been made through his accountant and me. His accountant reached my office this morning, and informed me that he was making his line of credit available to you. The transfer has been successful, and the deal has transpired quite smoothly."

There was only one person in the world who would do this for her, thought Soo-Ja. *Yul, you stubborn mule! How many times do I need to tell you I don't want your money?*

"Mr. Im, I'm afraid there has been a mistake," said Soo-Ja, with asperity in her voice. "Please cancel the deal. Right away."

"Don't be silly! You wanted the land so much and it's yours now!" said Gi-yong, in his trademark high spirits. Soo-Ja could hear the squeaky springs of his leather chair as he leaned back against it.

"Mr. Im!"

"Send your husband here to sign the papers tomorrow morning," Gi-yong interrupted. "Although I'd prefer if *you* came." He did not try to hide the leer in his voice. "I can imagine you'd prefer to sign papers yourself, in your name, but I know you're too clever a woman to emasculate your husband like that."

"Mr. Im, I'm serious. That money—"

"Oh, before I forget," Gi-yong interrupted, "your silent partner asked me to relay a message to you. He wants you to know that this is only a loan, and you'll have to pay him back."

Soo-Ja closed her eyes, taking this in. Yul knew that was the only way she'd accept his help. *But I'd rather have the man than the money. Is there no way to have an exchange?*

"Anyway, I do have to say I was surprised that you pulled through. You said you'd come back by the end of the month, and indeed you did, with three days to spare. Now, you may be interested to know about certain rumors circling around city hall. As I mentioned before, my original estimation was that they'd start building on the land in fifteen to twenty years, and that's how the lots have been valued, and priced. But . . . there are rumors."

"What kind of rumors?" Soo-Ja asked, furrowing her brow.

"I can't talk about it," said Gi-yong, his voice growing a little hushed. "I don't want to raise anyone's hopes if it doesn't happen. But the people are getting restless. New elections are inevitable, and the President's under a lot of pressure to do more for the cities. This whole *saemaul undong* movement to improve the countryside sure sounds nifty, but the government can't expect people to stay away from the cities. You know the saying, 'If you have a son, send him to Seoul.'"

"Well, that sounds very promising," said Soo-Ja, and she could hear the understatement in her own voice.

Gi-yong laughed. "By the way, are you going to tell me who your silent partner is?"

Soo-Ja swallowed. "Good-bye, Mr. Im."

Soo-Ja knocked lightly on Yul's door. When she got no answer, she hesitated, and then pulled out her master key. She went into the room, only to find it dark, with no one inside. Yul was gone, and so were his things. Before she could grasp what happened, Soo-Ja saw her daughter appear next to her, touching her arm lightly. Soo-Ja looked at her daughter's oval face, her eyes shining intently at her.

"They checked out a couple of hours ago," said Hana.

"They're gone?" asked Soo-Ja, taking in the emptiness of the room.

"Yes. Yul left this for you."

Hana handed her mother a note, and when Soo-Ja opened it, she read the words *Don't forget me.* Trembling, Soo-Ja closed the note again, the meaning of the words etching themselves into her skin.

As she exited the room, Soo-Ja noticed that Hana looked upset. She wondered how much her daughter knew about Yul and her. Children, Soo-Ja believed, had a sixth sense about such things. Soo-Ja tried to think of some explanation to offer her. It had to serve many purposes: it had to keep her from going to her father; it had to prevent the wound from scarring; it had to get her to forgive her for a deed she hadn't done.

"I'm glad he's gone," said Hana. "I don't like him."

"Why don't you like him?" Soo-Ja asked cautiously.

"He cheated on his wife, Mom," said Hana. In her voice, Soo-Ja could hear she was half accusing her and half testing the words.

"No, he didn't," Soo-Ja corrected her, deciding that she wouldn't pretend not to know what Hana was hinting at. "He was loyal to her."

"He is a bad man," said Hana.

"Don't say that, Hana. It's not true. He's a good man. Don't say bad things about Yul, please," said Soo-Ja. She realized she would not get a chance to thank him. She'd just have to add that to the list of things she'd never get to say to him.

chapter fifteen

With Yul gone, Soo-Ja began to think of him even more often. She imagined him next to her, offering that sad-hopeful smile of his as she did the most mundane of tasks. *How is it possible that Yul cannot be mine, when the pain of his absence feels like a cave inside my heart?*

Soo-Ja could tell no one about her feelings—Yul was a secret, the way any great love was, to some extent, a secret. But when she asked her own self, she heard the words loud and clear: *You are not finished with him, and he is not finished with you. Even if you two wanted to, you could not fight this longing.* Which led, of course, to the one person who'd most like to see the end of the bond between them: once, always, forever, Eun-Mee.

"Hana's mother, what are you doing this afternoon? It's Saturday, and it's the eve of the lunar festival. Surely you can't be working!" Eun-Mee stood before Soo-Ja in her fur coat, with a light pink embroidered top underneath and a long, flowing skirt. Soo-Ja put away her guest book, taken aback by her presence at the hotel.

"Happy New Year," said Soo-Ja drily.

"Happy New Year," said Eun-Mee. "Now, I know you may want to get a head start driving home for the holidays, but I'm inviting you and your husband to come to our house for tea, and to celebrate the Lunar New Year. You've been hearing about these renovations for so long, I'm sure you must be curious about the final result."

"You want me to come to your house?" asked Soo-Ja, in disbelief. She had made the mistake of trusting Eun-Mee before, but never again.

Eun-Mee kept her voice even, as if she couldn't imagine why that would be a bad idea. "Yes. This will give us a chance to say a proper good-bye after we checked out so hurriedly. You have to let us thank you for your hospitality. I'm very glad I got to stay here. Meeting you has been so . . . instructive."

Soo-Ja opened her guest book again and buried her head in it, trying to remain polite. "I appreciate the offer, but I don't think I can go. I have a lot of shopping to do before I head to my parents' for the long holiday."

"Oh, Hana's mother, aren't you the least bit curious to see the house? It won't take very long, just tea. Please, I know we had some . . . friction while I was here, but really I'm no monster. Give me an opportunity to prove that, and to make things up with you. I don't want to end things on a sour note."

Soo-Ja didn't know what Eun-Mee truly had in mind, but she didn't believe a word she had said. Nevertheless, Soo-Ja knew that their feelings for each other were more complicated than either would admit. Soo-Ja guessed that Eun-Mee hated her, but then hated herself for feeling hate, and tried to make it up to her. Eun-Mee wanted to dislike Soo-Ja, but for Soo-Ja to like her at the same time.

More important, Soo-Ja knew Yul would be at his house, of course, and try as she might, she could not really pass up the chance to be near him. If the only way to see Yul was to do so on Eun-Mee's terms, then so be it. She'd keep her guard up, she told herself, and remember Eun-Mee's old tricks. She called for Miss Hong and Min, and tried to ignore the confusion on Min's face as she explained to Miss Hong her duties during their absence.

● ● ●

And so the four of them ended up meeting in front of the hotel to walk together to Eun-Mee and Yul's new house. It was not very far, Eun-Mee explained, just four blocks west of the New World Shopping Center. It was too cold, actually, to walk, but the streets were alive with festivities related to the Lunar New Year, and they felt like losing themselves in the lively crowd. They looked well, too, Eun-Mee with her brown fur coat and Soo-Ja in a navy sweater with a low neckline and a camel's-hair jacket. Both Yul and Min wore knee-length overcoats, Yul's dark blue, Min's gray with small white dots. Eun-Mee and Soo-Ja walked ahead of the men; at one point, Eun-Mee interlaced her arm around Soo-Ja's, and smiled at her like a mischievous younger sister.

Seeing Yul again felt like an unexpected gift. Soo-Ja didn't think it would happen so soon—if ever. Yul's eyes seemed to say the same, a sort of bittersweet joy. Here they were, in this pas de deux, changing partners, trapped in a dance performance. Soo-Ja didn't trust Eun-Mee, but she liked this part, all of them walking together—she liked the ordinariness of it. She imagined couples did this with other couples all the time, going out to coffee shops and restaurants, the men talking about business while the women discussed their health. She felt grateful, in a way, to Eun-Mee, for giving them a context in which they could interact— they were all friends, Eun-Mee seemed to have decided one day—and she was more than happy to play along.

They had been walking for about ten minutes when they saw a large crowd gathered in front of an impromptu stage set up by the entrance to Royal Park. On the stage were a group of four *janggo* street musicians performing traditional village music, meant to celebrate the harvest. They played loudly, like some ancient tribe—the intense beating of the drums made it feel as if some kind of old religious ritual were taking place, never mind the modern, concrete buildings behind them. The men wore traditional janggo costumes: a black robe held down by a yellow sash across the chest and a red belt around the waist, all made out of silk. They also wore loose white pantaloons, which matched the white bands strapped on their heads. There were four of them onstage, sitting cross-legged, one behind a cymbal, another behind a gong; the other two were behind large drums, one shaped like an hourglass, the other barrel-chested.

Soo-Ja was wondering if they were going to stay and listen to them, when Eun-Mee suddenly stepped forward gaily and made her way into the crowd, like an excited child, trying to get closer to the stage. Min followed her lead and moved closer to the stage, too, walking past Soo-Ja. She was surprised that Eun-Mee would leave Soo-Ja and Yul alone like that, until she realized that Eun-Mee didn't know that Min had left them as well. Soo-Ja stayed in her spot, aware that Yul was right behind her. She did not have to turn to sense his familiar scent, to feel his body pulling her toward him.

Yul placed his hand on the small of Soo-Ja's back, and she closed her eyes, the sound of drums reverberating through her body. Each bang felt like a new warning, telling her to run. The music sounded like boulders cascading down a mountain, loud enough to be heard by gods. Soo-Ja opened her eyes again, looking through the crowd for Eun-Mee, who would be coming back at any moment. Soo-Ja knew she should tell Yul to move away, but she could not. The dappled shade cannot ask the tree to leave it alone.

Min was nowhere to be seen, either. Soo-Ja kept listening to the echoes of the drums, beating without stop, the players' hands magically flying from one end of the drum to the other. Then a sudden pause, and a four-man chant, and then the beating of the drums again, growing in intensity. The two drummers played first in perfect sync, then later against each other, sounds clashing, a kind of combat. Each turn of the head and each wave of the drumstick was carefully modulated, as if the music itself had shape and was being choreographed by their bodies.

Yul's surprisingly warm hand brushed against Soo-Ja's, and she quivered at his touch. They both kept staring straight ahead, their hands obscured by the crowd and their own bodies. Yul pressed a single finger, his middle finger, against the center of her palm, caressing it, almost burrowing into it. Her fingers closed in a little, and her hand was like the yellow forsythia whose trumpet-shaped petals can furl and unfurl, opening up to the sun, but then closing, to protect itself from cold winds.

Onstage, the drumming grew in intensity and the chants became more frequent. The players would pause for a second or two, letting a single beat of the drum reverberate fully through the air, then fall, promising an end. The crowd cheered; some people started clapping. Then, just when you thought it was finished, the drumming would start again, sounding more potent than ever, and you did not know if that was because their playing had grown mightier, or because they had made you miss it.

Soo-Ja had moved her hand abruptly to clap with the others, but then she returned it to her spot, eagerly, hungrily, searching for Yul's hand. His hand quickly returned to hers, and this time, as his finger pressed against her palm, she placed her own fingers on top of his, covering them with her warmth. They stayed like that, their fingers exploring each other's—caressing, squeezing, feeling—moving like naked bodies, skin next to skin.

Just then, Min returned, and Yul moved his hand away.

"It's a modern stove," said Eun-Mee, turning it on. "It controls the gas so it doesn't all shoot off into the air. With the normal *yentan* gas, half of it goes straight into your lungs."

Soo-Ja watched as Eun-Mee showed off her spacious kitchen. When Soo-Ja was growing up, kitchens reminded her of dungeons, lower in the ground than the rest of the house, suffocatingly hot, gray and dark, full of earthenware jars and ceramic pots and pans. Even in the hotel, the kitchen area was really just a sink and a small gas stove. Eun-Mee's kitchen, however, was like something out of a magazine. Eun-Mee had a seemingly endless countertop, rows and rows of cupboards, her own refrigerator, and a washing machine.

Eun-Mee set the teakettle on the stove and was about to unwrap petits fours from their packaging when the phone rang. It was a friend of Eun-Mee's from Pusan. As they started chatting, Soo-Ja excused herself and stepped out of the kitchen. Yul and Min were downstairs, in the garden, and Soo-Ja was able to wander around on her own. The house was enormous, especially by Seoul standards, and Soo-Ja walked through room after room: a dining room, a living room, a sitting room, and a room with a large window that looked out at some trees. Looking at the house where Yul and Eun-Mee would live out their lives, Soo-Ja understood, finally, the enormity of her mistake. She thought of that day—that cloudless day—when Yul stood before her on the eve of her wedding and asked her to choose him. If she had said yes, she would be married to Yul and living in this house with him. When Yul asked that single yes or no question—*Come with me*—and she said no, Soo-Ja did not know what she was saying no to. She did not know the size and weight of the consequences, how life is not set down like train tracks, and you don't just ride above it. The life she had could not be that different from the one she *could have* had, she had thought. *I am the same person, surely the story unfolds roughly the same way?* Each decision she made couldn't be *that* important, couldn't change her life *that* much, right? Otherwise she'd drown in the multiple possibilities of who she could have been and was not—the Soo-Ja who went to diplomat school and worked in the government; the one who found a post teaching at a school and found another man, neither Yul nor Min; the one who never married at all, and stayed by her father's side, a happy spinster—wouldn't all of these women crash and collide, eventually? How could all of these versions exist, three or four for each of us, and then more so, as they intersected? Soo-Ja wondered. How could the world fit so many lives, so many iterations? It couldn't be that big, it couldn't fit so much. We're only given one life, and it's the one we live, she had thought; how painful now, to realize that wasn't true, that you would have different lives, depending on how brave you were, and how ready. Love came to her that day—she was twenty-two—and wanted to take her, and she said no.

Why are we asked to make the most important decisions of our lives when we are so young, and so prone to mistakes? Happiness came that day—she knew nothing—and asked her to say yes and she did not. Why did she assume it would come back again, when there were so many others waiting for it to visit?

Stop it, Soo-Ja, she told herself, and she could have, if she had not made the mistake of looking out the window, and seen Yul down in the garden, showing Min around. He looked up and saw her the instant she got to the window, and with his eyes he confirmed everything she'd been thinking. It was not an accusing glance; it was wistful, a half smile on his face. It spoke of memories of things that didn't happen; full of nostalgia for a life together that they had never shared. She looked away, as if Yul were the sun, and it would hurt her eyes if she kept looking at him. What could she say to Yul? It wasn't just words she wanted. She wanted him to forgive her—for her cowardice and her fear, for having looked at happiness and turned away from it, afraid it would burn her, like the surface of the sun. She wanted him to know he wasn't crazy, but that she knew, too, and that in their knowing together they could feel some consolation—that would be something they could share. It was not ideal, not at all, but still, it was warm and neat and it could be pulled out in days of need, like a woolen blanket from a treasure chest.

Soo-Ja then heard Eun-Mee call from the kitchen, and she, like a good guest, headed back to help her.

Eun-Mee poured lemon tea for the four of them in the manner of a schooled hostess, with her back perfectly straight, bending only her knees. She seemed in good spirits, heartily enjoining them to eat petits fours and drink warm tea. Soo-Ja felt for a moment that she'd misjudged her, and that Eun-Mee really did invite Min and her there to express her gratitude. Soo-Ja thought of how she might return the kindness—perhaps send her a box of pears? That feeling, however, quickly dissipated as soon as Eun-Mee opened her mouth.

"I'm so glad I no longer have to sleep in that hotel!" Eun-Mee said, sitting down across from Soo-Ja's chair.

Min sat next to Eun-Mee, and Yul found himself next to Soo-Ja. The room looked quite luxurious, with sofas upholstered with white Mongolian fur and thick armrests made out of cherry wood. Behind them stood a stack of shelves where Yul had placed a record player, some ficus and spider plants, and an expensive-looking TV. It sat there like an after-thought, akin to a board game to be pulled out occasionally.

"Eun-Mee!" said Yul. "That's a very rude thing to say."

Eun-Mee suddenly became very quiet, a look of disappointment on her face. Soo-Ja did her best to stay above this.

"Nobody likes to stay in a hotel. I don't blame Eun-Mee. You always want to be in your own home, sleep in your own bed," Soo-Ja said, holding up her teacup.

"Oh, I don't mind hotels," Eun-Mee quickly corrected her. "In fact, I love the Plaza Athénée in New York, or the Napoleon in Paris, or the Fujiya in Tokyo. But where you work, it's not really a hotel, is it? It's more of an inn, or a motel."

"Eun-Mee, why are you saying such rude things?" asked Yul, looking at her with annoyance.

But Soo-Ja feared his reaction could only make things worse. "Technically, she's right. We *are* in fact more of an inn than a hotel," Soo-Ja said, making it clear that she was not bothered by Eun-Mee's comment.

"And a very dirty one, too. Dusty. And I'm telling you this as a friend, who really hopes that your little business can in fact become a real business one day."

"Eun-Mee is right," said Min, as usual taking sides against Soo-Ja. "You need to do something about that, Soo-Ja. We have to make sure rooms are clean. That is a basic rule. You listen well to Eun-Mee. She has a lot of valuable advice to share."

Eun-Mee smiled faintly, almost in distaste, as if she didn't care for the support of someone as inconsequential as Min. "I can't help it. I'm not one of those two-faced women who pretend to be one thing in public and are something else in private."

"Please stop talking to our guests like that," said Yul.

"She needs our help, *yeobo*. You can't think she wants to stay where she is forever. She'll want one day to have what we have, a house like this, with working appliances and nice furniture. If she is to make something of herself, she'll need to work somewhere better than her motel."

Eun-Mee then turned to Soo-Ja, still holding her teacup on her lap. She had not sipped a single drop, and the hot liquid kept threatening to spill over. "And I call it a motel because a place where men go to have sex with women *is* a motel. Do they ever ask you, by the way, to bring them girls to spend the night with?"

Yul put his teacup on the table, and then rose. "Stop it, Eun-Mee. What is wrong with you today?"

"It's fine, Yul. You don't need to defend me," said Soo-Ja, doing her best to stay calm. "Actually, it's not the men who ask, it's the women. They come to the hotel and ask if there are men looking for company. These women have small children, or are widows, or young girls without families. They're hungry. And yes, sometimes I tell them what door to knock on."

"The commissions must be nice," said Eun-Mee, smiling, looking vindicated, as if Soo-Ja had confirmed her suspicions.

"I don't ask for it, and they don't offer it," Soo-Ja replied. She drank her tea as if this were normal conversation for a Saturday afternoon. She would not make a scene; she knew that's what Eun-Mee wanted.

"Are you ever tempted to make some bucks yourself?" asked Eun-Mee.

"Eun-Mee!" Yul shouted. He looked at Soo-Ja, his eyes full of pain. She wanted to tell him, *It's okay, I can handle it.*

"No, Eun-Mee, I'm not," said Soo-Ja, looking at her evenly.

"Really? What if the guest were, say, not some ugly nincompoop, but a handsome fella, like my husband? Would you make an exception for my husband?"

Now all three of them looked at Eun-Mee, stunned. Soo-Ja could see her own hand shaking, and the tea spilling over from her cup onto her lap and falling onto the furry beige carpet. Yul rose again from his seat and walked to Eun-Mee, grabbing her arm and forcing her to rise. She resisted.

"You owe Soo-Ja an apology," said Yul.

Soo-Ja put her teacup on the table and rose as well. She did not want Yul to take her side—it would only make things worse. All she wanted was to get out of their house.

"I'm just joking! It's a joke," said Eun-Mee, struggling to free her arm from Yul's grasp, looking defiantly at him. "But I hope you can see now what kind of woman she is!"

"Thank you for the invitation, but we really should—" said Soo-Ja, turning to Min.

"A woman who steals other men's husbands!" burst out Eun-Mee, staring straight at Soo-Ja.

Soo-Ja felt her face turn hot. She understood, with no uncertainty, why Eun-Mee had brought her there—to unmask her, in the most public and embarrassing way possible.

"You've ruined everything in my life!" yelled Eun-Mee. Then, out of nowhere, as if to punctuate her words, Eun-Mee slapped Soo-Ja with the palm of her hand. The gesture made a sickening noise, and hit Soo-Ja so hard that it caused her to stumble and fall to the couch.

"Soo-Ja!" Yul shouted, jumping to her aid.

Her anger still unsatisfied, Eun-Mee reached toward Soo-Ja again, but Yul grabbed hold of her, restraining her with his arms. It took all his might to pull her away, as her body swung wildly in Soo-Ja's direction, her elbows and feet kicking into the air.

Soo-Ja put a hand on her throbbing cheek, her mouth agape in shock. She felt her eyes well with tears, blinking madly. The moment felt blurry and out of focus. When she wiped the tears from her eyes she saw Yul dragging a screaming Eun-Mee into the bedroom. Soo-Ja thought about the house, the afternoon at the park, the warmth of Yul's hand.

Soo-Ja's cheek felt as if it had just been burnt with coal. It would probably bruise later, Eun-Mee's palm leaving her mark. Soo-Ja shook slightly, her breathing deep and fitful. The same urge kept thrashing at her over and over, *Get up, Soo-Ja. Get up.*

Through all of this, Min said nothing, not moving from his chair. As Yul and Eun-Mee fought in the bedroom, their harsh words pounding the air, Min looked confused and out of place. The last few minutes, with all their commotion, felt unreal, the kind of thing you hear about second-hand, told in the form of gossip. It was strange to live it, to be a part of it, to be tossed and turned like Jonah inside the whale. Min would have to lie in bed for the rest of the day. He would feed off the events like a sick patient on a special diet, as if the wrong had been done to him.

After a few seconds, without helping Soo-Ja get up, Min rose from his chair. He headed to the kitchen, where he opened a cupboard and began taking out its contents. He found a tote bag lying on the floor and started filling it with packets of barley tea, jars of dried seaweed, and packages of anchovies. He added some peppermint candy, cakelike chocolate, and squid-flavored chips.

Soo-Ja got up on her own and joined him in the kitchen. "What are you doing?" she asked, using the wall for support.

He did not reply, just kept filling up the bag.

"They'll know it was us," Soo-Ja said. "And if you want things, we can buy them ourselves, or we can ask Yul if we can have some of this. But we can't just take it. We can't just take it without their permission."

Min stopped for a moment and glanced at her, registering the stricken look on her face. He then resumed his looting, reaching for more and more food. On the way back home, he made her carry the bag.

For hours, Min lay on the floor without speaking, staring at the ceiling and eating his food. He opened each bag one by one, emptying it, then moving on to the next bag. Soo-Ja sat a few feet away from him. All day, neither acknowledged what had happened.

"Stop eating so much. You're going to get a stomachache," said Soo-Ja.

Min said nothing, just kept opening more and more packages, his stomach a pit, his hunger unable to be satiated. Soo-Ja grabbed a bag of anchovies away from him.

"Stop. Go to sleep," said Soo-Ja, reaching up and turning the light off.

Neither of them moved.

"I've always been afraid of you leaving," he said in the dark, as if he'd been waiting for some way not to see her. "Every day of my life I have this fear. I wake up in the morning and ask, *Is it today? Is it today that she'll be gone?*"

"As long as Hana is here, I'll be here, too," said Soo-Ja. They were still in the same position as before she turned out the lights—Min lying on the floor, she still sitting.

"The only time I'll be able to rest is when you get old, and no one gives you a second look. Then nobody will want you, and I won't have to worry," he said.

"That day will come soon," said Soo-Ja sharply.

"From now on, when you walk on the street, keep your head down. I don't want men to see your face," said Min. "And no more skirts. And take off that jewelry you wear. You're not a girl anymore. You're not single."

"You know who you sound like?" asked Soo-Ja, without hiding the chill in her voice.

"They were right about you. I never regret listening to my parents. They're *me*. I talk to them and I hear myself. I should never have let you separate me from them."

Min blew his nose, and Soo-Ja wondered if he was crying. In the dark, she couldn't tell.

"You think it's hard being you, or being Yul?" he continued. "Imagine being me, or Eun-Mee. If you had to choose, would you rather be yourself or be Eun-Mee?"

Soo-Ja wondered at that moment what it was like to be Min. When friends greeted them, they always greeted her first. When guests at the hotel passed by him, they did not nod or say hello. When they went to church, no one sat next to him. His invisibility wasn't her fault, but surely it had grown worse after years hiding behind her strength. She wondered if Min would have been happier with a quiet, shy woman who would let him shine. A plump, stout wife who'd be thankful to have him, constantly cooking him his favorite dishes. He might have been happy, once, to have her as his captive, but over time he must have realized he was as bound as she was. The thing about capturing a prize fish is that everyone admires the fish, and soon forgets about the fisherman. You love the thing that makes you special, then hate it because it's the thing that makes you special.

The next day, Min refused to take the train to Daegu for the Seollal holiday. He also refused to let Soo-Ja and Hana go without him. Seollal was Hana's favorite holiday, when the entire extended family gathered to celebrate the Lunar New Year. Hana loved the sight of all the tables filled with food, as they feasted on mung-bean pancakes, steamed rice cakes, freshly cut apples and pears, sweet rice flavored with dates and honey, cinnamon punch, and rice nectar. She especially loved the ceremonial bow made to the elders, as the children wished them good luck in the New Year, and were rewarded with money in white envelopes. Hana was heartbroken when her father told her they wouldn't be going south that year. She took this hard; with every passing year, she'd worry that it would be the last chance she got to see her grandfather. Soo-Ja told Min as much, but Min did not express much sympathy, as he was deprived of his own father as well.

chapter sixteen

"I'm surprised to find you at home. Everyone's left town for Seollal," said Gi-yong on the phone. They had not seen each other in weeks, but Soo-Ja could easily picture his smarmy smile, his blue vicuña overcoat, and his cramped office with secondhand furniture. She was surprised to hear from him; she did not expect to sell the land for at least ten years.

"It's a long story," said Soo-Ja, sitting at the front desk.

"Well, I'm glad I caught you. I have news for you."

"You do?" asked Soo-Ja, intrigued.

"My hopes of making you my mistress are over," said Gi-yong. "You're going to be a rich woman, Soo-Ja."

"What do you mean?" asked Soo-Ja, her fingers nervously intertwining with the coils of the phone cord.

"The government wants to develop your land," said Gi-yong, rolling each word around his tongue like a lollipop.

"It does?"

"Yes. It wants to buy your land and start erecting buildings there."

"How much are they offering?"

"Five thousand *won* per pyeong."

"What? That's ten times what I paid for the land!"

"Yes, but you paid for an empty lot in the middle of nowhere. They're paying for what's now officially the site of a planned commercial zone.

It's still a bargain to them. We're hoping big business will follow their lead and turn the area into a commercial center. I've said this all along, Seoul is too congested. The city can't handle the traffic and the crowds."

"I can't believe it. This is wonderful." Soo-Ja started shaking her head in disbelief.

"If you sell the land, you'll make five million *won*. How much did you put in? Five hundred thousand *won*?"

"You knew this would happen, didn't you? When you sold me the land, you knew its value would shoot up."

"Yes, I had a tip from a friend in city planning. They were debating between a lot in Gyeonggi-do Province and ours. The lot in Gyeonggi-do turned out to be tied up in a family inheritance. Our lot would be easier for them to buy. They're eager to start construction soon."

"If you knew the lot would increase in value and so soon, why did you still sell it to me? Why didn't you buy it yourself?"

Gi-yong did not answer at once. "You think businessmen are so cold and calculating, and yes, we are, but when it comes to the heart, we're sentimental folks. I thought that if I helped you get what you wanted . . . you would like me."

"Oh, Mr. Im, I like you tremendously right now," said Soo-Ja, side-stepping his confession. "This comes at such an opportune time. It has been such a terrible week . . . Thank you for what you did."

"Don't be *too* thankful. There was, of course, a small chance they'd go with the other lot, in which case ours would probably sit idle and worthless for another thirty years."

"Thirty years? You said ten, or twenty at most."

"Never trust a businessman, Soo-Ja. Never."

Soo-Ja laughed. A guest came into the hotel. Soo-Ja gave him a quick nod, but kept her attention, rapt, on the phone. "I have to go. But one last question: Any chance we can negotiate with the buyers?"

"It's a tricky line there. The thing is, the government could, if they want, just seize the land. So what they're doing is a gesture of goodwill, too. It is only an offer, but it's assumed we'll all accept it."

"So everyone who bought lots is selling, too?"

"The ones I spoke to so far, yes."

"Add my name to the list. And oh, one more thing . . ."

"What is it?"

"I love you, Mr. Gi-yong Im," she said, in English.

Gi-yong laughed. Soo-Ja knew he could hear the smile in her voice.

"We're rich! We're rich!" Hana began to dance around the room, pretending to hit a wall, then falling on the ground, then getting up again, then hitting the opposite wall. Min, eating his dinner, stewed in his silence, sitting in his usual corner in front of a nong armoire.

"Sit down, Hana, and eat your dinner. You're going to get hurt," said Soo-Ja, waving her chopsticks at her daughter.

"How much did he say again?" asked Min.

"Five million *won*," said Soo-Ja. She was pretending to be nonchalant, but her heart was doing the same thing Hana was doing, just on the inside.

"Don't tell your brother it's that much. He may want a cut of the profits," said Min. Soo-Ja bit her tongue, nodding. One day she'd have to tell him the truth about the source of the original loan. "But you always had a lot of luck. This kind of thing only happens to you."

"I'm lucky? Is that why I've been working as a hotel clerk for the past six years? And before that, I was basically a maid to your parents," she said.

Min smiled. "My parents think we're barely scraping by. Imagine their surprise when they hear this."

"They *like* to think we're barely scraping by. They like the idea that they're better off than we are."

Hana, as if feeling neglected, stopped running around the room and landed on her father's lap, where she barely fit. Right now she was the giddiest twelve-year-old Soo-Ja had ever met.

"What are we going to do with the money?" asked Hana.

"What do you think we should do?" Min asked her, his head buried in her silky black hair.

"I think we should go to America," she said.

Soo-Ja immediately looked up from her rice bowl. But why was she so surprised, when it seemed like everyone she knew fantasized about immigrating to America? Why should her daughter be any different?

"Who put that idea in your head?" Soo-Ja asked gravely, figuring it was Min.

"Elizabeth Taylor and Paul Newman," Hana replied.

"Your America exists only in movies," said Soo-Ja.

Hana quickly got up and reached into the nong for a cylindrical can of Pringles chips, left behind by some American guests. She'd been saving it. She opened the lid, and pulled out a chip shaped like a wave, admiring it.

"*This* is America," she said, before biting into it. "I *eat* America."

"Ah, and of course, she can't travel alone, so you'd have to go with her," Soo-Ja said, turning to Min, letting him know she was onto him.

"I don't want to visit America, I want to *live* in America!" Hana almost yelled.

"Go. Go live with Elizabeth Taylor and Paul Newman. Hana, the life you want is a dream, a movie-star life. If we moved to America, we'd start at the bottom. I'd probably still be a hotel clerk, just in a place where nobody can understand what I'm saying. Nicer background, same life."

"But we have money!" Hana protested.

"Hana, I already told you before. We're not keeping all the money. We have to pay back your grandfather in Daegu." Soo-Ja smiled at herself, proud of being able to pay her father back for the money he had loaned to Min's father so many years ago.

"I thought you said the money was for me! You told me, the reason you invested was so you could invest in my future!" Soo-Ja heard an unexpected desperation in her daughter's voice.

"Yes. It is, of course it is. If we had sold the land twenty years from now, especially, all of it would be yours. But my father is still alive, and I want to pay him back."

"It's not fair! It's my money." Hana got up and ran out of the room, leaving the paper door open on her way out. Soo-Ja wondered if she spoiled her by letting her do whatever she wanted. How would she ever learn to appreciate their love?

Soo-Ja patiently rose and closed the door. She didn't want guests to look in and see into their room.

"My parents still offer to pay back what they borrowed from your father," said Min evenly, without looking up from his bowl of *doenjang* soup.

"What kind of insulting offer are they making this time? The exact same amount he borrowed, not adjusted for inflation, only enough to pay for a TV? Your father borrowed enough to pay for three houses!"

"You can't get back what you lost."

"What do you mean?"

"The years you spent with them. The money can't make up for that."

"I was their slave."

"I know, I know. But they're my parents you're talking about!"

"You want to go to America, too, don't you?"

"Of course," he said quietly, the pinched sound hinting at some larger sorrow.

"And if it were up to you, we'd fly there tomorrow, right?"

"But you won't let us," said Min, letting more of his anguish emerge. "You're trying to keep us away from them."

"I'm not," she said. "And I don't have my parents with me, either."

"They're four hours away by train."

"My father's too sick to travel. I hardly ever get to see him."

"But you see him. I haven't seen my parents in almost ten years."

Min was as restless as a cast-off lover. He would often talk about his plans to join his parents—plans that Father-in-law neither supported nor discouraged. In the past, whenever Soo-Ja listed the reasons why they couldn't go—Min's parents had betrayed them, she did not wish to live with them, she couldn't leave her own parents—Min only repeated, *But they are my father and my mother.* She knew at those moments that he did not, could not think ill of them, regardless of what they'd done to him. He rationalized the past, did elaborate somersaults in his head, concocted versions of the story in which his parents finally emerged as victims, and Soo-Ja—Soo-Ja, whom he had to live with, the one who was left—turned out to be the villain.

• • •

But the idea somehow took hold. It came back in the morning, in the bitter coffee and the spicy udon noodles. It lashed at her ears, tugged at her ankles.

"You don't have to come if you don't want to. I can go live with Grandpa and Grandma on my own," said Hana.

"Don't say that," said Soo-Ja.

"Why?"

"Because I need you to need me."

"It's America!" Hana yelled, like a mantra. Soo-Ja understood her daughter's frustration. She probably couldn't fathom why her mother was keeping her away from sun-drenched afternoons and wide-laned streets and air so clean you could drink big happy gulps of it. In America, no one would honk in traffic, or cut in line, or speak ill of you. In America, every day was a vacation, including the workday.

When it wasn't Hana, it was Min. Did they conspire to take turns cornering her? Soo-Ja wondered.

"She's not just being frivolous," Min said to her over lunch, between bites of thinly sliced beef and spiced cubed radishes. "She's worried about her future. She's not doing very well at school."

How awkward it was, to have to hear news of your daughter from your own husband! thought Soo-Ja. "She'll do fine. She'll spend the summer studying."

"In America, you don't have to be good at school. You just have to know how to smile brightly and shake hands firmly. Hana could learn how to do that."

"Listen, if she wanted to go to America to go to school, I'd give it a second thought. But you know Hana. She wants to sit by a swimming pool in a nice hotel, and marry some Kennedy."

"Fine. We just might go without you then," said Min, with his mouth full, pushing his empty plate away from him, the leftover chili pepper staining it red.

"I'd kill you if you did that," said Soo-Ja, heading back to the front desk.

Soo-Ja had no time to listen to either of them. She couldn't wait to tell her father that she could finally pay him back. She would go visit him and give him a check for the money.

For the last eight years Soo-Ja had lived full of guilt, thinking of all the money he had lost because of her. In his sixties, her father was supposed to reap the rewards of an industrious life, and finally rest while Soo-Ja and her brothers took care of him. But Soo-Ja had not been able to help him in this stage of his life; and not only that, she had moved to another city.

Her brothers still lived in Daegu, but the eldest, Tae, had turned against their father (he felt that his father played favorites toward Soo-Ja), and it had been left to Kwang-Ho, the youngest of the three, kindly but a bit reluctantly, to take care of their parents (which was the job of the eldest, not the youngest).

After Soo-Ja moved to Seoul, she tried not to think too much about the family she was leaving behind. She felt terrible when they lost their ancestral home and had to move into a small apartment. Now, finally, Soo-Ja could make it up to her father.

"Eomma, can you please put Father on the phone?" asked Soo-Ja excitedly.

It was late in the evening, and Soo-Ja sat in the alcove that served as her office. The day's check-ins and checkouts were done, and she knew she could talk to her father in peace.

"Soo-Ja, is this you? I don't remember what my daughter's voice sounds like," said Soo-Ja's mother.

"Eomma, please," said Soo-Ja, trying not to let her mother kill her good mood. "Just give the phone to Father."

"I'm just saying, it's been so long since you called. And you didn't come home for Seollal."

"I know, I'm sorry."

"If you won't even come home for the holiday, when will you ever come home?"

"Eomma, please put him on the phone. I have good news for him," said Soo-Ja.

Soo-Ja heard the faint sound of her father's voice in the background. Her heart leapt with joy, until she realized he was singing. She heard the hesitation in her mother's breathing, and then finally the sound of the phone being handed to her father.

"Soo-Ja? Is this you?" He sounded like a man who had swallowed a microphone. His words seemed to stretch for miles.

"Hello, appa."

"Your mother doesn't want to sing for me! Nobody wants to sing for me. But you will sing, right?"

"Appa, no, I—" Soo-Ja squinted her eyebrows, worried. The phone cord tangled in her hands, an unruly bracelet.

"Sing for me. Sing for me!"

"Appa, you're going to wake up Kwang-Ho. He has to get up early for work," said Soo-Ja. She heard some talking in the background, and she thought she could hear her brother's voice. She had not spoken to him in months.

"Kwang-Ho is not my son!" her father proclaimed loudly. "I have disowned him!"

"Appa, you live in his house. He takes care of you."

"He drags me out of the sul-jib, and embarrasses me in front of my friends. What kind of a son is that?"

Soo-Ja closed her eyes, mortified by her father's drunkenness. For a moment, Soo-Ja heard the sound of the phone changing hands, and then she heard her mother's voice.

"Soo-Ja, your father is tired. Why don't you call again tomorrow?"

"What's wrong with him? Why do you let him drink?" asked Soo-Ja, pulling the phone cord so tightly she almost broke it.

"Your father's been having a hard time. He doesn't like living off of Kwang-Ho. Your father never had to depend on others before. It used to be that other men came to him, asking for money. Now he has to ask *them* for handouts. He has nothing of his own. Remember, he was once the richest man in Won-dae-don."

When Soo-Ja was a little girl, and her father owned the biggest factory in their town, he would have her sit next to him when visitors—relatives real and fake, friends of friends—came asking for money. They'd plead their cases, explaining their reasons for needing help. Some claimed they had a daughter getting married, when in fact they had a mistress on the side. Or they talked about funeral costs for an in-law, when what they wanted was a holiday trip to Japan. A few had real reasons, like medical bills for a child, or the costs of sheltering a parent. Soo-Ja and her father would listen attentively. Then, her father would turn to her and ask her to make a decision. He already knew who to give money to and who *not* to give money to, of course, but he made her feel like she was the one with all the power. Soo-Ja had inherited both her father's compassion and his ability to spot liars. They always came to the same conclusion, and it was usually the right one. And when she bestowed the money, the supplicant would kneel in front of her and call her sage. And so she had spent her childhood.

By the time Soo-Ja reached Daegu, he had already passed away. As she sat in the train, staring out at the open fields, she wept—she'd been denied parting words, or a last look. For most of the journey, she prayed for the train to keep running forever, never stopping, never dropping her off, never reaching its destination at all.

Later, during the half-hour trip from the train station to her brother's house, she sat in the back of the taxicab with her body feeling frozen—it was the longest half hour of her life. The taxi dropped her off in front of a series of huge apartment complexes, an entire maze of them, all identical, washed white, with rows of small balconies; each building was set apart only by a giant three-digit number painted on the side. This was the new Daegu, rising upward.

Soo-Ja knocked on her brother's door, and he himself answered it. When she saw the expression on his face, she felt a lump in her throat. She took in the commotion behind him, the grieving women chanting and crying, arms rising and falling madly in the air. Soo-Ja and her brother did not say anything at all. They simply stood by the door and embraced, and when she felt his warm body against hers (he had their father's build), she felt her face flood with tears.

Soo-Ja ended up staying in Daegu much longer than she'd anticipated. Her days were busy, since there was always someone to visit with: distant relatives, friends of the family. They all wanted to see her. They said being around her was like being around *him*—the same smile, the same warmth. So she met with everyone who wanted to meet her, going to visit folks all over Daegu, and becoming her family's public face, while her mother stayed at home, retreating into her room, her pipe, and her silence.

Min and Hana came for the funeral, but left almost immediately. Min told Soo-Ja someone had to look after the hotel, and she couldn't argue with that. Soo-Ja didn't know what was happening with her husband and her daughter at that point. She didn't know they'd already decided what they were going to do. Later, when Soo-Ja would tell people about what they did to her, they'd always ask, *Why did you stay in Daegu so long? Why did you give them the opportunity?* This is really your fault, can't you see?

Soo-Ja liked it in Daegu; she liked the fact that everyone around her was mourning. They were all in love with loss—her brothers, her mother, and she. She liked the fact that their meals magically appeared, courtesy of countless friends, who brought the food not on aluminum or plastic plates, but on real tableware and silverware. She liked the fact that for as long as she was there, she could simply burst into tears at random times, and no one took pity on her, as if it were normal to start weeping while doing the dishes. At night, Soo-Ja read and reread the long, beautiful letters her father wrote her, the blue ink stained by tears, rendered nearly unreadable.

My dear Soo-Ja,
   I have not heard from you in a very long time. I can imagine you are very busy, working in that hotel and raising Hana. It hurts me,

sometimes, to think of you working such long hours. It is embarrassing to me, to think that I could not give my daughter a better life. Everything I worked for—the factory, the business—they were so that you could have a comfortable future. It seems to me that I have failed.

It pains me to know that I want to give you more, but I have so little left. All I can give you now is my love, and it seems so insignificant, so inconsequential. My love cannot get you a day off; it won't pay for a bowl of rice. My fortune is gone now, and so is much of my health. I see friends of mine turn to prayer for comfort—and drink, too, which you know I have always been fond of—but I want to tell my friends not to fear what lies ahead. I am not afraid of dying—I am only afraid of the hurt it may cause those I leave behind. If something happens to me, cry, but do not cry too long; mourn, but do not mourn too much.

Know that I count myself lucky that I have had so much love in my life—from your mother, your brothers, and from you. You especially— who keeps running away from me. But I will always find you, no matter where you go. I will always be a part of your life. I will always care for and protect you.

Your loving father

Soo-Ja was sitting on her father's old bed, looking at photograph albums, when she saw her mother appear by the doorsill. Soo-Ja's mother had always seemed old to her, even when she was younger. Now that she was a grandmother, she seemed to have finally fit into the role she'd waited for all her life. She'd been wearing the same outfit recently, almost like a uniform—heavy, padded brown pants held down by white socks, and a knitted green vest with white buttons.

"Why did you leave that money on my dresser?" asked Soo-Ja's mother.

"It's for all the phone calls I've been making to Seoul."

"That's more than just for phone calls to Seoul," said Soo-Ja's mother, entering the room. Soo-Ja moved aside slightly, so her mother could sit on the bed. "Phone calls cost a lot less than that."

"It's all right, Mother," said Soo-Ja. "You and I both know I owed Father a lot of money. And I will send you more, every month."

Soo-Ja's mother squinted at her daughter, as if trying to read her. "Are you still torturing yourself about your father's loan to old Nam Lee?"

"How can I not? Father living here. Losing all his money. It was my fault."

"No, Soo-Ja. Your father lost everything because he *drank* so much. He'd come home, and relatives would ask for money, and he'd give it to them. His brother once stole his signature stamp and used it to fleece one of his bank accounts. Some other scoundrel took money that your father meant to use to build a school, and ran out of town. The money he lost because of you was relatively little."

Soo-Ja did not reply at first, as she felt the blood drain from her face. She began to feel herself crack open; that detail of her life had long been as much a part of her as her arms and legs. "But I always thought that he had ruined himself because of me."

"Your father let you think that," said Soo-Ja's mother, with a sigh. She produced a bag from under the bed; it was filled with dried rolls of mugwort and incense. As Soo-Ja watched, her mother picked up one roll of dried mugwort and pressed its end against her finger, while lighting the other end with an incense stick. By the time she pulled the incense away, the heat had made the mugwort glue itself on her finger.

Soo-Ja breathed heavily, starting to lose her bearings. "Why did he do that? Do you have any idea how horrible I've felt all these years? Do you know how much guilt I felt, every day?"

Soo-Ja's mother reached for another roll of mugwort and placed it on her index finger. The smell of incense filled the room.

"You're so ignorant sometimes, it hurts my ears," said Soo-Ja's mother. "Behind his tough facade, your father was a cub. And he was terrified of losing you. You had just gotten married. He needed something to hold over you."

Soo-Ja began to weep. Her mother continued lighting the mugwort rolls, until every single one of the fingers in her left hand had one attached to its tip. Soo-Ja had watched her mother do this many times growing up. The mugworts would burn slowly, and were supposed to heal different ailments. In Soo-Ja's mind, those sticks were as much a part of her mother as her eyes and nose. They were the kind of thing she'd remember her by, long after she passed away.

"Don't be angry at your father. Now that you're a parent, you must know what it's like to fear losing your grasp over your child."

Soo-Ja looked at her mother, as the light smoke covered her face in a thin white layer. For a moment, she longed to touch her wrinkled warm hand and feel it against her own skin. Her mother was so small and hunched, but still so strong. Her mother's life was so different from hers.

Suddenly, breaking Soo-Ja's reverie, the telephone on the nightstand began to ring. Soo-Ja guessed it would be Min and Hana. It was late, later than the time she usually called them at night, and Soo-Ja figured they were concerned. Soo-Ja's mother motioned for her daughter to pick it up, as she excused herself from the room.

But when Soo-Ja answered the phone, she did not hear Min's voice. Instead, she heard the unexpected sound of Miss Hong's distinct cadences, the round, exaggerated phonemes of a woman from the countryside, sigol. She was half crying, half mumbling, and it took Soo-Ja a while to understand why the chambermaid was calling her. Still, even after the words became clear, Soo-Ja could not believe what she had just been told.

The shock almost made her drop the receiver.

PART FOUR

Bamboo

Hours Later
Seoul and Los Angeles

chapter seventeen

Soo-Ja arrived back in Seoul late in the evening and found a handwritten sign on the glass door of the hotel reading "Closed." She had some trouble with her keys and struggled to get inside. Right then, she regretted refusing her brother's offer to come with her. She'd been wrong to think she could handle all of this by herself. But during the ride on the train, she'd managed to convince herself this was simply a misunderstanding, and Miss Hong had alarmed her for nothing. Min and Hana would be in the hotel when she came in. They'd hug her from behind, and ask her why it had taken her so long to return home.

"Hana's mother?" Miss Hong's disembodied voice greeted her as she came in.

"Where's Min? Where's Hana?" Soo-Ja asked, turning the lights on.

Miss Hong's body came out of her room and joined her voice as she hurriedly put on her slippers and rushed forward in her hanbok, putting her hair in a bun.

"Hana's mother, I tried to stop them, I really did! Please don't be mad at me."

"What happened?" Soo-Ja asked her. "Where are Hana and Min?"

"I told you on the phone! They left," said Miss Hong, her eyes growing big.

"No, this can't be happening," said Soo-Ja, shaking her head. Had they lived in peace for so long that she had forgotten what her husband could be like? "Even for Min—he wouldn't do this to me!"

Miss Hong reached for her arm and pulled her toward Soo-Ja's own room. In there, lying on top of a sausage-shaped pillow, Soo-Ja found a sheet of paper where a sleeping head should have been. Miss Hong pointed to it, her face anxious, suddenly going mute. Soo-Ja quickly reached for the letter and began to read.

> *Dear Soo-Ja,*
>
> *So many people want to move to America, but can't. While we—we have family there and the money. That's why I decided we should immigrate.*

Soo-Ja put the letter down, gasping. Now she could no longer pretend that her family was still home. Miss Hong, seeing the stunned look on Soo-Ja's face, propped her up with her right hand and offered to bring her some water. Soo-Ja shook her head and reached for the letter again.

> *Now that your father is dead, I suppose the money from the land can go to Hana. We will spend it on her education. I promise I won't touch it.*
>
> *I have made arrangements with Gi-yong Im to transfer the funds from the sale to our accounts. I have also left behind some cash for you to buy a ticket to join us.*
>
> *I know we should have consulted you before we did this. And we would have. If you were here. Are you ever coming back? Isn't two weeks too long to be gone? Do you not miss us at all?*
>
> *Please don't be mad at me. I was afraid that if I asked you, you would never let us go. In a way, I'm helping you, so you don't have to make a tough decision. The decision has been made for you, and now you can look forward to a great future in a great country!*
>
> *I know I am doing the right thing, and I will explain it all to you once you get here. We'll be staying with my parents. The address is on the back. It is in English, but I think you can read it.*

Hurry to your new home.
Your husband,

Min

Soo-Ja made a mad dash to Min's desk, looking for her in-laws' phone number. Her mind raced with thoughts. She had been gone for too long. She had given Min too much time alone to plot and plan and go back and forth in his decision, until he finally began packing their bags. This couldn't have been a spur-of-the-moment decision—it took too long and too much work to get the tourist visas and plane tickets. Soo-Ja wondered if her absence had made him feel abandoned, and maybe she had, in fact, abandoned him, choosing her father's memory over his live, anxious body. Still, he'd done this in the most cowardly and hurtful way possible. Not even a phone call.

But why the sudden departure? Soo-Ja knew that for years Min had yearned to reunite with his father, but she never thought he'd act on his own like this. There had to be more to his decision. And how could he take Soo-Ja's own daughter away from her! Without consulting her! Soo-Ja asked herself how he could be so selfish. Hana must have been thrilled, of course, to go to America. She was too young to understand what her father was doing.

Soo-Ja found her in-laws' number on the inside of the back cover of one of Min's notebooks, scribbled in pen in his uneven handwriting. It was the longest number she'd ever had to dial, and she had to do so carefully, so shaky was her hand. Soo-Ja held the phone close to her face as it rang, breath caught in her throat. Miss Hong looked at her with anguish in her eyes, helping her sit down. When Soo-Ja heard the voice answer on the other end, she knew immediately who it was. She had not spoken to him in almost seven years, but it was the same hard voice, unsmiling and emotionless.

"Hello?"

"Father-in-law . . ." said Soo-Ja.

"Hana's mother," he said, like a reprimand.

"Is Hana there? I want to speak to her."

"She's outside. In the pool. It is still morning here."

"Tell her to come to the phone," said Soo-Ja, gripping the phone cord with her fingers. "And Hana's father, too. I want to talk to him."

"He doesn't want to talk to you. He's afraid you might yell at him. Or that you'll talk him into coming back," said Father-in-law.

"Are you saying you won't let me talk to my daughter, or my husband?"

Father-in-law sighed, as if Soo-Ja were simply too unintelligent to understand the situation. "I'm going to raise your daughter for you. The school district here is very good. Of course, once she finishes high school, she'll have to pay me back, but she can work in my warehouse for a few years and earn back the money I spent on her."

"She's not staying there, she's coming back home with me," said Soo-Ja, steel in her voice.

Father-in-law did not say anything, but he did not hang up, either. Silence followed him, and Soo-Ja assumed he'd gone to fetch his son. Although, knowing her father-in-law, she figured he'd probably just leave the receiver facedown on the counter, until someone inquired about it.

Soo-Ja felt suspended in time, each second an eternity. Finally, Soo-Ja heard Min's voice on the line. "Soo-Ja?"

"Considering all the things you've done to me, I still never imagined you'd take my daughter away from me," said Soo-Ja, practically yelling on the phone.

"We're going to start fresh here, Soo-Ja," said Min, also skipping any pleasantries. "We're going to start over again."

"How could you do this? Without even asking me?"

"I have every right to, according to the law. It is within my rights as a father."

"You're coming back here with Hana," said Soo-Ja, boiling with anger. "Right now, do you hear me?"

"This is our chance, Soo-Ja," said Min, his voice rising to match her intensity. "A lot of things didn't go right for us in Korea, but America will give us a new beginning. We'll get it right this time."

"No, America won't make any difference," snapped Soo-Ja,

interrupting him. "*You* are still going to be you, and *I'm* still going to be me. Can't you see that?"

"It's not just being in America. It's being away from Korea. It's being away from . . ." Min trailed off, stopping short of saying his nemesis's name.

So he's trying to separate Yul and me, thought Soo-Ja.

"It is our only hope, Soo-Ja. It is the only way our marriage can survive."

You're wrong, thought Soo-Ja. *Yul is not the reason our marriage is the way it is.*

"How many times do I need to tell you, Yul and I are not together," said Soo-Ja.

This did not seem to convince Min. "Hana and I are waiting for you here. We've left you money for a plane ticket. I don't know how long it'll take you to get a visa. Maybe a week, maybe a month," said Min, irritation in his voice.

"Put Hana on the phone," said Soo-Ja.

"No. You're going to try to—"

"Put her on the phone!"

"No. I can't. It's for her own good."

Soo-Ja felt the night grab at her, and she closed her eyes, to make herself blind. She hung up the phone and slammed it on the floor. The sound of a busy signal punctured the air.

"What do you think is going to happen when you get there?" asked Yul, looking somber. He was driving Soo-Ja to the airport in his gray Kia Brisa, making his way toward the departure lanes. He had not spoken to Soo-Ja since the Lunar New Year's Eve celebrations.

"I don't know. I haven't thought that far ahead," said Soo-Ja, looking out the window, her energy completely drained. A light drizzle had begun, and drops of rain hit noisily against the glass pane.

"What did they say when you called them?"

"I don't want to go over it again," said Soo-Ja. "But clearly Min thinks it's up to the husband to decide where to raise the children."

"He wants to stay there?"

"Does it matter? He won't get to."

"So you're bringing them both back?" asked Yul, skeptical.

"Of course," said Soo-Ja testily.

"What if Hana doesn't want to return? Are you going to stay in the U.S.?"

"A child can't dictate where her mother will live," said Soo-Ja.

"Well, if she's anything like her mother . . ." Yul smiled kindly at Soo-Ja, but she could not muster a smile back. Yul slowed toward the curb and parked the car. He looked at the rain, the clouds, and the bad visibility. It wasn't a good day to fly. "Will you call me when you get there?"

"Your wife is not going to like it."

Yul glanced at the planes landing in the distance.

Soo-Ja looked at him, noticed his reticence—he wanted to tell her something, but he was holding back. "What?" asked Soo-Ja, placing her hand on the door handle.

"Nothing, I'll tell you when you get back."

"How's Eun-Mee?"

"I'll tell you when you get back," Yul repeated, like a mantra. He turned off the windshield wiper and the engine. The glass pane soon became covered with rain, drops coming from all directions.

Soo-Ja kept her hand on the door handle, without opening it. "Did she leave you?"

"I don't want to talk about it right now."

Soo-Ja sighed. "This is a wakeup call for me. To stop indulging in fantasies. Min is helping me. That's what he's doing."

"What does that mean?"

"It means that whatever is happening between you and me has to end. Min could use it against me in a divorce. The judge would never let me keep Hana if he learned I've been unfaithful."

"You're missing an important detail. You have not been unfaithful."

"Yes, but I can't take the risk, can I? Hana is more important to me than anything else in my life, including you."

"So . . . I should drive away knowing not to keep my hopes up," said Yul weakly.

"I'm sorry, Yul."

"This is the end, then?"

"Yes. This is the end," said Soo-Ja, swallowing. She felt a tear run down her left cheek, and she wiped it off with the back of her hand. She kept her face away from Yul—if she did not have to look at him, she could do this.

Color drained from Yul's face, and he nodded slightly. "I wondered why you asked me to drive you here. This is why, isn't it? You wanted a chance to tell me this?"

"That's not why I asked you, but now that I think about it, I guess I owe you that, don't I? After all that we went through together."

"Do you really think the decision is yours alone to make?"

"I'm sorry, Yul."

"Well, I have something to tell you, too," said Yul. Soo-Ja could see his face rearranging itself, lines forming in odd places. He looked like a dam about to explode.

"I don't want to—"

"I can't just remain on hold forever," said Yul, speaking over her. "I'm not an object that you can keep on a shelf and pick up only when you feel like it. You've said no to me many times, and this is one time too many. So think about this before you leave the car: I cannot wait for you anymore. So when you say this is the end, make sure that you know what the end means." Yul stopped and waited for Soo-Ja's reaction. "What do you have to say to that?"

Soo-Ja shook her head slightly and looked away, reaching again for the door handle. The rain hit the windshield hard, and Soo-Ja felt that it lashed her own face. "Good-bye, Yul."

"She left with her father," said Yul, and for a moment his voice sounded like that of a stranger speaking to another stranger on the street. "Have you considered that maybe—you might have to accept that you're not getting her back this time?"

Soo-Ja turned back around and glanced at him, taking a deep breath. "Of course I have."

"Can't you see it? Either way you lose someone—me or your daughter. Or maybe both—maybe you'll manage to lose everyone. Amazing how much you lose when you play for high stakes, isn't it? Your high-mindedness and your virtue sure paid off—look at all the dead bodies on the road behind you."

"Yul! Stop!" Soo-Ja yelled, unable to stand the weight of his words.

"I'm beginning to wonder if maybe Min was right all along," said Yul rapidly. He looked as if he would regret his words, but he did not seem able to contain himself. "Maybe I've been in love with the wrong person and not known it."

"That's not fair," said Soo-Ja.

"What's not fair is that I spent the last ten years of my life pining for a woman who never intended to be mine!"

"That's not true," cried out Soo-Ja.

"Get out. Get out of my car. I don't want to see you again."

Soo-Ja felt the words push her out of the car, and she walked toward the terminal with her suitcase, the sliding glass doors beckoning her. She let the rain drench her clothes. It fell into her ears, her mouth, the spaces between her fingers. From the corner of her eye, she watched as the back-and-forth of the windshield wiper sliced Yul's face into slivers. His car pulled from the curb and slowly drove away, the tires skidding on the road, water splashing. In a matter of seconds, he was gone.

That meant Soo-Ja could stop walking, and finally let her pain show. Bending her knees, Soo-Ja rested her arms over her suitcase and let out the cry that had been bursting inside her heart. She freed a noise savage and broken, gasping madly for air, and let the raindrops pelt her body. Yul had been right. She had lost everything she could lose, an entire con-stellation. She watched the automated sliding doors a few yards away, smoothly opening and closing. Those glass doors led to the future, and to America.

So this is how it ends, thought Soo-Ja. *Min wins, Father-in-law wins; Yul loses, Soo-Ja loses.* She had thought there was nothing more they could take from her, until she found herself with no bones, no skin to cover her. They had taken away everything—even the air inside her lungs.

chapter eighteen

In Seoul, it's said that once you breathe American air, *migug baram*, you don't wish to come back. Soo-Ja could see why Min and Hana, like the children in fairy tales, might have been enchanted by the sweet, clean aroma of that country. As the taxi driver drove her from the airport to her in-laws' house in Palos Verdes, California, she, too, felt herself lulled by the wide-open spaces, the heaven-sized quiet, and the orderly merging of the cars on the road. God may not live in Los Angeles, she thought, but he must come here for vacations.

Riding in the car, Soo-Ja was amazed by the distance between buildings—all that empty space! Such luxuries—big parking lots, generous curbs, the mere existence of walkways. As the car drove on, she had the feeling they were standing still, so smooth was the ride, and it was the buildings that glided closer to them. It was her first time out of the country, and the irony was not lost on her.

I suppose I did, after all, get to practice diplomacy.

When the taxi driver arrived in her in-laws' neighborhood, Soo-Ja was astonished by the size of the homes—mansions really, full of room, with endless driveways, long enough for planes to land. Her in-laws' house sat on a slope, surrounded by shrubbery, and to her it looked more like a park than a residential street. In Korea, only the very wealthy lived like that, but, as she found out later, this was simply middle to upper middle

class. Soo-Ja glanced down at her clothes—a dark green one-piece
housedress stamped with prints of white flowers—and immediately
wished she had brought her pearl necklace. It was as if her daughter
and her husband had been adopted by a rich couple, and the couple just
happened to be her in-laws.

As Soo-Ja had expected, her first encounter in years with Min's parents
was tense, with long, bleeding silences. Fortunately, Soo-Ja had no time
to dwell on this, as relatives began to swarm over her. Soo-Ja arrived, it
turned out, on the day of Mother-in-law's sixtieth birthday, and the house
teemed with family and friends. Her brothers-in-law and her sister-in-law
greeted her effusively, with all the fervor of Christian missionaries meeting a native, telling her how wonderful Hana looked, and how she was all
grown up. Nobody mentioned why Soo-Ja was really there, though she
could tell by the nervousness of their smiles that they were well aware of
the circumstances under which Min and Hana had come.

Soo-Ja found Hana outside, in the backyard, emerging wet from the
glistening swimming pool. Soo-Ja ran to hug her daughter, and when she
saw Hana's grown body, in her borrowed swimsuit, wrapped in a huge
yellow towel, Soo-Ja knew she had already lost. She fought back a tear
as she held Hana against her, and let her daughter lead her to a recently
painted swing set, where they sat down.

Hana was eager to tell her everything about her grandparents' house,
and to show her around the garden. She treated her mother like a late-
comer to some party whose pleasures and secrets she'd already sampled,
and she would share them with her only if she promised to appreciate
them. Soo-Ja had lost her authority over her daughter, lost her to this
bright, three o'clock sunshine, and this giant backyard pulsating with
wildflowers, and the reclining deck chairs that promised long, lazy afternoons where you could sip the world through a straw.

Not too long after, Min came to them and stood by Soo-Ja awkwardly. If they had been business partners, they would have shaken
hands. If they had been boyfriend and girlfriend, maybe they would
have kissed. If they had been relatives, they would have hugged. But
they were husband and wife, and did not know how to greet each other.

Soo-Ja was keenly aware, however, that they were being watched. There were three dozen people milling around—nephews and nieces of all ages, all the wives who'd married into this clan, the select friends from church—but they moved around with the expediency of background extras.

"You always told me you were afraid to fly. Did that fear just go away overnight?" Soo-Ja asked Min quietly.

"Hana, go take a shower and wash the chlorine off your body," said Min.

Hana pecked her mother on the cheeks and left, a tearful expression on her face. Min took her spot, sitting on the swing next to Soo-Ja. They spoke quietly, watching the others gather by the barbecue grill, on the other side of the pool.

"Dad offered you and me jobs in his warehouse. They sell wholesale unisex sportswear. He said you could work the front area, and me in the back, but you'd have to learn Spanish. Most of our customers are from Mexico."

"He's very eager to boss me around, isn't he?" Soo-Ja looked toward the house, where she knew Father-in-law was sitting on his plush white leather couch, probably watching them. "Why would I work for him when I could just start my own business in Seoul?"

Min bit his lower lip, an old habit of his when he was nervous.

"Dad wants to keep our money for us. He said it's so we can contribute to the expenses here. He said we can't expect to live here for free."

Soo-Ja could not help letting out a small, rueful laugh.

"Look at this big pool, Min, this nice house. Who do you think is paying for all this? Do you really think your father would welcome you with open arms if you didn't have the money with you?"

"Don't talk like that. He's my father," said Min.

"The only reason that what I say bothers you is because you've wondered it yourself. Fine, keep the money, but give my daughter back. And by the way, I will never, ever forgive you for this."

Min looked at her with a bit of a start, and the look on his face confirmed it—he had felt no guilt about taking the money from selling the land she herself had originally bought; he thought of that money as his, the same way he thought of Hana as his, and her future, too—all his.

"Can we talk about this later?" asked Min. "It's Mother's birthday."

Soo-Ja closed her eyes, resting her forehead against the palm of her hand. An elder's sixtieth birthday represented a momentous occasion, with a number of ceremonial gestures. At which point, Soo-Ja wondered, should she confront her in-laws? Maybe after the "offering of the flowers," but before the "song of congratulations"—maybe that would be a good moment to ask them why ten years ago they had abandoned Soo-Ja, penniless, while they started a new life in America with her father's money. Or maybe after the "offering of the ceremonial liquor" but before the "congratulatory address"—maybe that would be the right moment to demand why they hadn't sent back their son and granddaughter to Korea, when they knew very well that Min had brought Hana there without Soo-Ja's consent.

"No, we can't talk about this later. I want everyone gathered here to know exactly what kind of people your parents are," said Soo-Ja, preparing to get up. She saw, not far from her, the banquet table covered in white and laid out with the traditional sixtieth birthday dishes: sliced rice cakes stacked almost four feet in the air, and shiny pears sitting on different rungs of a three-story silver platter.

Min's parents had taken their place on the other side of the banquet table, and in a moment, the ceremony would start. Each of their five children—along with their wives, or in the case of Na-yeong, her husband—were expected to bow to Soo-Ja's in-laws and offer them a gourd filled with red wine. By living to age sixty, Mother-in-law had reached a milestone. She'd completed the sexagenarian cycle of the zodiac, and, for the first time in her life, her animal element, the monkey, had finally aligned with her *yin-yang* heavenly stem, metal. The already revered matriarch would be even more so, and given more power and respect than ever.

"If you make a scene, no one will sympathize with you. Everyone here is on Mother and Father's side," said Min. "And as far as knowing what kind of people they are . . . we all know already. We're their children, remember?"

Soo-Ja took a deep breath, frustration running through her veins like water boiling in a cauldron. "Don't speak to me. I don't want to hear another word from you."

Soo-Ja sat on one of the lawn chairs, holding a thick paper plate filled with spicy radishes, sulfurous eggs, and rice wrapped in seaweed. She made a point of sitting apart from the others, and away from Min.

But not soon after, a woman not much older than her, perhaps in her early forties, plunked down next to her. She had a perm, and big, heavy locks of curly hair. She must have been a distant relative, for she seemed to know Soo-Ja, though Soo-Ja herself didn't recognize her.

"It's very nice of your father-in-law to bring you to America," the woman said, settling into her own lawn chair, and balancing the overflowing plate of food on her lap.

"Yes, he brought me here all right," said Soo-Ja, savoring the irony.

"But then again, he's always taken care of you, I hear. He gave you a business to run in Seoul, didn't he?"

"Is that what he tells people?" asked Soo-Ja.

"And I heard he gave you a house, too." The woman smiled broadly, revealing some gold in her back molars. Soo-Ja wondered if she did this on purpose, an older woman's version of a young woman flashing a diamond engagement ring.

"Oh, yes," Soo-Ja said, bewildered at her father-in-law's distortions. "He's so kind."

"So how do you like America?" the woman asked, playfully waving her hands in the air, as if she were a magician and had just produced this country, for Soo-Ja's benefit, for her to look at.

"It's very large," said Soo-Ja.

"I heard you just arrived from Korea. You're very lucky."

"Am I?"

"Yes. That country's so hopeless. After the war, we should've all just emigrated and let it stay in ruins." Soo-Ja looked at her closely, this middle-aged Korean face wearing Western clothes, a French logo emblazoned on her chest pocket: Pierre Cardin. "There is nothing good there, only pollution and people with bad manners. The local American paper here had a letter to the editor about how nasty Koreans are—they never smile, don't apologize when they bump into you, cheat you in business. I think that's all true."

Soo-Ja took this in and thought of simply letting go at first, but she couldn't. She stared straight into the woman's eyes and spoke, and though she did not know where the words came from, she felt them vibrate through the deepest parts of her body. "Did you know Korea was the first country in Asia to have a standing army? And even through decades of being colonized by foreigners, it still managed to create world-class art, literature, and the finest tradition of brush ink paintings you've ever seen? When I visit the magnificent, centuries-old temples of Naksansa or Shinhungsa, or drive past the Namdaemun Gate, or think of the astonishing *Tripitaka Koreana* and the thousand Buddhas of Jikjisa Temple, I am always proud that in my blood runs a tradition of great scholars and artists." The woman shifted, uncomfortable, but Soo-Ja held her gaze and did not stop. "Or when I hear a woman, dressed in a colorful hanbok, sing and dance the *pansori*, and do so beautifully, I find myself swooning with joy. This is what I like about being Korean: when we were attacked by all those different countries, and our names, language, and occupations taken away, we may have looked as though we were bound to our enemies, but deep down we never forgot our worth, we never let them into our heads. And that's why we'll be able to triumph in the end, and be proud to call ourselves Korean, and even a woman like you will be proud one day to call herself Korean."

Soo-Ja wandered through the bright and airy house on her own, as the sound of the party outside filtered through the sliding glass doors and windows. She noticed the high, sloped ceiling, and how the sunlight bounced against the walls, creating a bubble of warmth. She had not expected her in-laws to have such a large living room, full of so much furniture.

In the living room, Soo-Ja sat on the soft L-shaped pink couch and let it sink comfortably under her, like a pillow molding to her body. She glanced around the room, noticing the color TV with long rabbit ears and a large dial, the record player with numerous knobs, and a series of commemorative silver and gold coins. By glancing at the objects gathered around the room, Soo-Ja could see hobbies taken up and abandoned: golf balls, a badminton racket, some fishing line. On the bookcase shelves, Soo-Ja could make out some of the English writing: a thick world almanac, a stack of *Life* magazines, and Korean-English dictionaries.

Soo-Ja had been by herself for only a few minutes before she noticed someone else in the room. It was Min, standing against the wooden railing by the stairway.

"I'm glad you didn't start a fight, with all those people outside," said Min.

"Are you giving me an opportunity now? I'm more of a ticking bomb than you realize."

"I'm still not going to apologize," said Min, coming into the room, and sitting across from Soo-Ja. "I'm doing what I think is right for Hana."

"When did you ever do what's right for her?"

Min leaned forward on the sofa, his hands locked together.

"You think you're the only one who suffers for this family?"

"Name one thing you did for me or Hana," said Soo-Ja.

"I stayed with you when my parents moved here!" Min suddenly shouted.

"And you always remind me how you regret that."

"You think it's so simple. You think I'm a bad person. Do you think it's easy, to live with a woman who thinks I'm nothing?" Min's voice rose and fell, as if afraid others could hear them. But they couldn't. They were alone in this impossibly bright room.

"Then *make* something of yourself. I dream of the day you'll do something courageous, when you'll prove yourself," said Soo-Ja.

"What do I have to do to prove myself?"

"I don't know," said Soo-Ja, pressing against the pink couch with her hands, as if to measure the thickness of the foam.

"You've made sacrifices for me, I know," said Min. "You could've married someone else. But you stuck with me. Don't think I don't appreciate that. One day I'll be able to make a sacrifice for you, and you'll love me."

Min looked away, toward the party outside. He watched his parents and his brothers and his sister smile and laugh at one another. Soo-Ja, following his gaze, looked out at the sea of bodies in the backyard, at Min's big family. She noticed their laughter, their cheerful talk. She could see Min wondering what the joke was—the source of their happiness. She knew he would give anything to unlock it. If he lived here, he wouldn't be alone even if he tried. She realized then how lonely he must have been in Seoul, with just Hana and her.

"You don't need to sacrifice anything for me," said Soo-Ja.

"I'd like for you to respect me."

"I would have respected you if you had let me divorce you, all those years ago, and still keep Hana."

"Is that what you want? For me to let you go?"

"It doesn't matter now."

"Is that so you can go off with Yul?"

"I can't, even if I wanted to. Yul said he was tired of waiting for me. There's nothing left for me back in Korea," said Soo-Ja, fighting back the sadness growing inside her. "And anyway, it's not about me leaving you and going off with another man. It's about you becoming the kind of person who's willing to do what's right for me and Hana."

Soo-Ja noticed the sliding glass door open, and one of the guests made her way in. They would have to end this conversation for now. Min rose and turned his back to Soo-Ja, heading back outside.

"Yeobo . . ." Soo-Ja called out.

"What?"

Losing her father had been bad enough. Soo-Ja couldn't bear to add Hana to her list of losses. Hana was all she had left—if she had to stay in this foreign land and serve as her father-in-law's handmaiden in order to keep her daughter around her, so be it.

"If you and Hana really want to stay here, I—" Soo-Ja hesitated, her voice trembling a little, struggling to get the words out. It killed her to have to say it. "I'll take your father's offer. I'll work for him."

chapter nineteen

The party ended late, long past sundown, after the small caravan of Fiats and Cadillacs and Oldsmobiles noisily left the driveway, one after the other, like a procession. Soo-Ja retreated to the downstairs area next to the garage, a kind of fancy chauffeur's suite, with its own bathroom, separate from the rest of the house. Hana and Min had been staying there, Min sleeping on the floor, and Hana by herself in the large queen-sized bed. Now that Soo-Ja was there, she and Hana would sleep on the bed, and Min on the floor. There was also a small TV in the corner, on top of an old chest made of paulownia wood. Soo-Ja stared at its dark grain, made all the more noticeable by the lighter shades surrounding it.

"Grandpa wants to see you." Soo-Ja heard Hana's voice behind her. Soo-Ja rose, only to be struck by the incredible silence in the house. She realized that this was where she'd live, not the bustling house of a few hours ago, filled with sunlight and life; but *this*—this eerie home where unhappiness seemed to linger like dust on top of the furniture.

Soo-Ja walked up the stairs and found herself in the dining room, which had been turned into a kind of multipurpose area, with a second refrigerator, an old leather couch, a color TV, and a round white Formica table pushed against the wall. Father-in-law sat at his chair, waiting for her, holding a backscratcher that he tapped on his knees lightly, repeatedly, as if counting time. Mother-in-law sat on the floor, a few feet away, her back against the couch; she had a quilted blanket on her lap, and she was stitching the silk cover. Min and Hana sat on the couch, supposedly watching the TV, but the sound was turned too low for them to actually hear. As Soo-Ja sat down across from Father-in-law, she knew the others were just pretending to be busy, and they were there for this conversation as much as she was, like human props placed there for an important scene.

"I want to make something clear to you. You're not here on vacation. You're here to work," said Father-in-law. "Work starts tomorrow. Early. Six o'clock. It'll be a long day, twelve hours. You can have a little break for lunch, twenty minutes, but if a customer comes in while you're eating, you leave your food aside and go wait on her. The work is not easy. We sell in bulk, which means carrying ten, twenty pounds' worth of clothing at a time. All day. But I don't want to hear complaints. You understand?"

"Yes, Father," said Soo-Ja. She saw from the corner of her eye that Min and Hana's heads were bent down. She was speaking for all of them.

"If you don't like it, tough luck. Try showing up at an American store and asking for a job. You don't speak English and you smell of kimchee. You have nothing to offer, remember that. You're lucky that I even let you work for me. There are a lot of hungry people out there. At least here your stomach will always be full."

"Yes, Father. Thank you, Father," said Soo-Ja.

"We didn't become successful and rich by being idle. We made sacrifices. We worked very hard."

"I know, abeonim," said Soo-Ja, thinking of the money he had taken from her father.

"Remember, too," and this is when he changed his tone, to become the benevolent patriarch, "I'm not going to live forever. When I die, this house will be yours, and my business, too. So you see, even though I'm not paying you, you're not working for me, you're working for yourself."

"Thank you, Father." Soo-Ja knew already that when he died, Father-in-law would leave everything to his daughter, Na-yeong, and nothing to Min and her. She knew Father-in-law so well by now, she could tell when he lied—it was the only time he ever smiled.

"You've said a lot of harsh words to me in the past, but I forgive you. I forgive you because I live in a beautiful house and I have a lot of money, and that is so because I am a good person. You, on the other hand, you still have much to learn, but I can teach you how to be a humble, obedient daughter-in-law."

Soo-Ja turned to Min then, as she was about to respond. She expected to see triumph in his eyes, but she found only sorrow. And that's what made her voice quiver, when she finally said, one more time, "Yes, Father."

Father-in-law then dismissed her with a nod of his head.

When Hana went into the bathroom of the suite to take a shower, Soo-Ja and Min found themselves alone again. They looked at each other with apprehension in their eyes, sensing this might be the prologue to another stage of their lives. It would be easy to follow this road, and live in America, and work for Min's parents, and go on with things as they always had. Still, something in the air did not feel right, and it emanated from Min. Soo-Ja thought of the look of grief on his face during her conversation with his father. She saw how it hurt him, to see her abased like that.

"Why did you do that?" Min finally asked, sitting on the bed.

The only sound, other than his voice, came from the shower in the next room.

"Do what?" Soo-Ja asked, busying herself with pulling blankets and pillows out of the closet.

"Lower yourself like that."

"I had no choice, Min."

"What happened to you? You used to fight them. You used to stand up to them."

"Maybe I'm tired."

"I made a mistake, didn't I? Bringing you two here?"

"What's the use of knowing that, if you're not going to do anything about it?" asked Soo-Ja. "Let's go to bed."

Soo-Ja glanced at her bags. She did not have the energy to unpack them, and decided to sleep in some old clothes she found in the closet. She did not know who else had slept in this guest room before, but whoever they were, over time they had left marks of themselves behind: a book of maps, a broken eight-track player, worn-out shirts and pants. The room belonged to no one, quietly absorbing what others had cast away.

"Soo-Ja?"

"What?"

She heard him swallow a few times before he finally spoke. "If I had found someone else—if I had talked some other girl into marrying me, you would have had a very different life, wouldn't you?"

Min had broached the topic again, and this time she could not hide her feelings. Soo-Ja dropped the blankets for a moment and sat on the bed next to him. She felt the emotion rise in her throat, and soon her eyes welled up with tears. He had never hinted at knowing of her sorrows. This was only the tiniest of acknowledgments, and yet it burned deep like a welt.

"Don't be foolish," said Soo-Ja.

How could he possibly atone for the last thirteen years? How could she make him understand that her life so far had not been her inescapable destiny, but rather a choice she'd made? How could she tell him that all her frustration and disappointment in this marriage had not been set in stone, and did not *have* to happen? That she could so easily have been spared all of that, if only she had chosen Yul over him? It felt almost unbearable, to begin to explain to him the different life she could have had if she hadn't married him. She could never convey the magnitude of that loss—the loss of the woman she'd never been allowed to be. It was better not to ask for any apology at all.

You will never understand what I have given up.

"If I feel bad about it now, imagine how I'll feel forty years from now," Min said ruefully, as if joking.

"This is no time to talk about this. Let's go to bed. Your father said we'll need to get up early."

"All I'm saying is—I cannot change the past, but maybe I can do something about the future."

"What are you going to do? Are you going to talk to your father?"

The Min she looked at now reminded her of the Min who'd once told her not to ask for her father's money, the Min who had protected her from his own father's schemes. He lay there, waiting, underneath those layers of self-preservation, and on rare occasions she'd caught a glimpse of the man he could have been, if he could have chosen his parents.

The sound of the running shower stopped. Min had gone upstairs for a glass of water, and Soo-Ja sat in the room by herself. She could hear only the occasional noise coming from the bathroom: a comb being placed on the sink, a faucet being turned on and off.

Soo-Ja wondered if her daughter knew she was waiting, and wanted to avoid her. Finally, a few minutes later, Hana emerged, a towel wrapped around her head like a turban, and another wrapped over her adolescent body, tucked in at her breasts.

"Come here," said Soo-Ja, as she stood and reached for the towel on her daughter's head. She began drying Hana's hair, pressing her hands gently against Hana's scalp. "How is the shower here?"

"It's nice to have your own, and not have to go to a bathhouse," said Hana.

"You used to like going to the bathhouse. You used to like soaking in the warm tubs, droplets of warmth on your forehead."

"Tastes change."

"You like it here, huh?"

"Yes."

"Aren't you going to miss your friends?"

"I can make new ones," said Hana.

"But they may not love you like your old friends did."

Hana reached for the towel from her mother's hands. She sat on the bed and began drying her own hair, pressing it deeply against her scalp in fast, jerky strokes, instead of her mother's slow, gentle movements.

Soo-Ja sat down next to her.

"I don't like it when you're like that," said Hana.

"Like how?"

"You're staring at me."

Hana stopped drying her hair, resting the towel on her lap. Her hair hung wet and wild above her face. The sliding closet door in front of them was mirrored, and they could see their reflections looking back at them.

"Do you know that I love you?" Soo-Ja asked.

"Don't be so melodramatic."

"I don't mind not being rich, like our relatives here. Not living the good life they live. As long as I have you. Without you, what do I live for?"

"I'm not going back to Korea."

"It doesn't matter to you, my opinion?"

"The responsibility of a mother is to give her child a good life," said Hana a little stiffly, almost aware of how precocious she sounded.

"And you think you'll have a good life here?"

Hana looked at her mother as if she were crazy. Of course she'd be happy in America! Here, even people without limbs had smiles on their faces.

"You already told Grandpa that we'd stay, so we'll stay. And even if you said no, I'd still stay here, with Dad."

"Why do you listen to your father, but not to me?"

"Because he always spends time with me. You're always busy with other things."

Soo-Ja made her hands into fists, her arms shaking. She struggled for breath, and fought back a wave of emotion rising in her chest.

"I have to work!" said Soo-Ja loudly, her voice piercing through the air. "I work so that you can play! I work for *you*. For you."

"Mom, please stop. Somebody might come in," said Hana.

"Am I— Am I embarrassing you right now?" asked Soo-Ja, desperate for the love of the girl in front of her.

Soo-Ja stared at her own reflection in the mirror. She had never lived for herself, and in that, she found her greatest mistake and her greatest glory. Her selflessness had not been entirely chosen, but rather forced out of her, by her family. She had not been allowed to pursue happiness; only to try to find some meaning in her sufferings, and look for a way, however small, to make sense of her disappointments. How could she explain this to her daughter? she wondered. Hana already seemed to belong to another world.

Soo-Ja stopped looking into the mirror and stared, instead, at the carpet below her feet. It was light brown, and it reached between her toes. Her voice suddenly became very quiet, like a whisper. "All right, then. It's all decided."

"I know what you're thinking. But your life is your life, and my life is my life," said Hana. "You made your mistakes, but they're your own."

"Yes, I know," said Soo-Ja, forcing herself to smile. "You're right. Forget what I said."

"If you're not happy about being here, you can go back and just visit us later," said Hana. For Soo-Ja, each word felt like a lash against her bare skin.

"No, Hana. I'll always be where you are. No matter how much you try to run away from me, I'll always be where you are."

Soo-Ja thought of her father's letter. *You keep running away from me, but I will always find you*, he had written. She didn't think she'd be repeating his words to her own daughter, and so soon. She was so struck by this, she did not notice that Min had been standing outside the door, in the hallway between the room and the garage, listening in, making no sounds of his own. He was like a prowler, already inside the house, just trying to figure out how to get out.

It took her a while to fall asleep. Soo-Ja was used to random noises at night—guests lumbering to the bathroom, couples tossing harsh words like tennis balls—and the silence felt otherworldly to her, the prelude to some shaman evoking mountain spirits.

When she was twenty-two, Soo-Ja dreamed of donning a diplomat's suit jacket and flying through the atlas to dole out goodwill like peppermint candy from a bag. This was the diorama version of her life, the one you put in a magic snow globe and sell in souvenir shops. At the time, she was sad that she didn't get to leave Korea. But now she wanted to tell her twenty-two-year-old self that she was lucky, that she got to spend a little more time with her father (if she'd left Daegu then, she would have missed the last ten years of his life), that she got to know her own country and came to cherish it like a loyal friend. There was not enough time later to say good-bye to your parents and your youth; the old familiar rooms fall away before you know it. She wanted so much to escape, and marry, and leave. She didn't know back then that she had already found happiness, and that in going after it, she'd simply been walking farther and farther away from it.

Soo-Ja didn't know how long she'd been asleep when she felt someone nudge her. She opened her eyes only a slit and saw it was not morning, but not night either—the light outside, shy and bleached out, announced only the promise of sun, not its presence. Min stood over her with an anguished look on his face, and when he saw she was awake, he began to nudge Hana, too. Min had an amped-up energy about him, and Soo-Ja realized he had not slept at all. Next to the bed, she saw that he had placed two bags—the one she'd arrived with, and the other, a smaller one, which she recognized as Hana's.

"What time is it? What's wrong?" Soo-Ja whispered.

"I called a taxicab. It's going to be here in twenty minutes. It'll take you and Hana to the airport."

"What do you mean?" Soo-Ja asked, sitting up on the bed, struck by the urgency in Min's voice. Min reached for her and gently wiped the sleep off her eyes.

"I want you to get out of here," he said, pressing a note against her hand. "This is the account number, and the name of the bank. The money's still there. It's in a bank in Seoul."

"Min, what's happening?"

He looked at her as if he were taking a picture, as if this was how he wanted to remember her: in the dawn, with her hair falling softly over her face, her lips half opened, and her eyes, too, taking him in the way the sand takes the sun.

"What I did was wrong—bringing Hana here. I can see that now. And I hope that one day you'll be able to forgive me," said Min.

Soo-Ja swallowed and closed her eyes. The moment felt strange, unreal.

"Why are you up already?" Soo-Ja heard Hana's sleepy voice, her body turning in the direction of their voices.

"You're going back to Korea with your mother," said Min.

"What? No, I don't want to go back there," said Hana, rubbing her eyes.

"You're going to do what I tell you," said Min, firmly but kindly. "For once you will listen to me. You're free to disobey every other order I ever give you, but this one you have to listen to. You're going home with your mother."

"No. If she wants to go back, she can go back on her own. I'll stay here with Grandpa and Grandma."

"You think it's so great to be here, don't you? You don't know what it's like to live with them. I'm not going to let you go through what I did," said Min. His voice shook a little, and Soo-Ja was struck by the intensity of his words. Soo-Ja thought he might continue, but he was overcome by emotion. "Being with them again reminds me of so many things. No one knows what I had to go through as a child—"

"I *know* what you went through," said Soo-Ja quietly. She reached for him and held his head with her hands. Min had never spoken about his childhood, but over the years, Soo-Ja guessed the kind of torments he had suffered. "I know."

Min finally regained his composure. "Go," he said.

"Are you sure about this?" asked Soo-Ja.

"How much more can I take away from you, Soo-Ja? At what point do I stop?" Min's voice cracked a bit, and he took a long breath. "I deceived you, Soo-Ja. I tricked you into marrying me."

"Don't say that."

"I deceived you. And I can never give back what you lost, but I can stop making you lose."

Soo-Ja and Min sat in silence, and they could hear the birds chirping outside. It had become day while they were looking away.

"What about you?" she asked.

"I'm going to stay here."

"Why?" asked Soo-Ja, though she already knew the answer. "Why? What about Hana?"

"I want to be with my parents when they die. I want to take care of my father and my mother. It is my responsibility as the oldest. In spite of everything, I still want to be a good son."

"You are," she said. "I've always known that." He'd never change, thought Soo-Ja. "But you're making a big sacrifice."

Min took the back of her hand and placed it against his lips. He kissed it once, then left it there, so that she could feel his soft breath on her skin.

"Dad, no!" cried out Hana, who'd been watching her parents, weeping. "I'm going to stay with you. I don't want to go with Mom." Hana got out of the bed and jumped into her father's arms.

Min held her for a second, then he made her let go, made her look at him while he spoke. "If you ask yourself, deep down, *Can I really live without her*, the answer you hear is *No, I can't live without her.* Your mother did so much for you, and she loves you so much. Where would you be, if it weren't for her? Where would *I* be?"

Soo-Ja heard the sound of a car engine running outside. The taxicab had arrived. Seeing it outside the window made the moment feel more real, and Soo-Ja suddenly felt the urgency of it. She glanced at Min and saw the pain in his eyes.

"Maybe . . . maybe we can send Hana here for her summer vacation?" she asked, hoping to make this moment a little easier for him.

Min sighed with joy. "Of course. Yes. Hana, I'm going to call you every day, and write you every hour."

Hana finally let go of her father. Her face was wet with tears. She put on her clothes slowly, as if putting on an old self, once discarded, and now recalled to life.

Soo-Ja wondered if her daughter would hate her for the rest of her life. Of course she would. She was a teenage girl. She'd find reasons to hate her mother, and to love her, every day of her life.

And Min, who was this Min in front of her? Had he been there all along, and she had simply neglected to see it? Or did she make him day by day, inch by inch, build him lovingly and patiently, sparing him cross words, offering him a kind look here and there, so that one day, one day at last, he'd do exactly this and finally let her go? Soo-Ja did not love the man she married, but she loved the man she divorced. It just so happened that as she found her heart swell with joy for him, it was also time for her to leave him. She wanted to speak to this man, to get to know him, this man leaning over the window of the taxi, looking at her in the passenger seat, looking at her as if for the last time, but the words never got out of her mouth, as the taxi drove away, and she saw Min growing smaller in the distance, disappearing already into some nostalgic past.

chapter twenty

When they returned to Seoul, Soo-Ja and Hana resumed their lives as if nothing had happened. Soo-Ja went back to work, and Hana returned to school. They had the money. Soo-Ja had checked with the bank; it was all there. If she wanted to, she did not have to work again for a long time. But Soo-Ja longed for routine, for her life to be as close as possible to what it had been before. She had lost both her father and her husband, and she still felt the grief in her bones. When the divorce papers were finalized, Soo-Ja surprised herself by feeling sorrow, rather than relief. She didn't know many other divorced women. They were like ex-convicts—people you talk about but don't associate with. Did this mean she had failed, to some extent? She had always dreamed of the day she'd be free from Min, but when it arrived, it provided no joy.

At the time, Soo-Ja worried most about Hana, though her daughter seemed to take her father's decision well. She even joked about it, said it made her more like American girls, whose parents were all divorced. Soo-Ja knew then that she'd lose Hana to America eventually. First the summers, then college there, then she'd probably move west for good, and marry an American boy. And Min, Min kept busy—he liked being needed by his parents, driving them around to play golf, going on fishing trips, having barbecues. Soo-Ja suspected he might even start dating soon.

And Soo-Ja? Well, she worked a lot. She thought about Yul and Eun-Mee, how they had probably managed to work things out between them. She could not bring herself to hurt their marriage, so she stayed far from both of them. Now that she was no longer married herself, it felt wrong to speak to Yul. Once, she saw him in the street, coming out of the New World Shopping Center. She turned and walked the other way, before he could see her. If they stayed away from each other, thought Soo-Ja, maybe at least one of them could have a good marriage.

But that is not to say she didn't miss him. Soo-Ja thought of him almost every day, especially before she fell asleep in bed. And she figured maybe that was why she waited so long to return the money he loaned her—that was her last link to him, and once she gave it back, she would have no reason to speak to him. But finally she realized she had to learn to let go, and she gave Hana an envelope with a check inside in the amount he'd loaned her, and asked her to drop it off at his house. Hana went on the errand, curious but asking no questions. Soo-Ja waited anxiously for her daughter's return, hoping for a word from Yul, or a reaction, but when Hana came back, she said Yul hadn't been home, and she'd had to leave the envelope with the maid. Soo-Ja tried to hide her disappointment, as this felt a bit anticlimactic. No message from Yul, no final good-bye. Soo-Ja nodded and went back to work, and things might have stayed that way—calm, placid—if Eun-Mee hadn't burst into her life once again, for the third and final time.

Eun-Mee came the very next day, unannounced. She did not look as well put together as she normally did—her hair hanging long with no headband or pins to support it. Even her clothes were somewhat middle of the road: a purple shirt with a large collar that hung almost as low as her chest, creating a V-neck, with the collar white and blue in diagonal stripes, matching the stripes on her skirt. And Soo-Ja did not notice this at first, but when Eun-Mee placed it on the counter, Soo-Ja saw that Eun-Mee had the envelope she'd given to Hana to deliver to Yul.

"Your daughter dropped this off at my house, didn't she?" Eun-Mee asked, staring at Soo-Ja across the counter.

Soo-Ja closed her cash drawer and gave Eun-Mee the neutral look she reserved for difficult guests. "It's for Yul."

"You know Yul doesn't live at the house anymore. You have a lot of nerve leaving this for him."

Soo-Ja took the envelope from her and looked at it—its edges dirtied and worn-out—turned away, in limbo. By seeing its seal intact, she knew it had not been opened.

"Don't worry, I didn't open it," said Eun-Mee. "I have no interest in reading your pathetic love letters."

"What did you mean when you said that Yul doesn't live at your house anymore?"

Eun-Mee did not answer immediately. Instead, she simply stared at Soo-Ja, as if in disbelief. "Don't pretend you don't know that we separated. I'm sure your husband told you all about the scene I made."

"My husband?"

"Yes. When I came to the hotel after Yul left me. I thought he was staying here."

"When was this?"

"The week after Seollal."

"The week after Seollal? But only the week before, we had tea at your house—"

"Yes. Who'd think *that* would turn out to be a happy memory compared to what came later."

"And Min knew about your separation?"

"Yes. I made him open every room in the hotel, even the ones occupied by guests. But Yul wasn't here. He was at a different hotel. He told me when I saw him again, when he came back to pack things."

"Eun-Mee, I don't think we should have this conversation here. Do you want to come into my room?" Soo-Ja asked her, pointing inside.

"I was about to suggest that very same thing," said Eun-Mee.

Soo-Ja called out for Hana and asked her to watch the front desk. When Hana came out, a bit out of breath, Soo-Ja saw Eun-Mee caress

Hana's chin lightly, as if she were a pet. Hana flinched a little, though her attention was immediately distracted by the envelope on the counter.

"I'll explain to you later. Just put that somewhere safe," said Soo-Ja.

As they walked to her room, Soo-Ja thought about Min. Eun-Mee's story confirmed Soo-Ja's suspicions that his decision to move to America had not come out of thin air—Eun-Mee's actions must have given Min his sense of urgency. Min had hoped to keep her away from a newly separated Yul. To this day, Soo-Ja still didn't know exactly what had transpired in her absence, only that one day Min and Hana were in Seoul, and the next they were in America.

Soo-Ja slid the paper door open and led Eun-Mee inside. The room still had some traces of Min in it. Eun-Mee sat on the floor, and once she had moved some padded blankets and mats out of the way, Soo-Ja sat across from her.

"So you're saying you didn't know about Yul leaving me?" Eun-Mee asked, sitting cross-legged on a mat.

"No, Eun-Mee. I really didn't. I'm very surprised to hear it. He didn't tell me that when I saw him."

"I'm not sure if I believe you," said Eun-Mee. "I wonder if this isn't part of some plan you hatched."

"You're the one always making plans, Eun-Mee. Me, I don't look too far beyond the present moment. I can't afford to."

"So I'm supposed to act surprised when, by sheer coincidence, any day now, you happen to leave your husband, and find yourself conveniently unattached?"

"Eun-Mee, I can't leave my husband. My husband has left *me*."

"He left *you*?" she marveled.

"Yes."

"Just as Yul has left *me*. So we're going through the same thing then, experiencing the same pains and sorrows?"

"I suppose. It is a bit disorienting not to have Min anymore. I've been talking to myself a lot. I still cook for three, and have to throw away his portion."

"But can you sympathize with my sufferings? You can, can't you? Oh,

I was foolish to think of you as a rival, when you were in fact an older sister."

Soo-Ja held her tongue—she knew Eun-Mee didn't mean any of her words. Soo-Ja could detect the theatrical tinge in Eun-Mee's voice.

"Yes, I suppose we've both been left bereft," Soo-Ja said, trying to remain noncommittal.

Eun-Mee reached for Soo-Ja, and ran her right hand fast a few times over Soo-Ja's arm, as if she were undoing a crease on her shirt. This close to her, Soo-Ja could see her face was a bit swollen with past tears, and she realized Eun-Mee must have lost five pounds or so off her already thin figure since she'd last seen her.

"Now, older sister, if you could do something to assuage my pain, you'd do it, wouldn't you?" Eun-Mee asked.

"I'd try."

"There's a fear I have—this awful anxiety! It keeps me up at night. But you could put that fear to rest, and make my ordeal a bit more tolerable." Eun-Mee had come closer to Soo-Ja and taken her hand into hers.

"What is it?"

"I'd like you to promise me something."

"What?"

"I'd like you to promise me, that if Yul comes to the hotel, and asks you to be his wife, you'll turn him away."

Soo-Ja took her hand back from Eun-Mee and looked in the other direction. "Eun-Mee, why are you asking me that?"

"Because I know there's a chance Yul will come back to me. But he'd do that only if he knew he did not have a chance with you. So make it clear to him that you will never take him."

"I'm sorry, I can't promise you that."

Eun-Mee reached for Soo-Ja's hand again, but this time Soo-Ja did not let her have it. Soo-Ja could feel the nervous vibrations off Eun-Mee's skin, the way she seemed to shake from some core deep within.

"How can you not promise me that? He's still a married man, as far as the world is concerned. Promise me you will reject him if he comes to you."

"I would do no such thing."

"You mean that you'd take him? Knowing that if you did, he'd never come back to me?"

Eun-Mee's legs were now touching Soo-Ja's, and Soo-Ja felt like Eun-Mee was on the verge of moving even closer.

"No wonder your husband left you. You have no morals."

"If you're here to insult me, then you should go."

Eun-Mee remained quiet for a moment, as if trying to decide what to do. If Eun-Mee tried to hit her as she had done the last time, Soo-Ja would not hesitate to hit her back. Finally, Eun-Mee rose and excused herself, bowing deeply to Soo-Ja. Soo-Ja bowed back and wished her a good journey home. It amazed her, how polite and formal they were acting, when only a few seconds earlier, she thought they were about to do physical harm to each other.

"Is Dr. Yul Kim here?" Soo-Ja asked the receptionist, her voice barely audible. Decorated with ink brush paintings on the walls, and low brown leather chairs, the office was much larger than the one he'd had in Pusan. Outside, Hana waited for her.

"May I have your name, please?" the young woman asked, in a distracted manner. She sat behind a sliding window she opened only halfway, like a teller in a bank.

"My name is Soo-Ja Choi," she said. Her heart pounding, she smoothed down the front of her dress and brushed her hair with her fingers. Inside, her emotions—anxiety, excitement, joy—swirled around her like mad butterflies of different colors, their wings breaking as they clashed into one another.

The receptionist checked a list. "Are you a patient of his? Do you have an appointment?" she asked, without looking up.

Soo-Ja noticed a hint of North Korea in her accent. "No. I'm a friend of his. I'd just like to see him, please." Soo-Ja felt the anxiousness rise in her body; it had taken all of her courage to come here. She would not, in fact, have come if Eun-Mee hadn't gone to talk to her. After Eun-Mee

left, Soo-Ja simply could not keep still. Yes, she had to return the money
he'd loaned her, and she let that goal dictate her steps, but in fact she
was drawn there by an almost irresistible force.

"Dr. Kim is in the break room. We're having a party for him," the receptionist said.

"A party?" asked Soo-Ja, confused. *But it wasn't his birthday.*

"It's so sad he's leaving for Pusan next week," said the receptionist,
her manner around Soo-Ja growing more informal. "Are you here to say
good-bye to him?"

"Pusan?" Soo-Ja repeated. She had to put her hand over her mouth,
to hide the shock on her face. The receptionist could have said Mars,
or Russia, and her reaction would have been the same. Surely she had
misheard?

"I'm going to miss him a lot," said the receptionist, with a glint of a
smile in her eyes. "He's one of the nice ones. Too bad he isn't staying."

"Can you please—can you please tell him I'm here?" asked Soo-Ja.

The receptionist looked at Soo-Ja with concern on her face, and Soo-
Ja could see her own distraught emotions mirrored back to her. Soo-Ja
could not tell if the receptionist knew her reasons for being there, but it
didn't matter—the young woman rose quickly from her chair and rushed
to the door separating the waiting area from the examination rooms. She
bowed to Soo-Ja and pointed to Yul's office with her long, pale arms.
Soo-Ja was touched by her kindness—that she would let her in without
questioning her more, without making her wait.

Once inside Yul's office, Soo-Ja pulled out the envelope with the
check from her purse, and she placed it on the examination desk. She
made sure Yul's name faced upward. Soo-Ja was not sure whether to remain standing or sit on the chair, like a patient. She hesitated, afraid to
step too far into the room. Soo-Ja stared at the hospital bed, imagining
the various men and women who came to see Yul. So much sickness, so
much worry. Soo-Ja thought about what Yul did every day: he listened to
people's woes.

Yul came into the room only a few seconds after she did, and she
realized he must have rushed there as soon as he heard her name. She

took this as a reassurance—he could have hesitated, maybe even refused to come. Seeing him, Soo-Ja felt the air tickle her skin, as it traveled underneath her clothes, stirring up nerve endings. He had burst into the room so fast that the tail of his white coat flew up a little. He looked out of breath, as if he'd been miles away instead of next door.

Yul shut the door behind him and, like her only a moment earlier, seemed to wonder whether to sit or stand. Wanting to put him at ease in his own office, Soo-Ja walked to the patient's chair and sat down, allowing Yul to take his doctor's seat across from her. His knee bumped hers slightly as he eased into the chair, and she moved her legs to the side.

Yul noticed the envelope right away. "What is this?"

"The money I owe you," said Soo-Ja.

Yul nodded. "Is that the only reason you came?"

"No. That's not the only reason. Is it true you're going back to Pusan?"

"Soo-Ja, your timing is not very good," said Yul ruefully, almost sighing.

"So it's true. You're going back to Pusan," said Soo-Ja, the weight of the words feeling heavy on her tongue.

"Eun-Mee and I have separated," said Yul.

"I know. So have Min and I."

"You have?" asked Yul, surprised.

"Why are you going back to Pusan?" asked Soo-Ja, ignoring his reaction.

Yul blinked for a second, gathering his thoughts. "My old patients miss me, and my former colleagues invited me to return. They said they'd welcome me back to the clinic."

"I see," said Soo-Ja, feeling as if her gut had been punched. "So you're going back."

Yul directed his gaze at her, both love and anger flashing from his eyes. "Why didn't you tell me about you and your husband? Last time we spoke, you told me to forget about you. You told me it was over between you and me. Isn't that right?"

"And you believed that?" asked Soo-Ja, cracking a desperate smile. She realized they both wanted to shout, and this conversation belonged in an open field, or by the river. Anywhere but a small examination room.

"You told me that. You gave me no hope for a future. When you left for America, I never thought you'd come back. What was I supposed to do?" asked Yul, with a tinge of desperation in his voice.

"You were supposed to wait for me," said Soo-Ja, her fingers tracing the metal armrest.

"Wait for you? Wait for you to come back and tell me what? That you cannot be with me because it wouldn't be good for Hana? That I have to wait another ten, twenty years?" Yul spoke through gritted teeth, his words bouncing against the stark white walls.

Soo-Ja lowered her head and wished the floor would turn into water, so she could dive and swim to the bottom of the sea. "Don't go," she whispered.

"I don't think I heard you right," said Yul, staring at the top of her head.

After a few seconds, Soo-Ja lifted her head up. Her eyes were welling up with tears as she met Yul's gaze. She could barely mouth the words—*Sarang-hae*—but it was a beginning. She repeated them again, amazed that after so long, she was finally free to direct those words—*I love you*—to him.

"What did you say?" asked Yul, his breathing growing shallow.

"I said, don't go to Pusan. There's nothing for you there."

Yul swallowed, his hands trembling slightly. "What are you trying to do, Soo-Ja?"

"I'm trying to keep you from slipping away from me. I could not survive that, Yul," said Soo-Ja, her voice scratchy and flickering.

Soo-Ja reached for Yul and rested her fingers on his arms. She could feel the electric charge running through his body. She knew his heart would be beating as fast as hers.

"I have made so many mistakes in my life," said Soo-Ja, fighting the pain pushing against her chest. "But my biggest mistake was that I gave you up too many times, and I won't do that again." Her shoulders began to rise and fall, and her eyes flooded with tears. "If you want me, that is.

God knows I've hurt you enough. God knows it would be simpler for you
to be with someone else."

"Of course I still want you. I know I said some horrible things to you
the last time I saw you, but I didn't mean them."

"So don't go then. Don't go," said Soo-Ja, the urgency burning in her
tongue. Soo-Ja glanced at his face; it looked older than the last time
she'd seen him, and the lines around his eyes evoked in her a feeling of
tenderness.

"What about the patients who have already made appointments?"

"They can find another doctor. They can wait."

"Where has this resolve come from?" asked Yul tenderly, leaning forward toward her.

"It has come from living half my life without being able to touch your
face," said Soo-Ja, as she held her hand up and gently brushed his cheek
with the back of her hand. Yul closed his eyes and moved his head, so his
lips could meet her hand.

Soo-Ja angled to the side and leaned forward, so that their knees
were touching. Yul reached for her, and Soo-Ja let him rest his hands
over hers. She could feel him try to find the hole in her heart, try
to heal it. The kiss, when it came, happened blindly, without forethought. He pressed his lips against her mouth, his tongue gently
tapping hers.

As they kissed, Yul's body moved closer to her, and the room seemed
to grow quieter. Soo-Ja felt Yul wrap himself around her, until she wore
him like a favorite coat. After a while, they let go of each other's lips and
held each other without speaking. Soo-Ja could feel the vibration travel-
ing back and forth between them. She reached for his neck, which felt
warm and naked against her hand.

"Why didn't you just say yes to me all those years ago, when I first
asked you to marry me?" said Yul.

"I was young. I was a fool," said Soo-Ja, holding him tightly. "Forgive me."

Yul placed his head on her shoulder, and Soo-Ja did the same to
his. He could be a baby, asleep on her shoulder, a newborn with a soft

cranium and the promise of speech. Silent tears traveled down her cheeks. Soo-Ja let out a long, slow breath.

"I won't go," said Yul. "I won't go to Pusan."

Soo-Ja closed her eyes. She had made so many mistakes in her life, but in that moment, she forgave herself for them. She forgave her past, with all its bumps and imperfections, and let it go, pouring it into some beautiful gilt-edged box, wrapped with cellophane. The life she had was in fact the one she'd been supposed to have, she told herself. Without its lessons, how could she have become the woman she was?

When Soo-Ja finally came outside, Hana saw the tearful look on her mother's face, and she immediately reached for her. They were in the middle of a busy street, and arms and elbows brushed against them. They could barely hear each other above the din of cars rushing by on the road and buses coming to a loud stop.

"Mom, what's wrong? What happened?"

Soo-Ja smiled through her tears, wiping them away. "I'm all right. Everything worked out. Let's go."

"Was Yul there? What did he say to you?"

"Nothing. He wasn't there," said Soo-Ja.

"Then what took you so long?" Hana asked cautiously.

Soo-Ja nodded. How could she hide her joy from her daughter? She couldn't.

Hana squinted her eyes and looked as if she understood. "You have him, don't you? You have Yul."

Soo-Ja leaned forward, nodding, and kissed her daughter's head. Even though night was beginning to fall, surprisingly it wasn't cold. The weather had turned the day before, and a warm blanket of air enveloped them as they walked. Soo-Ja liked this—when she thought she might need a coat or a sweater, and she didn't, and for that she was grateful. Everybody in the crowded street seemed to be thinking the same thing: spring had arrived, at last. As Soo-Ja walked, she kept noticing the faces of the people around her, especially the women. Soo-Ja didn't know where they were going, or where she and Hana were going, for that matter. They simply walked together, Hana's arm around her waist, her head leaning slightly toward her mother's shoulder. The strangers who walked by and saw them may not have found anything remarkable about them, and she liked being ordinary, just mother and daughter. Straight ahead, construction cranes lifted steel bars onto bare scaffolding, while window-washers descended in their bosun's chairs. Store loudspeakers announced sales, and food shop greeters called for new customers. Bicycles and carts sped past pedestrians—bells ringing, horns blaring. Exhaust fumes rose from the ground, tinting the air black and brown for a second or two. The streets seemed to widen in front of Soo-Ja and Hana, and the two of them held hands tightly as they kept walking, joining the rest of Seoul.

ACKNOWLEDGMENTS

My agent, Lisa Grubka, at Foundry Literary + Media, is the best agent I could have hoped for, and I'm lucky to have her knowledge, hard work, and good judgment on my side. My editor, Kerri Kolen, at Simon & Schuster, is simply the best: her editorial guidance made this story better in every way, and, with unyielding enthusiasm, she served as this book's best possible advocate and midwife. Also at Simon & Schuster, many thanks to Jonathan Karp, Amanda Ferber, Tracey Guest, Rebecca Marsh, Sammy Perlmutter, Jackie Seow, and Wendy Sheanin.

In researching some of the historical and cultural details of mid-century Korea, I have relied on a number of studies and memoirs, and am especially indebted to the following: *Korea's Place in the Sun: A Modern History*, by Bruce Cumings; *Symbolism in Korean Ink Brush Painting*, by Francis Mullany; *Korea: A Walk through the Land of Miracles*, by Simon Winchester; *The Koreans: Who They Are, What They Want, Where Their Future Lies*, by Michael Breen; *One Thousand Chestnut Trees*, by Mira Stout; and *Home Was the Land of Morning Calm*, by K. Connie Kang. I also couldn't have researched this book without the *Korea Annual* volumes published by the Hapdong News Agency.

I have many, many people to thank for helping me with support, feedback, or both, during the time I was writing this book: Crystal Williams gave me a beautiful home in which to write. Jean Petrolle read an early draft with great attention and care, providing priceless insights and encouragement. At Foundry, "anonymous" readers Chelsea and Laurel. Hyunjung Bae, Michael Dwyer, David Lazar, Wendy Lee, and

Karen Osborne provided advice, information, and suggestions. Curtis Sittenfeld is the book's *fada madrinha* (fairy godmother). Her brilliance, wisdom, and generosity of spirit touched this book in all of its stages. For as long as I can remember, Maitraya Patel has been my biggest supporter and my best friend, and I could not have asked for a better one—his loyalty over the years has been unwavering, and his belief in me never-ending.

Finally, I am lucky and blessed to have the love of an incredible family. Kwang Ok Park has been the most kind and giving dad I could hope for. My sister Julie is the most generous and caring person I know.

My sister Mila delights me with her wisdom—her initial support for the book helped me keep faith in the darkest of times. My mother, Ryung Hee Park, whom this book is dedicated to and inspired by, is a heroic figure and gifted storyteller. A mother-lion in every way, she has sacrificed and fought all her life to give her children a good life. Without her efforts, this book would simply not exist.

ABOUT THE AUTHOR

Samuel Park is an Assistant Professor of English at Columbia College Chicago. He graduated from Stanford University and the University of Southern California, where he earned his doctorate. He is the author of the novella *Shakespeare's Sonnets* and the writer-director of the short film of the same name. He lives in Chicago.

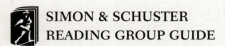

SIMON & SCHUSTER
READING GROUP GUIDE

This Burns My Heart

If you would like Samuel Park to visit your book club, please visit his website, samuelpark.com, for more information.

Set in South Korea during the 1960s, *This Burns My Heart* centers on Soo-Ja, an ambitious young woman who finds herself trapped in an unhappy, controlling marriage. She struggles to give her daughter a better life and to overcome the oppression of her husband, while pining for the man she truly loves. Ultimately, she must make her own way in a society caught between tradition and modernity.

TOPICS & QUESTIONS FOR DISCUSSION

1. Early in their courtship, Soo-Ja thinks of Min as weak: "But what she realized was that she wouldn't mind that, if she had to be the strong one. She'd like to swoop in and care for Min, who sometimes had the air of an orphan . . . He was the opposite of Yul, who seemed to need nothing and no one." (pp. 45–46) Is Soo-Ja's perception accurate? Does Min change throughout the book, or has he just masked himself during their courtship? Is Soo-Ja naïve to want such an unbalanced (and untraditional) relationship?

2. Soo-Ja is angry that she was tricked by Min, but her objective was to trick him as well. Is she getting what she deserved? Who had better motivation? Do their motivations matter?

3. Why do Soo-Ja and Yul have such a strong connection, even though they rarely see each other?

4. Discuss Soo-Ja's relationship with her parents. Which parent is she closer to? Which parent understands her better?

5. Compare Soo-Ja's relationship with her parents to that of Min and his parents. Do you see any similarities?

6. After hearing about Soo-Ja's ordeal when Hana was lost, her father tells her, "When you let me be your father and let me worry about you, care for you, and even suffer for you, you're not doing a favor to yourself, you're doing a favor to me. When you need me, I am alive." (p. 152) Discuss the significance of this statement. How is this true in his life and in Soo-Ja's? Do you think this statement applies to all parents?

7. Min asks Soo-Ja, "If you had to choose, would you rather be yourself or be Eun-Mee?" in an attempt to elicit empathy from her. Soo-Ja realizes, "The thing about capturing a prize fish is that everyone admires the fish, and soon forgets about the fisherman." (p. 251) Do you think Soo-Ja feels pity for Min? Do you? Why or why not?

8. When Hana tells Soo-Ja she should have done something about her unhappiness, Soo-Ja realizes, "She had never lived for herself, and in that, she found her greatest mistake and her greatest glory. Her selflessness had not been entirely chosen, but rather forced out of her, by her family" (pp. 290–291); she then tells Hana that it is indeed her own fault. Do you agree? What could Soo-Ja have done differently? What would you have done in her place? What forces were working against her?

9. Why does Min finally agree to let Soo-Ja and Hana go? What causes his change of heart, and why did it take him so long?

10. The title of the novel is *This Burns My Heart,* which is how Soo-Ja and Yul feel about their forced separation. Discuss the meaning of the title, and how Soo-Ja and Yul deal with their pain. What else does the title capture in the novel?

11. Throughout the novel, Soo-Ja regrets saying no to Yul's proposal back when she was twenty-two. "We're only given one life, and it's the one we live, she had thought; how painful now, to realize that wasn't true, that you would have different lives, depending on how brave you were, and how ready." (p. 245) How does this statement compare with her revelation that "the life she had was in fact the one she'd been supposed to have"? (p. 306) Reread both passages. Which do you agree with, or do you have a different philosophy? In your own life, can you see one monumental decision that changed the course of your life, even if you didn't know it at the time?

12. Discuss the role of women in the novel. How does their position in society shift during Soo-Ja's lifetime? Think about the increasing opportunities for Soo-Ja's mother, herself, and her daughter, Hana.

13. The changing society of South Korea after the Korean War provides the backdrop for the story, and one of the themes of this novel is the balance of traditional family roles with an increasingly modern society. Discuss examples of this conflict that stood out to you in the novel. How do you see the growth of the country evidenced throughout the novel?

ENHANCE YOUR BOOK CLUB

1. Learn more about the time period of *This Burns My Heart* and the struggles between North and South Korea. Read about Korean customs and history at http://www.state.gov/r/pa/ei/bgn/2800.htm#history and check out maps and photos at https://www.cia.gov/library/publications/the-world-factbook/geos/ks.html.

2. Try some Korean food at your book club meeting, such as kimchi (a vegetable side dish), bulgogi (Korean barbecue), or bibimbap (vegetables and rice). Find recipes and information about Korean dining customs at http://www.lifeinkorea.com/food/index.cfm. If you want to avoid washing dishes, try holding your meeting at a Korean restaurant instead!

3. The girls who stay at Soo-Ja's hotel are fans of the Korean band the Pearl Sisters. Check out the video for one of the band's most popular songs at the author's website, http://samuelpark.com/clips.

A CONVERSATION WITH SAMUEL PARK

This novel is based on your mother's story. What inspired you to write it down?

Something really extraordinary happened to my mother the day before her wedding: another man tried to get her to choose *him,* instead. She was equally attracted to him, but what woman in her right mind goes off with a stranger the day before her wedding? So she said no, and once her own marriage turned into shambles, she began to wonder, *what if* . . . As a writer, I thought that was an irresistible hook for a novel and couldn't resist fictionalizing it. Who was that man? What was their relationship like? Did they ever see each other again? The question that kept coming back to me was, what are the consequences and reverberations of our choices? What does it mean to pick X instead of Y? Do you still have the life you were supposed to have, or is it another life altogether?

Was your mother involved in the writing process? How much is true, and how much did you fictionalize?

My mother didn't know I was writing a novel inspired by her life. If I had told her, I would have become too self-conscious to continue. She turned out to be okay with it, which was a relief. My mother did ask me, however, not to tell people which parts were true, and I've—mostly—stayed true to my word. It's been a balancing act—being honest about my inspirations, but also respecting her privacy. I would say this is a book that is inspired by my mother's life and her spirit, but at the end of the day it's a work of fiction. The characters were born out of my imagination, and all the real-life events were rearranged for dramatic effect.

Did you have to do research on Korean language and customs? How much of your history and culture is a part of your life today?

I read a lot of books and spent about a year consuming only Korean-language films on DVD and VHS, and that was all I would watch. I especially loved discovering films from the period the book is set in, like *Madame Freedom* and *School Trip*. Because of their low budgets, many of these productions were shot on the streets, almost *vérité* style, and you get to see what buildings and streets looked like in the 50s and 60s. I also came across a pretty great resource: the *Korea Annual,* an almanac published every year by the Hapdong News Agency. If you want to know what kind of fish were being sold in the stalls in 1964, you can find that information there. I've also been to Korea twice, when I was younger, and have vivid memories from both trips—the maze that Soo-Ja runs through in the opening scene, for instance, really exists and is only a block from my uncle's old house.

You've written a novella, *Shakespeare's Sonnets,* that was published in 2006. How have you changed or grown as a writer? Why did you decide to branch into historical fiction?

In those five years, I grew a lot as a writer. In the beginning, I measured my success by how quickly people turned the pages—I wanted my stories to be page-turners. But while you do want the reader to keep turning the pages and feel immersed in the story and the characters, at times you actually need the reader to stop turning the pages and be swept by their own feelings. When the reader is struck by a burst of emotion, or inspired to reflect upon a thought—those are the moments when the novel actually works. And getting people to respond that way, especially emotionally, is the hardest thing to do. If I describe someone kicking a dog I can get cheap, easy emotion—but truly heartfelt emotion, where you feel genuine investment in the situation, is much harder to elicit, and requires more craft.

Shakespeare's Sonnets was made into a short film that you also wrote and directed. How was creating a film different from writing the novel?

I wanted to direct films when I was younger, and I used to love making shorts. I remember one day we were shooting in a friend's apartment, and it was nonstop drama: I had to herd my friend's unruly cats into a bathroom and deal with an angry building manager who wanted to kick us out. At one point I didn't know if we'd have a lead actor, since the person who went to pick him up called to say he wasn't answering the door. I don't know if this was good preparation for writing a novel, but a bookseller once told me that my writing is very cinematic. When I write, I want the reader to feel she can picture the action unfolding in front of her and see and hear all the characters. Ideally the reader feels she is right there in the room with them, and everything is happening at that exact moment.

Do you see yourself writing more contemporary fiction or historical fiction? How was the writing process different for each genre?

I see myself doing both, actually. Writing contemporary fiction is a lot easier, in the sense that you're free to use any metaphor or reference you wish, and so the range of tools available to you is much larger. But writing historical fiction can be very satisfying, in that the limitations placed upon you free your imagination, like a haiku. I especially like writing historical fiction when the focus is not on "famous" figures but on ordinary people whose lives illustrate historical shifts. When we discuss history, most people conjure up political events, economic policies, and important dates, but those don't account for the subterranean feelings and desires circulating through the citizenry—and to me, those are just as important. In the book, Soo-Ja's quickly changing life serves as a metaphor for her country's own transformation. She stands in, in many ways, for South Korea. The changes in her gender roles, for instance, from traditional daughter to more independent businesswoman, end up mirroring South Korea's own shift from a poor rural country into a rich industrialized one.

You maintain an online blog at your website (www.samuelpark.com). How is blogging different (or similar) to writing a book? Do you try to write every day?

Blogging is a form of speech, and reading a blog is like listening to someone on the phone tell you about her day. Reading a novel, on the other hand, is more like putting on your earphones and listening to music. The words have to do more than just provide information; they need to fulfill some unarticulated desire for beauty, comfort, conflict. They engage with your unconscious. When you write a blog, you're essentially transcribing conversation. But when you write a novel, you pour onto the page a much more complicated soup that's in your head and in your heart—the combustion between your past experiences, your emotions, and your imagination.

Why did you choose the title *This Burns My Heart*? You use the Korean word "chamara" to describe the pain between Soo-Ja and Yul. How is this word significant?

I suppose the title and the concept of *chamara* are intertwined—one is the condition and the other is the response to it. When you're in love and you can't have the other person, the pain can be almost physical—your heart literally hurts; it feels like it's burning. But there's nothing you can do but stand the pain. *Chamara* is a concept that I'm not sure you can fully translate; it literally means "hang in there," or "try to bear it," but a closer definition might be "swallow your pain." It implies that you really can't do anything about your sorrows—all you can do is try to persevere, which is essentially what Soo-Ja does through the course of the novel. Also, even though the words "burns" and "heart" are the more evocative words in the title, I actually chose the title because of the demonstrative determiner "this." What is the "this" that is burning her heart? Is "this" the longing that characterizes the life of someone who cannot have her true love? Is "this" the gap between the life we'd like to have and the one we actually do have? Or maybe "this" has to do with something even less specific, and just refers to the condition of being in the world, open and vulnerable to all the hurts and joys and pains that come with it.

You are an English professor at Columbia College Chicago. Does your teaching affect your writing? What inspired you to become a professor?

Teaching English lit to undergraduates can be old-fashioned at times, and you end up following the 1950s New Criticism model of isolating and analyzing important passages. For the instructor, this means reading and rereading the same passage hundreds of times, leading to different voices becoming ingrained in you. This can be useful in as heteroglossic a genre as the novel. For the character of Eun-Mee, for instance, I borrowed the voices of Lydia Bennet—Elizabeth's vain and boy-crazy younger sister in *Pride and Prejudice*—and that same novel's Lady Catherine de Bourgh, the haughty noblewoman whose speech drips with pretension and entitlement. My love for characters like them—and Lizzie, of course—inspired me to go on to graduate school and become an English professor.

Who are your favorite authors? What are you currently reading?

Some of my favorite contemporary authors include Curtis Sittenfeld, Sarah Waters, Ann Patchett, John Burnham Schwartz, André Aciman, Nami Mun, Ali Smith, Zadie Smith, and Michael Cunningham. My favorite "classic" authors are Jane Austen, Charles Dickens, Emily Brontë, Edith Wharton, Henry James, Virginia Woolf, and E. M. Forster. I'm currently reading a lot about a country that will remain unmentioned—it's research for my next book.

Who are some of your literary influences, and how did their work help to inspire you when writing *This Burns My Heart*?

I love all of Jane Austen's novels, as you can already tell, but *Pride and Prejudice* in particular influenced me. I've read and reread it about ten times, and a few years ago I decided to break it down scene by scene, and that helped me see what made each section work so well. Part of what she does so brilliantly is to find external means to articulate inner turmoil. In the scene, for instance, at Pemberley, when Lizzy realizes that she made a mistake in turning down Darcy, Austen dramatizes her discovery by having her engage with the external signs of Darcy's good character—the beautiful artwork in his estate, which mirrors the harmony of his mind. I really love how Austen's heroines are strong and spirited, but also prone to making self-defeating mistakes. Finally, she's brilliant at depicting insular, constrictive customs. In many ways, *This Burns My Heart* is *Pride and Prejudice* in Korea, imbued with a sense of sorrow that is uniquely Korean. Also, I enjoy reading nineteenth-century British novels, and *This Burns My Heart* has a Victorian triple-decker structure (though I cheated and added a part four)—it is really three novels in one, allowing you to follow a character over different stages of her life, much like *Great Expectations* or *Jane Eyre*.

Do you have any advice for aspiring novelists?

Give all you can, then give ten times more. Write the best possible book for you to write, then add three great scenes. Don't be satisfied with good enough, or with "publishable." If you think you can make something in your book—a character, a scene—better, then take the time to make it better. Ask yourself, is the book, in its current form, one that readers would tell others about, and that newspapers would review positively? Often enough, we stop too soon. Take the time to make it the absolute best book you can write, because you have to win the reader over line by line, page by page, scene by scene. You cannot take anyone's interest for granted. At the end of the day, you're asking someone to fork over thirty bucks and hand you six to seven hours of their time. You had better earn every dollar and every minute.